Requiem *for* Rosco

Peter Gallagher

AMP&RSAND, INC.

Chicago · New Orleans

ISBN 978-146754530-3

Design
David Robson, Robson Design

Published by
AMPERSAND, INC.
1050 North State Street
Chicago, Illinois 60610

203 Finland Place
New Orleans, Louisiana 70131

www.ampersandworks.com

Printed in U.S.A.

This novel is dedicated to:
Ruby Gallagher,
Michael Gallagher and
Thomas and Alexandra Gallagher

1

"M*y god*," breathed Miller, the detective in the gray suit. His voice was a slow controlled whisper.

For a moment he just stared, then he moved closer to get a better look.

"*My god*," he said again, now speaking quietly aloud at the foot of the bed. "Who found him?"

"Traffic detail," answered Sweeney, the cop in uniform. "A girl. Rita something," he continued, as he paged through a small notebook. "She's still here. You can talk to her if you want."

Around them six members of the lab team were conducting business. A bearded technician squeezing off flash photos had just waved them out of the way for the second time, but their efforts to comply only placed them squarely into the path of one of the guys dusting for prints. In addition to the traffic, somebody had a police radio tuned to an emergency frequency that periodically yielded a startling static-filled racket. To escape all of this, they moved away from the body to a corner of the room.

"Ah, here we go. Officer Martinez," Sweeney said, finally locating a note in his book. "Officer Rita Martinez, Traffic Detail. Writes parking tickets. Boots scofflaws, that kind of stuff." Sweeney stopped and looked up from his notebook. "You know," he said quietly, "This guy is number three. We're gonna be national news again. The papers and television and all, they're gonna all come down on us. But this time it's not our fault. We did everything we could. Unmarked cars, foot patrols. You name it. Plain-clothes *teams*. You even spit on the sidewalk around here and somebody's gonna call you on it. Christ, they crack down on everything from parking to dope to hookers in this area and," he said motioning to

5

the body, "The same goddamn thing happens *again.*"

Tow Truck Miller grunted an acknowledgment.

To anyone who'd met him, Tow Truck was a label that required little explanation. Just under six feet tall, Tom Miller was defined by his exceptionally broad and sturdy build. It was at the University of Illinois, playing left tackle, that he acquired the nickname Tow Truck, an enduring invention that fit him a lot better than his given Thomas Theodore. Throughout his 30-plus years in the Chicago Police Department, everybody knew him as Tow.

Now he considered business at hand. Everything Sweeney was saying was accurate. Despite all the publicity surrounding the two previous murders, another playboy had rolled the dice and chosen the wrong playmate–with terrible consequences.

"So what's our meter maid got to say?" asked Tow.

"Well, the way she tells it," said Sweeney, "She found him about 1:20 this morning after the storm passed through. Says the storm knocked a tree through a window and up against the front door. The dogs, two of them, were barking like crazy inside. That's what really got her attention, the dogs. You can still hear them out back now. They can't get them to shut up. Grissom from K-9 says they're trained shepherds. Guard dogs, you know. The real thing, Grissom says. Tear you to pieces. This guy wasn't taking any chances." Sweeney hesitated, listening for a moment to the racket the dogs were making. "Funny how animals know, don't you think? They actually know when something is wrong."

Tow could hear them, big dogs, barking and yelping. Demanding to be heard. Demanding like everyone else, thought Tow, an explanation for this spectacle. And that's exactly what it was–a spectacle. "Yeah," he said pushing ahead. "So what else did Officer Martinez have to say?"

Quickly refocusing, Sweeney continued. "Says she could hear the barking from the sidewalk. Then nobody answered when she rang the bell, but the front door was open just a crack, so she went in to investigate. You can talk to her now if you want."

"Yeah," said Tow. "Let's get to it."

Sweeney turned in the direction of the door. "Rita," he called above the several other conversations in the room.

After a moment, an attractive dark haired young woman in a Chicago Police uniform with a pistol bulging at the curve of her hip appeared in the hallway. She hesitated, came forward somewhat, and then stopped just short of entering the bedroom.

"Over here, Rita," said Sweeney.

She just looked at him, not wanting to come any closer.

"Just one more time?" he implored. "Could you …" Abruptly the police radio interrupted with an almost painful blast of sizzling static. Then Sweeney repeated, more gently, "Just one more time, Rita. Could you go through this once more? This is the last time, I promise. I know you've had a long night. The detective here has just a few questions for you, then you can get back to your beat."

Standing in the doorway of the bedroom, the girl regarded them silently for a long moment. Finally, resigning herself, she closed her eyes and blessed herself quickly with the sign of the cross. Then she entered, moving slowly and carefully, her knowing dark eyes already drifting cautiously in the direction of the brass bed.

Tow followed her involuntary gaze as it settled, then locked on the body.

The victim was a man about 55 years old, gagged and bound naked in his own bed. Dead of literally dozens of puncture-like stab wounds, he lay on a white satin sheet copiously stained with dark dried blood. His eyes, bulging in death, stared intently at the ceiling. His hands, their knuckles white and wrists bound with leather, still grasped the brass bed frame.

She had every right to be horrified, thought Tow. This was every bit as vicious as any street gang murder he had ever seen. The gangs were brutal and indiscriminate, routinely shooting innocent bystanders, frequently including children. This, Tow decided, was far worse. Nothing about this had been random. The attack had been furious—calculated and protracted. No mercy whatsoever. Quite the contrary. Pierced even in the soles of the feet, the victim had been meant to suffer until the very end. And from the unmistakable traces of the tears that stained his face, it could well have taken hours. The shocked girl, thought Tow, was reading all of this very well.

"It's okay now, Rita," said Sweeney, observing the same thing that Tow did. "Our friend here won't be feeling any more pain. It's all over for him. You okay now?" Sweeney encouraged gently. "You all right? Can we go through this one last time?"

The girl managed to look at him, smiled briefly, then nodded unconvincingly. Tow knew that a dozen or more detectives had already questioned her, and that she had been up all night and was exhausted.

"There, that's better," said Sweeney easily, putting his arm around her. "That's my girl. You know Tow Truck here–Detective Miller–don't you?"

The girl accepted this comforting from Sweeney, but lacking any kind of certainty, bit her lower lip as she turned to look at Tow. Her dark eyes, already filled with horror, slowly took on a look of dull recognition. She stiffened abruptly and reflexively withdrew toward Sweeney. She knew him all right. Though it happened almost a year ago, everybody in Chicago remembered the cop who shot the kid. It had been all over the papers and TV for weeks. Even *Time* and *Newsweek* had done articles. Tow wasn't surprised by the girl's reaction. It wasn't the first time another cop had looked at him like that.

There was another blinding flash from the camera.

The girl gasped reflexively and, turning away, raised the back of her hand to her mouth in defense. The camera flashed twice more. "Do we have to talk here?" she asked in quiet protest, still looking away.

Sweeney looked to Tow, but Tow didn't budge. "Tell me what happened," said he quietly. "Start at the beginning."

At this the girl seemed to withdraw physically, looking to Sweeney for help that was not forthcoming.

Tow waited, allowing the girl time to compose herself.

Finally she began in a quiet, flat voice, "I'm on parking and traffic assignment. The midnight beat. Because of the other murders the heat is really on in this area, especially the lakefront from Chicago Avenue to North Avenue. Everything is double or triple covered. My orders are to ticket every vehicle illegally parked, even if it is attended. No discussions, no exemptions. Lay down the law."

Here the girl hesitated, already not wanting to remember, but she would never be able to forget. This Tow understood very well.

Then she continued. "It was toward the end of my shift, just after the storm went through. I saw the damage the tree did when it fell against the building. I radioed for help, and then went in. I am trained and armed, and I felt I had to go in. It looked to me at the time a lot less like a crime and more like an accident. The tree had broken a window with some branches up against the door. I pushed my way through the branches to ring the bell or knock, but the door was already open. Just a crack, but I could see it was open. Some of the branches kept it from closing. Right then I knew something was really wrong. I drew my weapon and walked in and called out loud. There could have been someone in trouble in there."

Tow ignored the irony of this last comment. "And?"

"And there was no answer."

"What about the dogs?"

"They were barking. I found them locked in the laundry room."

Tow motioned to the bed, "Is that exactly how you found him?" He wanted the girl to engage the scene, to work for the very details that she was already trying to purge.

Now she had no choice. Forcing herself to turn again slowly in the direction of the body, she nodded emphatically. "*Exactly*," she said in an abrupt attempt to get it all over with, "Except that lights were out and the two candles on the dresser were still burning."

Tow allowed a long strained silence. "We can't find the murder weapon," he finally continued.

The silence had done its work. Now the girl could not take her empty eyes away. If she had anything more to say, she would do it now. "That's because," she said in a faint flat voice, "She always takes it with her. You know. Just like the other two. She probably keeps it in her purse, ready for the next customer."

Nobody said anything for a moment, then Tow nodded to Sweeney. The girl was close to breaking, and Tow didn't want that.

"Okay, Rita," volunteered Sweeney, suddenly protective again. "That's enough. You can be on your way now, you've done your part," he said soothingly. "Nobody could have asked for more."

Then as if on schedule, the radio blared again, popping and sizzling, blasting its urgent static.

• • •

Tow found Morrison downstairs in the living room.

It was Chicago Police Commander Anthony Morrison who had summoned him to this madness an hour ago. Seeing Tow come down the stairs, Morrison rapidly concluded his instructions to two other Homicide detectives, actually ushering them out the front door with a final command, "*Now!*"

Turning to Tow, Morrison got his eye and shook his head wearily. "This," he began, rolling his eyes upwards, toward the master bedroom, "is real trouble. You ever see anything like this in Street Gang Crimes?"

Tow had. Much worse. A dozen times a day, and then in his dreams at night. An innocent 11-year-old boy, dying with a bullet in his chest. A bullet Tow had fired in a desperate moment of fear and indecision. Yes, he had seen worse, but thought better of saying so. "Not often."

"Morri," called a uniformed officer from the door to the dining room, "You're wanted on the phone."

Visibly irritated, Morrison turned in his direction, "Alright, Lynch, I'll be right there."

Morri took Tow by the arm and led him to the vestibule where they could talk. The July sun coming through the delicate lace curtains had already bathed the hall in brilliant morning light. "Look, Tow," Morrison began earnestly. "This is a real bad situation. Bad for the victims. Bad for the department. Bad for the city. Bad for me. There is something going on here that we just *cannot* stop." Here Morrison hesitated, possibly considering the significance of what he had just said. "And it's bad for you, too," he finally went on. "I know you got to go back because they're bringing up this thing on the boy again next week."

"Morri," Tow interrupted. "The hearing is this Wednesday, that's the day after tomorrow. *Not next week*." With this crisis shaping up, Tow wanted to get the record right.

"So, okay, Wednesday," conceded Morrison. "That's right. Wednesday. I knew about that when I agreed to your transfer. Now with all of this going on, the timing on that is real bad, too. I'm sorry about that. There's nothing I can do except ask for your help in exchange for some advice."

"Morri," said Tow ignoring the suggestion of advice. "You know I'll do my best."

"*Look, Tow,*" snapped Morrison. "*You're in enough trouble.* I don't want your *best.* I want you to do what you're *told.* You report to me. Directly to me. Don't go solo, and don't get nuts on me here, Tow. I got enough problems of my own, as you can damn well see. I want your help. If you got a snitch who can solve this goddamned thing, well, fine. But this isn't Gang Crimes and it isn't the streets on the west side. This is the fucking Gold Coast. Christ, look at this place. Stained glass windows in the parlor? Come on. A place like this probably costs a million bucks. These people have *real* money, Tow. And power. Believe me. Just ..."

"Morri," called Lynch again. "*Telephone!*"

"*Just hold on,*" snapped Morrison, looking up.

Then he returned to Tow. "Now you listen to me a goddamned minute," he continued forcefully. "I'm sticking my neck out here for you, my friend. With your reputation, nobody else in the Department is gonna touch you. But I see it differently. What happened to you is wrong." Morrison's voice was now just an earnest whisper. "In my job, you have to understand politics because in Chicago politics is everything. These people giving you hell, well they're not cops. I know all about this O'Connor woman on the Police Board. Her father was a cop, but that was a damn long time ago. She married old money. Big money. So she can keep a condo on North Michigan Avenue just to satisfy the city residency requirement. She really lives out in Barrington with a summer house up in Green Lake. She has a goddamn chauffeur to drive her around, for Christ's sake. What the hell does she really know about drugs or guns or gangs, or going into the projects at night and getting your fucking head blown off? So I'm giving you a chance now to start over in Homicide. But Tow, you got to do your part here. I believe your story, but you can't fight this thing anymore. You say that there was a witness—some kid with a barking dog–and that this kid can corroborate your story that the boy pointed the gun at you? Well, if you haven't found him after a year with the kind of contacts you got, you're *never* gonna find him. And what the hell would it really change if you did? *Nothing!* The Police

Board ruled the shooting justified. Granted, this Madeline O'Connor pulled a lot of shit and you got thrown out of Gang Crimes and suspended for a year, but the Board still ruled for you and you got paid during your time off. You're cleared. *So put the boy behind you and move on.* They'll never let you go back to Gang Crimes, but is that so goddamn important? You're still a cop and you have a job in Homicide working for me starting now. Play by the rules and in 10 years you'll have a million murder stories and your pension. But one mistake–any rough stuff or other bullshit from you–*and you're out.* You understand me, Tow? *Not one fuck up.* You can't use your old Gang Crimes tactics here. These aren't gang-bangers. You can't smack them around, or put a pistol in their ear and tell them to talk. These people have money, and money buys lawyers, and lawyers make trouble. You have to read them their rights and go by the book."

Enduring all of this silently, Tow finally sighed involuntarily and nodded slightly. Morrison was a cop's cop, a veteran 10 years Tow's senior, and a friend. And, more importantly, Tow knew he was right. Right on everything. Tow knew he should put the boy behind him. But he couldn't. What he wanted was vindication. Not just the skeptical justification of the Civilian Police Board, but rather the kind of unqualified vindication that would come from a public revelation of the true facts. In an effort to find the person he was certain had witnessed the shooting, he had spent almost a full year, all of his savings and the remainder of his marriage. All for nothing. "Morri, you got it," said Tow. "Believe me. I appreciate what you're doing for me. I know you're taking a chance on me. I'll stay in bounds."

Satisfied now, Morrison allowed a long moment of silence. "Okay, then. This is one hell of a day to start in Homicide, I'll say that. So you know what we got here. A fucking *nut case* is what we got here. Sex murder number three. Cash, wallet and watch all missing, too. Just like the other two. But this guy got it at home. Big difference. Victim lived alone. Divorced, according to a neighbor. Rosco Mink is the guy's name. You probably never heard of him."

Tow admitted that he had not.

"Well, I have," said Morrison. "And what I was saying about money and power, that's our victim. I mean, look at this place," said Morrison clearly impressed. "Big social name. Political, too.

Big money," repeated Morrison. "Really big bucks."

"I believe it," acknowledged Tow, careful now to indulge the boss on his first day. The truth was that he *did* believe it. Anyone could see this guy had money. And with it came power and the rest. Morri was right. All the signs of trouble were here.

"Okay, listen. There's an answering machine in the study. Now be goddamned careful with this, Tow. Let the lab boys play it back for you, don't touch it yourself."

Tow nodded assuringly, "No problem, Morri."

"Rosco Mink was some kind of financial manager, we think. A broker, or something. I don't know exactly. But he has one very pissed off client on his phone machine threatening to sue him, and offering to come over and kick his ass. Get the name, then run the guy down. My guess is this Rosco Mink has an office in the city somewhere. Maybe they can give you a lead. Find this guy first thing."

"*Morri*," interrupted Lynch again. Justified in his patience, Lynch was bolder now, this time extending the receiver in Morrison's direction. "*You know you got a call here.*"

Very annoyed, Morrison growled, "*Goddamn it, Lynch.* I'm busy. Tell them I'll call back."

"*Shit, Morri*," protested Lynch again back in his place, his hand now over the receiver. "*It's the Mayor's office!*"

• • •

The heat of the summer sun immediately confronted Tow as he left the brownstone to check out his first lead. It would be another cloudless day; a pale, almost transparent full moon fading in the blue morning sky. Another high humidity July scorcher, thought Tow regretting now he that he had not found the time—or the money—to get the air conditioner in his car fixed while he had had the chance. Not yet assigned a police vehicle from Homicide, he was driving his own six-year-old Buick.

The moment of Tow's departure was especially timely.

A stretcher bearing the deceased was being unceremoniously loaded into the back of a city ambulance surrounded by seven uniformed police officers, present mainly to restrain the photographers and reporters. Beyond the yellow crime scene tape, a hushed crowd of spectators strained to get just a little closer. It was the predictable mix. Many of the curious appeared to be people already on their way to work that Monday morning. Most genuinely seemed to be shocked. With the ambulance as background, several local TV stations were conducting live mini-cam reports, and hovering above, two traffic helicopters competed for position.

Morrison was certainly right about one thing, thought Tow, as he watched them slam the ambulance doors on the corpse. This was bad for the city and for the department. Tow knew pretty much what everyone knew from the voracious media reporting surrounding the events. It had begun in early November with the sensational dual murders of two young call girls. Grim mug shots from prior prostitution arrests revealed both of them to be attractive, blue eyed and blonde, 19 and 20. They were found in a suburban motel, both bound naked to the bed, their throats slit. Two lighted votive candles were found on the dresser, suggesting a possible religious motivation in the slayings. Then, in late February the first conventioneer was murdered in a luxury Gold Coast hotel, followed in the same area by another victim in mid-March. These were ritualistic stabbings. The victims–gagged, bound and naked like the two call girls–had been tortured for some time. In both cases the murder weapon was thought to be a leather punch or an ice pick. In each case, the murderer had carefully avoided the victim's heart to prolong suffering. Cause of death in both cases was multiple penetrations of the lungs which filled with blood, slowly suffocating the victims. The best guess was that this was probably the work of a prostitute–possibly with the aid of an accomplice. In each case, two votive candles were found burning near the corpse, suggesting professional retribution for the slaying of the two call girls.

Five murders, thought Tow, all ostensibly by the same two killers. What if they couldn't stop it? Then what? But Tow knew they would stop it. Each of the killers would make a mistake and that would be the end. The real question was how many would die in the meantime?

Already the ambulance siren was wailing in the distance, and the spectators were breaking up. Brushing off a pack of ravenous reporters, Tow made his way through the crowd in the direction of his car. Half way to the corner, he had already loosened his tie against the morning heat and was removing his suit coat when he stopped and groaned out loud. Even at this distance he could see it. *"Damn it, Rita,"* he muttered looking down the block. The yellow parking ticket tucked under the Buick's windshield wiper was as unmistakable as the red and green fire hydrant next to the car.

2

From the very earliest hours, Monday was off to a good start for Richard Landon.

Vicki's call had awakened him a little after midnight. "Hi," she said softly. "I can't sleep."

With all that thunder and lightning, he was restless too, he admitted. "It looks like it's going to rain again," Richard said lamely.

"It sure does," Vicki agreed. "It really poured a little earlier."

This conversation went on quietly for a few minutes, a midnight reconciliation of a lover's dispute. They continued to ramble on about the weather, deftly avoiding those earlier issues. But Vicki, as usual, soon wanted more than to talk. "How about if I come over?"

"It's late," offered Richard. "I could come there."

"No, no," she protested quickly. "I'm up. I'll be right there."

Only four blocks away, her trip took just 10 minutes. She arrived before the storm broke. Lightning was dancing all over the apartment when Richard heard the key turn, then her heels brisk on the oak floors of the hall, abruptly slowing, and finally halting on the carpet as she undressed in the living room. There was a crack of thunder, and she appeared naked in the doorway of his bedroom just as a dazzling flash of white and blue lightning suddenly illuminated the living room behind her, freezing her for a long erotic moment. In the new darkness that followed, she made her way cat-like across the room and slipped into bed. The rain had just begun lashing the bedroom windows as she pressed herself against him, reaching and finding his erection. "Miss me?" she whispered.

• • •

He had missed her.

Their breakup had been brief, just three days. The same thing had happened a few times before. Another silly dispute of no consequence, this time over a game of chess. Thursday evening last week, Richard arrived at her place late after a few drinks with friends. In jeans and a sweater, Vicki had been drinking too, and was more than a little unhappy with him for being late again and for neglecting to advise her that he was still wearing a suit. "Now I'll have to change," she complained.

"We're not in a hurry," he said.

"You didn't make reservations?"

"On a weeknight we can have dinner anywhere." He kissed her, which seemed to placate her somewhat. She ended their embrace, and headed for the bedroom to change. "Take your time," said Richard, still trying to appease her.

While he waited, Richard poured himself a drink and idly considered the chessboard on the coffee table. The game laid out was their unfinished match from earlier in the week. He was white, and in his usual distress, reduced to a rook, a bishop and three pawns defending his very vulnerable king. Black threats were everywhere, but rather than forfeit he had proposed a temporary suspension which his ruthless opponent had uncharacteristically allowed, with the understanding that they would definitely complete the game at a later date.

Always quick to get ready, Vicki came out of the bedroom in a wicked little red dress, one of her favorites. *Streetwalker red*, she liked to call it. Her long blonde hair was loosely gathered with a large black satin bow. With a single glance at her, Richard dismissed all thoughts of chess, and stood up to meet her. Immediately he had his hands all over her, but she had other priorities. "Wait," she said breaking their embrace and focusing on the game before them. "We should finish this."

"We haven't even started," Richard countered, nuzzling her neck and backing her toward the bedroom. Of course, he was well aware that she was still upset with him.

She resisted. "*No, Richard.* The game. First we should finish the game. Unless, of course, you forfeit!"

Aroused, he almost agreed but instead pleaded again for a delay. "*No, Richard.* Now, or you forfeit. You didn't bother with reservations. You said we have plenty of time."

"Okay, okay. But first I need another drink."

"*Fine,*" she said, taking his empty glass.

She returned with drinks, and they settled down in silence to study the board. It was her move first. However, aware of his condition and too confident of victory, Vicki strung him along instead of going for the throat as usual. Toying with him, she neglected his advancing pawns, one of which recovered his queen, which in turn won the game for him in a series of ridiculously lucky moves.

His laughter was genuine, and not well received.

Unable to complain about his victory, Vicki began to provoke, digging elsewhere. He was late again, she began, and she was tired of it. Then came the real issue: *Katie's things were still around his apartment. Was he expecting her to return? Was he still seeing her?* One thing led to another and they never made it to dinner. Then later came the stonewalling. She pouting in her apartment; he, sullen and withdrawn, not answering the phone in his.

Until tonight.

Vicki's idea of kissing and making up required an urgent coupling. Not even their usual modest foreplay had been necessary this time. She was as eager as he was, and their passion lasted until the storm had finally spent its fury. This time she had really worn him out, her midnight performance completely uninhibited–aggressive even by her lusty standards. He had never seen her so excited–or exciting, with all that lightning and wind and thunder and rain.

They had just gotten to sleep when sirens–*screeching, screaming sirens*–wailing just outside, rudely shocked them awake around 1:30 in the morning. Now they were unable to get back to sleep. As the storm cleared, they began making love again, this time with a full silver moon looming in the window while even more sirens passed below, responding to some very nearby calamity. Then exhausted, they overslept, but were immediately at it again the moment they awoke. So they would be late for work. So what? It wasn't the first time.

As usual, she showered while he made coffee.

Richard was happy enough about this lusty reunion. Seeing the trail of Vicki's clothes strewn through the living room confirmed his smug confidence. Clearly she had undressed in a hurry. Her heels still lay where she had kicked them off, on the carpet near the door. Next to go was her skirt and blouse, then her pantyhose. Last, a lace bra and matching panties had been carelessly discarded on the chair nearest the bedroom. Fastidious by nature, Richard collected her things and arranged them neatly on the chair in the order she would require them. His confidence was soaring. He knew she would be back.

But the situation was complicated–very complicated. Ending one love affair, and immediately beginning another, naturally would be complicated. And there were other factors, complex in themselves. Some Richard's fault, some not his at all. Still, Vicki had been right about one thing in their argument the other night. He had to return the rest of Katie's things, and pick up his tools, videos and clothes from her mother's place out in Barrington. He simply had to bring this relationship to a final end. Katie O'Connor was history, and he resolved to clean up the remaining details, which consisted mainly of the few personal items she had casually accumulated at his place. A pastel hairbrush with those unmistakable long dark strands still bound among its bristles. An especially bulky pink sweater that she kept around because his corner apartment could be chilly in winter. A dozen romance novels with those ridiculous covers–he could never understand why she spent so much time reading such junk. Some expensive crockery for those occasions when she prepared meals at home then lugged it all to his place. There really wasn't that much. He had packed it all into a couple boxes that sat on the floor in the hall closet.

There wasn't much because Katie had never moved in, though they had been engaged for three months. That her mother would never have tolerated. Largely because of Madeline O'Connor, everything with Katie had been traditional and proper, from the introductions to The Question. Richard had met Katie through his boss who was married to her oldest sister, Eleanor. They had begun dating immediately, the relationship progressing almost a year until it was time for The Question. Of course Katie's response had been immediate and joyful, the conventional response to the conventional question. It was only at that point, with considerable reluctance on her part, that they began sleeping together. That was another problem. She seemed to be totally inexperienced. Patient, but not passionate. Nothing was quite right.

All of this had been over for almost four months now, enough time for Richard to realize that it had never really been love on his part. True, they always got along, but that did not constitute love. Their relationship never actually failed, rather it just never succeeded. Toward the end, Richard was profoundly unhappy, and Katie certainly knew it. Then came a particularly serious financial setback for Richard. An investment blew up, the disastrous Cambridge Fund, brokered by a close friend of the O'Connor family. That was the bad news, and it certainly was bad. Richard lost almost everything he had put into Cambridge. But the good news was that it had provided a convenient excuse to end the misery of their relationship, and Richard immediately did so, invoking an earlier covenant. They had agreed at his insistence that he had to have money in the bank before marriage and family. Then, suddenly, there was virtually no money at all–a profound shock.

For her part, Katie accepted his evasion, but obviously would have welcomed a reunion. They still spoke regularly on the phone, friendly conversations, only understandably strained. She knew about Vicki too, but never said anything. That had been just a little bad luck, he and Vicki at Dorati's one night, running into Katie's sister, Molly, just weeks following the breakup. Richard knew the engaging smile and polite greeting were mere diplomacy, and that a less generous report would be filed immediately with Kate.

This was regrettable on his part. There was no doubt in Richard's mind that Kate had been far more involved than he, and he felt badly about it. To a large degree, he blamed himself. His motives had been sensible, but perhaps not quite legitimate. More than anything in the world, trader Richard Landon wanted to make a lot of money. Really a lot of money. His employer, Paul Steward, had counseled stability. *You will trade better if you settle down. A wife and a family will improve your focus.* Such advice from a phenomenal trader like Paul could not be ignored. Then one day Paul, still trying to help, introduced him to his lovely young sister-in-law.

Still, much of the eventual failure, Richard was certain, was because Kate was simply too young–just 23. A history major, she had virtually no career aspirations, few interests and no friends other than Molly with whom she was very close. Neither were there any vices. Katie seldom drank, didn't smoke, and never fooled around with drugs. She didn't complain about anything. She had no serious opinions, made no unreasonable demands–strictly low maintenance. The ring and the cradle were all that Katie had ever wanted. That, and maybe to escape wealthy, controlling Madeline. The whole thing had been a sad mistake on both sides.

Now Richard wanted to ask Victoria Moss The Question, too. This proposal, however, had a more contemporary twist–not marriage, but an invitation to move in with him permanently. That would be commitment enough, he thought. And it was what he guessed she wanted as well. It was possible–even likely–thought Richard, that Vicki would actually scoff at any suggestion of a ring and a cradle.

· · ·

With a cup of coffee in each hand, Richard returned to the bedroom as Vicki emerged from the shower wearing only a bath towel wrapped turban style around her head. Teasing, she removed the towel and shook her wet hair back, then flaunted playful hands on her hips. "Like my outfit?"

He did like it. He liked everything about her. She was blonde, somewhat less fair in one place than another, but still obviously a real blonde. She had green eyes, creamy skin, a model's high cheekbones and smooth high forehead. Her mouth was wide with full lush lips. Lips that could pout. Lips that could smile. Lips that could do a lot of other things too, depending on her moods. At 31, she was almost three years older than he. A big girl, maybe five eight or nine, and sturdy from all that time at the gym. Large breasts, narrow waist, and full hips. And those long, long legs. Exceptionally great wheels. Yes, he liked her outfit all right.

But there was more. Vicki was extraordinary in another way, a beautiful woman who lived and worked in a man's world that Kate was acquainted with only from a distance. Vicki was a bond trader like Richard, and she understood the ruthless realities of trading. The punishing doubts, and the even more punishing consequences when your fears come true. The rewards when you win. And she was a winner herself, a big money maker. The real thing, not just an observer like so many women in the trading world. Richard attributed her success not so much to her considerable intelligence, but rather to her boldness. Particularly calculating, nervy Vicki actually took much more risk and made far more money than most men.

However, Richard already knew that money and trading–the very passions that dominated his life–were not the most important things to Vicki. Those things she already had in abundance, and seemed to take them for granted. She certainly liked money, and spent it in great quantities. But Vicki's greatest passion was for passion itself. Oddly, this was probably the biggest difference between them. While he loved sex, she lived for it. There was nothing she wouldn't do. And she always wanted to do it. She was always so lusty. And she was good at sex, actually skilled like a superb athlete. She was sophisticated, and very direct, and had a kind of sexual power that he had never seen in another woman.

Most importantly, Vicki completely comprehended the sexual aspects of the male mind, perhaps the secret to working her magic. This unquestionably was where things really became fascinating for Richard. She was an expert in seduction and eroticism. With that fabulous body, she could tease, she could flirt. She could seduce or merely tempt. But usually she meant business. After all, it had been *she* who had picked *him* up at the bar at the Pump Room late that rainy Tuesday evening in April. True, they already knew each other somewhat, acquainted only slightly from the small world of markets and trading. Still, at that time she was to him mainly this hot boozy blonde with a great set of knockers. And she couldn't have known much about him either. It had been Vicki's blunt proposition after four drinks at the bar to go back to her place, and it wasn't to play chess. Just inside her apartment and still partly dressed, they first fucked on the living room sofa, then moved to her bedroom where they spent all the next day and night. And even then, in their lust, they managed to be late for work the following day. Despite his money problems, Richard Landon felt a remarkable and sudden happiness–at last something spectacularly wonderful had come into his life. All of this was all so different from his dismal experience with reluctant Katie. This time, Richard knew, it was for real. Together now less than three months, Richard was sure that he was in love with high maintenance Vicki.

• • •

He was in the shower when she peeked in, nothing unusual for playful Vicki. She was only half dressed, just in pantyhose and heels, not yet wearing a bra. This eroticism–often so deliberate on her part–stirred Richard's desire, and he reached for her. "Hey, baby," he began.

"Richard," she said, completely brushing him off. "You had better come see this."

"What?"

"You know all those sirens we heard last night?" Her tone was flat, ominous.

Richard hesitated, a sense of dread already beginning to gather deep within him. "Yeah?" he responded slowly, cautiously.

"They were for Rosco. It's on television. He's dead. Just three blocks from here. *Murdered in his own home.*"

The significance of this development registered with Richard Landon with the speed and force of an arrow finally finding its mark. "Oh, no," he said. Then, with a moment more for reflection, his anger exploded. "*Fucking Rosco!*" he cursed, that feeling of dread now fully surging as he grabbed a towel. *Fucking Rosco,* thought Richard. First the Cambridge Fund, and now this. It was all his fault.

His luck, Richard Landon knew immediately, had changed.

It was all over the news.

They sat on the bed and watched. Prominent investment advisor Rosco L. Mink had been found murdered in his Gold Coast brownstone following the storm that had roared through the area late Sunday night. Apparently the third victim of a serial killer, Mink had been bound then stabbed numerous times with a sharp weapon.

The serial aspects of the murder drew much conjecture. The two previous victims had been conventioneers, out partying late, slain months apart in hotel rooms last winter in apparent retaliation for the dual slaying of two young call girls in the fall. Rosco Mink, however, was murdered in his own bed. Was the killer–sketchy evidence suggested a prostitute–becoming more aggressive? Did this constitute an error on her part? Surely the heat would be turned up now. And there was more. Reference to scandal was already surfacing. What was this respectable, divorced Chicago business man doing with a hooker in his own home?

In a city that loved scandal, it was a media celebration.

A helicopter report from Channel 7 revealed a large crowd and a dozen blue and white police vehicles jammed before the townhouse over on Astor Street. Channel 2 played then replayed a mini-cam report showing a hefty shrouded corpse being loaded without ceremony into the dark cavity of a city ambulance. Perspiring in the heat on the steps of the victim's townhouse, a very tense Chicago Police Commander Anthony Morrison conceded, in response to a reporter's question, that there were "no immediate suspects."

"Well," said Richard. "*That's that.*" He was angry and despairing, only beginning to organize his thoughts.

Vicki was more detached. "Well, I'd say Rosco got just what he deserved," she said casually, almost wistfully.

This was so like Vicki, thought Richard. No sympathy whatever for an adversary. All he cared about was his investment. Since March when the Cambridge Fund had bottomed out, he had hoped for at least some improvement. If not a rally, at least some compensation from Mink Capital Management for brokering the disastrous investment. "Now," said Richard. "We'll never get our money back."

"Come on, Richard, Rosco was never going to re-capitalize the fund."

"He could have returned his fees."

She laughed. "Get real. We were screwed from the beginning. He never intended to give any of our money back."

"I suppose you're right. But now we'll never know." Here he stalled, considering just how much he should say. Richard Landon was beginning to realize that he had a very big problem. "You know," he finally confided with casualness calculated to match her earlier comment, "I tried calling him last night, but just got his machine."

"I don't know why you bothered." Then a more entertaining thought occurred to her, and she laughed out loud. "Maybe Rosco's lady friend was a Cambridge Fund investor, too, maybe somebody we know," she said smiling, suddenly gleeful. "This is kind of exciting. Rough justice, you know. Maybe," she continued with smug satisfaction, "we should just think of it as class action justice. I think we should have a little celebration."

He knew of course what she was suggesting–so typical of Vicki– but Richard wasn't quite ready to *celebrate* yet. There was the money to think about. Vicki was probably right about that. They would never see their investments again. Like many Chicago traders, they had been introduced to Rosco Mink and, separately, each had invested in the Cambridge Fund over a year ago. The money they placed with Cambridge probably was gone, a much more serious problem for broke Richard than for prosperous Vicki. He should never have risked so much. It was only because he had been pressed. Nothing had been going right and on top of that, other serious problems now complicated the situation. If he were lucky, they might just go away. If he were not, he could be facing even more damage. What should he tell Vicki? What would she say? He had to stop and think.

The main problem was that he had been there last night.

When he couldn't get Rosco on the phone–Rosco had yet to return even one of Richard's many calls–he walked the few blocks over there to bang on the front door and confront the son-of-a-bitch, just as he had threatened in his phone message. After all, he had almost his entire net worth in this failing investment, and Rosco probably was home, just not answering the phone. As he approached Rosco's brownstone, a girl was leaving. She had a tissue in her hand, applying it to one eye as though it were injured. Still their eyes met. Richard immediately recognized her from a party months earlier. Her eyes held sudden recognition for him, too, but they passed without a word. The experience was so unnerving that by the time he walked up the steps of the brownstone, he had changed his mind about the urgency of confronting Rosco. He didn't even ring the bell, but by the time he turned around to leave, the girl was already closing the door on a Yellow Cab. Then it started to rain, and he had to jog all the way home.

That party. That bachelor party for Gordon Wells right before Christmas. God, he wished he had never been there. It was all so stupid, way, way out of hand. More than the conventional booze and chicks, this north suburban bachelor blowout included drugs—a lot of drugs. And a lot of women. Some were servers, and some were high paid talent recruited to satisfy your every desire. All so stupid, at least from Richard Landon's point of view. He didn't do drugs, and he would never drill a hooker. And he didn't need to be blamed when things got rough on some of the girls who apparently were not for sale. Like that black chick he saw leaving Rosco's last night. At the party she had been a topless bartender with stiletto heels and a Santa hat. This particular elf had a fabulous body that proved to be just a little too tempting. Who could forget that body? What a set of jugs! She was fantastic. The scene had been a spectacle. Somebody crammed a wad of cash in her hand, but she tried to say no, insisting she wasn't a hooker. The more she resisted, the more her pursuers were aroused. Richard could hear her muffled screams in an upstairs bedroom where someone had hung mistletoe on the headboard. And she wasn't the only one who was gang banged. There were at least three others. The real hookers ended up standing around watching, as he had. He had left in a rush when someone shouted that the neighbors had called the cops.

Thank god that Ricky Wells, Gordon's younger brother, had sense enough to talk to the police that night. Ricky was always a pretty smooth character. Charismatic, good with people. Magically, nothing ever happened. No questions, no nothing. Richard was as amazed as he was relieved. However a few days later, Ricky called to advise Richard quietly that his share of this *magic* would cost him two thousand dollars—cash. Richard paid up without a word. He didn't care if the money went to the cops or to the girls or to the neighbors. And it didn't matter that he was innocent. This was the kind of thing that could get you fired and ultimately ruin your career. He could not afford to be involved. That was eight months ago, just before Christmas.

And now this.

So, *this was the one.* The bartender with the great body. The one suspected of murdering those two conventioneers. It all fit, he reasoned. No doubt about that. The pattern made sense. A progression of desperation. From topless bartender to hooker to murderess. Then another thought occurred to him–a particularly frightening thought. Something had to have happened to cause this chick to go over the edge to murder. And not just one murder, but three calculated savage killings. *Could the rape have been the trigger that actually led to the murders?* Richard groaned at the thought. Of course, it all made sense. Perfect sense. A string of crazy events leading up to Rosco, the premier victim of chance. Richard had no difficulty believing that sleazy Rosco was indulging in expensive home entertainment without considering the possible consequences. Yes, it all fit. To his despair, he was unquestionably linked to this crazed serial killer.

But now, what to do?

If he told the cops about Rosco and the girl, all the rest was sure to surface in some way devastating to him. Accuse the girl of murder and she could finger him as a participant in the covered up rape. A high level investigation would no doubt follow. They would get all the facts. And when the cover up was uncovered, well then things could get very messy.

What was in it for him? This wasn't social work. It wasn't like he owed Rosco anything. Or anybody else for that matter. He resolved to say no more to anyone and let the cops track down the girl themselves, as they sooner or later would. He would be fortunate now if he could just stay out of the whole thing.

Yes, thought Richard Landon, his luck had certainly changed.

But his desire had not. As usual, Vicki knew exactly what he was thinking when he drew her closer. Clearly excited, it took her only seconds to slip out of her pantyhose and lie back for their celebration. And as usual, Richard noted, she was already more than prepared to accommodate him. They were working on her third orgasm when the phone rang in the other room. Vicki didn't even notice, but Richard did and was suddenly distracted. Then with a surge of relief, he remembered that he had turned the answering machine off days ago, stonewalling Vicki in his anger. The last thing he needed now was a message from Katie for present company to hear. Refocusing he returned to his task, and coaxed Vicki to another crashing orgasm just as the insistent phone finally stopped ringing.

3

Twelve-year-old Benjamin Foster was feeling the effects of the surging heat on that same early Monday morning. The effort of lugging six heavy bundles of newspapers up several flights of stairs to the train platform had caused his shirt to cling uncomfortably to his back and sweat to bead on his forehead. But Ben let none of this bother him. "That's the last one, Harold," he said, dropping his bundle with a thud.

"Good job, Ben," Harold Lamb told him. "I'll be back in an hour or so. You take care of things here for me."

This was the kind of thing Ben loved to hear. He had worked for Harold Lamb only two months, but already the boss trusted him completely. Now Ben would sell the papers and Harold would return to collect the day's cash and pay Ben his share. It was a good paying part-time job, and Ben especially enjoyed working with kindly Harold Lamb.

It was only a little before seven, but already business was brisk among the early Monday morning commuters at this west side rapid transit station. An impatient line had formed quickly, the kind of thing that usually happened when there was something big in the news. Ben was aware of a quiet murmur of concern among the crowd. A familiar white man, today in a dark suit and red tie, frowned as he scanned the front page. "Jesus," he muttered. Then to the woman he was with, "Look at this, Margo. *Another one!*"

Ben wasn't sure exactly what the big story was. The headline was political, Congress Overrides Veto. The photograph on the front page featured the President speaking before some indecipherable group. Columns on both sides of the page offered nothing of interest to Ben. It was a small item on the lower right that was probably the big story, he guessed. "Gold Coast Murder" was the heading. The story was brief, only several short paragraphs that referenced a crime just hours old.

Ben quickly sold 20 or so of his 150 *Tribunes*, and guessed that today would be a lucky day. His mother would be pleased. He'd most likely sell all the papers and make about $15, which they could certainly use. The same good fortune had come his way three or four times in recent months. Crime, Ben knew, was good for business.

Of course the kind of crime that sold newspapers was not real crime to Ben. Newspaper crime was distant, a little like the movies. And it always involved rich people. Rich white people, not struggling black people like he and his mother. Though he had never witnessed a crime, Ben knew that crime, real crime, was not a good thing. When his father walked out of a currency exchange into the fatal cross fire of a gang shootout one summer evening three years ago, there were no headlines for him. His death was, in fact, only briefly acknowledged in the back of the middle section of the *Tribune,* which Ben had saved and kept in a drawer. Neither had the police ever solved the crime, or even ever charged a suspect. No, real crime was not a good thing.

By 9:30 a.m. Harold Lamb returned and Ben was done for the day.

It was a perfect summer morning, hot already and getting hotter, but still perfect. Ben stopped at the bakery on Lake near Ridgeland, lingering for a half-hour over a jelly Bismarck and chocolate milk. Across the street was the familiar Oak Park Village Pool, already filling with kids shrieking in the inviting blue water. Normally he would have phoned his mother, and then gone swimming there all day. But now they had no phone, and he had no resident's pass for the pool. Instead he finished his chocolate milk and walked a few blocks north where he waited on Chicago Avenue for an eastbound bus. After a few minutes in the searing sun, he withdrew to the protection of the shade of a large tree and sat on a big rock in the grass still damp from last night's rain.

Until five weeks ago, he could have walked home from here, just five shady blocks back the way he had come. He and his mother had moved three times since his father's death. After his mother sold their house, they lived in apartments, each located progressively closer to the city, but still west of Austin Boulevard and within walking distance of the pool. But their recent move to Pine Street changed all of that. On Pine Street there were no bakeries and no swimming pool.

The bus finally arrived, and as Ben got on, a young man in a gray suit carrying a brief case got off. Ben took a seat near the back, and noticed that there were only three other riders, all of them elderly. All three got off at Austin Boulevard. Until they moved to Pine Street, his mother had never permitted him east of Austin. This was gang territory, and his mother had established a list of rules to deal with the threat. Most of the rules began with the word *don't*. Alone now, Ben slouched into his seat and watched out the window as the bus proceeded into the city.

The change in the neighborhoods was profound. This morning many traffic lights were without power, Ben noticed. A consequence of last night's storm. This was no longer shady Oak Park, with big watered lawns and wide quiet streets. Now just three miles east of Oak Park, Ben could actually see the tall buildings of the Chicago Loop.

Ben got off at Chicago Avenue and Pine Street in front of a liquor store covered with gang graffiti, its filthy windows protected by rusty iron bars. Sidestepping a muddy puddle that swamped the sidewalk, he abruptly noticed something, and stopped. Curled in the shade of the recessed entrance to the store lay a young boy whom Ben judged to be about his own age. Drawing closer, Ben saw no signs of injury, and guessed the boy to be sleeping, probably having sought shelter here from the violent storm last night. The boy was black, exceptionally thin and taller than he, and dressed in a dirty white T-shirt and baggy red shorts. He was lying on a flattened cardboard box. Still studying the boy, Ben was suddenly startled by a growl from the darkness further within. He froze, his heart skipping, then gradually made out the figure of a dog near the door. Not a very big dog of any discernible breed, it was just getting to its feet, teeth bared, its eyes locked on him. Ben did not move.

The dog stopped protectively just behind the sleeping boy, and stood there panting in the heat. Roused by the commotion, the boy looked up. Disoriented at first, he quickly assessed the situation. The dog was growling again.

"Doan worry," he said to Ben. "He woan hurt you none." Without getting up, the boy put a long thin arm around the dog's neck, closing his fingers around the dog's chain collar. "Down, boy," he said softly. "*Down.*"

Obediently, the dog settled next to his master who turned back to Ben with an expectant look. Ben slowly backed away, then, greatly relieved, stepped quickly in the direction of Pine Street and home.

• • •

Pine Street surely was not what Ben had expected when his mother had told him they were moving. Not only were there no pine trees as the name suggested there would be, but there were few trees at all. Neither was there much grass. Instead the few narrow strips of earth not covered with asphalt or concrete were barren and baked rock hard from the sun. And it seemed there was glass everywhere. Glass from broken pop and beer bottles was ground into the dirt or lay in wicked shards ready to menace children on the sidewalk and steps. Often where cars had vacated parking places on the street, small square nuggets of glass from shattered automobile windows glittered like diamonds in the brilliant morning sun. Evidence of such forced entry seemed to mark every access. In the building where Ben lived, many apartment doors were severely scarred and even gouged at their handles and deadbolts. Mailboxes seemed to be especially vulnerable to plunder. All of this suggested to Ben relentless predators just waiting for his mother and him. Beyond fear, Ben felt terribly ashamed by all of this, none of which would be happening if his father were still alive.

Ben and his mother lived in a small apartment on the third floor of a nine story building in the middle of the block. Like the others, Ben's building was in desperate need of repair. Its basic 60-year-old construction was brick and concrete, crumbling from time and neglect. The roof sagged, as did the wooden staircase that provided an exterior rear exit in the case of emergency. Decor–paint and carpeting–was completely expendable. This building was larger than most, but generally indistinguishable from the rest in the neighbor-hood. Its roof and plumbing leaked. Heating was inadequate, ven-tilation and cooling non-existent. Electrical service was vulnerable and susceptible to extended power shortages. The vacant lot next door, like two others on the block, was a depository for tires and other junked automobile parts, and sometimes even the stripped down cars themselves, which provided shelter to homeless wander-ers. Only the projects, located further east and closer to the city, offered poorer and more dangerous living conditions. Places like the LBJ Homes, where Harold Lamb lived. So dangerous, that his mother had specifically forbidden Ben ever to visit Harold at home. "He's a very nice man, and he's been an enormous help to us, but *don't you ever go there.*" In emphasizing this message, she grasped Ben by his shoulders and actually shook him. "*Don't you ever go there for any reason. Do you understand me, Benjamin? Not ever!*"

• • •

Ben could hear the television as he fitted his key into the door, and was barely inside when his mother was already scolding him over the volume of the set. "*Benjamin, where have you been?*"

Ben knew immediately that she was upset, a circumstance that was increasingly common.

"Do you know what time it is?" she went on as though it mat-tered. "I've been worried sick about you."

There was no question that she was very upset. Ben guessed that she had been crying again. "I made almost $15 today, Momma," he said, trying to appease her. From his pocket he pulled out two fives and four singles and some change. "I sold every newspaper I had."

Normally his mother would have acknowledged this accomplish-ment with considerable praise. Today, fixed on the television, she ignored it. "*I told you to come straight home. Those are my rules. There are gangs out there, didn't I tell you that?*"

The television was tuned to the news, the story of the Gold Coast murder, and Ben concluded that this far away violence had fright-ened his mother, suggesting and enlarging the very real dangers of their present situation. Then he noticed that she was applying a cold towel to the side of her face. "What happened to your eye, Momma?"

"*From now on, young man,*" she went on through the towel, not taking her eyes from the television, "*You come right home. Do you hear me, Benjamin?*"

Ben moved closer for a better look. "What happened to you?" he repeated, his face now close to his mother's and full of gentle concern. Suddenly she drew him close, hugging him, holding him. She was crying.

"What's the matter, Momma?"

She held him for a long moment, then finally drew a deep breath and composed herself, still holding him. "Oh, Benji. Nothing is the matter," she said smiling through her tears. "Nothing is the matter, really. We're fine. We're going to be just fine. I just ... I mean, someone—two boys—tried to grab my purse last night, and I fell. That's all."

His mother released him and Ben stood up. "Where did this happen?"

"Downtown. In the city."

"Did you tell the police?"

"It's okay, I'm fine, Benji," his mother said softly. "Really I am. It's just a bruise. The boys ran away and I still have my purse, so I don't have to tell the police anything."

Ben had cause to worry about his mother. Before, when his father was still alive, she had worked at a big bank in the city. That was safe. Nothing ever happened. But she was a model now, and went different places on each assignment. At first she worked in just one place. Like the one where they did the Sears catalogue. His mother was in 11 pages of Sears's photos, modeling dresses and coats. In several of these pictures, she was holding a golden retriever on a leash. But now she went from place to place. And though Ben was only 12, he was keenly aware that his mother was young and exceptionally beautiful, and he understood that that meant she needed special protection in a dangerous world. Only eight months ago, just after she had sold the car, she and her friend, Lydia, had been badly beaten in a late night mugging. It was a few weeks before Christmas and his Aunt Frances, his mother's sister, had come all the way from Milwaukee to stay for two days while his mother was in the hospital. When his mother got home, she was very weak for a while and spent a lot of time crying. No one ever found the men who had committed this crime. It seemed to Ben that no one even tried. Whenever he asked his mother about it, she seemed to become angry and often wept. This little bruise, Ben had to agree, was a small problem in comparison. His mother was okay, and she still had her purse. Justice, Ben knew from his father's experience, was a rare commodity, and certainly not the most important thing in life.

It was already very warm in the apartment. Ben turned on the fans in the living room and kitchen, and set about making a sandwich. In the heat the peanut butter had a syrupy quality, and the milk from the old refrigerator was only cool rather than cold. Impatient with the stifling heat, Ben wished desperately that he could go swimming at the pool. Of course without a resident's pass, that was impossible now. "I'm going outside for a walk," he told his mother who was again absorbed with the television.

"*You be careful, Benjamin,*" she warned removing the towel from her pretty face. She seemed angry again. "You do like I told you. You remember my rules and you stay away from trouble."

"I will, Momma."

• • •

With no particular destination, Ben wandered down residential Pine Street to commercial Handel Boulevard. Drawn by the distant yet unmistakable sound of a string of fire crackers popping, he turned the corner and squinted directly into the brilliant morning sun. Shading his eyes he could make out a sparkling jet of water shooting geyser-like, 10 or 15 feet straight up in the air. It was an open fire hydrant, and around it were a dozen shrieking kids playing in its silver spray. And romping among them, Ben observed as he approached, were the now familiar figures of a tall thin boy and a scrawny dog.

It was the dog, of course, that brought them together again.

Even from a distance, Ben could see that the dog was the center of the fun, darting from kid to kid through the spray of the open hydrant adjacent to a small playground. Obviously these were neighborhood kids, varying in age from five or six to mid-teens, all drawn to the playground. Ben counted three balls in the air at once, all competing for the dog's attention.

"Here, Scab!"

"Come, Scab! Come on, boy!"

Soaked from the hydrant games, it was clear how Scab had gotten his name. Several large irregular sections of his long brown coat, particularly on one side, were completely barren as though the hide had been peeled from his flanks. Soaked, Scab did not look so formidable now. The dog was slight to begin with, and appeared to be much thinner than he should be. Still he was fast, and very agile.

Out of this din, a yellow rubber ball the size of a baseball bounced in Ben's direction with Scab in vigorous pursuit. Ben easily fielded the ball, then extended it carefully to the eager dog, which halted a few feet before him. Ben stooped, then gently rolled the ball to the panting dog. Scab allowed Ben to advance and pet him briefly before bolting back to the action at the shriek of another kid.

"See? I tol' you he woan hurt you none."

Ben looked up. It was the boy, the tall thin boy from this morning. He was wearing the same baggy red shorts, but had removed the soiled white T-shirt. Before Ben could respond the boy spun neatly away to retrieve another bouncing ball. Spider, the other kids called him.

Spider, thought Ben. Another understandable label. The boy was not all that tall, Ben realized. Not much taller than he, and he was average for 12. However, Spider, like his dog, was exceptionally thin and wiry. His long limbs and narrow torso, with all ribs visible, manufactured the illusion of height.

A series of fire crackers started popping again, some sputtering, others fresh and live. The older kids shrieked with delight, while several of the little ones began to cry. Scab reacted with only the briefest alarm, then quickly refocused on the game. At first Ben couldn't tell who had the Lady Fingers, then he saw Spider toss a small flat sizzling package in the direction of a car parked at the curb. Again came the series of small explosions.

In response to this racket they heard a shrill angry voice from across the street. It was an elderly Chinese woman, standing in the door of the Handel Boulevard Dry Cleaners. "I told you to stop," she scolded, shaking an angry finger. "I told you over and over. *Stop*, I say. Many times I say *please* stop! Now I call the police. You hear me?" She was very upset. "You hear me? The police are coming!"

Ben was alarmed by this, but to his surprise, there was little immediate reaction from the other kids. They simply watched as the woman threw up her hands in disgust, and shaking her head, sought to escape the searing sun by retreating to the dark recesses of the shop.

The games quickly resumed, drawing a few more participants who arrived on bikes. These were older boys, three of them. Ben guessed they were around 16. They were big, and they looked and acted 16. They were loud and arrogant, and stuck together. Everything they did seemed calculated. They even dressed similarly, black Bulls hats turned left, black and red laces in their high top sneakers. Each had a small gold ear ring in his left ear. All very cool. They removed their shirts and, together, strutted defiantly into the spray of the hydrant. Soon however, even this icy unity faded, and all three showed pre-dictable interest in playing ball with Scab.

While the old woman's threats of police produced no concern among the younger children, Ben noticed most of the older kids had begun to drift away. Despite his doubts, Ben wanted to stay. He wanted no trouble with the police, but many others stayed. Spider stayed. Why shouldn't he?

Ben approached Spider, who was removing another string of Lady Fingers from a clear plastic bag that contained an assort-ment of fireworks. "Aren't you worried about the police catching you with that?"

The boy looked at Ben curiously, then laughed. "Ain't no po-lices comin'," he said shaking his head. "Po-lices doan bother with no fire crackers."

This rebuke had been mild enough, so Ben just stood there, still puzzled by the sudden departure of so many of the older, possibly wiser, kids. Still, under Spider's obvious scrutiny, Ben felt decidedly foolish.

"Here," said Spider, "Hol' dis."

Eager now to redeem himself, Ben took the string of fire crackers while Spider sought a dry match. After three failures, he finally coaxed life into one and lit a decidedly lively fuse to the block of Lady Fingers. Ben froze.

"Throw it," urged Spider calmly.

Ben could do nothing.

"Here," said Spider now with some urgency. "*Gimme.*"

And with that Spider flung the package to the curb where it was demolished in a series of rapid explosions.

It was just then that they heard a painful yelp from Scab.

And at a glance through the spray of the hydrant, they could see the problem. One of the three newcomers was awkwardly attempting to kick the retreating dog as it quickly limped, head down and whimpering, toward its master. This last attempt had missed badly, but there was no question that Scab had already suffered a solid blow.

All three of the teenagers followed the dog directly to Spider and Ben.

Spider immediately advanced to confront them. "*What you do to my dog?*" he screamed, instinctively shoving the closest one. "*Why you hurt my dog?*"

Ben was right behind Spider, then at his side with Scab barking furiously between them. Immediately Ben was hit hard, a blinding blow flush to the face. Then on the ground he was kicked repeatedly, a blizzard of black and red. Lying in a puddle of warm dirty water, Ben tried without success to roll away from this assault. Then he saw that Scab had one assailant by the back of the leg. Blood was running from the screaming boy's wound. For Ben it was a furious, painful blur. Then abruptly, the kicking stopped. As suddenly as it had begun, the fight was over, and everyone was running.

The Chinese woman was yelling again, pointing in their direction. Spider dragged Ben to his feet, shouting at him, "Come on, we got to get outta dis place. P*o-lices* comin'," he urged, "*Come on, we got to go.*"

Bleeding profusely from his nose, Ben staggered along with Spider and Scab down the block into an alley next to a restaurant where they sank to the ground behind a garbage dumpster. "We be safe here," Spider whispered. "Theys only two of dem, and dey took off after dem gang bangers."

In the heat, Ben felt like vomiting. There was something rotten in the dumpsters, the smell adding to Ben's nausea. Sweat and blood dripped onto his chest. "Where are they?" he managed to say through a cut lip.

"Gang bangers or the po-lices?"

"The police are here?" said Ben hopefully.

Spider nodded. "Theys chasing dem punks. Good thing theys showed up, too. This here be much worse for us ceptin for them po-lices. But, dem boys, dey gang members. You see how everyone go when theys shows up? You see theys hats turned left? You see theys colors? They got black and red laces in theys shoes."

Ben nodded. He had seen those laces all too well.

"Theys Devils Disciples. Lucky for us they doan live nowheres around here. Devils live east of Cicero. But we got to watch out for dem now, and theys friends too. Theys gonna come back lookin' for us."

"What about the police?"

"That right. We got to watch out for dem too," said Spider. "Scab bit one of them gangbangers. Po-lices can use dat. Put us all in the penitentiary fo' dat."

"The penitentiary! For what? They started it."

"Doan matter none to po-lices. Po-lices do what theys likes."

Ben was silent for a moment, considering all of this.

"You new around here, ain't you?" asked Spider observing him carefully.

Ben nodded.

"What you name?"

"I'm Ben."

"Well, we be just fine, Ben," said Spider. "We just got to be careful. Everywhere the same. It always the same. Gangbangers and po-lices. Po-lices and gangbangers."

"We could just go to the police and tell them what happened," said Ben sensibly. "We didn't do anything wrong."

"*I stays away from po-lices*," snapped Spider. "Deys already huntin' me and Scab."

"For what?"

Spider shot Ben a corrosive look. "*I stays away. Doan matter none fo' what.* Deys still huntin' me, dat fo' sure."

Ben had no cause to doubt this.

Spider turned to Scab. The panting dog lay on all fours, looking exhausted, but not injured. "I got to get some water fo' Scab here," he said getting up and sneaking a peek outside the alley in the direction of the open hydrant. Spider, Ben saw, had a cut over one eye and a substantial swelling over the other. His elbows and knees, like Ben's, were raw. They had both walked away from a furious beating, but Ben realized, feeling suddenly very sick, they wouldn't be so lucky next time the Devils showed up. He struggled to his feet, trying to compose himself. But the heat, the stench, the pain and the fear were all too much. Immediately he sank again to the asphalt, where, very nauseous, he finally vomited.

4

The office of Mink Capital Management was as discreet as that of an expensive law firm. The glass doors were thick and heavy, with brass handles that matched the brass letters of the firm's name prominently displayed on the wall within. Several oriental rugs on oak floors in conjunction with fabrics that covered the walls produced a heavy sense of decorum, too serious for anything except the tasteful baroque barely audible from unseen speakers. For the occasional waiting client, a comfortable sofa and a cluster of chairs surrounded a brass and glass coffee table. The late morning edition of the *Tribune* lay on the table among the *Financial Times* and *The Wall Street Journal*. "AGAIN!" screamed the *Tribune*'s headline.

The girl at the desk was on the phone, quietly explaining.

Yes, as far as they knew, it was true.

And of course, they were shocked, too.

No, they had no details yet.

Yes. Yes, of course. Please do call back later.

The girl was in her early 20s, blonde and particularly attractive. Before her, the phone bank was blinking wildly, and she already had a finger on the next call. Though polite and efficient with each caller, she was struggling to keep her composure. Calculating an opportunity, she looked up at Tow, then quickly began her practiced spiel.

Tow raised a hand to stop her. "Is there a manager I can talk to?" he interjected easily.

"There is, but she's occupied at the moment. If you could leave your name, she could get back to you later today. Unless of course it's really urgent?"

"It is," said Tow, showing the girl his credentials.

"*Oh*," she said suddenly at a loss. Her eyes took on a dull fascination as she studied Tow's badge. Then, recovering somewhat, she asked, "Can I say who is calling? Officer ... ?"

"It's Miller," said Tow. "Homicide Detective Miller."

Completely flustered now, the girl picked up another phone. "Beverly," she said very quietly, not taking her eyes off of Tow, "They're here."

• • •

Tow was shown by another young woman to an office to wait. "Beverly will be here in just a minute," she said, and promised to return with coffee.

Tow considered his surroundings. Not even the victim's townhouse had prepared him for the opulence of his workplace. Morrison was right. This Rosco character had a lot of money.

This was a large corner office, obviously the product of a professional decorator. And clearly it was a woman's office. Tasteful and very expensive. Real peonies resided in a crystal vase. This Beverly was probably someone who had moved up the ranks, thought Tow, imagining an elegant older woman. No doubt someone who knew her stuff to merit all this. Then his gaze drifted to the windows and realized that it was the view that made the office really spectacular.

From the floor-to-ceiling windows Tow could see for miles to the south and the west. Sparkling silently 63 stories below lay the prosperous North Michigan Avenue shopping complexes and luxury hotels. To the south, the Loop and the financial district–the banks and futures exchanges–where the city's real wealth could be found.

None of this had much significance for Tow, who turned away and instead looked to the west. There in the distant morning haze stood the city's housing projects, the clusters of primitive concrete shells that he knew so well. Even at this distance he could easily locate the LBJ Homes. They stood like worn bunkers in an endless grinding war of poverty and hopelessness and crime. It had happened in the middle building. On the roof. Yes, true, he had shot the boy that night, but what else could he have done? The boy had pointed what appeared to be a gun right at him. And somewhere out there in that hazy distance was the person he had spent the last year searching for. The one person who could exonerate him. The one person who could tell the truth about that night and give him back the life he had had.

Here in this marble palace, he was, Tow reflected doubtfully, well out of his territory on a mission for which he had no passion at all. His job now was to find a murderer, not a witness. And he realized that though it was necessary, this particular assignment was a wild goose chase. Standing at these spectacular windows, he knew that he was not so much inside looking out, but very much outside looking in on a world he knew nothing of.

"Good morning, Detective. We've been expecting you."

Tow turned from the windows.

"I'm Beverly Nickols," she said walking directly up to him and extending a business-like hand.

She was maybe 40, maybe 45. Not at all what he had expected. Her hair, which she wore to her shoulders was dark, but in the morning sun there were traces of red rendering an overall auburn appearance. She wore a pale green summer suit with a skirt that could have been longer and heels that could have been lower. Absorbing all of this at once, Tow automatically accepted her extended hand. "Detective Miller," he said, producing his credentials. "Chicago Police Department. Homicide."

Beverly Nickols waved his star away without a glance. "You seem interested in something out there, Detective," she said gesturing to the windows. "Spot a suspect?"

This was another surprise for Tow. In his experience, most people about to be questioned in connection with a murder usually didn't choose to provoke the investigator. "It's not as easy as that," he said.

Beverly motioned Tow to a chair, and as she sat down at the desk, the phone rang. She picked it up immediately and listened briefly. "I'm in a meeting," she said. "Tell him I'll call him back. And Lynn, hold my calls."

This Beverly was a classy package, thought Tow. Very nice stuff. Big job. Smart. Probably a lot of money. For sure, a lot of money.

Probably a lawyer. And the diamond engagement ring on her left hand suggested links to even more power and money.

"You'll have to excuse us this morning, Detective." Beverly's voice took a less confrontational tone. "It's pandemonium here. The clients are shocked, worried to death about their investments with us. I need to provide them with better answers. Do you—the police that is—do you have anything to go on?"

"It's too early to say much," Tow told her as the girl returned with the coffee. It was very good. Fresh, some kind of hazelnut blend, served in a china cup with a saucer. Tow realized that he was hungry.

"But there is no doubt then, about the identity? All we know is what we've heard on the news."

This was actually a reasonable question. "Rosco Mink," recited Tow. "Astor Street townhouse. I didn't get the address. Mid-50s, short, balding?"

Beverly nodded slightly, appearing still not completely certain. Or maybe just reluctant to believe.

"I'm sure we're talking about the same person, Ms. Nickols. The Mayor's office was on the phone at the victim's home when I left."

This seemed to resolve all doubt. Beverly then moved to the next logical question. "So then," she asked very quietly, "what we've heard on the news is true?"

Tow nodded, his eyes meeting hers. "I don't know exactly what you've heard, but I can guess." He knew what she was getting at. "It wasn't pretty."

She shivered, and looked away for a moment, then back to Tow. "So how can I help, Detective?"

"Can you tell me what your position is here?"

She seemed suddenly cool, obviously drawing on some earlier preparation. "I'm the managing partner of Mink Capital Management." She handed him a business card. "Mr. Mink is—*was*, that is—my partner. You're talking to the right person, Detective. And for your information, according to our agreement, the death of a partner automatically terminates the partnership, and provides the surviving partner the opportunity to buy the business, an option I certainly intend to elect. Right now, I should be ecstatic. I'm the big winner in all of this. Does that make me a suspect? I mean the killer was a *woman*. It could have been *any* woman."

She was just full of surprises, thought Tow. "Look," he said. "We just need some basic information."

This seemed to appease her, but Tow could tell that she wasn't through. She was just catching her breath, or maybe evaluating his reaction.

"It's obvious what happened to Rosco," she went on. "Improbable that he's a victim of this fanatic. But more improbable things have happened." She paused again. "So what's all this mean to me? Did I have a motive in wanting Rosco's death? Not really. He was what he was. A vain, selfish man, very hard to work with. A lot of people will tell you all about that. But he was a fabulous salesman, too, with superb connections. Certainly more valuable to me alive and well, generating new business. But I won't miss him. Business overall is very solid, and I'm sure I'm going to do just fine on my own. So, did I have a motive? You could say so. This is a fabulous business. And if you want to know where I was last night, you can speak to my fiancé. Now, what can I do?"

Tow let a moment go by, and decided not to comment again. Beverly was smart, he thought. Very well prepared. Get it all out right away–especially the flimsy alibi–and it's all over before it's even begun. Of course the murderer could have been any woman. But with Tow, Beverly would never have been a suspect, alibi or no alibi. She was too professional. Or too smart. Or too young. Or, most likely, too sensual. She was all of these, thought Tow already rebuking himself, which to any unbiased investigator would have made her at least an unlikely suspect. But already Tow was not unbiased and he knew it. Further, this very personal interest came as a curious and pleasant surprise. It had been a long time since he was interested in anything unrelated to that night. He needed to say something, so he reached. "Is there anything obvious that you can tell me? Anything we should know?"

"You mean about Rosco's personal life?"

"If that's where you want to start."

"I can't help you much with that. Rosco was a very private person. As am I." She placed her cup in its saucer. "I really don't have much to say." She lingered here for a moment, deliberating. Finally she made a decision. She did have something to say. Her eyes found his. "However because of the nature of this crime, there is one thing I suppose I should tell you. Sooner or later you'd find out, and I'd just as soon get it behind me now." She hesitated a few seconds, then began with new resolve, "Rosco and I had an affair. About two years ago. Very few people know this—my fiancé in particular does not know, nor do I want him to."

Tow nodded slightly.

With this tacit understanding between them, Beverly went on. "When the whole thing blew up, it destroyed what was left of each our marriages. His third, my first. Looking back it was such a stupid thing to do. For me, that is. My marriage was miserable and Rosco was very persistent. As others will tell you, what Rosco wanted, Rosco got. *Always*. For me the business was very exciting. Our clients were wealthy, powerful men running powerful institutions. I was just overwhelmed by the attention and the success. Rosco was incorrigible and finally I just gave in. We lasted only three months or so, really nothing to it at all. After that, with the business doing so unbelievably well, we just went on, and stayed out of each other's personal lives.

"After my experience with Rosco, I can't say that I'm terribly surprised by what's happened here. His life was empty. He had three failed marriages, all basically for the same reason. Sex was his weakness. He was an intelligent man, a very good businessman, but just obsessed with women. Generally younger women. After me the parade continued. Rosco just never stopped. Though he had no trouble finding women, I have no trouble believing Rosco was involved with prostitutes. People who didn't know him will be shocked, but I'm not. Not at all. It fits. It's really very sad. That's all I can tell you. You'll have to look to somebody else for more answers."

She finally released his eyes and waited for his reaction.

Tow looked away, comprehending it all. It was the oddest feeling of shock. Or was it arousal? Not from the references to sex and power, but rather from the intimacy of the confession he had just heard. Struggling to appear unaffected, Tow returned to her and lumbered on. "Okay, then. We have a lead." Here Tow had to consult his notebook where he had written the name from Rosco's answering machine. "Does the name Richard Landon mean anything to you?"

Beverly seemed somewhat surprised, then nodded. "Richard Landon is a client. How could he possibly have anything to do with this? I thought the police were looking for a woman."

"Well, we have to run down every lead. Richard Landon left a message on the victim's answering machine. It seems he was pretty ticked."

"Oh," she said after a moment. "So that's it. I can understand that. It's no secret that Richard is very unhappy with us, Detective. Actually I can't blame him for being upset. However I really cannot imagine him having anything to do with this. But you have to understand what we do here. Let me explain. Among other things, we raise capital for hedge funds. This is not investing in the conventional sense, not for the ordinary person. This is professional speculation for high net worth individuals and institutions. Always risky. Some risks are simply greater than others. Richard Landon himself is a professional trader. He of all people understands the risks involved here. The fund that he chose–the Cambridge International Fund– was very promising, but also very speculative, and has suffered disastrous results speculating in convertible fixed income securities and options. Many of our investors diversify their risks by participating in several funds. Mr. Landon, however, deliberately chose to purchase a significant portion of the Cambridge Fund.

"Though he had no obligation to do so, Rosco had been considering returning our fees to this fund because of its unusually poor results. Failure is not good for business. But of course there will be no contribution now. It is very likely that Richard has lost by far most of what he put into the fund. Unfortunate, but that happens.

"Most of our clients are very substantial, and are prepared for such adversity. Richard, however, cannot seem to accept this. He has called and visited here several times in the last few weeks. Very upset. Confrontational. Rosco finally had to ask him to leave and not return. Rosco suggested that Richard have his lawyer call in the future."

Tow had no choice, though he didn't really think this lead would pay. More likely, this would be a colossal waste of time. It was obvious to everybody that a woman murdered Rosco. "Do you know where I can locate this Richard Landon?"

Beverly seemed reluctant, but turned to her computer and typed something on the keyboard. The printer responded immediately. "I really don't think Richard could possibly have anything to do with this," she protested. "This is confidential information, you know. I shouldn't be giving it to you."

"If you would like to see my credentials," Tow offered once more.

"Not necessary. I read the papers, Detective," said Beverly handing him a computer listing. Then that personal coolness returned, her eyes meeting his, "I know very well who you are."

• • •

Vicki called from work right away. "Hi."

"Hi," said Richard sitting back at his desk. He was aware that his shirt was still clinging to the sweat down his back despite the heavy duty air conditioning of the trading room.

"It's almost 10. Any flak from Paul?"

"Nothing yet," said Richard. "I guess he's got his own problems. Paul's got a bundle with Rosco, you know."

"Oh," she said idly. "No, I didn't know that."

There was a lot she didn't know, thought Richard. Suddenly he wanted to tell her all about the girl leaving Rosco's last night, then just as suddenly decided that was a bad idea. She'd say go to the cops, and then he'd have to tell her about the party and all those reasons he didn't want to be involved. And in the end he would be no better off than he was now. Instead he limped along with the conversation, "Yeah, that's how I met Rosco, through Paul."

"Really."

Another mistake. Paul Steward had also introduced him to Katie O'Connor, a fact well known to Vicki. "Yeah," he backpedaled, "Paul gets around."

"So, anybody call?"

She meant the cops. "Nothing yet."

"And nothing is going to happen, Richard." This of course was the point of her call. "The police won't care about a phone message from an angry client. There are probably a lot of those. So why are you so worried? Everyone knows that the killer is a woman."

He considered this for a moment. "Yeah," he allowed. Another long moment of silence passed. Again Richard considered confiding in her, and again decided against it. "Maybe you're right," he droned on. Then silence again.

"Okay, so what is it then?" she finally prompted. She already knew his moods.

"I had an error Friday. They just found it this morning."

"Oh, so *that's* it. Poor baby. Bad luck. What happened?"

"I gave Larry an order to sell 15 bonds. He sold 50."

"It's slow. People get careless when it's quiet."

That was another problem, thought Richard. The markets were very quiet. Of the six screens displaying images before him, all were still, their charts frozen in place. Stocks, bonds, currencies. All like a Sunday morning. The Dow was up two points and the 30-year bond down a single tick. Even the ever volatile derivatives markets were stalled. Neither had even one of Richard's eight direct lines to various brokers and dealers flashed all morning. This was a bad situation. Richard Landon desperately needed to make some money, and that opportunity did not seem to exist anywhere in the world.

"So what's the damage?" Vicki continued.

"About $12 grand." He had to struggle to conceal his frustration with this painful error. He did not want her to know just how broke he was. "They're rewinding the tape now. I'll call you when they play it back. I'm sure I said 15. It's gonna be Larry's loss."

• • •

Then came another call. Richard had expected this one. He knew she'd try again. "Oh, Richard, it's just terrible." It was Katie phoning about Rosco. "I'm sorry to bother you at work," she went on. "I tried calling your apartment earlier, but your machine is off."

Somehow he knew it had been her. Was she able, he wondered, to guess what he had been doing? "I know. Pretty unbelievable,"

49

he commented about Rosco Mink. "How's your mother taking it?"

"She's devastated. You know, Rosco was so wonderful to us when Daddy died. She's really upset about all of this."

"Your father and Rosco were partners, was that it?" All of this was before Richard's time, but he somehow had acquired a vague understanding.

"For many years," said Kate. "They were such good friends. They were always going on golf outings together. And when Daddy died three years ago, Rosco arranged for a new partner to buy Mother's share of the business. Really, he was just wonderful. What has happened here is terrible."

That was true, but Richard wasn't feeling particularly charitable. "Yeah," he agreed. "Pretty terrible all right."

She changed the subject. "You know, Richard, things don't have to be this way. We could still try."

Suddenly he was impatient with her. He really didn't have time for this lost cause. Controlling himself, he allowed a long silence. He didn't want to hurt her feelings. Finally he said, "I don't know, Kate. We really didn't work out."

"Well," she said slowly. "If you change your mind, we can always talk."

"I'll think about it," he said evasively. "In the meantime, I'll drop off your things. I need to pick up my stuff, too. Oh, and my key. How about if I call later, after all of this is over."

"Yes, of course," she said, disappointed as usual. "Talk with you soon."

He signed off with, "Bye, now."

· · ·

When no one showed up by lunch, Richard had convinced himself that no one ever would. Maybe Vicki was right. The killer after all had been a woman. Finally Richard's courage rallied sufficiently to order a beef sandwich from Mondelli's. He was on the phone again with Vicki when Kathy at the front desk phoned him. "Richard, you have a visitor."

"Come on, Kathy," he grumbled thinking it was the delivery

boy. "For Christ's sake, just send the kid in."

"*It's not the kid, Richard,*" she said, suddenly very annoyed with him. "I think you better just come out here yourself. *Now.*"

• • •

They sat down in the conference room.

Richard immediately recognized Tow from television. The cop who shot the kid last summer.

"We got your name from his answering machine," said Tow, not bothering to explain how they got his work address.

Richard acknowledged this with a nod. "Yeah, I called about an investment."

"So they tell me," said Tow. "You called this Rosco Mink at home on a Sunday night. Isn't that an unusual way to do business?"

"Yeah, I suppose it is. But you have to understand that he wouldn't take my calls at his office, so I had no choice. This investment is a big loser."

Tow acknowledged this with a grunt. "Where were you last night after eight o'clock?"

The question was so direct that Richard hesitated before manufacturing a monosyllabic answer. "Home."

Tow was taking notes. "And home is on Dearborn, about three blocks from the victim's address?"

Richard nodded, a sense of full alarm rising within him. Christ, they had his home address, too.

"Anyone home with you?"

The questions were coming like punches. Richard had to clear his throat. "My girlfriend."

"And what's her name?"

Again he felt the need to clear his throat and wondered if he should call a lawyer. "Victoria Moss."

"Moss?" repeated Tow.

Richard spelled it for him.

But lawyers were expensive, thought Richard. Good ones, anyway. This was coming at a really bad time. He couldn't afford something like this now. Who could he call? Leo Brulet? Leo was an attorney at Doyle & Doyle. Leo was a friend. Still this was going to be expensive. *No,* he decided abruptly. He was innocent. And he wasn't even accused of anything. He could get through this on his own.

Just going through the motions that even dead ends require, Tow was getting all the details down, just as Morrison would expect. "You didn't pay Rosco a visit like you threatened in your message? You two were home all evening?"

Here Richard was careful. Of course he had paid Rosco a visit. He hadn't seen Rosco, but he had seen his killer so he had to deny being there at all. What was more, Vicki came over after midnight, just after the worst of the storm. Of course this meant nothing in itself, but still such a revelation would only invite even more questions. Vicki would be pissed. Worse yet, she might tell the cops to go to hell. That would be just like her, and that he certainly did not need. "Yeah," he lied easily. "That's right. I was just blowing off a little steam when I left that message. We were home all night." He could reconcile this with Vicki later.

For the first time, Tow took a few seconds to evaluate this kid. Didn't seem like a bad kid. Definitely not a punk, not a wise ass. Late 20s, like his daughter, Susan. Susan was a computer expert. He didn't understand computers, and he didn't understand Susan either. And like her, this kid was probably well educated and made a lot of money doing whatever the hell they did here. He had to make a lot of money to get into the Cambridge Fund. High net worth individuals, that's what Beverly Nickols had told him. This kid probably didn't know a goddamn thing about the streets or gangs or violence of any kind. He was obviously worried just talking to a cop. Finally Tow decided that he was done with this wild goose chase. "You knew the victim pretty well. So, any idea who might have done this thing?"

Richard felt himself color. Christ, this guy was direct. And his questions were right on. He shook his head and cleared his throat again and tried to lie casually. "Sure. The same hooker who killed those other two guys."

Tow considered the response for a second. Something bothered him now. He studied the boy carefully, then decided it must be the heat bothering him because this kid was clean. Nervous–understandably nervous talking to the cops about a murder investigation–but clean. "Okay," he said giving Richard a card with his new number penned in. "If anything comes up, you can reach me anytime."

Richard accepted the card without a word.

Tow rose to end the meeting, and as they walked out asked, "So what exactly goes on here?"

"Trading," said Richard gesturing widely to the many computerized trade stations. "We're traders. Stocks and bonds. You know, Wall Street."

Tow really didn't know, but nodded anyway. "Look, I need to call in, but I can't get a cell signal in here. Is there a phone I can use?"

"Yeah, sure," said Richard jumping at this opportunity to be helpful. "Use mine," he said withdrawing a respectful distance to allow some privacy.

Tow made two calls and was finished quickly. Just routine stuff. Richard rejoined him.

"That line was taped," said Tow.

"Yeah, they're all recorded so they all have that beep," said Richard suddenly reminded of his own error. They should have played the tape back by now. "It's an industry practice. When there is a dispute, you can always go back to the tape and see who screwed up. It's for everyone's protection. I had an error Friday, for example. I told the broker to sell 15 bonds and he sold 50. The tape will tell us who pays for the mistake."

"And every line is recorded?" said Tow gesturing to the large bank of phone buttons.

"Every one," said Richard growing uneasy. "You get used to it."

Tow grunted. Having concluded this routine interview by the book just as Morri wanted, he left, contemplating the scorching heat waiting for him outside.

• • •

Richard sat down, relieved to be rid of the cop. He realized he was perspiring. Christ, he thought. This was crazy. He had done nothing wrong. But, with a chill, he realized that there was indeed reason to worry. Maybe he didn't kill Rosco Mink, but he sure as hell knew who did. And to make that worse, he had just lied to this cop in response to direct questions about his own whereabouts and about the killer.

Richard Landon groaned aloud.

He wanted no part in all of this. Really, what had he done to deserve such grief? All he wanted in life was to make some money and to live with lovely Vicki. Was that too much to expect? At least, he told himself, there was comfort in the knowledge that he had nothing to do with Rosco's murder. Not directly. He had committed no crime. If anything, he was a victim of Rosco's mismanagement. In fact, he had had a vested interest in Rosco's well-being. After all, Rosco well might have eaten some of those Cambridge losses for him. No, he, Richard Landon, had done nothing wrong.

The peal of the phone startled him out of this self-righteous funk.

It was Fred in telecommunications calling to play the tape back for him.

Richard listened for a nervous moment until he heard the replay, then managed to suppress a groan as he heard himself clearly order Larry to sell 50 bonds. He–not the broker–had screwed up. And it was he who had left early on a dreadfully quiet Friday summer afternoon to play golf without bothering to check out with the broker. Unquestionably, the loss was his. With this fact established, Richard carefully ground out the arithmetic to determine the exact dollar amount he had squandered. "Oh my god," he breathed to himself, "That can't be right." He ran the numbers again. Same thing. He swore quietly. The damage was not 12 grand, but closer to 15. It was a disaster–this thought returned him to the cop. Abruptly, Richard grabbed the phone and dialed Fred. With practiced composure, he began, "Hey, buddy, thanks for digging that one out."

"You get stung?" asked Fred with friendly concern.

"Yeah, no big thing," Richard lied easily for at least the third time today. "Fifteen grand. Peanuts. Need a favor though, Freddy."

"Yeah, sure, what can I do?"

"The last two calls on my outside line, can you play them back for me?"

It took 10 minutes and Fred gave him the last six calls. Two from

Vicki, Katie calling to get back together, followed by the scorching he got from Kathy, then finally the two calls made by the cop. The first of these was to a Commander Morrison who was not in, and the other was to somebody named Lenny in Records requesting *pronto* background checks on Richard Landon and Victoria Moss.

Background checks. Pronto!

Shocked, Richard fumbled the receiver back into its cradle, then was slowly drawn to the card Tow had given him. His business card. A white card with blue lettering introducing Detective Thomas T. Miller of the Chicago Police Department and the words Gang Crimes followed by a phone number. This cop was in the Gang Crimes business, thought Richard searching for any kind of relief, no matter how irrational. He himself had nothing to do with gangs, so what was there to worry about?

There was also something on the back. Scrawled in ink was another phone number and a single particularly illegible word. Richard studied the handwriting carefully, then, with another chill, he was suddenly able to read it. It said *Homicide*.

It took only a moment of reflection for the gravity of his situation to sink in, and then Richard Landon reached for his phone directory, looking under the Bs for Leo's number.

5

hairwoman Madeline O'Connor finally gaveled the pro-
ceedings of the Civilian Police Board to order Wednesday morning. The hearing room was crowded and they
had gotten a late start while waiting for the arrival of
a key witness. Adding to the pressure was the relentless heat. It
was only 10:30 a.m., but the surging July temperature was already
challenging the ancient air conditioning of Police Headquarters.

"I don't like the looks of this," said Joe Guilliam, Tow's lawyer,
to his client. "No sir, I don't like this at all." Guilliam, a product
of Chicago's John Marshall School of Law was 37, black and well
regarded. Tow thought he had a lot of guts just for taking this high
profile racially charged case. "The new Chair is really on the spot
here," Guilliam went on. "This is her first day on the job and she
don't want nothin' to do with this circus."

Then, as if to emphasize this point, came the angry gavel again,
now louder and longer.

Like Tow's first hearing a year ago, this would be a quasi-legal
procedure administered by a panel of nine civilian political appoin-
tees. This wasn't a conventional court of law. Here different rules
applied, especially regarding evidence and discovery. Here cameras were allowed, but TV mini-cams and cellular phones were not.
And here the Chair held most of the power. Madeline O'Connor,
the influential Board member who had been so harshly critical of
Tow last year, was now the new Chairwoman. Her bias then seemed
to be mostly political at first, and this Tow could understand. After
all, the shooting had torn the city apart. But as the case against him
developed, Tow sensed a very personal chill from her. She more
than disapproved of his actions that night. Rather she generally

came to disdain him as though he were some kind of thug. A predator who deserved to be crushed before he committed an even worse crime–if that were possible in Tow's case. He was lucky the former Board and its Chairman, Mike Duffy, had stayed the course for him despite Madeline O'Connor's intense objections. It was solely because of her that a compromise was eventually required. Tow was suspended for a year and removed from Gang Crimes, but Mike made sure his salary was paid while he and Tow sought a transfer elsewhere in the Department. It took almost a year, but finally Mike persuaded Anthony Morrison to hire Tow. Things could have been a lot worse if his adversary had had her way.

Madeline O'Connor, Tow knew, was a wealthy widow and a big contributor to the Cook County Democratic Party. Further, she had a family history of involvement with the politics of the city and the Police Department. Morrison sure knew all about her. *Very influential, very powerful and very wealthy*, according to Morrison. *Has serious political ambition.* In Chicago that meant City Hall. *Mayor O'Connor.* Jane Byrne had already proven that a woman could make it. To Tow, Madeline O'Connor seemed all of these things. Especially wealthy. That brooch sparkling on the lapel of her tasteful dark blue suit this morning wasn't made of rhinestones. Neither was the clustered jewel ring on her right hand. And accompanying her wealth was a sense of purpose. Her every movement resonated with confidence. Seated at the center of the bench like the eye of a hurricane, she was a dynamic presence on the board. She was slim and tall and blonde, and unquestionably intelligent. Tow guessed her to be about mid-50s. Still, she seemed too stylish and too damned good looking to be a widow, and Tow idly wondered what had killed her husband.

Tow's surveillance drifted to the evidence. Displayed on a table centered before the Board laid the only hard evidence in the case– what appeared to be a small black pistol. This toy was the object that 11-year-old Calvin James had pointed at Tow one horrific night last July. It was constructed of cheap tin, and was entirely realistic to the eye although it was as light as a feather. Significantly, its receptive smooth metal surface had provided prints from at least two individuals. Several belonged to Calvin James, the remainder were unknown.

Tow stole a quick look to his far right where the boy's mother and her attorney were seated. Tow did not know the attorney, a slim balding white man around 50. Curiously the racial polarities had somehow become reversed in this case. And just as he had, Anita James had changed lawyers. More likely, her original counsel had refused this extension of the case, just as Tow's had. Like Madeline O'Connor, nobody wanted anything to do with the politics of this all around loser. Tow quietly studied the boy's mother. Anita James was a heavy, determined woman in her early 40s, but looked 60 in her anguish and her pain. She was divorced and on welfare, and there were six other children at home on the 26th floor of her LBJ apartment. She really couldn't afford legal expenses, but that didn't stop her. She clutched a framed photo of her lost son in one hand and a Bible in the other, and behind the thick lenses of her glasses she was fiercely angry. Her purpose here was justice. She wanted justice for the child Tow had destroyed, and would do anything to get it. Even, thought Tow, if she had to manufacture a witness. So, what if she had, thought Tow. Who could blame her? Not him.

Tow looked silently back to Guilliam. He dreaded the prospect of going through the testimony again and apparently Guilliam could see his discomfort. "Don't worry," Guilliam told him. "Trust me. It's gonna be all right. I got a plan."

• • •

When she finally had silence, Madeline O'Connor explained the purpose of the hearing. A new witness had come forward, she said. A witness late for this proceeding, but expected to arrive at any minute. A person who had witnessed the shooting of Calvin James a year ago. And further, she went on, for the benefit of the three new members of the Civilian Police Board, there would be a brief review of the case from the beginning.

For Tow, this was bad, but it could have been worse. Last July the hearing room was sweltering and every seat was taken. The media coverage had been pervasive. *Time* and *Newsweek* and the others sent reporters *and* photographers. Even *The Wall Street Journal* sent a couple guys to do a big article, which was generally favorable to Tow despite the decidedly unflattering pencil sketch of his thick profile. Now, overshadowed by the spectacle murder of Rosco Mink, the room was mostly crowded with spectators. The city papers and news stations elected to make only a token appearance. For the most part, everyone expected the same old hash rehashed. Still there was no mistaking the intensity here. Like the last time, the racial divide was obvious. Armed guards operated metal detectors at the door, and more twitched nervously at every column on both sides of the aisle. The severely overweight sentry off to Tow's left seemed to be especially jumpy as he scanned the seated crowd. With one hand he repeatedly wiped his brow with a handkerchief, with the other he palmed the handle of a holstered revolver he could barely see beneath his girth.

• • •

The lawyer for the family, Howard Bath, balding and 60-something, quickly took the initiative.

"Madam Chairman," he began. "Before the new witness testifies, we wish to emphasize that Detective Miller has a history of violence leading up to the deadly assault on Calvin James. A history that somehow was not developed here a year ago. A history, we argue, that actually predicted a tragedy like this."

Tow leaned toward Guilliam.

"Relax," Guilliam whispered without looking at his client. "He's just stallin', waitin' on this witness of his. I been all over that file of yours and did some research. We gonna be okay on this."

Howard Bath wasted no time launching into his attack. There were several incidents in Detective Miller's file that illustrated his violent nature, he said, but there was one incident that particularly stood out. An incident for which Detective Thomas Miller received an official Departmental reprimand for excessive force. He had brutally beaten a man accused of a DUI 14 years ago. The 52-year-old accused was treated at Mercy Hospital for a concussion, a broken nose and cheek, three crushed ribs and two mangled testicles, and subsequently sued the City of Chicago for police brutality.

Guilliam was immediately on his feet. "Is that right? Perhaps the

Board would like to hear about the circumstances surrounding this incident? How Detective Miller came upon the scene of an accident? How he was the first police officer on that scene at 1:00 a.m.? How he radioed for an ambulance? How he pulled the 52-year-old accused from the Lincoln Continental in which he was trapped, the same car that had failed to stop for a toll booth and struck at approximately 45 miles per hour the Ford Pinto stopped at the gate? How a father and three small children were crushed to death in that Ford Pinto? I have photos here for the Board's review," continued Guilliam, now sailing. He handed about a dozen black and whites to Madeline O'Connor who accepted them warily, and immediately withdrew in shock. "These came from the Illinois State Police," said Guilliam. "The *Tribune* ran a big story the next day. It seems that the accused was intoxicated when he failed to obey a police officer's instruction to sit in the officer's personal automobile," said Guilliam nodding in Tow's direction. "It seems that instead he got out of the car and retrieved a seven iron from the trunk of his Lincoln with which to attack the officer who was attempting to free the victims dying in the Pinto. Detective Miller was struck twice from behind before vigorously subduing the accused." Then for the benefit of the overwhelmingly black crowd, Guilliam casually added, "And don't be thinking this was some kind of racial thing either. The accused here was *white.*"

The photos had produced a ghastly silence among the Board. Several had turned to the windows for relief. So powerful were the pictures that Madeline O'Connor quickly snapped each face down before her as she received them back from the Board members who flanked her. Tow could see that she was very unhappy with Guilliam for shocking the sensibilities of her Board, and perhaps their consciences as well. He had seen that look from her before, and knew that it meant trouble.

Guilliam, however, either didn't notice or didn't care that he was upstaging the most powerful person in the room. "I'd like to add that according to this *Tribune* article, the paramedics—we're talking about three *veteran* paramedics here—the paramedics *wept* as they used torches to cut the crushed children from the car. It took almost three hours to retrieve the bodies."

The room now was silent. Madeline O'Connor glared at Guilliam, then at Tow where her gaze settled, then rested.

"And for the Board's information," Guilliam continued dryly, "The lawsuit against the City failed. And as for the accused, he got his license suspended for a year and three years' probation on the rest of the charges." Then an idle afterthought, something he was simply incapable of suppressing, "Don't hardly seem fair, do it? Must have had himself a pretty good lawyer."

Howard Bath was a pro, and not easily out-maneuvered. "Nevertheless," he insisted, "The Department's view was that the force used was excessive, and issued a formal reprimand in this case just as they did three years later when Detective Miller brutally beat three innocent young men who had lost their way and wandered into the LBJ area."

Guilliam cut him off. "You mean the three punks from the north suburbs who drove down to the projects one night to buy drugs, and made the mistake of trying to roll what appeared to them to be an old derelict who turned out to be a police officer under cover? *Are we talking about the same innocent young men here?*" Guilliam demanded. "Come on, it was three big strong boys in their 20s against one 45-year-old cop alone late one night. At best, three against one. And besides, anyone who bullies an old man *deserves* to get the hell beat out of him. Detective Miller took their knives and guns and drugs away from them and put them where they belonged–*in jail.*

"You know, what we all should be talking about here is Detective Miller's true record as a Gang Crimes police officer. We could call upon his partner, John Mercer, who is seated right over there," said Guilliam nodding in the direction of a black man of about 45, dressed in a dark gray suit without a tie. "I'm sure he would be willing to testify about Detective Miller's record."

Mercer nodded for the benefit of the crowd as well of the Board. But Guilliam's real intent was to make sure everyone knew that Tow's partner for the last seven years was black.

"Or we could call on Commander Anthony Morrison," continued Guilliam now gesturing in Morrison's direction. "Commander Morrison is Detective Miller's new boss in Homicide investigating this big Rosco Mink case. It is certainly good of Commander Morrison to take the time to back up his long time fellow officer while managing a case as important as this one. Still I don't think we need to call either of these officers because their presence here on this scorching hot day already tells us what they would say."

Having crushed his opponent's opening barrage, Guilliam instinctively went on offense, turning to Howard Bath and addressing him directly. "But what about this new witness we've been hearing about?" Here Guilliam struck a thoughtful pause. "*Why now,* is what I want to know? What took so long? Where have you been hiding this guy? We've been looking for him everywhere."

Bath was clearly shaken now, unprepared for the depth of his casual young opponent. "We haven't been *hiding* anyone," he said indignantly. "Our witness fears retribution. Perhaps that's why he's not here. Detective Miller has been combing the LBJ Homes for a year, pressuring residents with repeated visits and endless questions regarding the murder of Calvin James one year ago. The Detective has been relentless and provocative in his search, and highly unprofessional. Our witness lives in the LBJ Homes and is simply terrified of Detective Miller. It's only because Miller has finally been transferred out of the area that our witness has felt that it is safe to come forward."

Guilliam took his turn, looking around the room. "Yeah, well it's safe enough now, so bring him on. Where is this guy?"

Theatrically, Howard Bath turned to look to the rear entrance of the room, searching, as if he expected his witness to be walking through the door at that very moment. Finally conceding that no one was there, he meekly took his seat.

Guilliam continued his own theater, shaking his head wearily. "Madame Chairman and Members of the Board. This is all a sham. The facts in this case have not changed and never will." Then with deference to Anita James, Guilliam turned and looked directly at her. He now spoke softly and earnestly. "We do profoundly regret what happened to Calvin James that night, but Thomas Miller is a victim as well. He has spent all his savings, has been divorced, and has lost the career that he has built over 30 years." Then turning to address the Board once more, he quietly urged, "Ladies and Gentlemen, do the right thing here. Dismiss this hearing and return this unfortunate police officer to the Gang Crimes Unit where he wants to be and where we all need him to be."

Madeline O'Connor did not bother to consult her Board. "We can wait for the witness," she said. It was a rude body blow for Guilliam, a blunt personal message about who was in charge, for all to see.

In response to the rebuke, a murmur ran through the crowd.

If anyone had any further doubt about just who was in charge, it was now removed. "Detective Miller," continued Madeline O'Connor, "Will you please take the stand."

It was the moment Tow had dreaded.

"It's okay," Guilliam urged him quietly as Tow got to his feet. "I got a plan."

Tow was sworn in, and sat down ready for Madeline O'Connor's first question. "Will you please describe the events of the night of July 5 one year ago?"

This is exactly what Tow feared. He began slowly. "It was late, about 11:00 p.m." Tow realized that his voice was shaky and he had to clear his throat. "My partner, John Mercer, and I got a report of gun shots in the LBJ Homes. We were on Lake Street, just a few minutes away, and responded immediately. We both heard shots from the roof as we entered the building. We took the elevator to 14 and split up to enter the roof. I went around the back, and Detective Mercer went up the front. I was able to access the roof immediately, but Detective Mercer was locked out. As I entered the area, there was no sound of gunfire, but I became aware of some movement from under a staircase, and shouted, '*Police. Come out with your hands up.*'"

Tow's heart was pounding now, and he stalled briefly by reaching for the glass of water before him. Then he continued. "Someone stepped out pointing a gun in my direction. There was a moon, but it was pretty dark. I shouted at him to put the gun down, but instead the suspect pointed it directly at me. I shouted again, but he just took more deliberate aim. I shouted again as I fell to the ground. This person then adjusted his aim to where I was lying. I thought he was about to shoot so I finally fired one round, striking the suspect. I got up and found a young boy, wounded in the chest just below the heart. I knelt down next to him. He was still alive, and I called for an ambulance. It just was then that I heard footsteps running then retreating down the same stairs I had come up. These footsteps were accompanied by the sound of a barking dog. I stayed with the boy until Detective Mercer arrived. I then told him to follow the footsteps, which he did. But he was unable to locate this person who I am certain witnessed all these events, and could corroborate them in detail."

"After the ambulance arrived," said Madeline O'Connor, "Could you describe what you found?"

Tow hesitated, looking for the right words. Finally, he chose to be direct. "What we thought were gun shots turned out to be Fourth of July fireworks. Cherry bombs, M-80s, that kind of thing. Fairly high-powered explosives. Extensive residuals from these explosives were found throughout the area."

"And the gun the boy pointed at you?"

Howard Bath was suddenly on his feet. If he was going to have any chance of victory, this was it. "That wasn't a gun at all. Calvin James was 11 years old, mentally impared and partially deaf. This gun you're talking about was actually a toy that ignited a sparkler when fired. He couldn't possibly hurt anyone. You say this child pointed a toy at you so you had to kill him? I say this child was gunned down in cold blood."

Now the entire room erupted.

Chairwoman O'Connor again resorted to the gavel to restore order. As the hearing room gradually settled down, Tow realized Joe Guilliam was on his feet before the panel of the Police Board, standing passively in front of the Chairwoman silently pointing a pistol directly at her. The room gasped, then froze. Joe Guilliam did not move, but continued staring at Madeline O'Connor who sat grasping the arms of her chair. She finally gathered her composure and coolly told Guilliam to put the gun down immediately.

Still Guilliam did nothing.

Abruptly there was a shot, and the room became chaotic.

Several burly guards rushed Guilliam who made no effort to resist while surrendering the weapon carefully.

There was more disorder, then the gavel again.

Now Guilliam was shouting. "*Now do you see what it's like?*" he screamed at Madeline O'Connor. "*Now do you finally see?*"

Guilliam remained twisted in the grip of the guards. "That's not a *real* gun," Guilliam shouted, mocking Howard Bath. "Look at it. That is the same gun that Calvin James pointed at Detective Miller. *The same gun.*"

Tow looked. It was. Guilliam had lifted it from the evidence table during the commotion. The significance of this became apparent to everyone. The shot that had been fired had come from the over-weight guard posted near the Board. What had happened was embarrassingly clear. In his panic, the guard had pulled the trigger of his revolver before removing it from his holster, firing a single round into the wooden floor. Exasperated, Chairwoman O'Connor motioned to the guards to release Guilliam who straightened painfully.

Massaging his neck with one hand, Guilliam took the floor. "Now we all need to think. All of us. We're in a crowded room in broad daylight–protected by armed guards–and you all panicked. Right here! All because a black man pointed a toy at you–a sparkler toy– *not a real gun,*" again invoking Howard Bath's comment, "And you, Madam Chairwoman, you're an authority figure and you surely have reason to believe I might now be harboring some resentment toward you. How would you feel alone at midnight believing there were real gun shots being fired around you? How would you feel if a stranger pointed a gun directly at you? You told him to put it down and he refused? What would you do? That guard over there was convinced enough. I'm lucky he doesn't know how to shoot."

The guard attempted without much success to disappear behind a column.

Guilliam chose to push his luck. Turning to Howard Bath, he challenged evenly, "I think we have all had enough for one day. Now, before we all melt, where is this witness of yours?"

Bath turned and privately explained the situation to Anita James.

Guilliam turned to Tow and whispered, "What he is saying is that it's not his fault this guy didn't show up. What he means is they're lucky this guy chickened out because the rules of perjury still apply in this hearing."

Then Guilliam took another chance, addressing the Chair. "Madame Chairwoman," he said, "I move that the Board dismiss this hearing right now."

Desperate to end the spectacle that could terminate her political career, Madeline O'Connor turned to her fellow Board members, all of whom promptly nodded their assent. Then she announced that the hearing was closed, banged her gavel for the last time, and the room again erupted. Madeline O'Connor actually bolted from the bench in order to escape the cameras now clicking furiously from the media seats.

"Like I was saying, I had a plan," Guilliam told Tow.

"You did great," said Tow over the commotion in the room. Tow was making a concerted effort to maintain an upbeat appearance for Gilliam's sake, but the truth was that he was still in that unsatisfied limbo of being not guilty, yet not truly absolved. In his heart he feared he would now be chasing footsteps the rest of his life. Still he offered Guilliam his hand, and his congratulations. "You have a real talent for this work, son, and you have guts," he said. "You're going to do great things."

It was just then that a uniformed police officer approached them. "Mrs. O'Connor wants to see you two jokers in her office." Then he added pointedly, "*Now.*"

• • •

If Madeline had been angry governing the Board in public, she was enraged now in her private office. "That was an outrageous stunt," she fumed at Tow. "*Outrageous.* You tried to make me look like a fool out there."

Guilliam, ever willing to take a chance, shot back, "I did no such thing. The real problem out there today was this bogus witness who was smart enough not to show up. And I'll tell you another thing, double jeopardy should apply in these cases. Are we gonna have another spectacle every time somebody gets some bright idea?"

At this Madeline O'Connor became visibly furious, almost unable to speak.

Then Tow tried to say something, but she finally managed to cut him off, speaking over the noise of a window air conditioner. She addressed Tow directly, ignoring Guilliam completely. "You're lucky you have a high friend in Homicide, Detective. I suppose you're an expert in that department and perhaps that's where you belong. But you say you want to return to your old job in Gang Crimes? I'd say you're very, very lucky Commander Morrison is on your side because no one else in the Department wants you at all. You're just bad news where ever you go, beating people up and shooting children. You're a disgrace. You don't deserve to be a Chicago Police detective. And I'll tell you something else. My father was a police officer, as was his father. And I myself have some friends high up in the Department and in the Democratic Party as well. And I want you to know that I'm going to personally see to it that you never return to Gang Crimes. Do you understand me? *Never!*"

• • •

Outside the office now, Guilliam immediately tried to comfort his client. "Now Tow, don't you let her get to you," he began earnestly. "This morning everyone in that chamber got to see what you had to deal with that night. Now they understand what really happened. And I'll bet they're on your side now. Luckily there's nothing more the Chair can do to you. I know she'd like to, though. And she would if she could because she's nothing but a bully. Nothing more. And deep down, bullies are cowards.

• • •

"What we saw just now is really all about politics," Guilliam went on. "Madeline O'Connor wants to run for mayor, and that's what this is really all about. Nothing but politics. And after what happened this morning, I'd say, running for mayor just got a whole lot harder for her. Maybe impossible. That's really why she's so pissed. And I'll tell you one more thing about politics in this city. What goes around, comes around—usually just when you really don't want it to. Right now, I'd say she's the one who has got the most to lose."

6

orrison, thought Tow, didn't look good.

In the four days since Officer Rita Martinez found one of Chicago's most prominent citizens brutally murdered in his own home, it seemed that Morrison had aged years. His color was ruddy from an unhealthy blood pressure, and dark circles emphasized the bags sagging under his eyes.

The political and civic pressure was taking its toll. Five people dead in 10 months. It was outrageous. *Scandalous.* Two young girls, and three middle-aged men. The local media wanted answers. The national media wanted answers. But there were no answers, only scandal–to the delight of the tabloids. The victims and murderers were all, very likely, either prostitutes or patrons of prostitutes. It had become a circus and the strain was reflected clearly in the face of 63-year-old police veteran Anthony Morrison. As the morning evidence meeting began, the thought suddenly occurred to Tow that perhaps he, also, was too old for the job.

"Alright, let's get started," Morrison shouted over the din of the 23 detectives working on the five cases. It was warm and Morrison, standing at the front of the room, had taken off his jacket. "All the Rosco Mink lab reports and tests are back. Each of you has the reports. I know everybody already has all the basics, but I want to brainstorm this thing from the beginning–together."

The room grew quiet.

Morrison stood and walked to the chalk board.

"Okay," he began, "First, back in November, Tuesday the 8th, Margery Billings and Jessica Reynolds, 19 and 20 years old, were murdered together." At the very top of the left corner of the board, he wrote the first girl's name, and beneath it, the second's. Then, turning to face his audience, he continued, "Both were pros with major league rap sheets to prove it. They were found naked and bound, their throats slit. The girls were working out of the Excelsior Motel on the west side. A lot of bars in the area, that's where they got the business. Our investigation turns up a couple dozen characters who had been with the girls, but no real suspects. The only trace of the killer is his calling card, two small votive candles. We figure him for a religious nut.

"Next William McNamara is murdered in the Matterhorn Hotel on the night of February 8th, exactly three months to the day since the girls were killed. An anniversary message." Returning to the chalk board, Morrison posted McNamara's name under those of the girls', forming a chronological list including significant details to the right of each victim's name. "This guy is 38, from Detroit and is a big shot with Ford. He's married, got kids. No record. We find him bound, gagged with tape and stabbed 26 times. Cause of death is asphyxiation when his lungs filled with blood. Not a single witness. Watch, wallet missing. Lab says he was drunk on his ass. Two votive candles are found on the dresser. The candles and the anniversary date pretty clearly indicate that this is a response to the murder of the girls.

"Then on March 16, we find Robert Jankowski, 48." Morrison added Jankowski to the list. "Worked for some software outfit in California. Same profile. Married, kids, no record. We find him in the Langston North Hotel, blitzed, bound and gagged and stabbed about 30 times. Same deal. Big shot executive. Gold Coast area, solo business trip, late night drinking on the Street of Dreams. No watch, no wallet. Victim dies of asphyxiation, exactly like the first guy. The same pattern of wounds, the same careful plan for a slow, agonizing death. The dates don't work this time, but again, two votive candles on the dresser.

"But one *possible* clue on Jankowski. A hotel maid says she thinks she saw him with a dark haired woman about 11:00 p.m., and she thinks—she's not sure at all—she *thinks* she saw the same woman leaving the lobby in a hurry with another guy a few hours later. That's what she said, *Leaving in a hurry*. We're guessing she's a pro with a pimp, or maybe with an accomplice of some kind.

We just don't know. Not much to go on. The bindings differ, the tape differs and the candles differ. The only thing we're really sure of is that both McNamara and Jankowski were killed with the same weapon. No doubt about that.

"And for about five months, nothing. Then out of the blue, bam! Rosco Mink gets it on the first Sunday in July. Morrison chalked Rosco Mink's name to the list. "Looks like the same killer, but there are important differences. So now what I want to do here is go over the key points. There are three. First, the murder weapon here definitely does not match the one used on the first two victims. This time it seems the tip of the weapon has been slightly blunted or broken. And only slightly. It was plenty sharp. It left small squares where it scored the victim's bones. In itself, this might not mean a thing. It might be the same weapon. She broke it somehow. Maybe she just dropped it. Or she just used another weapon. We don't know. We're assuming the weapon itself is an ice pick. And we are advised that that the choice of such a weapon may have some psychological significance for a prostitute who wants to get even somehow. A penetration fetish or some damned thing. Now I don't know about that. Maybe, maybe not. The second key thing is the fury of this attack. Rosco Mink was stabbed approximately 47 times. The first two guys were 25 or 30. Forty-seven is more than a 50 percent increase. Maybe this means something. Maybe not. I don't know what to make of it. Maybe Rosco pissed off his killer. Who knows?

"The third and last point I want to make is that Rosco Mink suffered a fatal stab wound to his heart. That was the cause of death. The murderer finally decided to kill him after stabbing him 47 times just about everywhere *but* the heart. Now remember the other two guys suffocated when blood filled their lungs. In other words, the murderer let them linger until they drowned in their own blood. Could have taken hours. For some reason this Rosco guy was tortured for some time, then suddenly executed on the spot. Dead in seconds. We think the storm knocking the tree against the house may have panicked the killer and she had to cut the festivities short."

It was hot. Morrison took a long drink of water. "Okay, now the small stuff. Rosco Mink showed significant traces of cocaine as well as being very intoxicated. Lucky for him, I would say. More evidence here points to a prostitute. *Romance.* The wet spot. Lab report on the sheets indicates Rosco Mink, unlike the other two guys, got laid on the last evening of his life. And we found a lot of hair. Real ladies' man. The maid changed the sheets the previous Monday and we found traces of hair from eight different women in that time. Some of everything. Red, blonde, brunette and a couple in between. And one girl was black. At least eight different broads in a week."

This brought outright laughter from the group.

Even Morrison shook his head and laughed. "I couldn't do that," he said. "Could any of you guys do that?" More laughter, then Morrison went on. "Okay, prints. We have lots of prints. Too many prints. We figure the women were all over the bathroom, the kitchen and the bar. Apart from the maid and the victim, all unknowns. So what we have here is a puzzle. Only the murder weapons from the first two stabbings match. As for the rest, the bindings and knots and candles, none of that stuff matches at this point. I hope one of you guys has a snitch who will sell us the answer to this goddamn thing, because we are really nowhere."

This last remark brought complete silence.

Morrison went on. "Oh, yeah, missing items. I'm sure you already know this. As far as we can tell the murderer stole what most hookers steal. The victim's wallet is missing and so is his watch. We are told that he had a gold Rolex. A lot of cash is missing too. The maid said the victim kept large amounts of cash in a drawer in the bedroom. She wasn't sure how much. She says a lot, maybe as much as $8-10,000. Maybe more. The bank says this guy withdrew $5,000 in large bills every Friday morning, so we have to believe the maid was right. Makes sense, too. He had to pay for drugs and the girls. Oh yeah, one other thing. A hand gun registered to the victim is also missing."

There were only a few questions, which Morrison promptly dispatched.

The meeting gradually broke up with the usual murmur of voices as everyone shuffled out. These guys, Tow noted, really liked the veteran Morrison. Morri was a pro. He had been through these kinds of things before. He would figure out what to do.

As he made his way out, Tow realized that his own respect for Morrison had increased considerably. Homicide was not Gang Crimes, but it was no picnic. The pressure on Morrison was tremendous. And observing the blackboard, it seemed to Tow that the boss expected things to get worse before they got better. Morrison had carefully organized the names and details of the decedents to date in an especially cramped, condensed fashion that easily allowed for the addition of six or seven future victims.

7

After a delay of several days due to the extensive autopsy, the wake for Rosco Mink was held at a near north funeral home on Thursday and Friday with the final rites scheduled for Saturday. A very frustrated Morrison ordered Tow to attend the Saturday services for the purpose of observing the mourners as they arrived.

"The funeral is just the kind of thing this fucking lunatic might enjoy. You know, the thrill of checking out her handiwork," Morri told Tow. "I have the wake staked out too, but I don't expect anything to come of it. She might show up there, but I doubt it. Too social, I think. Way too risky. Somebody might approach her and then she's cornered. I think she's too smart for that. I figure the funeral would be a lot safer. I'm serious about this, Tow," continued Morri, sensing Tow's skepticism. "I'm thinking what we should do is get the whole thing on video. So that's what I want you to do. Go over to Equipment and draw a video camera with a good zoom lens, and film people as they enter the church. Then I want you review the tape and hang on to it. When we do figure this thing out, I'll bet you there she'll be–right on video, our killer, walking up the steps of the goddamn cathedral to say so long to her victim." Morrison took a manila folder out of his top desk drawer and handed it to Tow. "Here is a list of people we've talked to so far. Park across the street and see if you can get them on tape." Then, again defensively, "I'm not kidding about this. I'm willing to eliminate any of these people from our suspect list if they don't show up for the funeral. Just tell me who didn't show up. Hard to say just what else to look for. I know it's pretty crazy. Just keep an eye out for a hot broad who looks as nervous as a whore in church."

Tow laughed at this. "Sure, Morri, I'll do my best," Tow said, always ready to humor the boss.

At first Tow regarded the assignment as mostly busy work, but a little later he reconsidered. Though it was a long shot at best, there was actually some merit in the idea of a stakeout. It also was a poignant demonstration of just how desperate they really were. Five people were dead, and they had few leads and no suspects at all. The pressure was really on, and they were reduced, literally, to taking pictures and looking for a whore in church.

• • •

Following a brief thunder shower, Saturday morning cleared to become brilliantly sunny, and, by 11:00 a.m., blistering hot and dripping with heavy July humidity. Parked among the blue and white squad cars directly across from the Cathedral, Tow was well positioned to tape the arrival of mourners from his sweltering Buick.

Killing a little time, he opened the envelope that Morrison had given him. Besides the list of people interviewed in connection with the murder, there was the victim's obituary from a recent *Tribune*. The *Trib* gave Rosco Mink the royal treatment. A favorable photo of the youthful businessman from 12 years earlier, and a lengthy, flattering discussion of his life and career. Tow was surprised to learn Rosco had come to Chicago as a six-year-old child from Poland where both his parents had been research physicians. Of course it was well into the cold war then, and relatives, with the help of the University of Chicago, had paid off the Communists to get the family out. Once relocated in Chicago, Minkowski had been shortened to Mink. Both parents joined the U of C faculty where they remained until they were killed in an auto accident several years later. Rosco then lived with an aunt, earning scholarships to several top undergraduate colleges. Later he graduated *magna cum laude* from Harvard Law and then joined the prestigious Wall Street firm of Chambers, Lord & Fennel where he excelled in the field of securities law. Next, with six partners, he helped organize the Boston-based Canterbury Group, a major asset management firm. Five years ago he began his own firm, Mink Capital Management, a highly regarded Chicago

money management boutique. His death at 57 was described ellipti-
cally as *sudden*. Of course there was no mention at all of the scandal
swirling around the victim who, it was gossiped, was almost denied
a Catholic funeral and burial because of the alleged circumstances
surrounding his murder. That discussion, and more, could be found
on the front page not only of the *Tribune*, but every major newspaper in the country.

For the media, the murder, the wake, the funeral, and the scandal
engulfing it were a huge bonanza. The daily reporting was constant,
ripe with salacious references to prostitutes, hookers and whores.
And the funeral today was truly a summer carnival, the turnout tremendous. Reporters and photographers clustered everywhere in
small busy groups. Television mini-cam teams reported live from
the steps of the Cathedral, while dozens of cops directed traffic and
kept the vendors of souvenir T-shirts away.

In all this confusion, Tow, fumbling with the video camera, briefly
taped the inside of his Buick before finally getting into focus some
guy in a Cubs hat walking his ice cream push cart directly in front of
the Cathedral. The cart had a canopy and even a gaggle of high flying
bright balloons. An officer mounted on a magnificent horse ordered
him to move, which he reluctantly did. But this guy was determined
and when he returned later, Tow taped him again, now practicing
with the zoom lens. This time the guy was escorted away from the
church with a final warning, about which he protested vigorously,
insisting it was police brutality. Tow got it all.

• • •

The earliest arrivals included the ex-wives.

Tow had received general descriptions with their names. There
were three, the youngest just 26 and reputedly younger than the
deceased's only child, a daughter. The first two arrived together,
in respectful black, but bantering tastelessly in apparently jovial
spirits. Number three, the young blonde, showed up next looking
fabulous and toting a husband at least three times her age. Tow
panned them all as they walked up the sidewalk, and then zoomed
in as they entered the Cathedral. Then he reviewed the tape. Not

bad, but obviously there was a technique to using a video camera well. He felt awkward with the whole process of initially focusing, then panning and zooming. Instead of trying to be selective, he resolved to shoot all the film–there was two hours' worth. That reduced the effort to simply panning and zooming.

The mayor with his wife arrived like General Patton, hood mounted blue and white city flags displayed on an official limo, its high beams rapidly flashing in an alternating fashion just in case anyone failed to recognize His Honor. The flags wilted in the heat the moment the car stopped. The Mayor's entourage included half-a-dozen perspiring body guards conspicuous in their white shirts, dark suits and sunglasses, with discrete ear pieces wired down their backs. Numerous aldermen quickly appeared on the royal coat-tails. Then straggled in the business elite, identifiable to Tow only by their anonymity. In spite of the scandal, politicians and business leaders had to attend, if only to provide a solid front for a city with a big problem. A problem that could haunt the urban economy on which they all depended. Chicago is a convention city. And those convention dollars support airlines, hotels, restaurants and shops. This third murder was a serious threat to that support. Atlanta was a dangerous competitor for conventions, and just as eager was Atlantic City. Even New York claimed it was now safer than Chicago. Something had to be done, and done fast.

Tow knew that this pressure weighed heavily on Morrison who also had the normal business to manage. Earlier in the week there had been another mob killing. The victim was a long time hoodlum. Vito Morretti was dispatched in the traditional Chicago late night fashion for skimming prostitution and gambling profits. The body was found by hikers in a shallow grave in a southwest forest preserve. The deceased had been shot-gunned, both barrels. Of course one would have been sufficient, the second was just to make a point to colleagues about cheating the boss. The victim's wife, mother of four young children, expressed surprise and shock when she learned the true nature of her late husband's business.

Fortunately everyone tended to ignore the daily street gang murders, usually one or two a day as a result of drug dealing. Gang crimes were not Morrison's responsibility, but a surge in drug violence still added to the overall pressure. During the five days since the Sunday death of Rosco Mink, there had been 11 such killings.

Then there was the hammer murder. This involved a Hispanic couple in their late 70s. She used a hammer from her husband's very own tool box to curtail his endless philandering. A single blow to the back of the head accomplished the main objective. The claw of the hammer then proved to be especially useful in prying his skull apart so that she could examine the gray matter there. These murders, Tow knew, all had one thing in common. Their simple, obvious solutions involved business associates, family and friends–generally validating Morrison's strategy about observing the funeral. Most victims actually knew their executioners.

• • •

Soon Madeline O'Connor, flanked by two daughters, emerged from a new black stretch Lincoln with private tags–a trio in black dresses. In Tow's zoom lens, Madeline's diamonds glittered clearly in the searing morning sun. For the media, however, she provided only a clenched jaw and a frosty smile. Joining them from the same car were a man and a woman, both in their late 30s. Tow zoomed out and checked the list. That would be Eleanor and her husband, Paul Steward. Mrs. O'Connor, Tow noted, deftly kept her distance from the Mayor who was finishing his comments for television just in front of her. In Chicago, candidates for Mayor are seldom especially welcomed by the current administration.

The next personality in this parade of urban celebrities drew an instant and spirited response from the media. Rushed by reporters, the young black man with the stunning smile and the babe stopped to chat. "I've been following this case very closely," Joe Guilliam told the group, employing his expansive courtroom voice so that all could hear. "It's going to be the biggest story in years before it's over and I certainly expect to be involved at some point. I just gotta know somebody is gonna need a good defense lawyer and I will definitely be available, free-of-charge." These shameless theatrics at the very doors of the Cathedral were concluded with that fabulous smile and a wave for the cameras, including Tow's.

Beverly Nickols soon followed, escorted by her fiancé, a tall slim man in his late 40s. With a pang of jealousy, Tow zoomed in. They made an extraordinarily attractive couple. He didn't even try to tell himself he didn't care. She was gorgeous in black. In the zoom, he watched her intently until the door of the church closed behind her.

Among the very last to enter the Cathedral was another striking couple. Richard Landon, hurrying, with a blonde girl who was struggling to quickly negotiate the wide stone steps in high heels. In his lens, Tow could see that the girl was remarkably beautiful. They had arrived just in time. Tow could hear the mournful organ begin when they opened the door.

• • •

With Vicki's hand in his, Richard Landon stepped inside to the merciful cool darkness of the Cathedral. They slipped into a center rear pew and immediately sat down, his perspiration now surging from those last quick steps. However, Vicki, he noticed, was hardly flushed. But then she loved the heat and humidity that he could just barely tolerate. They had agreed to attend the funeral–she was perfectly willing to go to the funeral–but not the wake. Vicki had flatout refused to go to the wake. "Just too gross," she said. "I don't do wakes."

Of course they had been out late. After all, it was Friday night. He was slightly hung over and still needed more sleep. Vicki seemed fine. A night person, she was always up late, drank every bit as much as he did, yet seemed to need so little sleep. He didn't know how she did it. Only an hour earlier they had been in bed, hers, for a little extended romance that had, once again, made them late. Vicki just couldn't stop. She insisted that he coax her to just one more orgasm, her fourth, and then they had to rush. Of course it took time for her to get ready. Not bothering with a bra or stockings, she squeezed into a short black cocktail dress and black patent pumps. She put a black satin bow in her hair, pulled up and back. She did her usual thick black mascara and shadow much heavier than usual today. Appropriate for the dead, Richard supposed. He glanced at her now beside him. She was all in black except for her nails, a scarlet enamel that matched her lip gloss. Black, he decided with a rush of desire, was her best color.

Abruptly Richard was struck queasy by the instruments of ritual. The punishing organ, followed by waves of pungent incense interspersed with sweet–almost confectionery–fresh floral scents of every kind all conspired to make him nauseous. He leaned forward and breathed deeply, slowly. In their rush, they had had only toast and Gatorade. It was all she had. What he really needed, Richard determined, was a cold beer.

Finally recovering somewhat, he sat up and scanned his surroundings. It was a vast cavern, almost full; a sea of dark suits and black dresses. A soft murmur drifted among the mourners.

Vicki shuddered and, leaning close, whispered to him. "Churches give me the creeps."

"Me, too."

"My god," she said motioning to the altar. "Look at that thing." Suspended from the ceiling, a 30 foot cross featuring a realistic Christ crucified loomed for all to see. "Talk about barbaric. It makes me sick. Really, Richard, what is *wrong* with these people?"

Richard nodded. The thing was barbaric. The crown of thorns, the huge iron nails, the open bloody wounds. Even the figure's eyes rolled up in the head as the scourged body seemed to actually wither in agony. "Catholics enjoy their suffering, you know."

She shuddered again and shook her head in revulsion. It actually took her a moment to compose herself. Then she nodded to the wall and asked, "What are the little booths?"

"Confessionals," said Richard. "Anything you need to confess?"

Of this she was contemptuous. "Catholics are just so weird. Sin and guilt and penance and all. Priests and their celibacy. And what about the Bachelor of the Year and his 12 bachelor boyfriends? How do they explain that? Very strange, if you ask me."

Richard had to smile. "Catholics are bizarre, that's for sure." Then another thought occurred to him. "So what are you anyway?"

"Methodist." Then she added, "Lapsed."

• • •

A moment later, the organ signaled the beginning of the funeral procession, and everyone stood. The Requiem for Rosco had begun.
Off to their left in the very rear of the church, Richard could see
the white haired, red faced undertaker with his white gloves retreat
as the chanting priests in violet vestments with their incense and
holy water took charge of the immense copper casket. And as the
body was slowly rolled nearer, Richard felt a distinct chill. Abruptly,
the procession faltered and for just the briefest moment, the casket
rested at Richard's side–close enough to touch, with time enough
for reflection. Richard was profoundly chilled. Through no choice
of his own, he knew something everyone in the Cathedral, everyone
in Chicago, everyone in the country wanted to know. He, Richard
Landon, the most reluctant of all witnesses, could beyond a doubt
identify the killer of Rosco Mink who, just an arm's length away, was
now waiting for him to tell the world. Rosco continued to wait, yet
Richard did nothing. Undoubtedly Detective Miller was here somewhere–there were cops everywhere–yet Richard did nothing. And
there were numerous friends and associates among the mourners,
and still Richard did nothing. There, ahead of him across the aisle,
he could see Kate and Molly O'Connor with their mother, Madeline,
all in black, glancing back in his direction. Yet Richard refused to tell
a soul, not even gorgeous Vicki who was right beside him. Finally,
in despair, Rosco gave up, and with renewed footing, the funeral
procession slowly continued on its way to the altar and, for Rosco
Mink, to eternal rest.

8

The main Chicago Police station at Morgan and Maxwell was an ancient battered fortress of weathered brick and huge windows. Constructed in 1888, its original purpose was to serve the immediate area surrounding Halsted Street and Roosevelt Boulevard. Decades later, Maxwell Street became renowned for a thriving flea market. It was said that there was a time when you could buy anything on Maxwell Street, anything ranging from a solitary child's canvas shoe to an AK47. The flea market eventually declined, but at about the same time other doubtful enterprises were just beginning to flourish in the housing projects to the west. Criminal street gang activities eventually became the primary mission of the Morgan and Maxwell station. Tow's old office was on the first floor. Now with homicide, he was on three.

"Mail call," announced Sweeney bearing a string tied bundle in each hand. "There's gotta be a hundred letters in each one of these."

"Just put them over here," Tow told him pointing to a vacant desk. The mail was of course public response to the hearing just days ago.

"Want to go to over to Torino's for lunch?"

"Can't," said Tow. "I still have yesterday's mail to open."

"Morri's really making you go through all these?"

"Yeah. My fan mail."

Observing the three stacks Tow had organized, Sweeney asked, "So how do you sort them?"

Tow looked up. "Basically pro and con."

"Pro and con?"

Tow's disgust was evident. "Hate mail, from all over the country. Same as last year."

Sweeney picked up a letter. His face quickly clouded, and he picked up another. Then another.

"See what I mean?" asked Tow.

Sweeney grunted and then gestured to a third smaller stack. "So what's that?"

"Death threats," said Tow. "Same as last year."

"Man, it's a sick world out there. What do you do with the death threats?"

"Turn them over to Morri," said Tow. "Department rules. We do everything by the book."

Sweeney grunted an acknowledgement. "Hey, listen, here's something else," he said handing Tow a pink message slip. "I got a call this morning from a west side patrolman who read about the hearing last week. Frank Gillato. He said he thought about it for a few days, and the idea won't leave him alone. It's a long shot, but I think you should talk to him. Seems one day last week Frankie and his partner got a call about some kids raising hell on Handel Boulevard near Pine."

"That's way west," said Tow suddenly impatient. He was irritated with his mail and wondering what this could have to do with him.

"Yeah, right, pretty far west," said Sweeney, not deterred. "But let me finish. So they get over there and break up a fight involving a few young gangbangers and some local kids. A Mrs. Chang filed the report. Her number is here. She owns a dry cleaner in the neighborhood. Says one of the kids involved is forever shooting off fireworks in the playground across the street. Black kid about 12. And get this–the kid has a dog. Actually, they're looking for the dog. It bit one of the gangbangers. Frankie thinks it all fits. It's a long way to LBJ from there, maybe three miles. But still, a 12-year-old black kid? A dog? Fireworks? Maybe?"

Tow put down the letter he was reading and, a little more considerate now, accepted the message from Sweeney. "Maybe."

• • •

He couldn't reach Frank Gillato, but Tow had the report faxed to him within an hour. There wasn't much to go on, but as Sweeney had pointed out, there was just enough to merit checking out.

Tow found the Handel Boulevard Dry Cleaners in a particularly dilapidated section of the west side. No surprise, gang graffiti was everywhere, but what was a surprise was the trident signature of the Devil's Disciples, an eastern rival to several local gangs. No doubt this was an attempt to expand the Devil's drug trade. And of course there would be violent consequences as the locals resisted.

A year ago, Tow could have called on a whole network of informants for useful details regarding a development like this. His former network, concentrated mainly within LBJ, was remarkably extensive and imaginative, more than the usual gaggle of prostitutes, drug users, petty criminals and rival gang members. Included among the most effective participants were a barber, a high school principal, a grandmother and a newspaper stand operator. But this civilian alliance was no longer available to Tow. One by one, his best snitches had deserted him. Even ever reliable Harold Lamb, his best source at LBJ, had finally withdrawn in doubt and mistrust.

Harold's resignation was especially regretful. Harold Lamb was a projects veteran who had lost two sons to street gangs. Neither lived to be 20. The younger, Steven, had been shot-gunned by a rival gang member. His older brother, Mark, was the victim of automatic gun fire from a source that has never been identified. Harold's grief was such that on the day of Mark's funeral, he just walked into Tow's office and offered his services. Burning with rage and sorrow, he promised to do anything to oppose the gangs. And he was true to this pledge, working with Tow for almost five years. Now Harold felt it was Tow who was no longer faithful to the original bargain. Tow knew that, like the rest, Harold Lamb simply did not believe his weary story of a mysterious witness and his dog, and certainly questioned the wisdom of his relentless search.

• • •

Tow found Mrs. Chang behind the counter on the phone.

He waited patiently, sweltering. Opposing large fans driving hot air from the presses generated so much heat themselves that they only made the whole place warmer. Finally he flashed his badge and Mrs. Chang immediately hung up.

"Oh, yes," she responded to Tow's first question. "Yes, yes, yes. I know the one. Very thin boy. Such dirty clothes. Just rags really. Always playing with firecrackers. The one with the dog. I tell him a thousand times, '*Don't,*' I say. '*Very dangerous,*' I say. He just look away."

Mrs. Chang somehow reminded Tow of Madeline O'Connor. It wasn't their ages which were close, nor their circumstances, which could not have been more different. Rather it was a profoundly uncharitable manner that seemed to border on outright anger. More than just a willingness to seek retribution, but a cruel eagerness to employ any means to that end.

"When is the last time you saw this boy with the dog?" asked Tow.

"Maybe yesterday," said Mrs. Chang. "He is with another boy now all the time. I see them with the dog every day. All the time now, the two boys and the dog. Always together."

Suddenly something within Tow demanded he give up the chase. This had to be another dead end. He had already spent thousands of dollars that he couldn't afford on promising information from snitches, as well as months of patient footwork following up. All of it wasted. But something even stronger within him insisted he follow up this lead. After all, it was free. And Frank Gillato was right—it did all fit. "Okay," said Tow penning his new number on an old Gang Crimes card. "When you see them again, I want you to call me."

"You will put them in jail for a long time?"

"We'll see," said Tow and handed the woman his card. He really didn't like this woman. "Just call as soon as you see them."

Mrs. Chang put on her bifocals and studied Tow's card. She was taking his instructions very seriously. "I cannot read this. What does it say?"

Tow took the card back and wrote another for the woman, taking care to make his phone number legible. Then he read the number aloud. "Now okay?" he asked, repeating his number aloud.

"Number, yes," she told him. Then, she persisted, peering through her bifocals. "What this word?"

"Homicide," said Tow. "I am now a Homicide Detective, no longer in Gang Crimes."

"Ahh, yes, *Homicide*," said Mrs. Chang, exceedingly pleased. "Homicide mean murder. Very good."

• • •

Tow was already half a block down Handel where his Buick was parked across from a playground when he heard Mrs. Chang calling him. "Detective!" she called. "Detective Homicide!" She was loud and shrill, gesturing frantically to the playground. *"Boys and dog there! Look! Right there!"*

Tow looked to the playground.

Ever vigilant, Ben had earlier observed the white man in the suit ease his car in the no parking zone in front of the playground. That was just his first tip. When the man walked directly to the Handel Boulevard Dry Cleaners, Ben's suspicions peaked. By now he was fully prepared for trouble and quickly alerted Spider.

For just a moment, they watched Mrs. Chang shouting and pointing, then they saw the big man in the suit as he began slowly jogging in their direction.

"Po-lices!" exclaimed Spider to Ben. "We got to get Scab and get outta here fast!"

Ben turned to look for Scab, who was running among the other kids.

Tow singled out the thin boy as his primary quarry. The heat caused his heart to race, but there was another rush, too. The boy's obvious alarm was a good sign. Was this the kid? Finally? *Was this the one?*

Spider was moving now, with the policeman closing. Clapping his hands vigorously for the dog's attention, he called for Scab.

Tow was gaining, fighting the heat and fatigue of actually running for the first time in years. Finally he maneuvered the boy back toward a fence from which there was no escape. Tow was severely out of breath now, but had managed to corner the boy against the

fence. "*Don't move, police!*" gasped Tow, leaning and supporting himself with both hands on his knees. "I won't hurt you. I just
want to talk to you." Tow was so winded that he could hardly speak.
He tried to stand upright. "*Calvin James*," he said still gasping
severely. "*A year ago. LBJ, on the roof. Was that you? Did you
see what happened?*"

Spider ignored what the big man was saying and was still calling
for Scab who was now in a full run to his master's rescue.

In a desperate effort, Tow made a calculated lunge and just barely
managed to grab the boy by the back of his oversized T-shirt.

But then, suddenly, there was Scab, nipping at Tow's ankles.
This distraction allowed Spider to struggle out of his shirt.

In the end, still winded and unable to follow, Tow, holding the
limp shirt, was forced to watch as the thin bare-chested boy bolted
past an open hydrant for the freedom of the streets with the dog
and another boy at his side.

• • •

The shrink called it ruminating.

He still did a lot of ruminating–obsessing about the past–especially at night. Usually he sat at home, as he was this evening, alone
and drinking. He recalled the events of That Night, which he had
enlarged over time to include that entire day a year ago–his last
day of a Gang Crimes Specialist career that had lasted almost three
decades.

Tow began work that day with a late afternoon court appearance
in the case of *The People versus Tyrone Green*. Tow was the arresting officer testifying before Judge A. Marius Starita in Criminal
Court. Responding to a call involving a shooting, Tow had stopped
Tyrone (Tiger) Green's late model Pontiac as Green was fleeing the
crime scene. In the car Tow found three hand guns and a shotgun.
Returning Green in handcuffs to the scene, Tow found Isaiah Clinton, 16, in an alley, face down, shot to death. Two witnesses identified Green as the shotgun assailant, but later abruptly refused to
testify. The retribution was just too great. Green, it turned out, was
a member–in exceptionally good standing–of the Royal Maniac

Demons.

This was a jury trial before Judge Starita. Prior to questioning Tow about the crime, the Prosecuting Attorney drew on Tow's 27 years of experience in Gang Crimes, elaborating especially on his extensive training in police tactics and on his working knowledge of the west side Chicago Housing Authority projects, particularly the Lyndon Baines Johnson and the Martin Luther King Garden Homes. The whole purpose was to impress the jury, a dozen ordinary people, the extent of whose knowledge of the projects was the Sunday Magazine Supplement that periodically did articles that were intended to shock. "*Here,*" the Prosecutor was saying to the jury, "*here before you is a man who protects you and me from all of that evil. Now, when he tells you what happened, are you ready to believe him? Are you ready to exercise your power as a jury and send the accused to jail?*"

The actual questioning was direct and routine; the ballistics evidence compelling, but not overwhelming. After all, no one testified that he saw Green kill Isaiah Clinton. A verdict was expected in the next day or two.

After testifying, Tow made his way to the Cook County Jail, located in the same Court complex. He had been requested by Sterling Grant, a member of the Insane Vice Rebels, who was awaiting trial for murder. Grant had information and wanted to trade. He offered detailed info on the recent murder of Sheila Burke, nine, for a lesser charge. The child had been raped repeatedly, then beaten and strangled. Her body was found in a dumpster at the bottom of a garbage chute in King Gardens.

Only Tow would do. Grant trusted no one else.

At the end of the two hour interview, Grant was sufficiently satisfied to finger a notorious local drug dealer named Desmond Leopold, or Leo the Lion. Leo had actually done time for child molestation, and was currently a suspect in several murders involving west side children. Nailing Leo was a big deal–if they could get him before he ran, as he surely would when the word got around. The race was now on.

It was already eight o'clock when Tow left the jail and met his partner, John Mercer, to begin the night shift.

Their first assignment was Presidential detail. The President, extending the fourth of July weekend for 24 additional hours, had spent the festive red-white-and-blue day celebrating with the Mayor who was up for re-election the following year. Since the election of John F Kennedy, everyone understood the significance of Chicago in presidential elections. That morning in Washington, massive federal funding had been announced for Chicago's infrastructure—expressways, bridges, and an airport. This would be a pretty tough act for other mayoral candidates to follow. Naturally, the Mayor would assume certain obligations when the President himself ran for re-election—basic politics in Chicago. The Presidential motorcade left late, after 10, following a political bash downtown. For Tow and Mercer, this was a simple assignment. In their unmarked Ford, they blocked the Division Street entrance to the Kennedy Expressway while the motorcade passed, then fell in behind for the trip to O'Hare Airport.

They had just returned to their west side beat, about when they received a radio report of gun shots from the roof top of an LBJ address.

Tow's recollection became such that his mouth felt dry and his heart began to pound. The events in his memory took on an unwanted, surreal quality, speeding forward to the same horrible conclusion no matter how desperately he wished to avoid it.

They could hear shots as they got out of the car, and split up to access the roof. Tow made it to the top, Mercer was locked out. Tow drew his weapon, and announced that he was a police officer.

Then a threat, followed by a moment of fear and indecision in almost total darkness. In self-defense, he fired once into a silent figure. Then discovery, and shock.

Horribly wounded, the boy was still alive.

Footsteps retreated down stairs, accompanied by a barking dog.

Soon sirens and lights. Then finally, much too late, an ambulance.

A hostile crowd had gathered in the heat of the night.

Tow immediately surrendered his weapon—a nine millimeter Smith and Wesson semi-automatic pistol, heavy stainless steel with black grips—to the crime lab.

Then the finally irony. The boy's gun. Black, about the size of a Berretta, but as light as Styrofoam. It was a fourth of July sparkler. Just a toy. A tin toy.

Kids. They had been shooting off firecrackers.

Just kids.

. . .

Mercer drove him home. He stopped the car and shut off the engine. "Tow, now you listen to me. You know me. I am telling you here and now this thing wasn't your fault. If it had been you who got locked out and I got in, the same thing would have happened to me. You know that. So I'm just tellin' you what you'd be tellin' me."

Tow nodded. "I know, John. You're right. I know that. I know."

Mercer seemed doubtful, but let him out of the car.

"You call me any time. You hear me, Tow. Any time, you call. Day or night. You call me."

"You're a friend, John. Trust me. I'll call."

But first, he had to speak to someone else.

It was about 5:30 a.m. and he knew Ruthann would still be sleeping.

. . .

He had to tell her, but he didn't know how.

In the kitchen he splashed two inches of scotch into a water glass and belted it down. Then he sat and had another. Gradually the booze gathered, and abruptly, hit him hard. Fumbling for another drink, he knocked over the bottle which rolled out of reach, fell off the table and shattered on the gleaming tile floor. He was on his knees with a roll of paper towels when he heard Ruthann's quick footsteps coming down to investigate the racket. He had cut his hand, and now the blood dripped onto the floor where it mingled with the alcohol. Seeing broken glass, Ruthann was immediately angry, and started to chew him out, stopping in mid-sentence when she smelled the liquor. Then she backed away, one hand across her heart. She knew right then that something terrible had happened.

Still on his knees with paper towels, bleeding down his cuff, he looked up at her. "It was a boy," he said. "An 11-year-old boy. In LBJ."

He didn't have to say more.

"Oh, my god," she said. "Oh, my god." She was becoming hysterical. For the wife of a policeman, it was a nightmare come true. "Oh, my god," she kept saying.

He managed to calm her down, then he went into the bathroom to stem his bleeding, and there, sitting on the edge of the tub with his hand under the cold water of the sink, he put his head down and finally wept.

• • •

The next day, a lawyer for the boy's mother told Channel 6 that Calvin James, 11, was both mentally slow and nearly deaf, and demanded a full investigation, warning pointedly against a police white wash. Later the same day, the lab found the only bullet fired, embedded in a four inch wooden plank having passed through two cinder blocks and the slender chest of Calvin James approximately 12 feet away.

There were no witnesses, and no trace of the retreating footsteps and the dog. It was Tow's word versus an attorney for a grieving mother. The pressure grew until two days later, Tow was suspended pending a review by the Civilian Police Board. Then word came that Tyrone Green had been found guilty, largely on Tow's testimony. Later the same day, they even bagged slimy Leo the Lion at an Amoco station just outside Detroit.

Still, everyone knew that Tow was through in Gang Crimes.

• • •

Psychological resources were provided by the Department. The psychiatrist, a young woman named Jennifer Ryan, really tried to help. Police work was her specialty. Her husband, Sean, had been a Chicago cop, on the force for seven years until he pursued a lone gunman into an alley one night about five years earlier. They found Sean Ryan fatally shot in the back. The assailant got away.

They said she was the best, and, understandably, she was. She had almost 15 years of counseling police officers who had been confronted with all kinds of grisly trauma—guys who were first to arrive on horrific scenes of disasters like air crashes and fires and explosions and murders and suicides. Initially Tow was skeptical about seeing a shrink, but gradually he came around. He saw Jennifer Ryan twice a week for about six months.

At first she was worried about him. "How are you? I mean, are you okay?"

In those first days, he was still pretty numb. "Yeah, I'm okay," he'd say.

But she wouldn't leave it alone, probing continuously for indications of trouble.

After about a month, he simply told her to relax, he wasn't planning to shoot himself.

And he wasn't, although the idea had had definite appeal at first.

Then courage appeared from an unlikely source.

It was this guy, The Duke.

Duke was about Tow's age, a black man, alcoholic and homeless. Tow had known him for years. A big, normally gentle man, almost a head taller than Tow. A Vietnam vet, too fearful of detox treatment to seek the medical care to which he was entitled at the Veterans' Hospital. He lived on the streets, a ragged beggar with a grocery cart. Tow couldn't imagine how he survived the Chicago winters. About a week after the shooting, Tow was already conducting the first of many private surveillances of LBJ. He found The Duke staggering around with only one eye. Half blind, dizzy and nauseous as a result, he could hardly walk. And he had been badly slashed too, about the ear and neck on the same side, serious open wounds that still needed sutures. But the eye was profoundly shocking—a raw empty socket. Tow could actually see into the poor man's head. The white nerves, blue veins and red arteries, all throbbing away not an inch from his brain. "Jesus Christ, Duke," Tow said gently, struggling to keep his composure. "Now, come sit in the car and tell me what happened to you."

"I doan rightly know, man," said The Duke, weaving, awkwardly trying to steer Tow into focus with his good eye.

Finally Tow managed to ease him into the front seat of his Buick. "Tell me what happened to you," Tow repeated.

"Like I said, man, I doan rightly know. Somebody kicked me or somethin', awful hard. While I was sleepin', I believe. I just got hit awful damn hard. My eye, it just sorta popped out, man. I tried lookin' for it everywheres, thinkin' maybe I could just scoop it up an slap it right back in, you know, before somebody went an stepped on it. But I couldn't see to find it on the ground for all the blood. I couldn't help it, man, I just lost it somewheres."

The apology was heartbreaking, but Tow doubted the story.

The truth was no doubt far more chilling—probably a drunken alley knife fight in which the victor claimed a grisly souvenir.

Predictably, The Duke resisted the Veterans' Hospital, so Tow drove him to the emergency room at Cook County.

A few days later, Duke was wandering around with a patch.

"Thanks, man," he told Tow, smiling. "You saved me. I'm fine. Really, man. I'm jus' fine."

If The Duke could cope, Tow resolved, he sure as hell could, too.

• • •

"Gang Crimes. So why do you care?" Jennifer Ryan asked one day, zeroing in on an obvious question. "After all, it's a dangerous, miserable job in depressing conditions. You've done this for your entire career." She pushed him. "Haven't you had enough?"

He just looked at her. "No," he said lamely. "I don't think so."

He tried to explain it, but he really could not, not even to savvy Jennifer Ryan. On the surface, Tow wanted his job back. Having it taken from him made it all the more important to have it back. This was what he did, it had become part of his identity. It was how he thought of himself. And there was more. He knew that he, Tom Miller, made a significant difference in peoples' lives. The kind of people, like The Duke, who nobody cared much about, who got little help, and who had no hope of ever escaping the projects. The kind of people who were either too young or too old to protect themselves from gang predators like Green and Leopold who were themselves products of such abuse. He knew there were fewer gang bangers because of him—and fewer victims as a result of that. He made a real difference, and he knew it. These people needed him. And, while trying to explain all of this to Jennifer Ryan that day, he realized that he needed them, too.

• • •

He was never much of a drinker before, but since the shooting, he drank every night. Liquor eased the pain of it all, the futility. After a few drinks, the hopelessness usually faded and a fuzzy vision of successful resolution gradually emerged. Somehow, this process kept him going—a typical dialogue of hope and despair as he considered the events of the day.

Finally! he thought.

Tow actually sat up in his easy chair and punched one fist into his other hand. This kid has to be the one. He has to be. It all fits. And I had him! I actually had him!

But I let him get away.

He slouched back into the chair, idly considering the damage the dog had done to his ankles. But his year of pain and misery was about to end. He was sure of it. And thank god, because he had so little fight left—55 years old, and dead broke. Money was a real problem. He had blown so much of his savings on informants that there was just no end to the bills. Particularly annoying was a warning in the mail today from the City of Chicago to pay the parking ticket Rita Martinez had issued to him the morning of the Rosco Mink murder. Tow resolved to get the ticket killed.

Rosco Mink. What a story this was. All that money! The guy scores with Beverly Nickols, and that's not enough. He's got to screw around with hookers, too. This Tow could not understand. Beverly Nickols was gorgeous. He had been infatuated with her instantly. He couldn't remember being so attracted to anyone in many years. In a way he felt foolish about it. Beverly Nickols was completely unavailable to him. The gulf between them was vast. She was engaged, and wealthy. A professional money manager, absolutely out of his league. He was, at best, a washed up cop. Nothing had gone the way he had planned.

• • •

He had a degree in history from the University of Illinois where he had played baseball and football. After returning from Vietnam–he had been drafted like everyone else he knew–he hadn't followed up those ambitious plans for law school. Instead he married a girl from college and went to work in Gang Crimes while she became an editor of children's books. Within a year Susan was born. Now, suddenly, after 31 years, Ruthann had divorced him, something he really did not want, but could not stop. Mostly it was because of the shooting, and Tow didn't blame her. It had been a terrible thing for everyone concerned. No one was spared. The intrusive media coverage had been brutal. Reporters hanging around, taking pictures and asking questions of the neighbors. And because they were listed in the phone book, there was hate mail at home, too. Sick, scary stuff. And threatening phone calls at all hours until they finally got an unlisted number. They argued over his insistence on locating the mystery witness and his determination for vindication. When their savings were reduced by half, Ruthann had had enough. She was bitter at the end. Mercifully, the divorce was quick.

No one wanted anything to do with him now. Not his snitches, not his wife. Only Morrison was taking a chance on him–and savvy Morri had laid down the law.

Nevertheless, Tow felt a surge of optimism. Things were looking up, he told himself. Those kids couldn't go far. Even if they did, the trail was hot. He knew just what to do now. He expected difficulty identifying the boys, especially separately, but there would be no mistaking that dog with the badly scorched flanks. He'd find them again, and the next time, they wouldn't get away.

9

It was a steamy Tuesday summer evening.

Tow was working the night shift when the call came in. The initial information was sketchy, but enough: a young woman murdered. *Candles found at the murder scene.*

The attractive blonde was still slumped in her car when Tow arrived. She had parked on an upper level in a self-park lot adjacent to North Michigan Avenue, her purse and packages still on the passenger seat. The killer had jilted a backdoor lock and had been waiting in the back seat for her return, rising to attack when she closed her door. The wound was made in exactly the same distinctive grisly fashion that marked the killings of Margery Billings and Jessica Reynolds. A razor sharp knife drawn slowly and very deeply across the throat. The victim's head had been wrenched back for maximum exposure–and near decapitation. Mortally wounded, Joanne Rice had been released to thrash about until her death. There was blood everywhere. The killer of the two call girls had struck again, his signature votive candle was displayed on the console.

• • •

Tow was just about to leave around eight the next morning when Sweeney stopped him. "There's someone here you better talk to," he said, and ushered a young woman of about 30 into his office. "This is Mrs. Martin. She knew the victim."

"I'm Nancy Martin," the woman told Tow. Her eyes were red, and she was struggling to remain composed. "Joanne Rice was my best friend."

Tow motioned her to a chair.

She sat down and started weeping. "I can't believe this is happening. It's just not right."

Tow waited patiently. "Look, Mrs. Martin, is there anything that you can tell us that might explain this?"

The woman nodded emphatically and tried to collect herself. "That's why I'm here. To tell you about last night. We had dinner and went shopping at Water Tower. At dinner, Jo told me she thought someone was following her. She thought it was her ex-husband. They were divorced two years ago just last month. Chuck has such a terrible drug problem and had become so violent that Joanne had to divorce him. She even got a restraining order in Los Angeles before moving here with the kids. That was why she moved here. To get away from him. She said she thought he'd want money. Drug money. You know, she was doing so well here. And the kids loved the new house. She just thought he'd want money."

"What exactly did she say, I mean, about being followed?"

"That there seemed to be someone watching her. At a distance. It happened four or five times. There were always people around so whoever it was had to keep his distance. That's all."

"That's all she said?"

"Yes. And that she thought it had to be Chuck. He was never supposed to get within 100 yards of her, or something. It happened four or five times. She thought it had to be him. "You're pretty sure about all of this?" Tow asked. If it were true, it was a tremendous break.

She gave him a puzzled look. "Why, yes. Of course. Joanne told me everything. We were friends."

Tow looked at her skeptically.

"We were *best* friends," she explained.

Tow nodded his understanding, then picked up the phone. "Morri," he said, "Could we drop in on you for just a minute?"

• • •

Though he was exhausted, Tow had difficulty getting to sleep. He had worked the night shift regularly before, and had long ago mastered the art of sleeping during the day. The problem was something else. The murder of Joanne Rice was one of the most grisly, evil crimes he'd ever seen. That was the problem. He'd seen a lot of murders, most of them so senseless, most perpetrated by some miserable creep.

The last time he was so moved was about a year and a half ago— the murder of 14-year-old Jeffery Lane, a black kid from Maywood. His mother drove into a tough west side neighborhood to visit her parents. On the way home, they were stalled on a side street and finally came to a stop because of a garbage truck blocking traffic. Three teenage members of the Devil's Disciples approached the car and demanded that Jeffery get out, claiming that he was a member of a rival gang. The mother, streetwise, exclaimed that her son was not a member of the rival gang, or any gang at all. She told them they lived in Maywood, 12 miles away and that they were just visiting. She even showed them the address on her driver's license. That seemed to satisfy the gang bangers, who withdrew. The mother and the boy were just about free of the garbage pickup when one of the gang returned and shot Jeffery five times at point blank range. He died in his mother's arms. Tow never learned if anyone had ever been charged in the shooting. It was about then that he realized that there could be no justice in such a circumstance. Nothing could be sufficient. The incident stayed with him for months.

• • •

By the time he had gotten some sleep and returned, it was about seven o'clock.

Already Nancy Martin's story had largely checked out.

The victim's ex-husband certainly had had a history of drugs and violence. Charles Rice had been arrested twice for beating his wife. She finally divorced him two years earlier in Los Angeles, but this promising lead fizzled when the suspect's alibi proved to be impeccable. He was doing three-to-five for narcotics in a San Diego prison.

Tow's instincts had been correct. It couldn't be that simple.

• • •

Joanne Rice was the 32-year-old divorced mother of three, executive vice president of the Chicago branch of a London import-export firm called Bradley & Company. She owned an expensive house in a northern suburb, held an MBA from UCLA and was active in several charities. What she clearly was not was a prostitute like the killer's first two victims.

Motive was subject to all kinds of conjecture.

Why choose two hookers, and then the suburban mother of three?

Nancy Martin provided the names of several men the victim had been dating, but interviews with them also went nowhere. More solid alibis. Her British employer, lamenting the violence in American cities, said she was professional, extremely well respected, and in line for yet another promotion.

Tow interviewed Nancy Martin an additional four times in the next week, pressing her for any other possible information regarding the crime. "You knew her best," he emphasized. "Is there anything at all that you can tell me? Anything that might link Joanne to the killer?"

But Nancy Martin could think of nothing more.

So the puzzle persisted. Why Joanne Rice? Had she actually been stalked? Was she selected at random? Or was there a reason?

• • •

Wherever Tow went, everyone had something to say.

Even at Chou Lei's speculation was put to him about the situation. Chou Lei's was a storefront converted to an oriental restaurant which Tow patronized three or four nights a week. He liked the place because it was in the neighborhood, the food was cheap, and the beer ice cold. His menu always included egg rolls and varied narrowly between chicken fried rice and moo-shoo beef. Of course chop sticks were always provided, but he preferred a fork and knife. Usually the Cubs or Sox were on television and no one ever bothered him as he ate alone with a newspaper at the same corner table. The proprietor of course knew who he was, and seemed to understand his desire to establish a personal boundary. Tow was always polite, and Chou Lei's staff of three daughters was equally considerate. That was it–little chit chat, no unnecessary engagement. But now even the ever respectful proprietor Chou Lei had broken this solitary ritual, months in the shaping, to address the crimes. While rendering a check one night, Chou said, "Excuse me, please, Officer. Excuse me, I am very sorry to disturb. I am still learning about America. Please, sir, how can such terrible things happen in Chicago? And when will police make them stop, please? I fear for my daughters. Three daughters, as you know, sir. All three work here with me, as you know. I have no fear for myself, and my wife has died. But for my daughters, sir, I have much fear."

The man's humility and sincerity was so moving that Tow took a moment to compose a suitable answer, but found that he had none. Long ago he learned not to counsel hope when there was none. "I'm sorry," he told Chou Lei. "I understand your concern, but there is not a lot I can say. These criminals will eventually be apprehended, but until then the girls should take precautions. Don't take any chances in dark or lonely places. Stay together. Be careful in every way. I wish I could say more. Just be careful and take precautions." Pretty lame advice, thought Tow. But the best he could offer.

Chou Lei regarded Tow silently for a moment, and then thanked him profusely.

The next time Tow visited Chou Lei's, the door was locked, and admission was obtained by recognition on the part of a daughter posted at the entrance.

• • •

On buses, in bars, at the grocery store, Tow observed people as tense and unnerved as Chou Lei. And naturally the heat made it worse. The penetrating cold of a Chicago winter could be truly brutal, but the city's suffocating summer heat was even worse. Night and day, the crushing, punishing heat defeated the patience of the most tolerant people. There was just too much to contend with–mind numbing traffic, squealing tires, blaring horns, obnoxious radios, screaming emergency sirens, exhaust and pollution hanging heavy in the air, scorching sun, blistering winds and never enough rain. Crime of all kinds was always higher in the summer months, and new records were being set in homicide, rape and other staples of city violence.

But it was the serial murders that truly were out of control. The consensus was that it was a sick competition. The general media referred to the murderers in short-hand fashion: He and She, or Him and Her. WQQX, a provocative Chicago FM rock station, created a controversy when it gleefully declared the game a tie. *Three up.* Two hookers and Joanna Rice for Him. Two convention-eers and Rosco Mink for Her. Further, it self-righteously proposed to the contestants an end to the grisly competition with a period of *sudden death,* in which the next to kill would be regarded the final victor.

This proposition drew a tremendous amount of criticism. The FCC threatened an investigation. A *Tribune* editorial excoriated the management of the station. The Mayor personally issued a scathing statement, condemning the station's proposal as irresponsible and reprehensible. In the end, a few heads rolled at ever defiant QQX while the station's popularity skyrocketed. A *Sun-Times* poll demonstrated that many Chicagoans actually approved of QQX's basic suggestion, provided it would end the spree of violence.

10

Becoming a trader was a natural career choice for Richard Landon.
Richard grew up in a Chicago suburb where he was raised with his sister by his father, a tax accountant. Richard's mother died of cancer when he was five. Caroline, his sister, was seven at the time. Widower Richard Sr., a diabetic with serious related illnesses, constantly preached to his children, offering hard earned advice on life. *Do what you're good at. Work hard, save your money. Be prepared. Don't do anything foolish. Marry a good partner. Don't smoke. Take care of your health.*

Caroline adopted these principles and became a lawyer to the delight of her father. She married a CPA and they now lived happily in Philadelphia with their three children. Richard, however, had no such talent for the law and no interest in debits and credits. For a while he considered careers in engineering and architecture. He could easily manage the required mathematics, but neither occupation seemed to inspire him. Neither did marketing or management. Both required inter-personal skills that he simply did not possess. Dismal summer sales jobs had demonstrated that. Then for a while he had considered the sciences–biology and chemistry. This led to the possibility of medicine, but again he just didn't have the people skills required to be a doctor. Neither could he write particularly well. His heart was not in letters. Literature, politics and debate bored him. What finally did inspire Richard was economics. His father questioned this selection, asking what he would ever do with it. Richard couldn't say. But the choice fulfilled the foremost requirement on his father's list: in economics, Richard had found something he was very good at. In fact, it was fun. At the University of Illinois, Richard actually enjoyed this subject that so many considered dismal and arcane. He looked forward to the lectures that others dodged, and actually read the text books others disdained. Richard was astonished by the mysteries unraveled in *Money and Banking*. He was dazzled by the science of the theoretical *Firm* and its hypothetical product, *Widgets*. He liked the many charts with their intersecting bold demand curves and dotted supply lines and all that they represented. Richard Landon was a born numbers guy.

Richard excelled in economics and liked statistics as well. "You don't know much about a subject unless you can measure it," his high school chemistry teacher had once told him. Richard listened and in college, employed this observation to the fullest. He enjoyed collecting statistical data, cleansing it of distortions and plotting the results to illustrate the dynamics of the relationships. Statistical analysis was essential to economics and economics, micro and macro, provided a natural route to trading. In his senior year Richard was recruited by the prestigious Wall Street trading firm of Young, Goodman & Brown.

It was there in YGB's elite training program that Richard learned how to trade. First he was schooled in the essentials of every financial sector on the planet. Following these fundamentals, they taught him how to model risk, and then how to trade that risk model. Employing these modeling techniques, they taught him to trade currencies of all kinds. They taught him to trade equities and corporate bonds. And U.S. Government securities. All the derivatives, too–futures and options, and options on futures. He traded them all, and he traded a lot of them. Richard eagerly learned everything YGB was willing to teach him. He did exceptionally well at arbitrage, selecting risks that he desired and hedging out those he did not. Being long Italian bonds, for example, included a currency risk in the Lira that could be offset by selling futures contracts against the bonds. But it was necessary to sell exactly the right quantity or else a net long- or short-currency position resulted. Not so simple. The work was in fact always difficult, unforgiving and filled with crushing time pressure. Typically he arrived early, ate a sandwich at his desk for lunch and was among the last to leave in the evening. An excellent, eager student, he read, he studied. He asked questions. He related one market to another to another. Richard did everything YGB wanted him to do, and he did it well.

There were several factors that contributed to Richard's decision to leave. First, New York proved to be just too aggressive for him. It was a profound culture shock. Manhattan, Richard quickly came to understand, meant commerce. And that meant everything and everybody was commercial. It was all for sale. This wasn't the Midwest where people were friendly and generally trustworthy. It was too intense, everybody on the make. Of course, Richard was on the make, too, though in a more conventional way. He didn't fit into the culture at YGB, and didn't want to. Another serious problem was money. He could save no money in New York. His salary at YGB was substantial, but it wasn't that much in New York. Everything from rent to food was expensive. Every penny he made was consumed by the high costs of the city. He was saving nothing, a major violation of his father's standards. Lack of incentives at YGB insured that this situation would not change in time. No matter how much money he made for the firm, his salary was still the same. Competition on Wall Street was such that prestigious YGB had no difficulty attracting first rate talent. Still, Richard wanted money, not congratulations from impressed managers.

He was further disenchanted with Lynn, a girlfriend there who pressed him to get married. Richard was crazy about Lynn, but not ready to get married. He had the potential for a successful career, but, as his father pointed out, that was not the same thing as money in the bank. Lynn, however, didn't share Richard's priorities. She told him either to marry her or say goodbye. He was 23 and just too young to be pressured. He said goodbye. That was the last straw for life in New York. The loneliness was too much. And it was at that time that his father, whose health was never good, died following a short illness.

Soon afterwards, Richard decided to return to Chicago where, at 24, with a superlative resume, he joined the Steward Trading Company. Richard just wanted to succeed, and he did. Unlike many traders there, Richard was not a speculator. Las Vegas type bets were not for him. An excellent architect of complex trades, he was energized by the careful analysis and structuring of risk that he had learned at YGB. In his first two years at Steward, Richard made a lot of money. In addition he was generous with his time in helping younger and sometimes even much older traders. Richard's year-end bonuses demonstrated Paul Steward's recognition of Richard's contribution to the firm. Finally, he was putting some serious money in the bank.

His general desire for success soon became more specific and more intense. Richard wanted more money. A lot more. He had been to New York, and had had enough of power and glamour. Now he did not care about having an office, a casual work environment, long vacations or other perks. He did not even want a salary. He proposed instead an incentive deal where he could get paid a grad-uated percentage of what he made for the firm. That suited Paul Steward, and Richard did very well until, in the last few years the markets grew quiet. Opportunities were becoming increasingly scarce. During this time of low volatility, conservative Richard–and many other traders as well–were struggling.

Taking all of this very personally, Richard felt that he had some-how lost his focus, and was falling far behind in his career. A grate-ful Paul Steward tried to help. First Paul introduced Richard to Rosco Mink, with whom Paul himself had placed a great deal of money with extraordinary success over the years. Paul had made the introduction, but it had been Richard himself who chose to invest in the Cambridge International Fund which traded in com-plex convertible fixed income securities and options. Next, asso-ciating family with focus, Paul introduced him to his lovely young sister-in-law, Katherine O'Connor. Now, a year later, Cambridge was bankrupt and his dismal relationship with Kate was in its final death throes.

• • •

It was early one overcast afternoon that Richard Landon drove out to Barrington to return Kate's things. They had been boxed and sit-ting for months in his hall closet–those very items that Vicki had so objected to earlier. That bulky pink sweater, a bunch of crockery, a dozen paperback romances. It all fit in two cardboard boxes. The drive was long, and severely hampered by drizzle and by summer road work on the Kennedy expressway. It was time to get this over with, resolved Richard. He didn't want his failed relationship with Katie to louse up his red hot affair with Vicki.

He knew it was going to be awkward at best with Kate, and hoped to encounter neither her sister, Molly, nor her mother, Madeline. The sisters, often mistaken for twins—which they were not—still lived with their mother on a spectacular estate on 80 wooded acres northwest of Chicago. Turning into the discrete private drive that led to the house, it occurred to Richard yet again that he was leaving a lot of money on the table by breaking up with Kate. Still, it just had to be done. Nothing was worth such misery.

Richard slowed at the gate where the guard recognized him and waved him by with a friendly smile. Security surrounding the estate was subtle, but substantial. During the winding drive to the house, Richard encountered one of the three unobtrusive mounted guards who patrolled the perimeter with dogs around the clock. Initially such precautions had struck Richard as extreme, but Kate explained that there had been several incidents over the years. For the most part these had been limited to vandalism and petty thefts. But alone now with two young daughters, high profile Madeline O'Connor was taking no chances.

The Barrington estate was magnificent. The house was a Tudor, dating from the 1920s, restored about 10 years earlier. New construction was built over and around the original house, seamlessly matched its splendor, and more than tripled its living space. It was then that the swimming pool was added and the stables enlarged and relocated opposite the guest house. There was even a putting green for those inclined.

And in addition to Barrington, there was much more. A few hours away was a summer home on the Green Lake in Wisconsin, and in order to escape the midwestern winters, there was a much bigger home on the water in Boca Raton. Richard had seen it all. These were just the toys. Robert O'Connor was not a self-made man, but had certainly maximized the fortune he had inherited from his Boston family. From Katie's comments, Richard understood there had to be at least a couple hundred million altogether and maybe a lot more. Molly, always more calculating than Kate, said it was closer to 500. Much of it was in commercial real estate, much in U.S. equities. The rest in commodities, as Molly had observed, had recently enjoyed huge advances. Kate actually knew very little about it. But she did know that it would be a long time before she and Molly or their older sister, Eleanor, would receive a penny of it. And Richard could expect to execute a pre-nuptial agreement at her mother's insistence. Madeline ruled with absolute authority.

It seemed to Richard that the issue of money was only on the surface. Both girls were unmarried, and that was the real issue. Their mother wanted them at home under her constant scrutiny. Her maternal manipulation was shameless. She provided them with a spectacular home and an unlimited wardrobe allowance, but gave them little cash, and permitted them to do social work only. As a direct consequence, the girls themselves were often so dead broke that Richard actually felt sorry for them. Desperate, they devised a scheme of selling newly purchased clothes at severe discounts, price tags still attached, for cash. Even basic transportation was a problem. Madeline flatly refused to provide them with the modest Ford they proposed, though she did allow them the liberal use of one of her luxury sedans. They simply could not afford to move, though they desperately wanted to escape their oppressive mother. Who in her right mind would risk being drummed out of the will with an inheritance like this?

The sisters were twin-like mostly in appearance. A year older than sweet Katie, Molly was far more bold and aggressive. Often, it occurred to Richard, Molly was a lot like Vicki at her most provocative. Still, they were as close as real twins, intuitive and very protective of each other. This defensiveness had its origins in the dynamics of a complex mother-daughter relationship, and not a happy one as Richard learned one wintry evening last year when they were still just getting acquainted.

They were at his apartment, drinking wine and listening to music.

Molly, who had had an argument with her mother earlier in the afternoon, was moody to begin with. After a couple bottles of chardonnay, they were all a little drunk. Molly really let go, refusing to be restrained by Katie. "Everything changed when Daddy died. It was just a couple years ago, but everything changed. Now we don't even have a car. We have to beg to use the Widow's."

That's how she referred to her mother, "The Widow." Or sometimes as Madeline.

"That's right," echoed Kate, more out of support for her sister than anything else. "It's true. Everything did change when Daddy died."

"In our home," said Molly, "he was the boss. He let Madeline run the house, but that was all. He managed the finances and the businesses, and she had to stay out of it. He was so generous. He gave us everything. And he spoiled the Widow, too. Believe me, Madeline has nothing to complain about.

"Daddy was from Boston, you know. From a really wealthy family. He was old money. She is nothing but a good looking gold digger who struck it rich. She was a Fitzgerald from the south side of Chicago. We hardly even know her relatives. She keeps them away. Really, she's worried that they'll ask for money, so she shut them off years ago."

"Molly," said Kate. "Richard doesn't want to hear this kind of thing."

"Well," said Molly, "it's the truth."

Even Kate could not argue with this, so Molly went on. "Madeline grew up in a family of Chicago cops. They're all retired now, but her father, grandfather and several uncles had been cops. Nothing wrong with that, but she owes everything she has to Robert O'Connor. Without him, she'd be working for the city instead of running for mayor."

This was pretty personal stuff, and Richard was privately gratified that they had come to trust him to this extent. Still, it was very troubling.

Kate, typically averting unpleasantness, returned to her father's passion for life. "Molly, remember how much Daddy loved to ride? He taught both of us how to ride," she told Richard. "It was such fun."

"And he loved golf, too," said Molly. "All the things the Widow hates. Look at the stables now. She got rid of all the good horses."

"Well," said Kate. "That's mostly because of my accident. She's afraid someone might get hurt."

"Come on, Kate," said Molly. "Get serious. That was just an excuse and you know it."

"What happened to you?" Richard asked Kate.

"I fell," she said simply. "A slight concussion. Really minor. Riders fall all the time."

"The Widow just hates horses, that's all," said Molly. "And look at the putting green Daddy put in. It's all weeds now. She hates golf, and everybody and everything that our father loved."

Richard understood that to include them. "So why don't you two just leave?"

"It's not that easy," Molly assured him. "Believe me. Wherever we might go, she'd find us. Then something would happen. Something would go wrong for anyone who helped us, or hired us. Believe me, the Widow would have her way. It's too bad she didn't die instead of Daddy. Life would be fabulous! She's probably the reason he did die—he was only 54 when he had a heart attack. He probably just wanted to get away from Madeline. I think about it all the time. I think she was happy when Daddy died. She couldn't wait to control everything. And everybody."

Kate admonished her sister. "*Molly!*"

But Molly could not stop. "The truth is that I'd kill her if I thought I could get away with it."

Katie was embarrassed. "Really, Molly. That's a terrible thing to say in front of Richard."

Richard tried to put them both at ease. "It's okay, she should say what she thinks. I don't mind." Richard did not mind, but he did wonder. All that money. Good god. And they were so miserable. It was extremely hard to understand. To have so much, yet be so unhappy.

According to them, the only person to escape Madeline had been their older sister, Eleanor. Richard had known her a few years before meeting Kate. She was his boss's wife. She had married Paul Steward some six years earlier. That much Richard knew. What he didn't know was that their father had wanted to provide a substantial share of Eleanor's inheritance in trust as a wedding gift, but stingy Madeline adamantly opposed the idea. In fact, she wanted Paul to execute a prenuptial agreement, but Robert O'Connor vetoed that, noting that Madeline herself was never required to do so before their marriage. Fortunately, Eleanor really didn't need the money. Paul Steward did very well as a trader and sole proprietor of his own firm. Kate and Molly revered their older sister for the life she had made on her own. She had a handsome, successful husband and three lovely children. She didn't need Madeline for anything.

The dispute about Eleanor resulted in an enduring rift between Robert and Madeline, and according to Molly, things were never remotely the same again. "We think he had a few girl friends," said Molly. "We sure hope he did, anyway. He deserved better than Madeline. We think she knew. She actually hired a detective agency to follow him. We heard her on the phone one time, telling them what to do. We actually checked to be sure. We just hit redial after one of her calls, and who do you think answered? '*Covington Security, may I help you?*' Isn't that the lowest thing you've ever heard of? Your husband can't stand you, so you hire private detectives to follow him? I think it's pathetic."

Richard nodded slightly. It was more than pathetic, he thought. It was outrageous. He pitied them all. Kate had been right. He didn't really want to know.

The most significant consequence of that winter evening was that Richard had been accepted and trusted in the most personal sense. And now that made everything so hard. Kate had almost made her escape as well, and the failure of the engagement still caused Richard a troubling sense of concern. But all of this was about over now. Their failure had been mostly Rosco's fault, Richard decided. Fortunately for him, he had lovely, willing Vicki to think about now.

• • •

Already alerted by the gate keeper, Kate answered the door immediately. "Hi," she said pleasantly. "Come on in."

"Hi. Brought you a few things," said Richard lugging a cardboard box. He leaned forward to receive a friendly kiss on the cheek. "Where can I put this stuff?"

She peeked inside the box. "Kitchen, definitely kitchen. Follow me. I have some things for you, too. I've got Molly checking around in case I've forgotten anything."

As Kate led the way, Richard could see she had gained weight, a development that surprised him greatly. She had always been so slim. Of course that was because she ate so little, and she, like Molly, had had her mother's great trim figure. Now her pretty face was fuller, and she was actually busty and heavier too in her hips. In the kitchen, Kate had a group of several boxes organized for him as well, including his tools. During happier times while they were engaged, he had once tried to be helpful repairing a garage light fixture. In a household of pampered women, they could not even locate a screwdriver of their own. Even Madeline had been clearly impressed with his resourcefulness. Richard supposed she was pleased only because she was cheap. He also recalled it as the only time Madeline had ever shown any approval of him in all the time he was engaged to her daughter. Oddly, she seemed to regard him more after he broke the engagement. She didn't seem to care a bit about Kate's feelings. It was as though a mediocre business deal had just fallen through.

"How about some lemonade?" Katie asked.

"Sure," he said lifting the tool box. "I'll just put this stuff in the car."

She nodded, "I'll help in a minute. I think the rain has stopped."

Richard opened his trunk and placed the box inside. After several more trips to the kitchen, he had everything packed. He heard the door close behind him and there was Kate with several shirts on hangers and a glass of lemonade. He took the shirts and accepted the lemonade.

Then Molly appeared a few minutes later with a hammer and several other tools. "Hello, Richard," she said.

The last time he'd seen her he had been with Vicki. What a disaster that had been. "Hi, Moll," he said.

"I found these, too," she said handing the tools to him. "Kate and I tried to open that stuck window in the Widow's study," she explained. "We ended up breaking the glass and calling somebody in to fix it before she found out."

They all laughed.

Richard dropped the tools directly into the box, and took a drink. All of this was so awkward. He really wanted to get out of there.

Molly, of course, knew to make a quick departure.

"Take care, Moll," said Richard as she left.

"You take care of yourself, too, Richard," Molly responded giving him a curious smile.

Molly was like that, thought Richard. Strange.

"Mother has been so upset lately," Kate said, re-engaging him. "Did you read what happened to her in the papers?"

"Yeah," he said with a smile. "I'll bet she was ticked. There goes city hall, I guess.

"Really, she has been *so* upset. She feels so sorry for herself. She thinks no one wants her in Chicago now. After all she has done for them, too. Now she is talking about selling this place and the condo in the city. If she doesn't need a Chicago residence, she can make Florida our permanent home and she doesn't have to pay state income taxes. She says it'll save millions. She says she wants to travel. But I think she doesn't really care about the taxes. And she hates to travel. She hates airports and flying. She hasn't taken a trip in 10 years. I think she's just rattled. First there's Rosco, then this lawyer points a toy gun at her in a courtroom the other day and the guard fires a real gun!" She laughed out loud. "Politics! Sounds dangerous to me!"

"Pretty crazy," Richard agreed, also laughing. "Why does she do it?"

"You know mother. She's just bored, really. Nothing to do but keep after Molly and me. Politics makes her feel important. I know it's not very nice to say, but she can throw her weight around and they have to listen."

"This thing with Rosco," said Richard. "So weird. The cops came to see me about it, you know."

Kate was visibly concerned. "Oh, Richard. *Why?*"

"Nothing to be alarmed about. Just this detective asking me some questions."

But she was alarmed. Richard wasn't surprised. She was like that. "But why ask you?" she said. "I mean, what did they want? How could you *possibly* have anything to do with it?"

"No big thing, really. They got my name from Rosco's answering machine. I left him a nasty message early the Sunday evening he was murdered."

"Oh my god, you did?"

"Well, I was angry. And Rosco refused to return my calls. So I left him a blunt message."

She seemed spacey, her mind wandering. Not terribly unusual for dreamy Kate. "I had no idea," she said.

"Kate, it was no big thing. I just left a message on the guy's machine. That's all. General stuff. It's not like I went over there and killed him."

She gave him a quick look. "But still, Richard. The *police*."

"There's nothing to worry about. They were just following up on leads. It's already over. I'm done with them."

She seemed relieved and after a brief silence, was composed again. "I'm so sorry about what Rosco did to you, Richard. I mean, what happened between us, the money and all, it wasn't your fault at all."

Richard accepted this absolution with a slight nod. "Still, Rosco. Murdered. Very weird."

Katie nodded. "The world is a crazy place, Richard. You never know about things. You've got to make the most of what you have. That's what Molly always says. And I agree. Maybe it's not too late for us."

This is exactly what he had dreaded. "I don't know," he stammered. He could barely look at her. "Maybe. Sometime, maybe."

She hesitated, then accepted this evasion and released him with a smile. "Let's stay in touch," she said pressing the key to his condo into the palm of his hand.

He gave her a kiss on the cheek. "For sure. We'll do that."

• • •

It was over!

He had his key back, as well as the rest of his things. Finally, it was officially over!

Richard could not get out of there fast enough. Once past the guard house, he hit the gas, leaving all his troubles behind him.

11

The recent attack by the police confirmed for the boys that they must take much greater care to protect Scab. Not only had Scab bitten a member of the Devil's Disciples, but he had most certainly drawn the blood of the big cop who had chased Spider. And they themselves, as Spider had often observed, would have to take serious precautions in order to avoid many years in the penitentiary as a result of these crimes.

Ben was especially concerned about the cop in the suit. "You know who he is, don't you?" he asked Spider following their narrow escape.

"Yeah," replied Spider. "Him a scout. That him job. Scout for other po-lices."

But Ben knew better. He had read his *Tribunes* and had seen the pictures. "That's the one who shot that boy last year. He got in a lot of trouble about it last week, but they let him go free. He might shoot us too, just like that boy."

Spider seemed to take little notice of this. "Me an' Scab, we seen him before. He doan scare us none, an' doan you worry about him neither."

Ben was impressed with Spider's confidence, but this cop really frightened him. "So what are we gonna do if he comes after us again?" he asked.

"Follow me," said Spider.

• • •

Their route through alleys and side streets terminated at a crumbling concrete bridge over a wide swath of railroad tracks about a mile from Ben's home. Spider surveyed their surroundings, then, with the coast clear, said, "Let's go." With Scab between them, they crawled under a rusted wire fence and ran down the grass to the tracks at the bottom. Quickly they ducked into the shady recesses of the bridge itself. "Where we going?" Ben asked.

Spider pointed to several box cars under the bridge. Clearly abandoned, the weathered box cars sat on a spur of rails so rusty that they could not have been used for years. The word *Alberta* was painted in huge gold letters on the side of each car. Spider knew just where he was going. He led the way to the end-most car, then, lifting the latch of a small door, climbed inside. Ben lifted Scab in, and then climbed in himself and looked around. He could not have been more astonished had it been filled with toys, or had it been the inside of a movie theater or had it opened to Disneyland. The car in fact was empty. It was huge, really enormous, larger even than all the rooms in his apartment combined. It was wide and long, and the ceiling was more than twice the height of a normal room. The construction was basically wood planking supported by a metal frame. It was just a big empty room, with bright morning sunlight penetrating the large cracks on the sides near the roof. "No one find us here," Spider said. "We be safe here."

Ben's regard for Spider, considerable before, was skyrocketing. "How did you find this place?"

"Doan matter. Now you know, too. It a secret."

For Ben, there came a thrill with Spider's willingness to share a secret with him. It was a sign of Spider's respect for him. His trust in him. Ben was growing, learning, achieving. It was an exhilarating boost to Ben's confidence.

Eager to employ their new resource, the boys sat down on either side of Scab, both petting him and talking to him at the same time. "What happened to his fur?" asked Ben.

"Burned," said Spider. "Burned bad. I had to pull him out of a fire in an empty apartment. Whole place burn up. His brothers and sisters all burned daid. His owners, they doan wan him, so I take him wid me. Took long time before he could walk. Scab burned real bad."

"Burned," repeated Ben, gently stroking the dog's barren side and thinking what a terrible thing that must have been.

"Yeah," said Spider. "I found him right before my little brother died. Same day. I found Scab in the morning. Jason shot in the afternoon."

"Your little brother was shot?" asked Ben fondling Scab's ears.

Spider nodded. "Gang bangers shot him right off a swing. Shot right in the face. Fell off daid."

Ben was shocked by this. "How old was he?"

Spider held up four fingers.

Ben felt as though he had heard an obscenity. "*Only four years old?*"

Spider showed nothing. "Lots and lots of real little childrens shot in the 'jects."

"'Jects?"

"The projects. Like King Gardens," said Spider.

"King Gardens?"

"Where I live." Spider was disappointed. "You doan know much, do you?"

Feeling defensive, Ben guessed, "You mean like LBJ, right?" This was where Harold Lamb lived, and it was at the top of his mother's list of forbidden places.

"Yeah," said Spider, pleased with this response. "That right. Just like LBJ."

"That's where that cop shot that boy."

Spider's eyes held Ben's carefully for a long moment, then he looked away and patted Scab's flanks firmly. "Doan you worry none about that old cop. Me an Scab knows jus' how to take care of *him*, right, Scab?"

Taking his cue, Scab barked to prove the point.

"Yeah," agreed Ben, now eager to please again. "Scab will bite his arm next time, and he won't ever be able to shoot anyone again."

They both laughed, then Spider got quiet and serious again. "You know what happen to little childrens kilt in the 'jects?"

Ben didn't.

"Theys come back. The babies, theys little birds. Mostly pigeons. Theys live under the L tracks at night and come to where theys was shot during the day. Theys lookin' fo' theys' mommas. That why you see so many pigeons huntin' around all the time."

Ben didn't know that. "What about your brother?"

"Right. I'm comin' to him. The little kids is dogs now. Like Scab. That where dogs come from. Jason somebody's dog now. Somewhere. I always watchin' for a dog to come around to the swing where Jason shot. Maybe it be him and I can give him a nice bowl of cold water to drink."

Ben didn't know about any of this, so he returned to Scab. "Scab must have been a real brave kid." This was a legitimate reference to Scab's defiance of the Devils and the dangerous cop.

"Right, fo' sure," agreed Spider. "He be the bravest one. And good at runnin' and ball."

"Probably was the smartest kid in his class, too," Ben went on.

"You know a lot 'bout dis, doan you?" asked Spider, now impressed.

Ben shrugged and both boys again petted Scab.

Like the natural leader he was, Spider had offered no proof of his beliefs, and like the natural disciple he was, Ben had required none. But he did have one last question. After a while he asked, "What happens to the gangbangers when they get killed?"

Spider had this figured out as well. Now his anger surfaced. "Theys comes back, too," he said without hesitation. "Theys flies and cockroaches. The leaders is always rats."

Ben nodded, agreeing contemptuously. "My father was killed by a gang. He was just walking across the street one night and they drove by and shot him."

"Ah," said Spider. "So you like me. You and me da same. Da gangs got Jason and you daddy."

Ben considered this connection solemnly. "That's right. It was the same thing."

"So we brothers," said Spider extending a thin arm for a street handshake.

Ben accepted the firm hand. "Brothers," he agreed.

• • •

Later, before he fell asleep, Ben thought about his father, as he often did.

He recalled his dad as a big man, a really big man. Strong, with calluses on his hands from hard work. And tall, like a lumberjack. Ben remembered him so often coming home from work in jeans and work boots and shirts that revealed his powerful arms. He often lifted his mother straight up into the air for a kiss as though she were light as a feather. This was just over three years ago, when Ben was nine.

Would his dad have liked Spider?

Ben was sure he would have. His dad liked people, and was always happy and fun to be around. Everyone liked him. And he would have liked Scab too, Ben was certain, because he loved animals of all kinds, especially dogs.

His father knew how to do a lot of things. He loved to build things. And so did Ben. *"Like father, like son,"* his mother always liked to say. For his seventh birthday, they built a go-cart together, and painted it a bright shiny blue and put a big number seven on it. And then there was the Saturday morning that they bought the garage door opener from Sears, and put it up the same day. This was back when they had a car. It took all afternoon to do, and they worked together. This Ben remembered very well. His father had continuously praised his help. They had measured, straightened and bolted all that Saturday afternoon. And then his mother came out of the kitchen with sandwiches and cookies and lemonade, marveling at their accomplishment. His father insisted she be the first to operate the remote control. He put the batteries in and handed it to her. She pointed the remote and sure enough, like magic, the door went right up. To celebrate, they went to the movies that night. And when they got home, they got out the big telescope that his mother had given his father for his birthday and all of them watched stars for an hour. His father loved stars and knew all about them. Astronomy was his father's special interest, his mother told Ben. She also said that this star knowledge made his father, in her view, very romantic. To Ben, the stars were fascinating and he loved watching with his father and listening to him. One brilliant night on a camping trip in Utah, his Dad had explained in some detail just how the Milky Way galaxy rotated with its gigantic spiral arms, and even showed Ben the dense galactic center through the telescope. Ben was dazzled.

The last memory Ben had of his father was the picnic they had the Sunday before he died. That morning his mother had cooked fried chicken–Ben's and his Dad's favorite–with potato salad and corn on the cob. And she had baked a cake in a flat pan. A yellow cake with wonderful chocolate frosting, thick and actually heavier than the cake itself. All these goodies his mother had packed into a large wicker basket which had been made, she told him, especially for family picnics.

It had been a Sunday picnic at a forest preserve. Under the huge trees, his mother spread several blankets on the grass. A red and white checkered one with matching napkins for eating, a large blue one for sitting and reading or listening to the radio. His father loved baseball, and often listened to it on the radio. His mother was always reading. Books, magazines and newspapers. But she loved music, too, and so did his father, and they both listened at home and in the car. And Ben liked to listen, too. Some, anyway.

Before their picnic lunch began, his mother instructed him and his father to fill a jug with water from the pump. Icy cold water came quickly in large quantities when his father worked the pump. This assignment took longer than his mother expected because his father chose to help other people who found the pump very hard to operate.

Finally it was time to eat.

His father sat right next to his mother, teasing her, making her laugh. This was back when she laughed a lot. He was always kissing her and making her laugh back then. Then finally, the feast! After eating, his father teased his mother–straining and groaning, pretending she had eaten so much that he could no longer even lift her. In response she scolded him, and began to chase him with a big wooden spoon until he gave up and they both laughed.

A little later they all joined in a softball game that went on forever. It was one of those really big softballs that were hard to hit and you had to catch with both hands. It was the Cubs against the Sox. Luckily, Ben had worn his Cubs hat that day. It was the Sunday Picnic World Series. They were the Cubs and had won, 42 to 36. His dad had smashed a home run so tremendous that they had to stop the game while everyone helped look for the ball in the tall weeds.

Then the rain came and they ran for the car. Ben and his mother and father quickly gathered everything into the wicker basket and they were all running and laughing as the rain started. *The rain, the laughter and running for the car.* It was the very last true memory that Ben could summon of his father, and he already knew that this was a treasure to which he must return regularly, so it did not slip away like so many other things in his life.

• • •

Recalling these events was a routine preface to his dreams, but that night Ben did not dream of the picnic. Rather, he dreamed of trains. He found himself waiting alone with his suitcase in a cavernous railroad station as many trains arrived and departed. Finally his train was announced, and he walked out to board in the freezing night. Ahead Ben could hear the steady chug of an idle engine. Then suddenly through clouds of steam he could see it clearly. It was a tremendous gleaming black locomotive that belched huge clouds of steam. Ben watched for a few minutes, then a conductor called "All aboard!" and instantly Ben found himself seated comfortably in a brightly lighted coach. Then, abruptly, without seeming even to leave the station, he had arrived at some mountainous destination and was eagerly stepping down from the coach into vast clouds. A big man stood waiting there to greet him. "So, this is where you've been!" cried Ben over the idle chug of the big engine.

"Yes, this is where I've been," said his father, smiling and gathering him up with one powerful arm. "It's been some time now, Benjamin. Have you been taking good care of your mother for me?"

12

Vicki's month-end itinerary required her to arrive in New York on a Wednesday morning and return late Friday afternoon. For this mission, she planned with professional efficiency. Over time she had acquired an extensive wrinkle resistant wardrobe that she squeezed into designer luggage. The Chanel carry-on was hardly a necessity, rather an indulgence that she could not resist. The $3,500 cost seemed ridiculous to Richard, but Vicki just loved it when she saw it at Neiman's. Of course she planned her business agenda as mindfully as she traveled. Most of her Wall Street meetings would be scheduled for Thursday, allowing plenty of time for obligatory lunches and dinners with clients. It was one such Wednesday afternoon that Richard twisted his knee playing full court basketball. Ice and aspirin allowed him to hobble home for more traditional pain killers. He had already had more than enough to drink when Vicki returned his call late that evening. "Hi, Honey," she said. "I just got in and got your message. Poor baby. How are you doing?"

"I'll live," he said. "Really, it's nothing. I'll be better in the morning." He was getting drunk and wanted to tell her that he already missed her terribly, but stayed with the no big deal line. "So how's the trip going?"

"Oh, Sweetheart, just great. Everything is really coming together so well. Just could not be better." Then she quickly returned to him. "You poor baby," she kept saying. She was playing with him, making him crazy for her. "Oh, you poor baby, you're just so brave," she cooed. "I'll be home soon and I'll kiss it and make it all better."

All of this naturally had its intended effect on Richard.

· · ·

The next morning, Thursday, he couldn't walk.

The knee was badly swollen and painful. Missing work was no great loss because there was nothing to do anyway. So Richard concluded he just had to be patient, eat aspirin and wait for Vicki. Bored, he channel surfed. There were a few videos he would have enjoyed still in the boxes from Katie's, but then he realized that he had forgotten to take the boxes out of the trunk. No matter. He had magazines and books. The internet was on his laptop. Food was no problem, but preparing it was, so he ordered in. The doorman brought his mail. This was the depressing part. Bills, bills, bills. Ironically a disability policy was due. This premium was extremely expensive, and he considered canceling. It was too much money right now.

Thursday evening he was drinking again and thinking of Vicki, waiting for her call. He got out photos from a recent weekend trip to Toronto, and more taken at her place the night of the black tie dinner at the Bond Club. God, she looked great in that black formal gown. All that blonde hair, in curls for the evening. Drop dead gorgeous. Then there were the pictures of them together at the cocktail reception. Just the two of them, *together*. The photos only increased his longing for her. He replayed her earlier phone messages just to hear her voice, then saved them, and played them again. He couldn't wait for her return. Despite all his problems—that fucking Rosco, the pushy cop, dead markets, too many bills, and a now a banged up knee—his relationship with Vicki provided Richard with an unreasonable happiness, the intensity of which he had not known possible. He resolved to tell her that he loved her.

He did love her, he was sure about it now. Not that he knew everything about her. She seldom spoke of her family, only brief references to her mother who lived in a suburb outside of Houston. Her parents had divorced, she told him. And she continued to contribute significantly to her mother's support. Richard got the distinct impression that she didn't get along with her father, and knew to leave well enough alone. Her family, after all, was her business. She told him that she had gone to the University of Arizona where she had majored in political science. "Back then I loved the whole idea of politics," she said. "I was active in student government and imagined going to law school and running for Congress someday."

"So are you a Republican or Democrat?" he asked her.

"Well, back then I was a card carrying Democrat. I mean, you could say I was a zealot, very pro-Democrat. But now I'm an Independent. What are you?"

"I don't know exactly. Independent, I guess. So why did you leave the Democrats?"

"I suppose you could say I grew up. It was one of the great disappointments in my life. Politics is a dirty, lousy business, Richard. You can't imagine. A lot of those people just want to use you. After a little taste of political reality, I was disgusted. I gave up all my dreams and went back for an MBA. So now I believe you have to help yourself, and if you have the means, you should help others, too."

This last comment suggested to Richard a touch of nobility about her. She wasn't a do-gooder or a flake. Rather a young woman of purpose and standards, serious about her world. Someone with high expectations for herself. Someone with depth. Someone endlessly interesting.

• • •

Richard had been completely blown away and he knew it. Vicki was overpowering. However she wasn't, he knew, *perfect*. She was vain, that was certainly true. But vanity was understandable for a woman with the kind of killer good looks that Vicki possessed. Still for Richard, her vanity often added to her sensuality. For example her obvious preoccupation with her hair, her gorgeous naturally blonde shoulder length hair. She was always employing her hair in a manner that made her sexier. She played with it constantly, often twisting it while deep in thought, tossing it back when she laughed, hiding behind it when she smiled. She wore it in every conceivable fashion. Up, in order to look more sophisticated; down to appear more approachable. And within this considerable range, there was more. With one side pinned up and back, the other loose—she seemed stylishly polished and professional. Businesslike. With both sides tucked behind her ears, she achieved a healthy college girl look. She would often change this arrangement several times a day according to her moods. Worn down and loose, her hair was light and had a full natural rolling curl that caused it to bounce lightly as she walked. This, together with everything else that bounced, produced a fairly stunning effect.

Beyond her hair, her signature was her makeup, particularly her eyes–light green with, looking closely, specs of brown. She made them up meticulously every morning. The light liner and mascara with traces of various shadows contrasted with her fair skin to riveting consequence. It seemed to Richard that she reapplied her lipstick at least a dozen times a day. Even while driving she frequently did her makeup in the rearview mirror at stoplights. One time while touching up her mascara as she crawled in heavy traffic, she rear-ended the minivan ahead. The consequences of this were many. First she had mascara running down one cheek, and a ticket from a cop who not only had refused her pleas of innocence, but who had actually laughed at her. Upset, she wrote a letter to the Superintendent of Police. Then her Jaguar was in the shop for almost four weeks waiting for parts, and when it was done the final bill was so stupendous that her insurance refused to cover almost half. But she refused to change. On the way home from the body shop she almost had another fender bender while brushing her hair.

Vicki loved jewelry, with a special passion for pearls. Necklaces and earrings, bracelets and rings. She simply loved pearls–the diamond serpent brooch, however, was a favorite exception with its fiery ruby eyes and tongue. Of course she also had numerous scents, and was always trying something different. Real perfume, numerous elegant bottles, sat on a silver tray on her dressing table.

And naturally she had closets full of clothes, yet was always shopping for more. She especially liked leather and suede, but of looked fabulous in anything. Vicki was never inappropriate. She was constantly changing outfits to fit the occasion. Tasteful suits for work, a black dress for dinner. Jeans for Saturdays. For a sexy evening at home, a short leather skirt, real stockings and heels. She loved shoes, mostly heels, which she had in stupefying abundance. Recently, after dinner, she dragged Richard to Michigan Avenue and purchased black alligator heels and the matching purse–$850! Then she left them in the shopping bag next to her dresser until she had time to make room for them in her jam-packed cedar closet.

Vicki lived in a pricey condo on Lake Shore Drive. She bought it primarily because it was vintage and for its outstanding view overlooking Lake Michigan. Richard considered the cost outrageous for a place with as many problems as this one. The biggest drawback to her apartment was that it was not big enough. But it had other problems, too. It had no air conditioning, but she didn't care for AC anyway. And the lights actually dimmed whenever she simultaneously employed two hair dryers, as she often did when she was in a hurry. But she didn't care about electrical service or blown circuits. And, located just off the Drive, her condo could be noisy. But she didn't care about any of these things. She wanted what she wanted. This place had high ceilings with elaborate moldings, and the huge gothic windows, in what she called the parlor, opened onto the Lake. It was too bad that it wasn't bigger, thought Richard, because it really was outstanding. Her bedroom, one of three, was almost entirely occupied by the enormous bed she had somehow gotten in there. The other two rooms were filled with her clothes. But without a doubt, the biggest attraction of Vicki's condo was the master bath, which she had gutted and enlarged to the detriment of the bedroom next to it. And she had spared no expense. Richard was astonished when he first saw the Italian frescos that surrounded the Jacuzzi and her dressing table. "Say," he commented, hung-over and disoriented the morning following their first night together, "Aren't these the same as at Florentino's?"

Florentino's was Ristorante Florentino, an expensive Northern Italian place on Rush Street. Dusty frescos on the walls and columns placed diners into a bustling fourteenth century marketplace among hardy street merchants offering their wares to a well-dressed clientele.

Vicki confirmed that indeed, she had sought out the same artist to do her custom job. Drawing selectively on the marketplace scene, she had populated her bath exclusively with the same smooth-bodied young men–though without their swords and little skirts–all surrounding a golden haired goddess wearing only a string of pearls. Significantly the fruits in the baskets offered the goddess by her many masculine admirers paled in unavoidable comparison with their own robust genitalia. All-in-all, remarkably original, undeniably stunning, and very Vicki.

Richard's own condo was fairly new and several blocks from the Lake. There was nothing artsy about it, but it was huge. Fortunately it would be big enough for both of them, and all of her stuff.

Of course all of Vicki's extravagance came at a high cost. She had a pressure cooker job as a bond trader for Byatt & Morgan, the huge New York based hedge fund. In this role, she was an unqualified star. Bold and cunning in the markets, while businesslike and convincing with clients. She steamrolled her competition. In the male-dominated world of trading, most of her colleagues were in fact intimidated by her. Vicki took no shit from anyone. And she didn't have to. She put up the numbers. And she was extraordinarily obliging with clients, never failing to attend the sales meeting in Manhattan at the end of every month. Trading was hard enough, Richard was well aware. Trading *and* travel were double duty. Vicki, with her little Chanel suitcase, was busting her ass for Byatt & Morgan.

But away from the job, she liked to party. She loved ethnic restaurants and spicy food, the spicier the better. The kind of stuff Richard could barely tolerate. Greek and Mexican were her favorites. She wanted to try everything hot from Mexican peppers to five alarm chili. At 31 however, Vicki was careful with her diet. She was ruthless about her weight, and quite self-conscious and humorless about any suggestion of gains. These unfounded fears lead to regular jogging, swimming and weight training at the health club as well as and golf and tennis. She even had roller blades, and loved to blade up and down the lakefront. In connection with all of this, there was one word that was absolutely forbidden. *The F word.* The F word, of course, was not to be confused with fuck. *Fuck*, she had no problem with, and used the word casually. The F word, however, she never said, and didn't want to hear. Richard thought this focus ridiculously unwarranted. Vicki was a big girl–in heels she was as tall as he–but nothing bounced that shouldn't have. She was absolutely gorgeous, and Richard told her so all the time.

At this stage of their intense relationship, her more personal inconsistencies were becoming evident to Richard. She would blow $10,000 on the theater and shopping in Manhattan, which she certainly could afford, but at the same time she was frugal in irrational ways. Potatoes would go on sale and she would clip the coupon and chase across town to find them after a hard day at work. And just as inexplicably, she often carelessly paid her bills late, resulting in occasional interruptions in service for electricity or telephone. These inconveniences never prompted her to change in the least. Mail continued to sit unopened, ignored for weeks in stacks on her desk. And there were other instances of silly economies. She'd feed the meter instead of valeting her Jag, then spend a hundred bucks at her hair appointment. And woe to anyone providing truly inadequate service. If you took Vicki's hard earned money, you better produce. Her standards for herself were her standards for everyone else.

Even more inconsistent was her generosity. There were big tips for waitresses, particularly black or Hispanic, routinely. She of course wouldn't give a penny to the Republicans, who constantly solicited her, but she would astound local shelters and soup kitchens with spontaneous donations. Women's causes were the largest beneficiaries. The Chicago Shelter for Battered Women and Children actually called, bringing her attention to what they thought was an error. No, there was no error, Richard heard her say. She had indeed intended to contribute $5,000, not the maximum request of $500.

And her habits were so much different from his. Vicki was truly a night person. Richard could hold his own drinking until 2:00 a.m., but paid a heavy price for it. The hangover, the headaches and the requirement of 10 hours of sleep in which to recuperate. But Vicki just thrived on night life without any noticeable penalties. In fact she often drank more than he did, but was always ready for work, the gym, or sex at dawn. She thought nothing of jogging along the Lake front on a 90 degree July morning after a late night.

Sexually she was dynamite, easily reaching and often surpassing Richard's own lust. And Richard's lust was such that he often was not completely capable of truly rational thought until those exact moments after he ejaculated. It was only then that, suddenly, he could think, really think clearly and objectively. One of his earliest, purely rational questions regarded birth control. After all, they were screwing two or three times a day, *every day*. "Don't worry, Sweetie," she had told him. "I'm on the pill."

So Richard never gave the subject another thought. It was a license for sex. She was so physically fit that she could fuck for hours, and then do it again. On those occasions when markets were slow, she would sometimes call Richard to propose a nooner at her place. They would literally begin to undress as soon as they set foot in the apartment, fuck like crazy, and then rush back to the office before the markets closed. It seemed to Richard that Vicki was always ready to fuck. And for her, five or six orgasms were typical. Her orgasms, as she explained this intimacy to Richard, were usually either vaginal or clitoral and occasionally both simultaneously. And as a diligent lover, Richard made his best efforts to please her. But when he assumed that she preferred the combination, she corrected him. "No, actually the best orgasms for me are vaginal," she told him. "Very deep, very slow. The deeper and slower the better." This indeed seemed to be the case. There was nothing she liked better than a slow hot fuck on a sweltering Saturday afternoon with all the windows open. Then she'd want to go out the same night and come home late and fuck all night. What a treasure she was!

She had a few girlfriends and numerous acquaintances, but like Richard himself, she seemed to have little time for friendships. They had time only for each other. Of course there was a lot he still had to learn about her–and she about him. And, he was just being honest with himself–not all of what he already knew was good. There was, foremost, that temper to consider. That he had seen before, and it was truly wicked. Here was an independent woman, no question. Complex, emotional and determined. But, above all else, exciting. Never had Richard known a woman so exciting, so unbelievably desirable.

And the attraction seemed to be mutual. Since their first encounter back in early April, they had been together almost continuously. They had spent their first day-and-a-half together in bed. This in itself was definitely a good sign. They had dinner together and slept together. They spent every minute of the weekends together. They worked out together, they golfed together. They shopped for groceries together, and did errands together. The only interruptions to this togetherness were mandatory. She had no choice about those brief month-end trips to New York while he too was required to make an infrequent overnighter on business.

Most recent of these, just a few days earlier, was the Pittsburgh trip he had made with Paul Steward who was considering a new trading venture with a firm there. They flew in for a lunch meeting that went extremely well, concluding with a short meeting back at the office. Paul stayed overnight, but Richard, eager to return to Vicki, planned to fly home alone early that evening. He should have arrived in Chicago about 9:00 p.m., but it had become the flight from hell. First, the plane was late arriving from Atlanta because of storms in the southeast. Then they were delayed for almost two hours on the runway in Pittsburgh waiting for clearance in Chicago where the weather also had turned to heavy rain and they were unable to land at O'Hare. They were diverted to Milwaukee. There Richard called Vicki and explained what had happened. Of course he should have just gotten a room, but his desire was such that he rented a car for the two hour drive back home. This of course took him directly into the weather that closed the Chicago airport. It was one hell of a storm. Sweeping rain, pounding hail, and 40-miles-per-hour winds. The highway was virtually devoid of other cars. Richard hustled the entire way, *thinking of Vicki*. He sped, *thinking of her*. He slowed to a crawl, *thinking of her*. He just kept going, *thinking of her*. It was nearly 1:30 a.m. when he opened the door to her apartment. All the lights were on, as was the stereo. Vicki was in the kitchen preparing steaks for broiling. She came out wearing just her pink heels and a lace apron, handing him a scotch as if he were just a little late from the office. "Welcome home, lover," she whispered pressing herself against him and linking her arms romantically around his neck for a long kiss. "Miss me?"

Yes, he knew then that he loved her.

But did she love him?

• • •

Richard awoke Thursday night in a great deal of pain. There was so much pain that he wasn't sure where it was coming from. Had he turned in his sleep and twisted the knee again? No, it was something else. It was his jaw that hurt. Somewhere on the right side of his lower jaw. Then he got it. A loose filling in that molar that had been bothering him for months. For months! And it had to blow up *now*. He cursed out loud, and reached for the aspirin bottle. He tried to relax. Don't move and nothing hurts, right? Somehow he got back to sleep and awoke actually refreshed about 9:30 Friday morning. Very soon though, son-of-a-bitch, that molar started throbbing again. He dragged himself into the bathroom. Now his knee was really stiff and tender, probably from putting his weight on it yesterday. Even taking a leak required a huge effort. No matter. Vicki would be home soon.

Too many aspirins and too little food conspired to make him drowsy. The dentist agreed to see him the next day at 11:00. Friday afternoon was a scorcher, and in the heat of the day, he napped fitfully for an hour at a time. It was her key turning the lock that woke him. Then there she was, standing before him in a dark blue business suit with an ivory blouse, her blonde hair pinned up and back. "Oh, you poor baby," she breathed without moving, unsure if he was awake.

Through the slits that were his eyes, he stared at her. She looked so goddamned terrific. "Don't move," said Richard. He swung both legs out of bed, stood up, walked over, embraced her and kissed her on the mouth. "I love you," he said. "Take off your clothes."

Never needing any real encouragement in this connection, she undressed immediately.

• • •

It wasn't until later, when they were done in bed, that Richard's brain began to function rationally, scrolling quickly through his problems. He still felt guilty about Katie, but was happy that it was finally over. Then there was this crazy thing with Rosco and the homicide cop to worry about. He was just about broke. His knee was killing him again and his filling began to throb worse than before. Still he felt wonderful. Vicki was home. And in their passion, he had told her over and over that he loved her, and she had responded that she loved him, too.

And she said it over and over again.

13

W orking for Morrison in Homicide was nothing like Gang Crimes where Tow had enjoyed great autonomy. Now, not yet assigned a partner, he continued to report directly to Morri and took orders from him alone. Despite this demotion in rank, Tow was lucky and he knew it. When no one else in the Department would touch him, Morrison had stepped up and saved his neck. And there was precedence for Morrison's trust in Tow. Their association went back some time. It was almost nine years ago that they collaborated in a case the media labeled *The Golf Lesson.*

The Golf Lesson officially began with a baffling series of seemingly independent murders. First there was the brutal slaying of a west side hoodlum named Marty DePaulo, a street enforcer for Louis Brattificanno who ran all west side drugs, gambling and prostitution for the Chicago mob. Late one evening Marty was found in an alley behind his favorite restaurant with his throat slit. Then in an apparently unrelated murder, a member of the Insane Disciples of Satan was found shot through the forehead in a park near Austin Boulevard. Not until later did anyone consider the fact that the park bordered the territory of the Disciples and the mob. On the west side of Chicago, the Mafia and street gangs had co-existed with mutual disdain and distrust for decades. The Italian mob considered themselves professional businessmen, and despised the black gangs as a gaggle of inept amateurs and criminals. The street gangs regarded the high living gangsters of the mob generally as soft and not nearly as competitive as they, and lusted over their lucrative turf. The gang bangers had kept their distance until now. One by one, the killings on both sides had accumulated. Independently, Tow in Gang

Crimes counted six dead Disciples in four weeks while separately, Morrison's crew watched six hoodlums get whacked. Because they were buried in the daily violence statistics, the tolerant media barely noted the killings. Anyway, who cared about black street gangs or Mafia violence among themselves?

It was Tow who first saw the highly improbable link. He noted the pace of the murders, which suggested that the killings were reciprocal, while in general the proximity of the violence made the unlikely link harder to deny. In a top level secret meeting, Tow presented his theory to Morrison and seven other Homicide officers: the Insane Disciples of Satan were moving in on the drug turf of the Chicago Mafia. Tow had even recruited a snitch, the girlfriend of a big talking gang member who enjoyed beating her up. According to the girl, Kadeem Clay viewed his rival, Big Louie Brattificanno, as old and soft—an easy target for Clay's Disciples. Among law enforcement officials knowledgeable about the mob, this gang versus the mob suggestion—no matter how well organized and developed—was completely ludicrous. Tow was actually laughed out of the meeting. Later it got back to Tow that Morrison himself had solidly supported Tow's unpopular proposition. And following that, there was a little professional retribution within the Department—a discrediting rumor that Tow himself was working with the FBI in order to embarrass the Chicago Police Department.

Then abruptly one evening, only days later, seven Disciples were shot to death inside of 30 minutes of each other. Neat, efficient killings that seriously decimated the gang. A single slug in each case. Not a clue as to the killers.

There was one message, however.

The headless body of Kadeem Clay, the ambitious leader of the Disciples and critic of soft Louie, was found buried to his neck in a sand trap on the thirteenth hole of Maple Links out in Fox Valley. The location was 30 miles from the turf of the larger confrontation, but the message was crystal clear. A mob informant later explained what happened. Clay's *old and soft* strategy had somehow gotten back to Big Louie who took profound offense and decided to provide Clay with a lesson. While his Disciples were being ambushed, Clay himself had been carefully abducted, bound hand and foot and gagged for the drive out to Fox Valley. There he was buried to his shoulders with only his head exposed like a golf ball in the sand. Under the high-beams of his Cadillac, Louie himself administered a lesson about the soft good life of a mob chieftain.

For this purpose he selected his favorite driver, not the normal club for sand shots, but particularly effective in this case. Of course Louie's intention was clear to the hysterical Clay. When his gag was removed, Clay begged to be shot. Big Louie simply ignored his pleas. As Clay floated into a kind of dementia, Louie took his time. After calmly taking a few practice swings that whizzed by Clay's ear, he stepped forward theatrically to address his subject. First there was the rush of the swing, followed by the solid whack of a good clean drive. Then Louie, now enraged, repeated this demonstration a couple more times. Finally, when there was nothing left to club, he urinated down the bloody hole in the sand.

A year later, with the help of Tow's snitch and the mob informant, Louie was doing hard time for the kidnap murder of Kadeem Clay. The golf lesson with its implications of the good life of a soft mob boss terminated the Disciples' expansion plans, and pretty much made Tow's reputation within the Department.

• • •

That was nine years ago. Now Morrison had him doing trivial things.

This morning, prior to returning the video camera to Equipment, Tow had made a copy of the Rosco Mink funeral video. Tow thought that it had come out quite well. He reviewed the whole thing carefully at home, noting that everyone on Morrison's suspect list had attended the services. The effort, therefore, had told them nothing. Still, as Morri had instructed, he kept the tape in a safe place at home.

This afternoon Morri wanted him to check out another message found on Rosco Mink's machine from the evening of the murder. Nothing threatening, like the angry Richard Landon message, but an unusual contact just the same. Joseph Brennen was a commodities trader who was in the process of negotiating the purchase of two polo ponies from the victim. The message was decidedly blunt.

"Listen, I'm tired of all your bullshit. This is my final offer, take it or leave it."

Tow wasted the entire morning on this assignment, driving out to Brennen's Orland Park home southwest of the city. His original hunch proved to be correct. Trader Brennen was very blunt, but wasn't that exactly what to expect from a man who made his living negotiating all day long? And Brennen had outright contempt for the victim's business ethics, but this was consistent with other comments Tow had heard. Brennen considered himself lucky the deal had fallen through. Tow's efforts had been a predictable, but necessary, waste of time. When he got back to his desk that afternoon, there was a phone message from Beverly Nickols. She had called late that morning asking Tow to meet her at 7:00 the same evening at her office. Something had come up, she said, nothing urgent, but she thought he ought to know about it.

• • •

At 7:00 p.m. the office of Mink Capital Management was dark, but there was a bell.

Tow didn't have to wait long. Beverly Nickols appeared promptly out of the shadows of the reception area to greet him. Then she locked the door. "Thanks for coming on such short notice, Detective," she said leading the way to her office. There she motioned him to a cluster of chairs around a coffee table. "Please have a seat," she said. She closed the door and took the chair opposite him.

She looked spectacular in her gray business suit and bright scarf. Even after a long day at the office, her makeup and hair were perfect, her upbeat manner professional and engaging. Tow even noticed her perfume, and had to resist the notion that she had carefully prepared for his visit. For him! Was that possible?

"I'll be direct. I requested this meeting because I have a problem," Beverly Nickols told him. "A big problem actually, and I thought it best to discuss it alone, after business hours so we wouldn't be disturbed."

Tow nodded, allowing her to go on and only just then realizing that beneath this practiced composure, she was upset.

"I expected to lose some accounts," she began, "but I figured the publicity about Rosco would blow over and that would be the end of it." Here she hesitated doubtfully.

"But?"

She took a moment. "Let me reframe all of this for you, Detective. Generally, I try to head off trouble. Try to get ahead of problems. That's why I called you. There is something I want to tell you before you read about it in the papers."

Tow nodded, trying to be patient and just let her get it out.

"But first I should apologize for the way I spoke to you when we first met. I mean, I was shocked. Really shocked by what had happened. But that's no excuse. I was very hard on you. I'm sorry for the way I behaved. I really am. I hope you will accept that."

Tow nodded. "No need to say anything more," he assured her. "A terrible thing had just happened."

Still she wouldn't accept the easy way out that he had provided. "I don't just mean Rosco. I read about you in the paper last week. After the hearing. And I really am sorry for what I said before, about knowing who you were. And the way I said it. Now I think I understand a lot better what happened to you, and I want to apologize." She hesitated, looking for words. Finally she simply said, "Can we start over?"

All of this was completely unexpected. "Sure," he said automatically. "No problem at all."

"Okay, then. I'm happy to hear that. So as I was saying, I have a problem. Rosco's murder has had consequences far worse than I expected. I've lost a lot of business, and that's got to stop. But the media just won't let go of this story. I mean it's on the national news every night. The nature of the whole thing is so scandalous. It's bad enough that Rosco's name is always involved, but now I'm afraid I'm personally going to be dragged into this thing."

"You're referring to your relationship with the victim?"

She was very still for a moment, and cool, considering exactly what he had just said. "Yes," she said quietly. "Of course, there was my affair with Rosco." Her remorse about this was visible. "Andrea was so nosey. She found out about that, too. But the problem now is something else, actually." She hesitated again. "This is very hard to talk about. Just bear with me."

"It's okay," Tow assured her. "Take your time. I understand."

She gathered her courage, and then began. "My problem is that I am being extorted. Or, rather, someone *tried* to extort money from me through the firm. An employee. Someone who was close to Rosco, and who had access to my own personnel files. Someone who knows everything that is to be known. Her name is Andrea Berger. She is no longer with the firm. I fired her last night."

"She tried to extort you?"

Beverly nodded. "Basically, she wanted a ridiculous raise and a bonus. Just ridiculous–$350,000 a year, plus an immediate bonus of $500,000. This is a woman who Rosco paid $55,000 to run personnel."

"And if you didn't pay?"

"Exposure." Beverly looked away. "Something personal. Something from a long time ago. Something that can really hurt me now."

Tow waited. Finally, she went on. "I did something stupid when I was 19. I needed money badly for college and for other things, and did something foolish. My roommate at school knew some people who knew some people who ran an escort service. One thing led to another and we spent a summer in Las Vegas where we were part of a large escort group. And that's all Linda and I ever did–we were escorts, nothing more. One day a vice sting came crashing down on the service and eventually we were all charged with prostitution. In Vegas, that's like a ticket for doing 40 in a 30. It was so stupid on our part. Some really bad characters. Guns, drugs. Of course Linda and I never actually did anything, but didn't have money for a lawyer and foolishly pled to a lesser charge. We got probation. I'm lucky that's where it all ended. Many others were not so lucky. I actually had my record expunged, but Andrea really drilled down deep."

Beverly waited for Tow's reaction, but he was careful to show nothing. So she continued to explain, "Rosco wasn't very thorough when he hired people, but when Bob O'Connor died, Rosco arranged for me to buy Madeline's share in the business. Rosco had to guarantee my loan with the bank because I could never have afforded the deal. That's when he found out about my record, when he had Andrea check me out. So that was her angle yesterday. *Pay or I tell the newspapers that you were a hooker in Vegas.* I'm sure you'll be reading all about it tomorrow. And given the unfortunate facts surrounding these murders, my criminal record will look particularly scandalous, don't you agree?"

"Not really, Ms. Nickols. I mean this goes back quite a while."

"Will it make me more of a suspect in the view of the police?"

"No, not at all."

"If the media asks, will you tell them that?"

"Yes. You in fact are not now and never were a suspect in this investigation, and I'll confirm that."

Beverly Nickols was visibly relieved. "Thank god," she said. "Now maybe this nightmare will end. I never really thought I would be considered a suspect even though I had a great motive. This is my firm now. And I have a solid alibi–I was with my fiancé the night of the murder. Still the publicity is a problem even if there is nothing behind it. Investors demand professionalism. Sordid publicity like this–if it continued–could ruin my business." Then another thought came to her. "I don't know how you managed with your own situation," she said. "It must have been hell."

"I know what you're going through with the media," said Tow. "It's no fun." Then he changed the subject. "I would like to talk to this Andrea Berger. Where can I find her?"

"I'll give you her number and address, but Andrea is no fool. Everything she has done is deniable. I have absolutely no proof of any of this. She'll deny everything if you ever do catch up with her."

Tow made a note of the woman's name.

"Still," said Beverly, "I've decided it's time to bury Rosco before Rosco buries me. This thing has to be solved and off the front pages or the publicity is going to cost me this business. I've already lost my fiancé. I told him about all of this last night. Attorneys in practice don't marry ex-prostitutes. He ended our engagement just like that."

Tow's gaze drifted to her left hand. The rock was gone.

"I figure I have to help myself now," she went on. "As I explained in our first meeting, I had the option of buying out Rosco's heirs. Well, now I'm committed to doing just that. I elected the option the Monday I spoke to you, the day after Rosco was killed. Now everything I have is in this business. I put everything on the line for this.

As soon as the legal work has been filed and approved, this will be Nickols Capital Management. That'll take a couple months. Right now I've got to make it work with Rosco Mink's name on the door. And it will work if I can just bury Rosco. That's why this publicity is so damaging. I've got to get it behind me and move on. You asked for my help when you were here before. Well, now I'm ready to help. I knew Rosco better than most. Where do you want to start?"

Tow thought for a moment. "You mentioned Madeline O'Connor."

"Yes," said Beverly. "And I saw from the papers that you know Madeline, too. Let me tell you something. I know why Bob O'Connor invested in this firm. Bob and Rosco went way back, Harvard Law. Bob was a very wealthy guy. Tons of money. And I mean tons. He came from a Boston family that has billions. Mostly commercial real estate in Florida. Big investments in shopping malls and that kind of thing. They must own half of Boca Raton, and a good part of Naples, too. But the connection here wasn't financial. These guys were pals. The deal was that Rosco would arrange for Bob to see other women safely. Young women, very discrete opportunities. Then Madeline found out. She had hired some private detectives. She had them follow Bob and Rosco, too. This had to be about two or three years before Bob died. I have to say Madeline was cool about it. Very cool. There was no scandal, no divorce. In fact very few people ever knew. Rosco told me only because he was scared to death of Madeline. But Bob and Madeline settled it all between themselves. The business connection here was really irrelevant. When Bob died suddenly like that, everything changed. Madeline wanted out. She detested Rosco. Really despised him. I remember thinking, boy, she really got that right. And Rosco wanted no part of Madeline either, believe me. That's why he went to such lengths to arrange for me to buy her interest, even after he learned about my arrest record–not that he was offended or anything."

· · ·

They had been talking for more than an hour, and now the sun was setting. It was almost a Caribbean sunset. A blue horizon mingled with vast gray and scarlet streaks. Stunning from Beverly's 63rd floor office. When the conversation had run its course, Beverly commented, "Beautiful, isn't it?"

"Terrific."

"Would you like a drink?" she asked. "After all, I'm not a suspect and we're both off duty."

When she wanted to, she had this way about her, thought Tow. This attractive way of personally engaging him. "Sure," he said. "Scotch?"

"No problem," said Beverly gesturing to the bar in the elegant bookcases against the far wall. "I have everything."

• • •

They were on their third drink, just a rambling conversation, when she changed the subject. "You know," she said, "I really am glad I'm not a suspect in this thing. I don't think I could bear that for real. At first I thought I might be, but I was so excited because of the financial windfall Rosco's death provided me. I really thought the police would consider that a motive and start investigating me. What really worried me was that they would find my record and that would sink my ship on the spot."

"There wasn't much chance of that. Motive alone isn't enough to merit investigation. There has to be more, some compelling evidence. With you, there wasn't any. And," he added, "there still isn't. Besides, you have an alibi. You were with your fiancé." She really didn't know anything about police work, thought Tow. But then, he didn't know anything about business.

"So who *is* a suspect now?" she asked picking up her drink in one hand and pushing her long hair back behind her ear with the other. "Not Richard Landon, I assume." Then she hesitated. "I hope I can ask that."

"You can," said Tow. "But first, what can you tell me about Victoria Moss?"

Beverly hesitated, already sensing trouble. "She's in the same fund as Richard," was her flat response. "Why?"

"I was afraid you were going to tell me that," said Tow. "As you know, Richard left a threatening phone message on Rosco's machine a few hours before the murder. Victoria Moss is Richard Landon's alibi. We're doing background checks now. It doesn't look good for those two."

Beverly repeated what she had just heard. "Richard threatened Rosco? And Vicki is Richard's alibi?" She seemed surprised by this. "Richard and Vicki? You mean they're a couple? I didn't know that. I thought Richard was engaged to one of the O'Connor twins. So now it's Richard and Vicki together? Are you sure?"

"That's what he told me. He was home all night with his girl-friend, Victoria Moss."

Beverly idly considered this development. "Richard and Vicki. A couple now." Then she got it. "*Oh, you don't think!* Because of the losses? The two of them? *No, I don't believe it.*"

"Believe it," said Tow. "Things like this, you don't have to like them, but you do have to believe them."

"But this is ridiculous," she protested. "I've seen losses in this business that would break your heart. People get very upset, but nobody kills over them. And Richard Landon is really such a nice young man. And Victoria Moss? I can't believe it. I don't believe it. It's just a coincidence."

"I understand what you're saying, but people do really crazy things. Motive always makes more sense to the perpetrator."

"But to kill someone over money? And go to jail? Or worse? For money? I can't believe it."

"Well, I remember a case about two years ago. Happened in a grocery store near LBJ. A woman, an elderly woman, black, on wel-fare. Bought two chickens, cut up in parts, from the butcher. When she got home, she found she had been sold eight wings, but no legs. She brought everything back and explained her complaint to the butcher who also owned the store. He pointed to a sign on the wall that said 'substitutions allowed,' and refused to do anything. So she took out a hand gun and fired six rounds in his direction. Only one hit him. Right between the eyes. She'll never live to get out of jail."

"But Rosco was killed by this fanatical woman. The one who killed those other two guys."

"Rosco could have been staged to make it look like her work."

"Staged?"

"Yeah, could be. It's a long shot, but Rosco Mink's murder could have been staged to look like the work of the other killer. It could be a very effective strategy of misdirection. There is no question that Richard Landon threatened the victim, has a motive and not much of an alibi. And besides that, there are possibly significant differences between the murders of Rosco Mink and the other two victims. It is entirely conceivable that Richard and Victoria could have committed this crime together. And maybe even some other crime, too. A hotel maid, in the case of the second victim, Robert Jankowski, thinks she may have seen a man leave the hotel with a possible female suspect. You just never know about possibilities. These crimes could be related. That's why we have to investigate further."

Beverly became quiet, thoughtfully considering her drink. Then she looked at Tow, who could see how worried she was. "It's all so crazy. But somehow," she said, "I really don't think Richard Landon or Victoria Moss had anything to do with this. I know them both and I don't believe it." And then she added a more personal afterthought. "I just hope you can put an end to this thing. And soon."

14

They usually met every morning.

Ben would finish selling papers by 8:30 a.m. or so, and Spider and Scab would be right there waiting beneath the L tracks. But today they weren't there. Harold Lamb had recently changed Ben's elevated train stop to another location closer to his Pine Street home, and actually only three blocks from the bridge over the train tracks. So Ben went directly to the box car, but they weren't there either. He even tried the playground–considered enemy territory since the attack–but no luck. With his options exhausted, Ben went home alone, taking special care to avoid both the gangs and the cops.

Ben knew at once that his mother was not at home because the television was not on. Weary of her unending interrogations, he was pleased to have a little time to himself. His mother, he knew, was just not the same as before, back when they lived in Oak Park. Since the move to Pine Street her emotions varied wildly. One minute she was laughing, the next she was crying. She would scold him severely, invoking one rule after another, then she would hug him warmly and tell him everything would be okay. And there were other things. She had changed her hair twice in recent weeks, cutting it short and dyeing in blonde highlights, then red. He approved of neither, and was sure that his father would have agreed with him.

Ben also knew that his mother was increasingly worried about their safety. One day while looking for a flashlight he found the hand gun she had recently acquired in the drawer of her night stand. The gun was ugly, sort of bluish in color, and very heavy. Upon closer inspection, he could see the fat copper bullets in their chambers. Ben was unhappy that his mother felt they needed such protection, but still relieved that they had it. If his father were alive, this precaution wouldn't be necessary. Recalling his recent dream, his father clearly expected him to take good care of his mother for him. Scary as it was, Ben resolved to use the gun if he had to.

But recently there were some good things that Ben could not account for either.

Ben had a PC, but no internet access. Now his mother said they would soon have a phone again, and proposed that he subscribe to a new service provider in order to have access to the internet and email. And now, all of a sudden, they had groceries too, and a lot of them. Not that his mother cooked the way she used to when his father was alive. Until she started working full time, there was always something good baking in the oven. Oatmeal raisin cookies, his favorite, often still warm when he got home from school. And for dinner, roast chicken with apple stuffing, or broiled cheeseburgers dripping with gooey cheddar and real fries a lot better than McDonalds. His mother seemed so happy when she was cooking. She loved being in the kitchen, baking while she talked on the phone with her friend, Lydia. Or fussing with her china or the many shiny copper pots that she displayed from the ceiling while something delicious simmered on the stove. On Sundays, she always made something special. Lamb with that green jelly, or roast beef with potatoes, or salmon with pasta. All of these goodies made even the accompanying salads and steamed vegetables seem tolerable. Then at Christmas, she would make a gingerbread house and use the special china with the green holiday wreaths. But all of that was before. Now Ben was happy that there was fresh sandwich bread and sliced turkey in the noisy old refrigerator.

But there was more recent good news. His mother and he had made several trips to Sears for summer clothes for him. With school only weeks away, she had also bought him shoes and a new backpack, and had paid cash for everything. Of course he never wore the new shorts or shirts because he felt conspicuous around Spider who wore the same soiled clothes for days. Now he was around Spider most of the time. The truth was that he admired Spider, and wanted most in the world to be just like him. To look like him, to talk like him, to act like him. Ben longed to bring his friend home, but he knew instinctively that his mother would crush the friendship on the spot. Spider was a street kid. A kid from the 'jects. He was rough, talked tough, and was dirty. And then there was Scab, too, to consider. There was no way, Ben knew, that his mother would allow it. Rather, she would cite her next rule: stay away from that boy *and* his dog.

• • •

The knock on the door immediately told Ben that he was in trouble.

It was more like pounding than knocking. Startled, Ben quickly linked Spider's absence with this. Probably the police, he thought, now coming for him. A gruff voice called, "*Patrice Foster, I'm National Credit and I know you're in there.*"

Ben did not know what to make of this, but in his fear, withdrew to his mother's bedroom where he squeezed under the bed. There was the sound of someone fumbling with the lock from the outside, and to his terror, Ben suddenly realized that he had neglected to bolt the door from within. Another of his mother's rules forgotten. He could hear the door open, and the footsteps of someone walking inside. "National Credit, lady," the man announced as the door closed behind him. "You know you're behind in your card payments. I know you're here."

Ben didn't make a sound. The man was looking for his mother, and there was, he knew, no way for anyone to know he was here. But his mother could be in real danger. Now presented with this threat, he recalled his dream of a few nights ago, and his father's last words to him. "*Have you been taking good care of your mother for me?*"

Heavy footsteps quickly walked across the living room and stopped at the door of the bedroom, then moved on. It was just then that he heard the lock again, the door open, and his mother walked in. Ben could hear her humming, and he could hear the rustle of the paper grocery bag she carried. Then she screamed and drop the bag with a thud. "*Who are you? What do you want? Get out. Get out of here immediately!*"

The male voice was unafraid. "You're behind, lady. National Credit. You're way behind." Then the voice took another tone. "Well, looky here. Now what do we have here?"

"You stay away from me," warned his mother. "You get out of here now, before I call the police."

"You don't have a phone," the man said. "Besides, we can make ourselves a deal and resolve this matter right here and now. Whatta you say, Sweetheart? Me an' you right now."

"You take your hands off of me!"

Ben needed to hear no more. He was on his feet in a flash, opened the drawer and dashed out with the gun.

He was a big man, black, and his back was to Ben.

Ben took careful aim for the center of the man's torso, and said, "Let my mother go or I will shoot you six times and feed you to the rats."

The man turned instantly, allowing Ben's mother to pull away. Then he made a move in Ben's direction. In an instant Ben had pulled the trigger twice.

The man reversed his direction, falling to the floor and rolling to the safety of the most distant corner of the room. There he lay unhurt, squeezing himself into the tight corner, his hands raised and his eyes full with panic. "*Don't shoot*," he pleaded steadily. "*For Christ's sake, don't shoot.*"

Ben took more careful aim while stepping directly toward the terrified intruder until the man was looking down the barrel not five feet away. "Next time I won't miss," advised Ben.

Then his mother was at his side and, with some force, took the gun. Holding it with both hands, she pointed the barrel directly at the man who, now completely terrified, put his hands on top of his head as he awkwardly got to his feet. "Look, lady," he pleaded. "You gotta be careful with that thing. I'm only doing my job. You know you're way behind in your payments."

"Now, you listen to me, Mister, and you listen good."

The intruder, withdrawing again, nodded his co-operation vigorously.

"Now *I'll* make *you* a deal," Ben's mother said still aiming the pistol carefully, "You get out of here and don't you *ever* come back, and I won't shoot you dead right now like I ought to."

• • •

Later, Ben wondered why his mother had let the man go, and had not asked a neighbor to call the police instead. After watching him leave, she fussed over Ben, praising his bravery and kissing him, but she made no effort to report the break-in. Neither was she concerned about the two small bullet holes, one in the wall and the other in the ceiling.

• • •

Of course, Ben was relieved that she had not called the police.

And when he finally met Spider later that day, Spider agreed it was lucky that the cops hadn't come because they surely would have arrested Ben and him and Scab, too, for their parts in that earlier confrontation with the Devils. "Then we be just like Roosevelt," said Spider.

"Who is Roosevelt?" asked Ben.

"Roosevelt my big brother," explained Spider. "When him in a gang, he kilt another gangbanger. Judge give him 45 years fo' dat. My mamma take me to visit him in the penitentiary and Roosevelt say to me, 'Look, don't never do nothin' wrong or judge put you in the penitentiary like me. An' I ain't never gonna get out of dis place forever. You hear me?'" he say real mad. *"Doan never do nothin' wrong, else you be just like me."*

• • •

Gun or no gun, Ben went to sleep that night wishing his father were still around.

And for the first time in his life, he felt real hatred. Whoever had killed his father had not been sent to the penitentiary for many years like Roosevelt. Whoever had done it had gotten away with it, and had condemned his mother and him to this terrible place.

15

She said it would be bad, and it was.

Two days later, the *Tribune* had the scoop, complements of Andrea Berger, and ran a small factual story. The surviving managing partner of Mink Capital Management, Beverly Ann Nickols, had a Las Vegas prostitution record dating back 20 years. Basically that's all it said, stressing that the police had confirmed that Ms. Nickols was not a suspect in the Rosco Mink murder case. In this environment, however, prostitution was an explosive word. That night, the story was national news again. Later the *New York Post* somehow linked the Rosco Mink investigation to a Vegas mob inquiry into gambling and prostitution. And taking that a step further, an imaginative national tabloid, invoking the Profumo scandal in Britain decades before, somehow introduced a California congressman and three Soviet spies into the mystery.

• • •

On the morning of the day after, a Friday, Tow got a phone message from Beverly.

I've been working from home for a few days, she said. I told you this would be bad. And I also told you I want to help get this thing over with.

She left her home number, inviting him to call any time.

He toyed with this notion for a while before working up his courage. Beverly Nickols' home number. He studied it for clues. She had a Chicago area code. That meant she lived downtown. What would he say? Should he comment on the story? What could he say? It was a hell of a scandal. Lurid and salacious. The papers were full of it, and so was television. Feeling like a nervous school boy, he finally forced himself to dial the number, which he had already memorized. "Beverly," he said. "How are you doing?"

"I've been better," she said. Then softer, "I'm really glad you called, Tom."

He could tell she had been crying. "It's my day off," he said. "What are you doing for lunch?"

She brightened. "I'd love to have lunch," she said. "Really, that sounds great."

Now Tow had a lunch date, his first date in 30 years. This realization made him feel foolish. What did he know about dating?

• • •

They had agreed to meet an hour later at Carmichael's, a small café on Erie Street. Her choice.

Tow arrived 10 minutes late. She was already seated at a corner table on the crowded outdoor patio, and waved when he looked in her direction. At first he wasn't sure it was her. Finally, she stood and, waving again, called to him. "Tom."

"Sorry," he said lamely when he sat down.

She was wearing a light blue summer dress with flat white sandals. Her long hair was gathered into a limp pony tail, and she wore large black sunglasses with dark lenses. "I'm incognito today," she said. She took off her sunglasses and tried to smile. Her eyes were red and she looked tired. This was not the cool capable executive from their previous meetings. She looked smaller without heels, and vulnerable. Girlish, thought Tow. Afraid and hurting.

Tow returned her smile. "You okay?"

"I've been better, but I'll get through this."

"So what's the damage?"

"It's bad. I've lost two more accounts so far, and I'm guessing three more will go next week. It's just becoming too embarrassing for them."

"I'm sorry to hear that."

She was quietly frustrated. "It has nothing to do with performance, you know. We're doing okay, the funds are making money.

It's a publicity disaster. A complete disaster. And the rumors and gossip are vicious."

Pretty much what Tow expected. "I'm sorry," he said.

"You see, all of this humiliates me in the eyes of sophisticated clients. It just looks so bad. It's causing real problems for my ex-fiancé too. He called asking if I'll please stop embarrassing him. His law firm is losing business, too. He's just furious. I mean, he almost married an ex-hooker. So he has a right to be angry. I know I should have told him about it—and some other things, including my affair with Rosco. But how much does a girl have to confess at this point in her life? Actually, now I have to say I'm glad the engagement is over. I really had my doubts before. John pressured me so much to get married. But we had other problems too—too many. I don't think I would have gone through with it. Still, I can't blame him for being frustrated about all of this."

"Doesn't sound like there's much you can do right now."

"Not much. Just get through it." She smiled again, making a real effort. "My lawyers tell me that I do have some recourse against Andrea Berger for violating the confidentiality agreement she signed when she was hired. Not that I'll recover any damages, but I could return the favor. I have to think about it. More bad publicity, you know. I doubt that it's worth it. I don't know how you managed your situation. It must have been very hard."

"You have a pretty good idea, I think. No mercy from the media, you know. After all, they have a job to do."

She seemed to be considering something for a moment. Finally, she said, "I have a confession to make."

Tow waited. "Yeah?" he said easily.

"Yes. I told you I read about you in the papers. Well, I did, but I also went to the hearing last week. I was there. I saw the whole thing."

"Is that right?"

She nodded. "Of course I already knew Madeline, and I had met you. You didn't seem to be what the papers and all had said. I wanted to see for myself. And I'm glad I went. It's what changed my mind. I have to tell you your lawyer did a fantastic job. Talk about wild!" Here she could not resist a smile that became a small laugh. "Really, that guy was unbelievable! I mean, what a show! It was like a Shakespearian play." She shook her head, unable to suppress her smile while trying to return to the gravity of the situation. "But really, he did do a great job. He showed not only what really happened, but how and why. I really understand now. So did everyone in that room. They all came out of there on your side. And I don't blame you for trying to find your witness. Probably just a young kid, but he could corroborate your testimony."

Tow waited again. "I'm happy to hear you say that." His spirits were soaring. She was interested and she was on his side.

"There is something else."

Jesus, he thought. What now?

"I also know that you're divorced. Your lawyer said so at the hearing."

He nodded. "That's right."

"I was married once. For a while, when I was young. Too young to be married. I was lucky, no kids. Do you have children?"

"A daughter. Susan is in computers. I don't really understand what she does, but she likes it."

"And your ex-?"

"Ruthann is an editor. Children's books. She lives in Baltimore now. We had our problems before, but after the shooting we really fell apart."

"Do you mind my asking all these questions?"

"Not really," he said easily. "It's okay. It seems I asked you a few."

• • •

After lunch, they sat in the sun, lingering over iced tea while the crowd dwindled.

"Okay, so now it's my turn," she said, and told him about herself.

She said she grew up in southern California, and went to USC for undergrad where she received a degree in accounting. Afterwards she went to Northwestern for her MBA. She didn't like Chicago at first because of the winters, but now she loved the city. Her dream was always to own her own business. Be the mistress of her own destiny. She had been in the managed money business her entire career and knew many people in it. It was a great business, especially for a woman. Her mentor was a Bill Redmond, a founding partner in the Wall Street investment firm Redmond, Blatchford and McCauley. Her best friend was Lisa Paley whom she had met at Redmond, Blatchford and now worked for Bank of America in L. A. Her mom still lived in San Francisco near her sister, Carolyn, and her kids. Carolyn's husband had been killed in Desert Storm. A helicopter accident. Her dad died six years ago. Cancer. It all happened very quickly.

She had a condo in the city and a cottage in Michigan. She played tennis and golf for exercise, and loved to cook. And she also loved to read. Fiction, mainly, and was determined to write a mystery novel of her own one day. She'd love to have a dog, but she worked long hours and had no one to take care of it. She also traveled a lot. Some for business, but mostly for pleasure. She *loved* to travel. It was her passion. She had been all around the world. "I could draw you a map of London, Hong Kong and Milan," she told him. Her last trip was to Rio just four weeks ago. She'd been there before and couldn't wait to go back.

"So, now," she said in conclusion and feigning out of breath from her unbroken speech. "How are you going to stop all this craziness and rescue the damsel in distress?"

Tow didn't say anything at first. "Well, I don't know."

"Well, how do crimes usually get solved?"

"I have to tell you, real crime solving isn't like what you see on television," Tow told her truthfully, "It's usually not discovering some small clue that breaks the case. That's for the movies. Mostly it's hard work. A lot of police officers knocking on doors, asking questions of a lot of other people. Sometimes an informant surfaces—informants can make an enormous difference. But in my experience, the big breaks come when criminals make mistakes. Until then, we just have to wait."

16

"I can't believe what I'm hearing on the news." It was Kate calling him one afternoon at the office. "They're making this so scandalous. I mean, it's embarrassing to listen to. Las Vegas prostitutes and the mob and the Russians. And this is supposed to be about Uncle Rosco? It's crazy!"

"Yeah," agreed Richard, dismayed to hear from her so soon. "It's pretty crazy alright."

"And poor Beverly Nickols. She bought Daddy's share of Rosco's business, you know. What they're doing to her is just not right. I mean, the poor woman. Digging up her past like that. Molly and I met her, you know. A few years ago, right after she bought us out. She was so nice. It's just not fair."

Not happy with Rosco or Rosco's partner, Richard tempered his comments. "No rest for the wicked, they say."

"Well, I hope the police have finally left you alone."

"Yeah, pretty much. I think they're just following up on every lead they can find. I'm not really worried, if that's what you mean. I didn't kill Rosco. Asking me all these questions is really pretty ridiculous. Everyone knows this crazy lunatic murdered Rosco and those other guys. I have nothing to hide."

"Of course you didn't do it. But I think it's a shame what they're doing to innocent people."

"I suppose so. But I'm not worried. I'll just roll with the punches."

"Good for you," she said.

This conversation rambled on for another minute or two, when, mercifully, Richard got hit on a resting order and had to hang up.

Kate was such an unusual person, thought Richard. Washed out, that's what she was. In a way, what he felt for her now was pity. He had seen her actually happy on only one occasion, a wedding they had attended last Thanksgiving weekend in McHenry County. Brimming with enthusiasm, Kate wanted to take the train from the city rather than drive.

He balked.

"Oh, Richard, the train will be fun," she pleaded. "You'll like it. I promise."

Her preferences were so few that he couldn't say no.

So with their luggage stacked on the seat in front of them, they snuggled together for the two hour ride on a virtually empty late-afternoon coach. Once beyond the grimness of the city, they sped through neat suburbs that featured crowded neighborhoods and gridlock traffic. Gradually they passed into open fields where autumn colors lingered everywhere. Finally in a splash of golden light, they plunged into endless rolling farm land. It was kind of an Impressionist dream. Distant hazy grain silos, and fields that lay fallow with the harvest just over. Kate stayed close, watching as the encroaching darkness finally enveloped them. Gradually the window of the lighted coach provided a mirror image of themselves rather than a view of the landscape. She was radiant. All Katie could talk about was this wedding. She just couldn't wait for this ceremony; hers would be next.

Richard guessed that she wanted to escape her home.

He had come to realize that Kate, more than either of her sisters, was not so much herself as the product of a stern mother's expectations. She was like a doll, a paper doll fashioned according to a rigid matriarchal origami. Most people certainly would have rebelled.

"When I was very little, about seven, Mother started me on piano lessons," Kate confided to Richard one time. "I had to practice every day. Usually a couple hours. Saturday and Sunday, an hour in the morning and two in the afternoon. If I didn't want to play, I had to sit there until I did. For hours. I took those lessons until I was 10. Daddy finally ended them."

"What about Molly?" asked Richard. It was a natural thing to ask. He wondered how Molly coped with such discipline.

Kate just smiled. "You know Molly. She refused. Whenever Mother sent her to her room, she tore it apart. Everything would be on the floor." Kate laughed at the recollections. "One time when she was about nine, she had this terrible argument with Mother and was sent to her room. Molly locked herself in and this time, she threw everything out the window. I mean everything that a nine-year-old could move. All her clothes. A couple lamps, toys, books, a stereo. Her new camera and a little television with a built in VCR. Tooth brush, towels. The throw rugs. Everything. And this was from a second story window. All of it landed on the roof of the garage."

"So then what?"

Kate hesitated. She was considering just how to answer this. "Well, after that, Molly had to see a specialist. That's what Mother called him. She found this Doctor Larsen, who, she said, specialized in children with learning disorders. Later we found out he really was a specialist in child behavior." Though they were alone, Kate lowered her voice to an embarrassed whisper. "He was a psychiatrist actually. A child psychiatrist. He still practices today."

Richard nodded in an understanding way, but said nothing.

Kate went on. "So Molly had to see Doctor Larsen every Saturday afternoon. The doctor's office was in the Loop. Mother drove her while I practiced piano."

A difficult silence followed. Finally Richard said, "Sounds just like kids' stuff. Kids outgrow that kind of thing, you know. Molly seems okay to me."

Katie nodded. "Well, *of course* she is, Richard. But she had to put up with all of this therapy off and on for quite a while. You know, she always told me all about it. The last time she went was her senior year of high school. Really, not that long ago. Molly said the guy told her she was angry with her mother." Kate genuinely laughed. "All this effort! Can you imagine! Just to hear that! You know, like tell us something we don't know!"

"But you still had to take piano lessons for three years?"

Kate nodded. "Eleanor kind of set the standard. She took lessons even through college. She's really good, let me tell you. She loves it."

"But you didn't?"

Kate hesitated, considering her answer carefully. "No."

There was abundant bite in her flat response. It was the only time Richard could recall Kate really being bitter.

She looked away. "I had no talent for it and I hated it," she said. "And I hated her for it. I hated my own mother." Her gaze returned to Richard. "Isn't that terrible?"

Richard had to restrain himself. He was tempted to say that such pressure on a child was cruel, and that her mother should have been the one to see a shrink, but wound up making a banal comment that parents sometimes make mistakes.

Richard hardly knew Eleanor, but he certainly knew Molly.

As close as they were, overbearing Molly put much pressure on Kate. And frail Kate, ghost of a personality, had no defenses with which to resist. Molly dominated and Kate submitted. Molly lead, Kate followed. Although they were not twins, in many ways it was as though they were joined at the hip. Always together, always sharing their interests and hopes. They certainly were unusual in their "twin-some" relationship, despite the intense regard that they had for each other. As personalities, they simply could not have been more different. Only together did they comprise a single complex person.

The person Molly most resembled, thought Richard, was Vicki. Those two were the real twins.

The two of them, Molly and Vicki were remarkably similar in so many ways. Each was a forceful personality, each capable of fierce anger. Both possessed a blazing intellect. Both independent minded. Both exceptionally attractive.

The truth was that Richard was more attracted to Molly than to Kate. He'd known that for a long time. It had been just a fluke that he had been introduced to Kate, rather than to Molly. Neither had been attached. Richard guessed that Paul Steward had yielded the match making to Eleanor who nominated Kate, a decision that he himself had second guessed many times. Kate was just so hard to relate to. It was like she was walking on eggshells even when she didn't have to. Richard couldn't guess what she was really like. Then again, maybe it really had been the best match possible. Life with Molly, Richard admitted to himself, would have been a roller coaster. But then, maybe not much more than with Vicki. Both seemed so militant in what they believed. Clearly, they were both feminists. Neither accepted any grief from men. Molly in fact seldom let any men get close.

When Molly did need a date, it was usually this guy Steve. Richard had met him at the McHenry wedding. Nice guy, quiet and very bright. He had recently earned his doctorate in physics, and worked at the big government facility at Fermi lab. Seated at the same table, they made small talk. Steve was intrigued about trading and Wall Street, and Richard was curious about the science Steve was doing, and the rigorous mathematics that supported it. It was in mathematical modeling that they shared a common interest. "We should have dinner some time," proposed Richard.

"Sure," agreed Steve. "If Molly wants to, sure."

Oddly, this suggestion was never acted upon.

When Richard inquired about it, Kate at first stalled. Later she admitted that Molly reserved her relationship with Steve for less optional occasions.

At first Richard didn't quite get it. "He seems to be a terrific guy," he said. "Really bright. How long have they been going out?"

"Oh," said Katie. "They went to high school together."

"They've been going out for more than five years?"

Kate nodded and shrugged defensively. "More like seven. Molly isn't ready to get attached yet. And Steve travels a lot in his job. You know he just got back from a conference in Leningrad, then stopped in London for another on his way back. He's away about half the time. So, actually, they're perfect for each other. Everything is just fine."

Richard wasn't so sure.

Basically one boyfriend in her entire life, and Molly kept him at a distance during the time available to them. All pretty strange, he thought.

17

F inally they got a break.

A couple hookers working in a west side motel had only barely survived a murderous attack.

The significance of this was tremendous: *live witnesses.* Witnesses can provide information that can lead to an arrest and, further, to a conviction. For the first time, one of the killers had made a serious mistake.

Its siren blaring, an ambulance was just leaving as Tow arrived. He braced himself, recalling the killer's work on Joanne Rice. *Crazy son-of-a-bitch,* thought Tow, suddenly angry. *Crazy murderous god-damn son-of-a-bitch!*

The pair turned out to be a mother-daughter team. The 17-year-old daughter had been badly slashed about the face, neck and chest. Her mother had saved her life, knocking the attacker over and recovering the razor sharp knife that he dropped causing him to panic and flee. Tow's mental preparation proved to be justified. Blood was everywhere in the squalid motel room. They had taken Beatrice Lopez to Cook County Hospital just as Tow arrived, but he did attempt to question the mother, who was unharmed.

Carmen Lopez, a heavy woman, about 35, knew only a little English, and did not want to employ that. It was a pitiful circumstance. Both she and her daughter were in the country illegally, and now they were involved in a criminal activity.

Refusing to talk to Tow or anyone else, she sat on the bed weeping.

• • •

Fortunately Morrison soon showed up with a translator and an artist.

"Tell her we don't care about immigration or prostitution," he instructed the translator. "Tell her we need her help to arrest the person who attacked her daughter. Tell her we'll forget about all the rest."

This seemed to work.

When asked if she could describe the attacker, the woman nodded and said she could. A young man, she said. Long hair. Marks on the face. Very drunk.

When asked if she knew his identity, she said she did not.

Then came the big break. There was something else.

She went on to explain that she and her daughter were working together because the daughter had had an abortion at a west side clinic five months earlier and they feared that the violent protesters there might hunt them down. Now she was certain the protestors had had something to do with the attack.

With the help of the translator, the police artist began a rough sketch. A male of 25 or so, long hair, poor teeth and a bad case of acne quickly emerged. The drawing was just completed when word arrived from County that the girl would survive, but she had received almost 200 stitches. When the translator delivered the first part of the message, the mother brightened. When advised of the last part, she started weeping again.

• • •

Dr. Roger Simon, Director of the Westside Women's Clinic, began with a caveat about the privacy of his patients. "You saw what our patients have to deal with when you came in the front door, Detective. It's a very threatening situation."

Tow agreed. "It's bad. No question. Are they always out there?"

"Rain and shine. Night and day. The only change is that some are more troublesome than others."

"Well, somebody out there may have been a little too troublesome." Tow told Simon about the attack. "I have a sketch."

The doctor accepted the drawing, and his face clouded immediately. "Oh, no," he said.

Tow's heart actually leapt. "*You know this guy?*"

The doctor nodded. "That's Eddie. He's our night watchman."

Finally, thought Tow. We're finally going to get this throat-slitting, murdering son-of-a-bitch. "What time does he start work?"

"Normally about 10:00. But ..."

"But, what?"

"He's not here. He took an emergency leave of absence last week. Something about '*a sudden death in the family.*'"

• • •

It was a crummy apartment building in a lousy neighborhood.

The name on the mail box was E. Chambers, 5b. They went in with guns drawn. Front and back doors. Six uniformed police officers, several armed with shotguns, and three detectives. It was the first time Tow had drawn his revolver since firing it just over a year earlier. Now he was relieved that there was no one home, and holstered the pistol.

There were only four rooms, and the place was a mess. A sink full of dishes soaking in dark, cold water; the garbage pail more than full, spilling over onto the floor; several liquor bottles evident. Another fifth of cheap bourbon sat open, almost empty, on the kitchen table. He must have been swigging it out of the bottle, thought Tow. Also there were numerous vitamin bottles and a salt substitute. Health food products dominated the refrigerator. The living room was furnished with only a soiled easy chair and a grimy matching sofa. Crooked shades covered the windows that overlooked a parking lot. Various free weights cluttered most of the room.

Religious paraphernalia seemed to be all over the place. A bible open on the sofa, rosary beads discarded on the floor nearby. On the walls, grotesque plaster plaques featuring a suffering Christ. Each plaque had a protruding candle holder at its base supporting a small votive candle. In the kitchen, they found a box of three dozen such candles for which the killer evidently had found a dual purpose. The plaques themselves were numbered, and Tow finally recognized these to be Catholic Stations of the Cross organized throughout the apartment. Soldiers of the Lord propaganda littered every room, including the filthy bathroom.

In the bedroom they found stacks of pornographic magazines, many open on the bed and the floor. There was a small amount of cocaine on the nightstand. A shaky card table supported a small computer. A printer sat on the floor to the right. Stacked high on the table beside the computer were numerous unpaid bills, and among these, Tow noted, were at least a dozen City of Chicago parking tickets.

What they found last was truly evil. A notebook in long hand detailed the killer's sexual fantasies about each victim. They were all there. Margery Billings and Joanne Rice had been patients at the Clinic. Jessica Reynolds apparently had been only an unfortunate companion of Margery Billings, just as Carman Lopez had been with her daughter, Beatrice. And now the mystery surrounding Joanne Rice was resolved as well. No doubt she *had* been stalked.

• • •

Morrison was pleased. Now things were really coming together. Now they knew who they were looking for. Edmund Chambers was a 23-year-old high school drop-out who had lived on the south side of Chicago all his life. He had been arrested three times before, in connection with violence toward his former girlfriend, Martha Grant. According to the girl, Chambers was a rough drunk who liked to beat her up. She said she wasn't surprised by what had happened, nor would she be surprised by any other violent act that he might commit. She herself had decided to move, and refused to say where out of fear for her life. Eddie, she emphasized, was crazy.

• • •

In the days that followed, the police lab confirmed that the killer's signature candles exactly matched those found in the suspect's apartment. Size, weight and manufacturer were identical. Also, a lab examination of the computer revealed detailed patient information obtained from the Westside Clinic. Names and addresses of each victim. Normal medical information: home and work phones, next of kin for emergencies. Insurance information. Physician references.

Tow was dismayed to see that Joanne Rice had listed Nancy Martin as her emergency contact.

When he again questioned Mrs. Martin, she finally admitted she had known all about the Clinic and had indeed agreed to be Joanne Rice's emergency contact. In fact she had accompanied her friend to the Clinic. She said that the implications in all of this had caused her much anguish, but she had decided that she simply could not reveal to the police and the newspapers something so personal about such a good friend. Then she broke down. "It's just not fair," she sobbed. "It's just not fair."

And it wasn't, agreed Tow. It wasn't fair at all.

18

I t was the cop again.

This time calling him at home in the early evening.

Richard Landon was instantly alarmed.

Tow had just received the results of the background checks. "Look," he said, "I have some conflicting information here. Do you think you can straighten this out for me?"

"Well, yeah," Richard stammered. "Sure, I'll try."

"Okay. The people at Mink Capital Management tell me you have to be a high net worth investor to participate in their funds. High net worth, right?"

"Right," confirmed Richard, his heart already fast.

"So I have a report that contradicts that. It says you have a serious credit problem. You're behind on your car and condo. You have creditors looking for a lot of money. Is that right?"

So that was it, thought Richard. This was something he could explain. "Okay, I'll tell you something," he began. "The truth is that I've been having a tough time trading. Last year was terrible. And I have already had some big losses this year, too. Now the markets are quiet. It's really hard to make any money. This kind of thing can happen to anyone, you know. Losing money is not illegal, and I'm not the only trader struggling."

"Well, it still sounds to me like you lied on your subscription agreement last November. It says right here that you say you had a net worth of $1.4 million at that time and an income of $300,000."

"Listen, so I stretched the truth back then," admitted Richard. "I wasn't trading well, so I sort of hired Mink Capital Management to trade for me. Only the fund I was in blew up. I lost everything I had in it."

"According to the subscription agreement you put $275,000 in this fund. And you lost it all?"

"Not quite," said Richard exhaling. "I got about $30,000 back."

"So that explains the phone call to the victim Sunday night," said Tow. "That's a pretty serious motive."

With this, Richard lost his patience. He stood up and walked to the window. "*Look*," he snapped. "*I didn't do anything wrong*."

"You threatened the victim on the night he was murdered."

"A fucking hooker killed Rosco Mink." Richard was almost shouting. "Everybody knows that."

Tow stalled for a moment. Then factually, "At this point, nobody knows that for sure. The whole thing could have been staged."

"Staged?"

"That's right, staged."

Exasperated, Richard continued slowly and deliberately. "Now listen to me. I didn't *stage* anything. *I did nothing wrong.* I never harmed that son-of-a-bitch. Would I be so stupid as to leave a message on his machine, and *then* go over there and kill him?"

Tow snapped right back. "Stranger things have happened."

"You have got to believe me," implored Richard. "I did *nothing* wrong."

"Yeah, well, you have a motive and you threatened the victim. Not a good combination. And your only alibi is that you were with your girlfriend, Victoria Moss. Is that right? All evening and all night?"

"Right. That's right."

"Well, the report on her is another problem. She has a record in Texas. Eight years ago she tried to kill her husband with a kitchen knife."

It felt like a punch. "*What?*" Richard had to sit down.

Tow went on. "Yeah. The guy beat her up so she stabbed him six times. I've got the report right here. Jack Fortis testified that she tried to kill him. Said his wife was crazy. A mental case, anger and rage. Convinced the judge. He had her take a battery of psychological exams. It doesn't say what the test conclusions were. In court she claimed it was self-defense. She got off."

"That's impossible," said Richard. He had to sit down again. "I don't believe it."

"Yeah, you better believe it" said Tow. "And there's more. Mink Capital tells me she's a loser, too. The same thing as you. The same investment. Exactly."

Richard couldn't contain himself. "That's no secret. There are dozens of losers in that fund besides us."

"Not good at all," said Tow again. "I'm going to have to talk to her. Stabbing charge, motive, and I suppose you for an alibi. You two could have staged this whole thing together."

"This is crazy," protested Richard. "I don't know anything about this at all. I didn't even know that she had been married before."

"Listen, son," said Tow relenting somewhat. "No one is charging you with anything yet. But this is very serious and I need to check it out. I have to talk with her. Do you know where I can find her?"

"She's shopping. I'll have her call you as soon as she gets home. Is that okay?"

"Okay," said Tow. "*Tonight*."

"I'll tell her."

• • •

"Hi, Honey," said Vicki closing the door. She was carrying several shopping bags. "Wait until you see what I bought. Oh, I just can't wait to show you."

He glared at her.

"What the matter, Richard?" she asked immediately. "Did something happen?"

"It's that cop again."

"Oh, no." She sat down next to him with her shopping bags. Now she was concerned. "What did he want?"

Richard shook his head solemnly. "He thinks we killed Rosco."

She hesitated for a moment, then she laughed. "Richard, that's ridiculous. I mean, really insane." She was brimming with contempt.

"He doesn't think so. He did some checking."

Suddenly she was not so secure. "And?"

Richard continued, direct and very serious. "Well, there are a few things."

"Like what?"

"Well for starters, he says I lied on my subscription agreement with Rosco. The truth is, Vicki, I have to tell you that I've had some serious financial problems lately. And because of that, it appears to this Detective Miller that I have more of a motive to take the fund losses out on Rosco."

This took a few seconds to compute with her. She chose to ignore it. "That's silly. Everyone is having a tough time." Her composure was gaining. "What else?"

"Yeah, there is something else." Richard didn't know how to go about confronting her, but finally chose to risk everything. "He says that you almost killed your husband in Texas eight years ago. You stabbed him six times with a knife, he says."

She looked away, abruptly very distressed.

"You know, Vicki, you never told me about any of this."

She colored severely, but did not move. Her anger was gathering. Richard would not have been surprised if she told him all of this was none of his goddamned business and slammed the door on her way out. That would have been very Vicki. Instead she looked directly into his eyes and nodded. "But I *would* have told you, Richard. I actually planned to do that. When the time was right. I certainly would have told you everything. It was ruled self-defense and that's exactly what it was."

There was a difficult silence which Richard finally broke. "Okay," he said accepting her explanation. "I do believe you would have." With this resolved between them, Richard returned to their mutual problem. "Now the cop also says you were in the same losing fund as I am. That's your motive."

"So?" She was striving to be reasonable again. "None of that means we actually killed Rosco even if we had wanted to."

"Yeah, but think of it from Miller's point-of-view. The losses are our motive. I have a money problem. You have a stabbing conviction. It all just looks bad."

Her response was so typical. A rush of anger. "*This is ridiculous*," she snapped.

"Well, when he asks you, I think you better tell him you came over about 8:00 the night Rosco was murdered."

"Why should I say that?"

"Because that's what I told him."

"Why?"

"Because I needed an alibi when he questioned me the day after the murder. So I told him you and I were home together the entire evening. So now we better be careful to stick to my story. Besides, what's the difference? Alone. Together. Neither of us killed Rosco."

Vicki was very upset. "All of this is crazy. Rosco was killed by this lunatic hooker."

"The cop says we could have staged the whole thing."

She laughed, now genuine contempt surfacing. "They think we *faked* it to look like a hooker murder? Crazy. Just crazy."

"This cop, Miller, he wants you to call him. Tonight."

She looked at him. "Tonight?"

"Yeah. I told him I'd have you call as soon as you got home."

She thought about it for a moment. "I've had enough for one night. I'll call him tomorrow."

"He's giving us a chance to cooperate. He said tonight."

"Well I didn't do it, so he'll just have to wait."

• • •

Tow didn't wait long.

The next morning, with Morrison's approval, he obtained a search warrant.

Given the meager grounds, it was a warrant limited to a search of only the apartments of Richard Landon and Victoria Moss in order to locate evidence in connection with the homicide of Rosco L. Mink. This meant the murder weapon, binding materials, candles or drugs. Further, he also obtained a subpoena for the taped phone recordings from the suspects' respective employers.

• • •

Admitted to each apartment by building management, they found nothing incriminating.

Tow phoned in his report to Morrison. "Sorry, Morri. I struck out both times."

"Worse," said Morrison. "The print report shows no matches either."

This was a reference to the suspects' finger prints long on file with the SEC and CFTC. None matched the prints lifted from the scene of the murder.

Tow groaned aloud. "Then there is no point in Hair and Fiber either."

Morrison agreed with Tow that Richard Landon probably did know more than he was saying, but the fact was that they had nothing to tie him and his snotty girlfriend to the scene of the crime. Absolutely nothing. Further it now appeared unlikely that they actually had anything to do with it. The phone message was indeed their best defense. It was too incriminating to be the scheme of any rational person. Richard Landon was right. Everyone knew who killed Rosco Mink. The same hooker who murdered two of her other customers. The victim in this case was emerging as a particularly loathsome character, but the suggestion that the Mink killing was staged was preposterous. Morrison agreed that it was a dead end. No hair samples would be required because the investigation of these two suspects was now over.

• • •

That evening, Vicki was furious.

"*Who does this Detective Miller think he is?* They asked me a lot of questions and subpoenaed the tapes from all my lines this morning. I thought for a minute that they were going to make me empty my purse on the table. They did everything but pat me down." Her anger then grew a notch. "*This thing about Rosco is flat out absurd.* And insinuating that I had anything to do with killing those other two guys is outrageous. How am I supposed to remember where I was one or two nights last winter? And then poking around in my life when I was married, what gives them the right? Everything was okay back then with the state of Texas. Jack got drunk and beat me up and raped me. And he did it all the time. I was always bruised and hurting. Once he even broke my collar bone. He liked to fuck me when I was scared and bleeding. Finally I fought back. This time it was self-defense. That's what the judge ruled. The prosecutor told me it would have been rape, and Jack would have been convicted, except in Texas a man cannot be convicted of raping his wife. I should have cut the s.o.b.'s balls off while I had the chance. Still even in Texas you can't get away with punching your wife around. But I suppose it's okay for a 200 pound drunk to beat up women in Illinois." Her anger was slipping into a rage for which she had no further words. Finally she exhaled in frustration, shook her head. "I'm sorry," she said and grew quiet.

Richard did nothing to break her silence.

"If Byatt & Morgan finds out about my charge, my career is toast," she said softly. "They were very supportive today, but they could have a problem with what happened in Texas. I'll never make managing director."

So that was what she was worried about. That he could understand. "You told the SEC and CFTC though?"

"No. Regulators only ask about convictions. I was never convicted of anything."

Richard nodded.

She really was agonizing. "I just can't believe the cops think we did this thing. They must really need a scapegoat. We can't prove we didn't do it and they have nothing to lose trying to prove we did. Now they're never going to stop."

Richard did not want to tell her, but now there was no choice. "Well, actually there is something we can do."

She looked at him skeptically. Then quietly asked, "Like what?"

"I have something more to tell you," said Richard.

She gave him another curious, unhappy look.

"That night, Sunday night? I walked over there. To Rosco's."

It took a moment for this to compute with her. "But you said you told the cops you didn't."

"Yeah, well, I had to tell them that. But I did go over there. And as I walked up Rosco's sidewalk, a girl was leaving. I'd seen her before. At a party last Christmas. Some of the guys got a little rough with her, and we had to pay off the cops."

Now she was staring at him, disbelieving.

"Don't you see? *She's the one.* She killed Rosco and those other two guys."

"Oh my god, Richard."

He wasn't sure what she was thinking.

"Oh my god," she said again.

He wondered if she had had enough of him, and was prepared for her to get up and leave.

"You know who did it. You know the killer!"

This was much better than he had expected from her. "No, I don't know her at all. But I can identify her, that's all."

She just looked at him. She was thinking. "So what's she like?"

"A black chick, a babe. Late 20s," said Richard.

"Well, good lord, Richard." Now she was relieved, greatly relieved and back to being reasonable. Even forgiving. "Why didn't you just tell that cop what happened?"

"Look, at the time, I didn't want to get involved in this thing at all. If I pointed the finger at this chick, she'd point it right back at everyone there that night. Including the cops we paid off. And me, too. I didn't have anything to do with that, and I didn't want anything to do with this. After all, I didn't have anything to do with Rosco's murder."

She considered this silently.

"Now I guess I have to tell that cop what really happened that night, but I don't have to tell them about the party."

"Yes," she said. "Yes, by all means. Tell them what happened that night. Let the police talk to her and leave us out of it."

• • •

Vicki's relief was such that she was exceptionally quiet the rest of the evening. And when he joined her in bed late, Richard found her crying.

19

There was a lot of train traffic on the rails adjacent to the box car, and for this reason Spider often cautioned Ben to take great care. And this Ben did, following Spider's lead as in everything else the three of them did. One brilliant afternoon, Spider proposed they buy chocolate milk and donuts at Marshall's Deli located down the block on the opposite side of the bridge. The most direct route was across the half dozen tracks and up the shallow embankment on the other side. The boys and Scab scrambled out of the box car, and in his haste, Spider nearly stepped into the path of an oncoming freight train. Only a quick shout from Ben prevented disaster. The three of them watched impatiently until the long freight finally rumbled past, then Spider immediately took the lead again, only to be jerked back by Ben who then stepped quickly onto the tracks to grasp Scab by the collar to drag him out of the way of a commuter train speeding from the opposite direction.

• • •

Spider seemed unable to talk about these events, very quiet and not at all himself. This troubled Ben, and the whole episode had caused him to wake several times that night. The next day, he found Spider and Scab waiting for him in the box car. Spider pushed him and said, "*Hit me. Go on an' hit me.*"

"What?"

Spider shoved Ben harder this time. "*I said hit me.*"

"I'm not hitting you."

Spider shoved him hard against the side of the car. "*You better, 'cause I ain't stoppin'."*

Ben was baffled. "Why are you doing this? I never did anything to you."

"*You better fight fo' you life,*" shouted Spider, shoving Ben again.

This time Ben responded reflexively by pushing back. But Spider was ready, and cuffed Ben hard along the side of his head. The blow knocked Ben to the floor where Scab licked his face. "*Get up, chump,*" snarled Spider.

Angry now, Ben quickly got to his feet and rushed his opponent crashing him into the side of the car. Both boys punched as they rolled around the floor with the dog jumping all around them. "*You better fight for yo' life, punk,*" taunted Spider as he climbed to his feet. "*Come get me.*"

Ben did, rushing Spider again.

Fists flailing now, Ben was furious, actually landing serious blows to Spider's head. Then suddenly Spider was hurt, blood all over his face.

Shocked, Ben stopped. He was truly shaken by damage he had done to his opponent.

In real pain, Spider screamed at him, "No! Doan stop! Doan never never stop!"

But Ben did stop, his anger instantly gone and now suddenly full of concern for his friend.

Spider sank to the floor. Ben did as well, with Scab whimpering and making his way between them.

"You cain't stop," said Spider very quietly through bloody lips. "You too nice. You strong alright, an' you smart, but you ain't tough. Around here you got to learn to fight for you life."

• • •

Only later did Ben figure it all out. The fight had been a gift, a lesson he needed to learn. He was strong and smart, but needed to be tougher. A lot tougher. He wasn't nearly tough enough. And significantly, this was also the only way that Spider knew to repay him for saving his life.

20

A few days after the apartment search, Tow got a call from Richard Landon proposing a meeting at Richard's home that night. "Sure, I'll be there," said Tow instinctively, although they had already closed the case on Richard and his girlfriend. Even the report on the subpoenaed taped telephone lines tended to absolve the two of them. Their conversations involving Rosco had been few, though especially irreverent on Victoria's part. Still the tapes yielded nothing suggesting a crime.

Against the consistent advice of his attorney, Leo Brulet, Richard chose to talk to the cop alone. An attorney, he reasoned, would only complicate the situation. And so would Vicki. This was something he had to do on his own. He had nothing to fear himself. After all, neither had he done anything wrong, nor had he even been accused. And this Miller was a straight shooter. No doubt about that. Richard trusted him. All he had to do was to explain the situation.

Tow arrived 10 minutes late.

"Can I get you something to drink?" Richard asked.

"Thanks, no," said Tow. "I'm fine."

"So how's the Rosco investigation going?" Richard began.

"Not too bad," said Tow. This kid, he thought, preparing himself for a shocker. He always knows a lot more than he tells.

"Well, maybe I can help some," said Richard already reconsidering his decision not to have Leo there. "That is, I'm sure I can. I just want you to know that Vicki and I had nothing to do with Rosco's death. I mean, in spite of our personal problems which you already know about. We did nothing wrong."

Here we go, thought Tow. The disclaimer usually precedes the shocker. Tow knew to just let the kid get it out. "Yeah," he said easily. "Okay, so what's on your mind?"

"Well, there is something." Richard stalled a moment and looked away. "Look," he blurted, "I should have told you this before, but I just didn't want to get involved." He hesitated again, full of doubts now about the wisdom of telling the cops anything. "I hope you can understand that."

Nodding, Tow agreed. Witnesses never want to get involved. And he really did understand on the most personal level. After all, there was a witness to another event a year ago who still did not want to get involved. "Sure," said Tow, "No one wants to be involved with something like this."

It was Richard's turn again. He took the plunge. "Well, I went over there that night. The night Rosco was murdered. I called earlier and left that message, then when Rosco didn't return my call, I just walked over there when the rain stopped. I mean, you know I owe a lot of money, and Rosco ..."

In absolute disbelief, Tow cut him off. "*When I asked you before if you went over there, you told me you didn't.*"

Richard felt himself color, and the cop could see it. Now he wished Leo were there. "Look, I just didn't want to get involved."

Tow backed off a bit. "So what happened?"

"*Nothing*," snapped Richard, actually raising both hands in defense. "*I did nothing wrong.* I just walked up to the door. I didn't even ring the bell. It was starting to drizzle again, so I left."

"That's it?" said Tow. "You got me over here to tell me that?"

"Well, not exactly," said Richard. "I did see something. Someone. Someone important. A girl. The one who did it. I saw her. She was leaving Rosco's as I approached."

This brought Tow to the edge of his seat. Something so provocative required at least a challenge, certainly a reconciliation with prior accounts. Tow was controlled and to the point. "*But you told me before that you didn't know who had done this thing. I asked you that directly.*"

"I *don't* know who did it," protested Richard. "I didn't see her do it. I don't know her name or anything."

"But you could recognize her?"

"Yeah. I mean, I think so."

Tow really had to control himself. "You should have told me earlier, son. This is very important. Why didn't you just tell me in the first place?"

"I already answered that question. I didn't want to get involved. I have my own problems, some of which are due to Rosco's mismanagement. I just didn't want to get involved in his murder. Then you dug up all my money problems and all that stuff about Vicki and her husband. It made us look bad. So now I'm just trying to set the record straight."

Here Tow took a moment to evaluate the kid. His earliest convictions about his likely innocence remained, but this was still pretty messy. This kid wasn't lying when he said he didn't want to get involved, but other than that, he was really hard to believe. "I don't know," said Tow. "I just don't know what to think now. You lied to Mink Capital on your subscription forms and you lied to me at least twice. Now what am I supposed to think?"

"Look," implored Richard. "I'm telling you the truth now. Vicki and I didn't do it. It was the girl, the black girl who did it."

Tow shot Richard a quick look. "What did you say?"

"The girl did it."

"No. You said she was black."

"Yeah. Absolutely gorgeous too."

"Let's go over this again. This black girl was leaving as you approached the door."

Richard's spirits were recovering. "*Right*," he said with new conviction.

"And where did she go?"

"Good question. She walked by me, holding a tissue to her eye. She walked down the sidewalk to the street and hailed a cab."

"She got right into a cab and took off. That's what you want me to believe?"

"Well, yeah, because that's exactly what happened. She hailed a cab, a Yellow Cab. I remember because the driver–a black guy, young–about stood the cab on its nose stopping for this hot chick. Guy couldn't believe his luck. She got in and he took off. That's all I know."

"But you could recognize her if you saw her again?"

"Maybe. I guess so. I think so."

"Okay, now *think*," said Tow as if talking to a child. "Is there *anything* else that you can tell me? Anything at all that I should know about this girl, or about what happened that night?"

"No," lied Richard Landon, still protecting the cover up. "Not a thing."

• • •

As much as he wanted to, Morrison didn't buy a word of it. "The kid is lying," he told Tow. "He's scared stiff, that's all. He thinks we have more on him than we do and he's scared."

"Yeah, he's plenty worried," agreed Tow. He expected this rebuttal from Morrison. But his job was to report directly to Morri, and that's what he was doing. "Maybe he is lying. But he could be telling the truth. The lab does have hair from a black woman. How would he know that was even a remote possibility? If I were gonna lie, I'd be a little more predictable."

Morrison took a moment with this. "Yeah, maybe," he said. "But this kid looks like a habitual liar. You told me that yourself. We can't go chasing every crazy lead we get." Morrison was frustrated. "You know how many bullshit leads we get? And I don't want the media hearing anything about this. It's just too goddamn racial. Besides, I don't buy it." Morrison stalled again, his gaze drifting out the window. "Shit, the truth is that I don't know what the hell to think. This kid could be a home run for us. Damned if I know anymore."

"How about if I have him look at some pictures?"

"Sure," said Morrison. "Quietly. Have him look at everything we have. But I want this quiet. You tell this kid his ass is on the line here."

• • •

After leaving Morrison, Tow's next stop was the lower level of police headquarters over on State Street where he was told traffic tickets were processed. He had gotten several more notices to pay his original fine for parking next to a fire hydrant. Now he had three warnings and it was time to do something about it.

Systems and Records was a vast expanse of bright lights, computers and desks. Tow had to wait. At least it was mercifully cool down here. Another waiting customer, an officer in uniform, struck up an idle conversation with him. "This place is really something," said Officer Barnnet.

Obviously, Barnnet recognized him, so Tow introduced himself.

"Yeah, they do it all down here," continued Barnnet. "Prints, mug shots, rap sheets. Everything. Custom reporting. Damned near anything you can think of, they can do it."

"Is that right?" said Tow, just being friendly.

"Oh, yeah," said Barnnet. "Everything is going hi tech now. I'm having them do a report on all burglaries in a five square mile area in Hyde Park. I want to see all break-ins occurring between 10:00 p.m. and midnight for the last three years. They can do it. Pretty amazing. Just like Sherlock Holmes, you know," said Barnnet smiling.

Of course, Tow knew about the department's computer resources, but in Gang Crimes, he had never had much use for them. He made a mental note to discuss possible future applications with his daughter, Susan. At least it was an excuse to call her.

Officer Barnnet collected his report and signed off, leaving Tow next in line.

Finally a young boy with long hair waited on him.

Tow showed him his badge and then laid the notices on the counter. "I got the original on the job," he told the boy. "I just want to kill it so I don't get these notices anymore."

The boy was doubtful. "Hold on," he said. "I'll be right back."

He returned with his superior, a slight man, about 60. "Sorry, Detective," said the man. "No can do. I need authorization to cancel a parking citation. Get this form executed and bring it back, and I'll take care of it for you."

Not at all acquainted with these departmental regulations, Tow was actually surprised. It seemed like such a trivial request. Then another thought occurred to him. Office Barnnet's comment about custom reporting. If Rita had been as vigilant with others as with him, maybe the murderer had also received a ticket. Eddie Chambers had certainly collected enough of them. It was a long shot, but why not check it out while he was there? "There's one other thing," he told the supervisor. "I need a report."

The older man nodded toward the boy. "Barry here can help you with that."

Barry stepped forward again. "Sure," he said. "What can I do for you?"

"Okay," said Tow. "Can you give me a list of all the parking tickets issued on particular dates for a specific area?"

"No problem," said Barry. "As long as you're not in a big hurry."

He wasn't, said Tow, and gave him the dates of the first Sunday and Monday of July, and the Gold Coast area from Division Street to North Avenue. "And I need names," said Tow organizing his request as he went along. "I need to see the names of the owners of the ticketed cars." This seemed possible. After all, they had his name.

"Okay then, you need the report listed by name of registered owners of the vehicles." Barry was writing all of this down. "That it?"

"That should do it." Tow gave the boy his card, with his new number penned in.

"Okay, I'll call you when it's ready," he said. "This is a sub-sort of a special sort. A programmer will have to write a routine to do it. It'll be at least a week."

Tow left, annoyed with the bureaucratic inefficiency involved with such a trivial request.

• • •

There was another assignment on Tow's agenda before knocking off for the day. Motivated by his sleuthing with the parking tickets, he resolved to apply the same technique to the issue of the availability of an ice pick to the general public. His first stop was the mall. At Baroque's, a high-end outlet for crockery, he was approached by a salesgirl with a badge that read Debbie. "Can I help you?" asked Debbie.

"I'd like to buy an ice pick," Tow told her.

Debbie was immediately doubtful. "An ice pick?"

He nodded. "Yeah, an ice pick."

Debbie couldn't have been more than 20. He thought for a moment she was going to ask him what he wanted it for. Actually this was the question he anticipated. What would anyone want an ice pick for these days?

"Well," said the girl. "I'm new here. I'll have to ask someone."

A few minutes later Debbie returned with a middle-aged woman who wore a look of concern. "I'm so sorry," she told Tow. "That's not something we've ever stocked."

"Well, can you suggest anyone who might carry something like that?"

The woman thought for a moment. "It's not really a culinary item. Not something most people use in the kitchen anymore. You might try a hardware store though."

Tow thanked the woman and left, having smugly confirmed just what he expected. Who had use for an ice pick anymore, and just what would that use be? Ownership in itself could narrow the list of suspects. Suggestion of an occupation requiring the use of one might point to a suspect.

• • •

The next day Tow stopped at Collin's Hardware on Handel Boulevard.

"An ice pick?" the clerk asked "No problem. Follow me. We have everything."

And to Tow's dismay, they did. They even had three different sizes, making it difficult for Tow to find some excuse to avoid actually wasting five bucks. "So who buys an ice pick these days?" he asked, still unwilling to give up this angle.

The clerk was growing skeptical now. "Look, mister, if you want to buy one of these, well great. But I got other things to do."

Tow showed the man his credentials. "We're just trying to understand something," he said. "So who buys an ice pick?"

Intimidated, the clerk told him, "Businesses, mainly. We sell a lot of picks. Produce guys. Fish guys. Go over to the Fulton Street Market. You'll see what I mean."

• • •

An hour later, Tow was walking down Fulton Street. Inside of four blocks, he counted 11 people working with ice picks. Some were packing for delivery, others receiving deliveries. Mostly fresh fish, poultry and some vegetables. Much of it in temporarily packed ice chips on a scorching summer afternoon.

So much for that idea, thought Tow, climbing back in his own sweltering Buick.

21

fter three days of looking at mug shots of prostitutes, Richard Landon finally gave up.

The only photos that Richard did recognize were those of Margery Billings and Jessica Reynolds, the two blonde victims who were murdered at the beginning of the whole thing. The glossy black and whites had been highly publicized for months. "I don't know what to tell you," Richard told Tow.

"No luck, huh?"

"I wish I could find your killer," said Richard, "But she's not here."

Tow tried another angle. "I'm checking with Yellow Cab drivers to see if one of them remembers this girl. Any other ideas about how we might go about finding her?"

"Not a clue," lied Richard once more, well aware just how deliberate Tow was being with him. His only hope was that if the cops got the girl, the cover-up would be a minor issue if it surfaced at all.

• • •

"We're on our own," Richard told Vicki later that night. "The cops can't even begin to find the girl. I looked at hundreds of photos without a clue. And all Miller can think of is talking to cab drivers."

Vicki was troubled, but very cool. "I think you should consider telling them everything, Richard."

"I couldn't do that now even if I wanted to. I already told them that that was all I knew. Miller barely believes me now."

She took a moment, and then spoke quietly. "Well, we better do something. This invasion into our lives is intolerable. If they don't find the real killer, they're just going to come back to us and start digging again."

"I know, I know, I know."

• • •

All this pressure had an unexpected effect on their relationship.

Despite the injustice–the cops and their ridiculous accusations– Vicki had proven her loyalty and her love. The craziness had some- how brought them closer together. Richard tried to reconcile the situation philosophically. It was a life test. One of those things that happens for no good reason. Something that must be endured and survived, after which you're stronger. That's how you grow. They were growing together, he determined. Clearly Vicki was making a courageous effort to control her temper, to be a friend, to be a real problem solver. They conferred, rather than argued about finding the Mystery Girl–the unquestioned real killer of Rosco and those other guys, the girl who they would turn over to Detective Miller and Company. Christ, what a nut case she must be. From doing bache- lor parties–where she was raped–to prostitution to murder. But that was not Richard's problem. He didn't do it. True, he knew about it. He understood it. He even saw it, but he didn't *do* it.

Richard Landon was now on a mission. More than anything, he wanted vindication. He had done nothing wrong, and had told the cops so. And to accuse Vicki, that was truly crazy. Well, okay, they were never really *accused* of anything. Just investigated. Even that was reprehensible. The cops were derelict in their duties, the buf- foons, antagonizing innocent people to the point that they had to do the cops' work for them. He relished the moment Miller slapped the cuffs on the real killer. Maybe he'd file a law suit, or give inter- views to the press. Then maybe Vicki and he would just take off somewhere and get married. Maybe at last he'd finally get some peace. He couldn't wait.

But first they had to catch the Mystery Girl, and Richard Landon knew just where to start.

• • •

They shook hands at Ricky's desk.

Ricky Wells was a Vice President at a loop bank. "Hey, man. Good to see you," he said, pumping Richard Landon's hand. "You here for a loan?"

"Is there some place we can talk?" Richard asked him.

"Yeah, sure. Let's just walk over to the new mural over there."

It was a good suggestion. The new mural took most of the interior wall of a building that covered half a city block.

Ricky was already nervous. "So what's up, buddy?" Very direct, forever smooth Ricky.

Richard was just as direct. "The girl. From the party. The black chick with the great body. I have to find her."

First a precautionary glance all around, then a quick nervous smile, then a brief meeting of the eyes. "You gotta be kidding, man." Ricky was making an obvious effort to be upbeat. "That's history. We spent some serious cash putting that matter to rest. We can't just dig it all up again now."

"Look, Ricky, I have to find that girl," Richard said.

"I told you, man. *That matter is dead and buried.* Forget about it."

"I can't forget about it. I have to find her. *Now.*"

"You in some kind of trouble?"

"You could say that."

"You want to tell me about it?"

Richard did not. "I just have to find that girl. Where do I start?"

"Sorry, man," said Ricky Wells coldly. "It's like I told you. It's over. The cops got paid. The girls got paid. Now do yourself a favor," Ricky told him firmly as he turned to walk away. "Leave it alone."

Richard grabbed him by the arm and jerked him back. "Now you fucking listen to me. If I don't get some answers pronto, I'm giving your name to the cops. This son-of-a-bitch from Homicide will walk right into your goddamn bank and sit you down and start asking questions in front of all these people. And he won't stop just because you tell him to. He'll tell your boss he's questioning you about the murder of Rosco Mink. *This is Homicide,* Ricky, not suburban cops looking for a handout. These guys aren't fooling around. And I imagine that in your case there are other things that might come up that you'd rather see forgotten." Here, Richard paused a moment, just to let the threat sink in. "Now are you going to tell me where to find the girl, or not?"

Ricky Wells regarded him sullenly for a moment. "The Grayson Agency. They're in the book. They say it's a modeling agency, but it's really just a high priced escort service. Her name is Patrice Foster. That's all I know. Enough?"

Richard nodded. "Enough."

"Now do me a favor, man," said Ricky Wells, wrenching his arm from Richard's grasp. "*Drop fucking dead.*"

22

Tow was busy, Beverly was busy, but they managed to see each other regularly. They'd often meet for lunch, usually at some busy place where they hurried like everyone else to return to work. When this was no longer enough, lunch became a drink after work. At Beverly's suggestion, they met at her office for a while. This arrangement had a business-like quality about it, providing cover from gossiping observers. It had been Beverly who had grown impatient to move on. One night she proposed a drink at Cavanaugh's, the open lounge in the atrium of her office building. Then afterwards she suggested trendy Florentino's on Rush for dinner. There, typical of their conversations, she quizzed him about progress on the Rosco Mink investigation, and in turn he inquired about her business. Neither seemed to be doing very well. Gradually, however, another problem surfaced. People were staring. At him at first. Then at her. Then they turned to whisper about them both. Toward the end of the evening, they couldn't wait to leave.

The next day she called, proposing dinner at her place on Friday.

• • •

For Tow, his developing relationship with Beverly Nickols had an unreal quality. Infatuated as a school boy, he was thinking of her more and more. But it all seemed so hard to believe. The cop and the executive. The *broke* cop and the *wealthy* executive. One night when some kids raising hell in the alley woke him at 2:10 a.m., he found that he had been dreaming about her. Disoriented, he thought that the whole thing–dating gorgeous Beverly–was only a dream. When he realized that it wasn't, he couldn't get back to sleep for two hours.

It was the oddest thing. He wasn't a school boy. This wasn't kid stuff. Still for the first time in about as long as he could remember, he felt happy. He had found something that he wanted. Something important. Something he already cared about profoundly. Something that even competed with the emotions of that night and deflated the burning urgency of finding vindication. Something he had not even thought possible. Something wonderful that was impacting his life in all sorts of ways. He even caught himself humming a couple times and of course felt foolish. But he was trimming down too, knocking off almost 20 pounds—and that felt pretty damned good. Apparently it showed. People were commenting. Even Sweeney had noticed. "You working out, Tow?" he asked the other day.

It was only because Beverly was so extraordinarily genuine that it all worked. At a distance, she appeared to be unapproachable, almost like Madeline O'Connor. Extremely attractive. Wealthy and connected, a determined, forceful woman. But that's where the similarities ended. Beverly's success had come on her own, not through a wealthy husband. And that experience made her different. She was easy to talk with, easy to be with. She was fun. And she wanted to know all about him. Who did his laundry? Could he cook? No, then where did he go to eat?

One night, after finally showing her his apartment, Tow took her to Chou Lei's.

Of course the door was locked, and Chou Lei's youngest daughter, Mei, who was about 10, had to look twice just to be sure it was grumpy old Tow who had always been alone before. Now there was this beautiful woman, smiling and chatting beside him. When Mei finally recognized him, she fumbled urgently with the lock, and then led them directly to Tow's usual corner table opposite the television in the almost empty restaurant. Chou Lei, when he saw them squeezed together like that, was appalled and hurried over to address them. "Good evening, Officer," he said bowing. "Please, sir, you and lady take window table. Please."

Tow tried to decline, but Chou Lei insisted. "Please, sir. You and lady sit at window. Thank you, please."

Beverly, smiling, was positively gracious as they relocated to the window table. "This is really very nice of you," she told Chou Lei. "Thank you so much,"

Chou Lei himself stood by to take their orders.

Beverly chose to study the menu, and suggested that Tow order first. He of course promptly chose his usual egg rolls with chicken fried rice while Beverly, with Chou's enthusiastic approval, eventually selected Szechuan Shrimp with vegetables. Predictably Tow used a fork and knife. Beverly preferred chopsticks. And of course Chou sent all three blushing daughters out to fuss over them the entire meal. Then, when they weren't serving dishes, all the girls hovered directly behind the flimsy Chinese curtain watching with their father. The tea and fortune cookies afterwards were complementary.

Beverly insisted they read their fortunes. His was *the cosmos is yours whenever you are ready to believe.* Hers was *romance and riches are only for those who dare.*

"I'm ready to dare," she told him happily, "if you're ready to believe." Her laughter, Tow knew, was genuine. In so many ways, she was girlish and happy like this, and could often make him smile in spite of himself. He was, he knew, falling in love with her.

They lingered for a while over the tea and cookies, just talking. Mostly she asked questions about him, drawing out his sketchy answers. She seemed so keenly interested in him. And unbelievably, she was fascinated with his job, though apprehensive about its dangers. How long had he been a police officer? And then, why Gang Crimes? Here, however, he resisted her good intentions, and politely sidestepped her questions. It was already his decision that she be spared some things. So he resolved never to tell her about that night and 11-year-old Calvin James. Nor about The Duke whose profound courage Tow himself had embraced, nor about young Jeffery Lane who had died in his mother's arms. Nor would he tell her about Harold Lamb who buried two sons murdered by gangs, nor about the evil child molester, Leo the Lion, or even about Soft Louie and the gruesome Golf Lesson. Neither would he tell her about vicious gang warfare over drug turf. Or the effect of drugs on people and a community. Or what the expectations were for a 12–year-old boy growing up in housing projects like King Gardens–death or imprisonment for so many by the age of 20. Or how apart from his high powered semi-automatic hand gun, the most essential requirement for safe navigation of the projects, was a reliable flashlight, necessary even in the daytime because desperate drug users had stripped aluminum lighting fixtures from their concrete cradles to sell for scrap metal in order to feed their habits. It was too sad and grotesque. So instead he drew on other stories, some lame and some actually funny, like the time he and Mercer were attacked while driving down the expressway by two hornets that had been nesting in their car. Of course she realized what he was doing, and why, and never really pressed him on anything. Basically, she just seemed to want him to like her. This conclusion was too good to be true.

· · ·

On Friday, in an effort to be on time, Tow found himself actually a little early for his dinner date with Beverly.

Now just to kill a little time, he got off Lake Shore Drive at North Avenue and doubled back a few blocks to drive past Rosco Mink's brownstone on Astor. He slowed to a stop at the curb before the home. Two little girls were playing hop scotch on the side walk. They were dressed identically in red dresses, unaware of the careful eye of their mother standing by. Tow watched them happily taking turns at the game. Good god, he thought, the evil that had played out here. *Tragedy. Crime. Insanity.* Like the Joanne Rice murder–so senseless–there was no way to explain this one either. He had seen it all in his three decades as a cop, and he had no answers. Before he grew any more morose, Tow eased his Buick back into the narrow street and head over to Beverly's, just a mile away. Clearly, Rita Martinez was still on the job. Cars parked illegally on both sides of the street had tickets.

· · ·

"Ms. Nickols, yes sir. That would be the 37th floor, sir," the doorman told Tow.

Tow got off the elevator on 37 and rang the bell.

"Hi," Beverly said opening the door. She gave him a warm smile. "Come on in."

She was in jeans and a pale pink blouse. Her lipstick matched her blouse and there was about her just a hint of perfume. She wore her long hair up, casual and chaotic, with a pink scarf somehow involved. All very understated, but there was no mistaking the effort. It had been a long time since anyone had made an effort for him. Christ, thought Tow, she looks fabulous.

"We're having lamb chops on the grill. Hope you like lamb."

"I like anything on the grill."

"Let me show you around."

"Some place you have here. You do this yourself?"

She laughed. "Yeah, if you don't count the four decorators I went through." First she took him to the kitchen. "The center of any good home. I just love to cook."

"Great," he said. She probably did love to cook.

She smiled.

That was the thing, thought Tow. Beverly was so goddamn sincere.

They moved on. "And this is my study." It wasn't a large room, but available space was reduced by wall-to-wall book shelves.

"Looks like somebody likes to read."

"Oh, I do. I love it. But I don't have much time for it."

Her briefcase, overstuffed, sat on the desk chair before the computer. "Homework?" he asked.

"Afraid so. I'm going to have to lay off some staff people next week." Now her cheerful look faded. "I really hate to do it, but I badly misjudged the consequence of Rosco's death. I mean, *murder*." Here she cringed. "I only calculated what Rosco's absence would do to revenues. I never considered what his *murder* would mean to the business. You know, the media spectacle, and now this crazy competition thing with this other maniac. It feeds on itself. The fact is that because of the resulting publicity, I paid too much for Mink Capital Management. Probably a lot too much judging by the decline of revenues. Before revenues were growing, now they are declining sharply and that's a big problem. Everything I have is either in the business or collateral for the business. Now I simply have to make it work. And fast." After a moment she regained her earlier composure and, despite the tears in her eyes, smiled brightly. "I'm sure it'll all work out."

Tow wanted to gather her up and kiss her, but hesitant, instead tried to reassure her. "Beverly, whoever did this thing is going to be caught. You know that, don't you? Nobody can escape the kind of saturation this case is getting for very long."

She nodded appreciatively, and smiled again. "I know."

She took him across the hall to a solarium where she had an exercise bike and some free weights lying on a mat. "I don't have much time for this either. It's crazy. I belong to two business clubs that have health clubs, and I also belong to another exclusive health club. And the building here has a small exercise facility. I just don't have time to go. So I did this. You know, thinking I could find a few minutes here and there. Big mistake." She smiled. "Now I have no excuse at all."

They passed through the dining room to the balcony. She stepped out first. It wasn't much more than a 12 foot ledge with a railing. Tow followed her lead into the twilight. From there Lincoln Park opened below and the blue gray of the Lake beyond. "Wow," said Tow. He could easily see Rosco Mink's town house to the south.

"Yeah, I know. We're half way to the stars," she said. "I never get tired of it."

They were leaning against the rail. When she stood and turned to him, he kissed her. Then he kissed her again. She smiled and took his hand. "Let's have a drink."

They settled in the family room. It was warm, the air heavy and very humid. She had the balcony doors and all the windows open, and the breeze was wonderful. "This place was built in the '30s," she told him. "I love it. They gutted it and completely restored it about five years ago. I've been here almost three years now. It's way too much room for one person, but I couldn't resist. Not many places where you get a whole floor."

Tow wondered what a whole floor cost in a place like this—$1.5? $2 million?

She rambled on. The Park, the Lake. Finally she returned to the investigation. "Anything new?"

"No, not exactly," said Tow questioning the wisdom of giving her false hope. Still he went on. "*Richard Landon.* There seems to be no end to Richard Landon's involvement in this thing. Morrison actually closed our investigation on him and his girlfriend after our warrants failed. We were done with them. But the other day he calls and wants to talk."

"Really? Richard called you?"

"He's scared. Worried. Didn't know he was home free." Tow felt the need to finish his drink.

"Here," she said. "I'll get you another scotch."

She returned and handed him the drink. "So what did Richard want?"

"Says he didn't kill Rosco and neither did his girlfriend, but he says that he saw a girl leaving Rosco Mink's that night and can identify her."

Beverly looked at him pointedly. "Well, that's great," she said suddenly enthused as the significance of this computed with her. "Do you really think he can? I mean, this is something new, right?" Then she seemed puzzled, and abruptly very doubtful. "Why didn't he say this before?"

"Good question. Says he didn't want to get involved."

She thought for a moment, and then seemed to accept this. "Oh, Tom. What does it matter if this thing ends now. I really can make this business work. It can be so good, if all the publicity just ends now. I won't lose any more accounts. Do you really think Richard can do it?"

Tow was hesitant. "I'm not sure. I wouldn't get my hopes up too much. But maybe, just maybe, he'll come across. He's worried. He thinks we consider him a suspect. He thinks his only way out is to find the girl who did this thing. It might just work."

"Oh, I hope so. I really do."

Tow was feeling very protective of her. "Well, I'll tell you a little secret. I think Richard Landon might finally be telling the truth. The reason I say that is he said that the girl he saw leaving Rosco's is black. Hair and Fiber determined that there had been a black female among seven other females in Rosco's bedroom and bathroom the week that ended with his murder. That's a one in eight chance that a black woman murdered him. But if Richard's story were not true, how would he have guessed? See? I'm betting he does know something."

She did see, and was immediately brimming with hope.

And Tow, too, was encouraged. He suddenly realized just how much he cared for her. Not that he was ever denying it to himself—but now he knew without a doubt that he was already in love with her.

• • •

It was late when they finished dinner.

A storm was gathering. The breeze had cooled and had begun to gust, causing the draperies to billow and flap wildly. They went around, closing the windows and doors. It was almost 1:30 a.m., and they were more than a little drunk. Then the rain came.

They watched from the sofa, her head on his shoulder. The room was dark except for a single lamp. It was quite a show with sheets of rain against the big windows, lightning all over the lake.

Tow was exhausted. Finally he moved to stand up. "It's late," he said quietly. "I'd better be going."

She also stood, and came close. "Wait."

He kissed her.

"I don't want you to go," she told him. "I want you to stay."

So he did.

23

Spider was an enduring mystery.

Of course Ben knew only what Spider chose to tell him, and consumed by a constant wariness regarding po-lices and gang bangers, Spider did not volunteer much. Ben knew virtually nothing about Spider's home–King Gardens–wherever that was, and nothing about his family. But there was more that tended to differentiate them. In many ways there was so little they had in common. One day when Ben gave Spider a piece of the banana bread his mother had baked, Spider had asked, "Now what dis?"

"Banana bread. My mother made it."

Spider was truly baffled. "Banana bread?"

"Yeah. You know, it's bread you make from bananas."

"You make *bread* outta bananas?"

"Try it, you'll like it."

Spider was doubtful. He looked closely. "It gots seeds in it."

"Yeah, well, so do bananas if you look."

So Spider broke a small piece off for Scab who wolfed it right down, and ate the remainder himself.

"So, now how do you like banana bread?"

Spider smiled. "It good."

Ben knew him well enough to realize that Spider really didn't accept his explanation about making bread from bananas. But when Ben told him that a cow has four stomachs Spider didn't believe that either. Neither had Spider ever heard of e-mail, for example, producing a truly inane discussion about sending letters through a phone line.

"Yes," Ben told him. "*Email.* It's electronic mail. You get letters through your computer."

"The mailman, he put the letter in you computer?"

"No, there is no mailman. The letter comes through the telephone line from the other person."

"The envelope, too? It all come through the telephone line into the computer?"

Ben was exasperated. "Look, you just get the letter part. *There is no envelope.*"

"Then where you put the stamp?"

This discussion, following the banana bread episode, had both boys questioning the other's sanity. But there was more that divided them. Spider knew nothing of the arithmetic of baseball, and could not understand how the Cubs could be 17-½ games out. "How can dat be?" asked Spider. "Theys only three outs."

"That's different," said Ben. "The Cubs are 17-½ games out of first place."

Spider gave this a little thought, and then asked, "What a half game?"

Ben gave up on baseball, realizing that there was much more that separated them. Spider had never been bowling, had never installed a garage door opener with his dad, and had never been on a family picnic or played 16 inch softball in the park. He knew almost nothing of the stars and nothing at all of the Milky Way. He knew so little, in fact, that it took Ben repeated evenings to explain what his Dad had taught him. Spider showed no interest in math, or history or school plays. And remarkably, he had never even heard of Oak Park.

What Spider did know however was the streets. About street life, Spider was the consummate professional, a student of the highest caliber. Skeptical and savvy, Spider was a roving database of street wisdom. Still he often had difficulty articulating this knowledge to Ben, frequently invoking events or even whole stories in order to make his point. But about the streets, Spider had never been wrong. Ben greatly envied this adult knowledge, and worked diligently to improve his own skills. In one way, thought Ben, Spider had a great advantage: his mother had not burdened him in his quest with a lot of rules. Accompanied by Scab, Spider came and went as he pleased, hitching rides whenever he needed them, accountable to no one. And about this freedom there lingered a sweet sense of adventure that Ben relished.

• • •

Ben found himself copying much of Spider's behavior. There was, for example, the day Spider started spitting. The three of them were just wandering down Handel Boulevard when Spider slowed to a stop, then leaned to one side and spit on the filthy window of Collin's Hardware. Only a block later, he did it again, this time anointing the hood of a parked late model Pontiac with chrome wire wheels. His next subject was a mailbox.

Clearly it was time for Ben to step up. For his initial salvo, he worked up a cheek full of saliva that he let go in the direction of a vending machine featuring a local paper. Unfortunately, Ben– with only an amateur's experience–succeeded only in hitting his left foot. Scab actually had to leap out of the way.

"Practice," advised Spider. "We both gots to practice to get good."

So practice they did. Everywhere they went for the next three days, they each worked up a load of saliva which they projected at whatever they could target. However this eventually proved to be so taxing that they finally grew weary, and converted their efforts to simply leaning over a rail or a bridge, and just watching their spit fall.

On the heels of this indisputably cool innovation to their life-style, Spider began to pepper his language with various obsceni-ties. "Fuck dis," he announced one day as they loitered on a street corner. "Lets us jus' get the fuck outta here."

Initially Ben was a little uneasy with this sudden change in Spi-der's behavior. After all, there were his mother's rules to consider. Ben decided simply to wait and see what developed with Spider.

But Spider persisted, finding occasion to experiment at every turn with this new form of empowerment. Still Ben did not join in, while Spider continued to flower.

"Goddamn," observed Spider. "It hot."

"Scab," commanded Spider. "You get you damn ass over here."

"*Ben*," confirmed Spider. "*You fuckin'-A-right.*"

This went on until Ben could stall no longer. The pressure was tremendous. Still, he wanted to show some originality, and therefore proceeded thoughtfully in search of a special opportunity.

• • •

The next day Ben got his chance.

That afternoon, he found Spider in the box car absorbed in a magazine, slowly studying each page before turning it. This was the first time Ben had seen Spider interested in reading. Then he realized that Spider was simply looking at the pictures.

"Hey, whatcha got?" Ben asked.

Spider held up an open page. The girl was young, blonde and lying naked on a bed.

He handed the magazine over. There were many more photos, all in color, all young girls, naked, in various poses, looking directly into the camera. "Son-of-a-bitch," said Ben slowly turning the pages. "*Son-of-a-bitch.*"

"Yeah," agreed Spider, panting over Ben's shoulder. "Som bitch."

• • •

It was right after the magazine that the trouble happened.

They were hungry, all three of them, and together they marched down to Marshall's Deli, a small grocer where they had been many times before. Ben took a sandwich out of the refrigerator which old Mr. Marshall, on both knees, was just stocking. Separately Spider was getting chips. Abruptly Mr. Marshall stopped what he was doing, and looking up, stared into one of the several curved mirrors that were suspended from the ceiling around the store. He cursed under his breath, and struggled quickly to his feet.

In the same mirror Ben could see Mr. Marshall rush up from behind Spider in the next aisle. Suddenly he was yelling, "*Hey, what are you doing, you little monkey? What have you got there?*"

"Just chips," said Spider, obviously startled.

"Do you have any money?"

Spider pointed to Ben who was now standing behind Mr. Marshall. "He do."

Mr. Marshall turned on Ben. "*And what have you got there?*" he snapped.

Ben held out the sandwich.

"Well, together all this comes to $4.98. I suppose you have $5.00?" he said full of contempt.

Ben counted only three crumpled singles and less than 50 cents in change.

"Why, you little jungle bunnies. There's less than $4.00 here. You were going to steal the chips, weren't you? Little black bastards, rippin' me off all the time. I'll bet you done it a dozen times. Well, I'm callin' the fuckin' cops this time."

At this, Ben placed the sandwich on a shelf next to the bottled water, and slowly backed up toward the door.

Observing Ben's withdrawal, Mr. Marshall, his face now very red with anger, snarled at Spider, "*Well, go on. Get!*"

Spider, however, didn't move a step. Ben drew a sharp breath, thinking that Mr. Marshall was going to strike Spider. But Spider just stood there with the chips in his hand, looking up at his much larger opponent. "I didn do nothin'," Spider said defiantly. "I didn steal nothin'. An' I ain't no monkey or no jungle bunny or no *bastard* or nothin'. An' I doan want nothin' you got so you ain't got to call no fuckin' cops." With this he tossed the chips on the nearest shelf, turned and joined Ben and they calmly walked out together.

• • •

Following that, Spider's language was notably absent of vulgarities. And Ben, now in complete awe of his courageous friend, of course followed suit.

24

A sleazy escort service would never disclose the real names and addresses of their girls to just anyone. Clients would certainly call the girls directly, or competition would steal them. But if threatened by some authority, argued Vicki, Grayson would fold right away. And who would be the scariest of all authorities? The cops, of course. But impersonating a cop was dangerous business, she warned, all of a sudden quite knowledgeable about cops. So who is most threatening next to the cops? The IRS, of course, stated Vicki. We'll call Grayson saying we're the IRS investigating this Patrice Foster without saying just why.

Her plan required Richard to call using the fax phone line of his printer. If Grayson insisted, he'd leave that call back number. She would answer like a switchboard operator forwarding the call to Richard who would simply pick up the same line. If Grayson ever called back, the line would be connected to Richard's printer, anonymously, never to be answered again.

• • •

After several theatrical rehearsals, they finally called.

Richard identified himself as Agent Balinski, Internal Revenue. Was there a manager he could speak to in personnel?

There was, he was told, but he was unavailable at the moment. Could the manager call back?

Of course.

The phone rang a few minutes later.

Vicki answered, "Internal Revenue Service. Can I help you?"

Everything was working smoothly. A man asked for Agent Balinski.

"One moment," said Vicki.

After a slight delay, Richard picked up. "Balinski."

"Yeah," said a voice. "This is Bill Norbert at The Grayson Agency. You called about one of our employees."

"Yes," said Richard. "I've got that here. Just one minute." Here Richard stalled for effect, then, "Right. *Foster*. Patrice Foster. I'm looking for an address or a phone number."

There was a pause, then Norbert said, "I'm sorry, we can't give that to you over the phone. Besides she quit about six or eight months ago."

Vicki had coached Richard for such evasion. "Well, the IRS as well as another bureau of the federal government have a serious matter to discuss with Patrice Foster. Look, Mr. Norbert, if you can provide this information, this is your chance to do it without any inconvenience to you."

Norbert stalled. "I don't know. Our policy is to respond in writing to these kinds of things."

"If you prefer," said Agent Balinski, "I can have our attorneys subpoena the information." Richard was prepared to bluff even further if necessary. He would threaten to shut Grayson down immediately. He'd have the phone company cancel their lines, and agents would padlock the doors. Vicki had thought of everything.

But none of these theatrics were necessary in the end.

Norbert was sufficiently intimidated. Of course, Patrice no longer worked there, and he obviously wanted no part of Agent Balinski and the IRS. He gave Richard an Oak Park address and phone number, then hung up without another word.

• • •

Vicki was ready with phase two of her plan. Somehow they had to be certain, absolutely certain, that they had the right girl, and they had to pinpoint her location so that the cops were certain to find her without causing her to flee. An error of any kind could blow the whole thing. They had to set things up perfectly so that the cops got their killer. It was the only way to free themselves of suspicion. The plan required Richard to stay in the background while Vicki approached the girl on a pretense of some kind.

Plan A was to call the phone number, prepared with a solicitation scheme designed to confirm the girl's name and address. This plan fizzled because the phone had been disconnected.

Vicki had anticipated that and moved to plan B–ring the bell, then apologize for a mistaken address. They drove out to Oak Park. What they found was a modest frame house on a wide residential street with a small garage at the end of a long drive way. Vicki rang the bell, while Richard waited in the car, carefully screened by the newspaper he was reading. She rang again, but there still was no answer.

A neighbor was out getting the mail.

Immediately recognizing an unforeseen opportunity, Vicki improvised. "Excuse me," she called to the neighbor. "I don't have Patrice's phone number. I wonder if you could tell me when she usually gets home."

"Oh, the Fosters don't live there anymore," the woman said. "They moved a few years ago."

"I'm an old friend," Vicki explained. "Would you know where I can find Patrice?"

"I have her newest address, but she doesn't have a home phone, you know. She usually calls from her neighbor's on weekends though. We still exchange recipes. She's really such a good cook, as I'm sure you know. Just terrible what happened. Her husband killed like that. So sudden. Just terrible. And poor little Benjamin, such a nice boy. Took it so hard."

Vicki continued to wing it. "Oh," she said sympathetically. "I didn't know. I wonder if you could give me her address. Benjamin was so little the last time I saw Patrice. It's been so long. I'd just love to see her again."

That did it. "Yes, yes, of course. That girl needs all the friends she can get right now," said the neighbor. "I'll be just a minute."

• • •

They took Handel Boulevard all the way into the city, bantering happily now that they were so close to their goal. Detective Miller would be eating crow soon. But as the neighborhoods deteriorated before them, their conversation lagged and finally ceased. In silence Richard turned onto Pine Street. Handel was bad, but Pine was worse. The address they were looking for was in the middle of the block that looked something like a slice of some third world documentary. Richard pulled to the curb just ahead of an abandoned car. "This is it," he said. Already people were staring.

Vicki prepared to open her door.

"No way," Richard told her. "You wait here. I'll just be a minute."

"It's okay," Vicki said. "I'll go." She was determined.

He shook his head. "No chance. I'll just check for her door bell. That'll have to do. I mean, look around you. We can't stay here."

Richard stepped quickly to the door. Inside he found a battered mailbox that read Patrice Foster, 3D. He came out immediately, giving Vicki the thumbs up sign as he approached the car. "Bingo," he said, smiling. "Our troubles are over."

25

The first team of seven detectives and uniformed police found Patrice Foster at home alone about 4:30 p.m. The second team to enter the small apartment specialized in evidence search and collection. They quickly found Rosco Mink's wallet still jammed with credit cards as well as a gold Rolex hidden under a loose floor board in the kitchen. Also stashed there were almost $17,000 in cash and a supply of cocaine. The victim's loaded hand gun, short two rounds, was actually in the drawer in the night stand.

Weeping uncontrollably, Patrice Foster offered no resistance, but near hysteria, she denied the murder repeatedly. After being advised of her rights, she refused to talk about anything except her son, Benjamin, who was not present. Tow then arrested her for the murder of Rosco Mink.

• • •

His job essentially complete, Tow took a few minutes to look around.

Until a few hours ago, he had never even heard of Patrice Foster. Coincidentally though, the Handel Boulevard Cleaners and the playground were only a few blocks east. This connection made Tow decidedly uneasy, as though he might be looking directly at something he could not see. It was this sense of uncertainty that accompanied him as he wandered through the apartment.

It was only four small rooms. The living room was the largest, then a cramped kitchen and two bedrooms, one smaller than the other. One obviously belonged to a young boy. It was neat and orderly in a sort of messy adolescent way. In the closet was an expensive telescope and quite a lot of camping equipment. There was nothing special about the other bedroom. Very organized. White lace curtains had been added to obscure the yellow window shades, cracked and stained with age. On a night stand sat a large color portrait photo of a family. A solid young man of 30 or so, seated on a sofa with a beautiful wife, somewhat younger. The boy, beaming between them, maybe six or seven. The innocence was disturbing. Patrice hardly looked like a prostitute serial killer. She looked more like a suburban housewife and mother. Beautiful. Happy. Not a demented murderess.

The kitchen was predictably small, but absolutely jammed with appliances and utensils. The kind of professional equipment that you might find in a restaurant. Then it occurred to Tow that although the rooms were not large, they seemed especially small because they were so filled with furnishings. There was a whole house full of furniture within these four rooms. And somebody sure liked to cook. There were at least a dozen cookbooks neatly organized on a shelf above the counter. Tow opened a cabinet door and counted place settings for eight. The china was real.

. . .

Outside the media coverage was accumulating, drawing a crowd of on-lookers.

Among the crowd on the other side of the street were two young boys and their dog.

"Just a drug bust," somebody said, dismissing the event. But Ben knew better. Clearly the police were there to arrest him. His concerns about his mother surged when she appeared in handcuffs among a group of police officers who put her in the back seat of a dark blue car and drove away.

Spider was the first to identify the big cop who emerged a little later. Now there was absolutely no question. Ben knew this was all his fault and moved to come forward, but Spider stopped him. "No, we gotta get outta here."

. . .

Tow hardly had time to call Beverly to cancel dinner. "Sorry," he told her. "Gotta work tonight. That's the bad news. The good news is I think your problem has been solved. We just charged a suspect with the murder of Rosco Mink."

• • •

It was later at her place that Tow told Beverly all about the arrest.

He was hardly in the door when she came into his arms. "I'm so glad this thing is over," she whispered. "And I'm glad you're here, and I want to hear all about it."

They settled in for drinks in her family room where the bar was.

"What don't you already know?" asked Tow. "The papers and television, they pretty well covered the whole thing."

"I know, but I want to hear it from you."

"Well, as I'm sure you know, her name is Patrice Foster. Black girl, late twenties. A beautiful girl. Prints and hair match those at Rosco's place. No question. Richard Landon identified her in a line up. We found Rosco's wallet, Rolex and hand gun in her apartment. Plus nearly $17,000 in cash and a bag of cocaine. Pretty incriminating stuff."

"And?"

"And, what?"

"And there's more. There's something bothering you. I can tell."

Here Tow hedged. "Well, I'm not sure. The evidence so far is overwhelming, but I'm just not sure."

Beverly was puzzled, and understandably not eager to see some issue delay the resolution at hand. "What do you mean?"

"Well, first, we didn't find the murder weapon. That's the main thing. Richard Landon saw the girl leaving Rosco's place, but he didn't see her kill him as any decent lawyer will point out. The murder weapon would have been strong evidence that she did it." Tow shook his head. "Richard Landon knows a hell of a lot more than he is telling. I'm sure of that. He's the lead to the girl. Now he says he saw her at a club the other night and followed her cab home. Says he saw the girl go into a building late that night, but the door was locked. The hall was too dark to read the mail boxes and he was getting some bad looks from the locals anyway. So he went back after work the next day, and found the girl's mailbox. That's when he called me."

"What's the difference how you got the information?" asked Beverly. "You still got the right person."

"Yeah," agreed Tow. "But inconsistencies like that bother me."

"Something else?"

Tow nodded. "Yeah," he said, sort of stalling. "I don't know. It just doesn't look right. Something is not quite right here."

"How so?"

"I'm not really sure. I looked around the apartment, you know. Carefully. This girl just doesn't fit the profile of a killer prostitute."

"Is there such a thing?"

"Yeah, and it isn't her."

"What exactly doesn't fit?"

"Well, to tell you the truth, not very much really does fit. First, she doesn't have a record. Nothing. That surprises me. Obviously she was there that night, and she grabbed the cash and the rest, but so what? That doesn't mean she killed him. It's all circumstantial."

"There must be something else bothering you."

"You're right. There is. She doesn't look like a killer. She just doesn't fit. Her background isn't right. She was married, and has a kid. The apartment is in a war zone, but it looks like she was baking cookies every day. The place was immaculate. Real homey. A house full of furniture. All the kid's clothes were clean and even pressed. New things for school. Lots of kitchen appliances. There were shelves loaded with canned peaches, that kind of thing. Homemade jam. And the refrigerator was stocked with all kinds of stuff. A sealed case of wine three years old, no other booze of any kind in the entire place. This is somebody taking care of things at home."

"You said she was married. Where's her husband?"

"Dead," said Tow. "We found an old *Tribune* in the boy's room. His father was killed in a gang crossfire three years ago. I intend to check the case file soon as I get a chance."

"Where is the boy?"

"Nobody knows."

Beverly was silent. Finally she resigned herself to the truth. "I think you're right," she said. "There's something wrong with this."

26

This was an exceptionally warm and humid Sunday in September. They had played 18 holes that afternoon and had bickered on the golf course. The course was slow, jammed with couples in chatty foursomes. From the first tee, Vicki was not on her game, and immediately fell behind him. On four, back-to-back missed putts placed her further behind. Then on seven, she drove out of bounds and had exceptional difficulty escaping the trees. Out of habit, Richard began to humor her. In the end, her focus and his general mediocrity produced the usual consequence. She shot in the low 90s while he, as usual, was unable to break 100.

They were late leaving.

Vicki drove, and the trip back to the city brought them into heavy weekend traffic. She was insistent, *"Of course Patrice Foster is guilty.* Really, Richard, you can't be that naïve."

It had been just a week since the cops arrested the girl, but already new tensions had come between them. Richard was doubtful now. He had not been prior to her arrest, not in the least. He had seen this girl leaving Rosco's and was certain she was the killer. It all fit. Desperate, resorting to prostitution, seeking revenge for rape. It had made sense—before. But now he had nagging doubts. "Her lawyer says all the evidence is circumstantial. This Joe Guilliam is on the news all the time."

"Look at this. Brake lights as far as you can see," said Vicki annoyed. "Well, naturally, he's going to say that, Richard. Besides Joe Guilliam is all about theater. Especially after that thing with your detective buddy. He's on a roll, just trying to make a name for himself. He's a great actor for the cameras, but I think his client is going to get fried."

"Well, Joe Guilliam says there is no proof. The prints and hair and the watch and stuff link her to Rosco–and I saw her leave about 9:00–but nothing at all links her to those other two guys. *Nothing.* I think that's strange. I would have bet the ranch she killed all three. You know, revenge for rape. I was flat out sure. Now I don't know. It just doesn't fit. I mean, she could have staged Rosco. The same thing they tried to say that we did. That's possible. But now I'm not so sure."

She was really annoyed with him. "Well, she looks guilty to me. What more do you want? Blood on her hands?"

"The cops didn't find the murder weapon. If she had the gun and all that other stuff in her apartment, why wouldn't she have the murder weapon, too? You know, ready for the next customer?"

Vicki was contemptuous. "These cops are such a bunch of fuck-ups, Richard. She probably keeps it in her purse, not that Detective Miller and his pals would ever think of that." It had been a long day and she really was at the end of her patience. "You know, Richard, you can take all this bleeding heart liberal stuff too far. But even these cops already have everything they need to send this chick to the electric chair."

● ● ●

She showered as soon as they got home.

He made the gin and tonics, strong. She did her hair, and came out wearing just a short black silk lace robe. She started dinner while he took his turn in the shower. Soon they were on their third drink. She had the windows open, and it was very warm and humid, just the way she liked it.

What really worried Richard now was the coverup.

"I don't think it will come up," Vicki was saying. "It's not the issue here. Patrice Foster has more serious things to think about. So do the cops."

"Maybe," agreed Richard with little conviction. "But it all still bothers me."

"You said you had nothing to do with it."

"I didn't. But I really had nothing to do with Rosco's murder either and look what happened to both of us because of it."

"Yeah, well, the last victim deserved what he got." She stopped. "Pasta or potatoes?"

"Potatoes," said Richard from the balcony. "I'm hungry. I'm starting the grill."

"Good. Put the chicken on low now. It'll take almost an hour," She took two large baking potatoes out of the fridge, and then she continued. "Rosco was a real piece of work alright."

He nodded in agreement.

"He cost us enough–$250,000 for you, $350,000 for me. That's $600,000. *Gone*." The gin was affecting her mood. Talking about these serious losses allowed a subtle anger to rise. "I wonder if he had some scam going there. You know, I wouldn't put it past our friend Rosco."

"I agree."

"Really pisses me off, to tell you the truth," she said, penetrating the potato in her hand with a small knife, preparing it for the microwave. "I think he fucked us. That's what I think. *Prick*."

Richard was watching her.

The penetrations were deeper now, and slower. More vengeful.

• • •

It was later that evening, after dinner, that they were concluding a little romance.

They were still intensely coupled when they finally came together. But it was only after he unloaded, those exact few seconds afterwards–without even time to disengage–that Richard Landon's lusty mind cleared sufficiently to think. If Patrice Foster did not kill Rosco, then someone else did. Now he could no longer ignore the obvious. Vicki's anger over her losses was much greater than he had ever guessed. And it was she who had picked him up that rainy night last April in a Gold Coast hotel bar. And she really was ruthless and experienced. Her knife attack incident in Texas demonstrated that. And she had come over late that Sunday night. It had been after midnight–the murder had been between

9:00 p.m. and midnight. She absolutely insisted Patrice Foster was guilty, having devised a clever plan right down to the last contingency in order to escape further scrutiny by the cops. And the way she stabbed those potatoes earlier, well, that really bothered him. "*Prick*," she called Rosco. *Prick*–did that have some special significance for her?

His lust satiated for the moment, Richard Landon was forced to conclude that he was intimately connected to a very big problem.

27

Following the arrest of Patrice Foster, Morrison was like a new man.

The media now did flattering articles on him, shamelessly ignoring all those earlier criticisms. The Mayor himself acknowledged Morrison's dedication and police savvy first before the Channel 6 cameras, and then again at a big political dinner held at the Conrad Hilton Hotel. There even Madeline O'Connor joined him in endorsing Morrison's efforts. His career was at its peak. And most significantly, thought Tow, Morri looked good again. Everything was going his way. Patrice Foster was in jail, charged solely with the murder of Rosco Mink. The Mink charge was enough, but the unspoken assumption was that she was indeed the prostitute who had also killed in vengeance twice before. Reconciliation of those crimes was not necessary for all except her *pro bono* attorney, Joseph Guilliam, who never stopped carping about her innocence. Further, the other killer in this deadly competition was between the cross hairs of law enforcement officials in three states. Edmund Chambers certainly would be found soon.

Tow's own perseverance was paying off as well. Even his long shot effort at locating the driver of the Yellow Cab that Richard Landon had testified about also had come through. The man, a young Algerian student, had been out of the country for almost seven weeks. Just returned to work, he read the circular Tow had distributed among cab offices and maintenance facilities, and called two days earlier. As Richard had predicted, the driver had definitely remembered this fare, immediately identifying Patrice Foster in a line up. Though he could not recall the exact location or time that she had entered his cab that night, he did remember her Pine Street address and his reluctance to drive through that neighborhood at night. In response to his protest, his fare had offered him a $20 tip to drive her to her front door. It had rained hard most of the way, he recalled, and he had to pull over twice.

Out of a sense of obligation, Tow searched the cab which had been in continuous use and, of course, found nothing. The location of the murder weapon remained a frustrating mystery for Tow. At least all of these developments tended to absolve Richard Landon in the eyes of Morrison and Tow, and publicly galvanized his credibility.

· · ·

Then another long shot was ready for his consideration.

When Barry Stern called from Records and Systems, Tow was at first puzzled. "Records and Systems?" he asked.

"Yeah," said Barry. "The report you requisitioned is ready. You know, the parking ticket sort?"

Then Tow got it. "Oh, yeah. Sure, Barry. I remember now. That was a few weeks ago."

"Sorry it took so long, Detective. We had to have a programmer write some special code for this custom sort. So it's ready when you are."

"Thanks anyway, but I don't really need it anymore."

The boy hesitated. "I'm really sorry about that," he apologized. "I know it's late, but we still have to charge Homicide with 2.25 hours of systems programming and .5 hours of computer time all the same. That's about $575."

"I'm sure that's okay," said Tow.

"You can pick up the report any time you want," said Barry. "Just ask for me."

· · ·

Tow knocked, then walked in. "Morri, you wanted to see me?"

"Have a seat, Tow," Morrison told him pleasantly. "How you

doin'?"

"Not bad. I'm okay. How about yourself?"

"Good. Just fine," said Morrison, about to get to the point. "I asked you to come by to tell you something. You did a hell of a job on this Rosco Mink case, Tow. I mean, you did one really professional job. And you made me look good to the brass."

"Shit, Morri. You stuck your neck out for me. That means a lot to me. You know that. Nobody else was interested in taking a chance, believe me. You saved my neck."

Morrison could have let it go at that, but he didn't. "Yeah, well I wanted to talk with you some about all that. And I want you to know I mean it. I have to tell you I regret being so hard on you before, at the Mink place that morning. I really am, I hope you understand."

Tow's already high regard for Morrison rose yet another notch. In a way, this reminded Tow of that early conversation he had had with Beverly at her request. Not many people had the character to apologize when they didn't have to. "Morri, you did what you thought was right. I just appreciate the job."

With that behind them, Morrison commented, "A hell of a business we're in, isn't it? We see the worst of the worst. The thieves and the thugs, they're bad. The rapists, and all those lunatics. They're bad, too. But homicide is the worst."

Tow could only agree. "A pretty grim business, that's for sure."

Here Morrison allowed a moment of silence. "You don't think she's the one, do you?"

"I have my doubts," said Tow. "Right now, we have a fairly circumstantial case."

"That's what I expected you to say," Morrison told him. "But I think she did it. And right now, that's the way I have to play it. We'll just have to keep looking for more proof. There's a murder weapon out there somewhere."

"That would do it," said Tow, just rolling with the rambling conversation.

"Look," said Morrison, suddenly buoyant. "Take a couple days off. Forget all about homicide. Go fishing. Have some fun."

Tow agreed that he could use a little free time. "Actually," he said, "There's something I've been looking forward to doing."

• • •

On the first of his days off, Tow returned to Pine Street and Handel Boulevard. This time he took infinite care in the preparation and execution of his plan. Most important was an undercover disguise he'd used a hundred times in the projects. Rags, literally, consisting of soiled gray pants much too short for him and a threadbare long sleeve shirt with a shiny down vest too small to button. In addition he wore a wig of long stringy gray hair with an equally matted glued-on beard. His accessories featured a walking stick and a green plastic trash bag half filled with scrap tin cans. He achieved exactly the image he desired. An aging homeless man. A convincing street target. Defenseless, yet predictably safe only because he appeared slightly more repulsive than vulnerable. In pockets on both sides of the vest Tow had stuffed dog treats. The rest, he figured, would be easy.

With his Buick parked blocks away, Tow wandered down Handel to Pine, rummaging through trash cans along the way. This route eventually took him past Mrs. Chang's dry cleaners to the general area of the playground where he selected a bench to sleep on. Tow's strategy proved to be so convincing that in a short time competition showed up in the form of an elderly black man who complained to Tow that the park was his since he had been coming there for months.

"Just passing through, friend," Tow told the man, hoping to appease him quickly and without making a scene. "Just passing through."

"Well, don't be bothering these kids then," the old man said. "There's crazy things going on here these days. One day a while ago, some fool in a suit was chasing young black chirrens all around the fence here. Got hisself dogbit doin' it too. That kind of thing brings complaints from store owners and gets police cleanin' up the neighborhood and such. Which I don't need because I ain't got nowhere else to go."

Tow assured the man he had nothing to fear from him. "I don't want no police trouble either," he said. "I just need to rest some."

This the man seemed to understand. He just nodded and found a distant bench for himself.

. . .

Tow, however, didn't just pass through. He wandered the neighborhood, returning to the park from time to time during the day. There were dozens of kids of every age, but no sign of two boys and a dog. When he repeated his pathetic routine the next day, Mrs. Chang came out with a broom to chase him away. A short time later, two cops pulled up to the playground in their blue and white cruiser. First they roused the old man Tow had spoken with the day before, and banished him from the area. Then they approached Tow. "Time to shove off, Buddy," Officer Gillato advised him. "You can't stay here."

"Look, I'm a cop," Tow told Gillato. "And I know who you are. Ed Sweeney gave me a message to call you. I'm Tom Miller, and I really appreciated your help. Now just let me hang around a while longer."

Gillato was truly baffled by this. He just could not reconcile what he saw with what he heard. "Lemme see your badge," Gillato insisted.

"Not now," said Tow.

"Like hell," said the other cop.

Finally Tow fished out his credentials, and the two cops meekly apologized as they retreated, having made a complete spectacle of Tow's undercover effort. Still no real harm was done. Tow just changed his look for the next couple of opportunities. But still no luck. It was nothing he was doing. That wasn't it. It was rather that the trail wasn't hot as he had thought.

This trail was stone cold.

28

I t was a Blackhawk exhibition game against the Flyers on a Tuesday night.

Vicki had gotten great seats, Byatt and Morgan's best. All seemed well with the firm. Understandably Byatt did not want to lose a producer like her, and had not investigated her any more than they had been required to do. Still, there were other pressures at work.

The Hawks were ahead seven to six with about five minutes to play. "Let's get a head start on traffic," Richard suggested.

But Vicki wasn't ready to leave. "We're in no hurry," she said. "We won't have any trouble getting a cab tonight."

He made no response to this.

She was right, but he was annoyed with her. And they had argued earlier at dinner. It seemed that they argued all the time now. Usually over small things, stupid stuff really. Things that really didn't matter at all. The real problem was something else. His problems. Cops, lawyers and more cops. Pressure, pressure, pressure. When would it ever end?

At the final buzzer, he realized that she was still unhappy with him, too. Silently they followed the crowd to the exits and the parking lot where it was drizzling and very misty. Before them the city had disappeared in low lying fog. Only the tops of the highest buildings were visible like distant lighted peaks of an unfamiliar mountain range bounded by the Sears Tower on one end and the John Hancock on the other. She was wearing heels from work, but had not chosen to take his arm. Still not talking, they walked across the gravel parking lot to the street in search of a cab, but found none. "Christ sakes," Richard cursed surveying the weather. "We have to go back."

It was just then that she noticed that she had lost a pearl ear ring. "Oh, damn," she said. "Damn. These are *real* pearls." She didn't know where to begin looking. The gravel of the parking lot made a search impossible. She shrugged then sighed, profoundly frustrated.

"Now, what's the matter?" said Richard cryptically.

She turned on him immediately. "This isn't all my fault, you know, Richard. You got yourself into this mess with Rosco, so don't take it out on me."

"Look," said Richard. "I'll tell you the same thing I told the cops. I did nothing wrong in any of this. The girl, the party, Rosco. I didn't do anything wrong."

"Then don't be such a baby, and it will all work out."

"A baby? Really. I'm a baby? Well, I have a question for you, Sweetheart. Something I've wanted to ask you for a long time. *Just where the hell were you that night?* The night of the murder. Before you called me at midnight. *Where were you anyway?*"

She took a deep breath. "I was home, if you really want to know. I'm so disappointed in you, Richard. I just don't know what to say. You can't possibly think I really had anything to do with Rosco. These are your problems, not mine. I've just tried to help you get through them. You ought to be more grateful."

They were making a spectacle of themselves, and now passersby were watching.

"You're the one who ought to be grateful that I saved your ass by telling the cops you were with me all night. I'm your alibi, you know."

"Richard, for your information, I don't need you or your help or your lies to the police. I don't have to hide anything about that night, so you don't have to do me any more favors." Furious, she stormed off in the direction of the cab stand near the Stadium, deserting him under a yellow street light in the dense mist.

29

It took only a few days for Ben's $16 to disappear, all he had with him the day the police invaded his home. Since then they had hidden in the box car. Ben and Scab, the two latest and most specific targets of the police, had remained secluded while Spider made periodic trips to the grocery store for chips, cakes and cola. Now they needed more money. Even if he could not return home, Ben hoped that he might still be able to work. Cautiously, they made the trip to the elevated train walking separately on either side of the street, Scab with Spider, and Ben a block ahead of them but well within sight.

Harold Lamb seemed surprised to see him. "Are you alright, boy?" he asked Ben anxiously. "Where have you been staying?"

"I can't go home. There is this policeman after Spider and Scab and me," he explained just as Spider arrived below the tracks with Scab. Ben looked down and returned Spider's wave. Harold Lamb followed these gestures until his gaze settled on the thin boy with his dog.

"You sure the policeman wants you?" asked Harold Lamb, still staring. "I think it was your mother they want to talk to."

"No," Ben insisted. "That policeman is chasing Spider and me because Scab bit a gangbanger a few months back. Then Scab bit the policeman, too, in the attack."

Harold Lamb was listening intensely now as Ben spoke, his attention still focused on the boy waiting below with the dog. "This policeman," said Harold slowly, returning to Ben, "Now tell me, was he a big man?"

Ben nodded. "He's the one in the newspapers. The one who shot that boy."

This seemed to have some significance for Harold Lamb. "Are you sure?"

Ben nodded vigorously. "I'm sure."

Ben noticed that Harold had stopped listening to him altogether, and was saying something. "Oh my god," he was saying. "Oh my god." He grasped Ben firmly by the shoulders and shook him slightly. "Listen to me, Ben. Now how long you known that boy?"

"Who?" asked Ben.

"That boy right there," said Harold Lamb nodding slightly in Spider's direction. "The boy with the dog."

"Spider?" asked Ben perplexed by questions about the obvious. "He's my best friend. Him and Scab."

"Where do they live?"

"King Gardens," said Ben. "My momma said I can't go there though."

Slightly out of breath now, Harold Lamb only grasped Ben more firmly. "Now you tell me where you met this boy and his dog."

Ben thought for a moment, recalling the day of the fight. "At the park. On Handel. By the fire hydrant. We were shooting firecrackers until the gangbangers made the police come."

"Oh my god, firecrackers," whispered Harold Lamb again. "Good god. And King Gardens. All this time. King Gardens, not LBJ. I been lookin' in the wrong place. All this time."

• • •

Just seconds later, Ben spotted a uniformed policeman among the crowd and slipped down the stairs leaving Harold Lamb looking for him in all directions.

• • •

Following his few days off, Tow was back on the job. Harold Lamb's call found him at his desk talking with Sweeney.

"Tow," Harold began, "Thank god I found you. Gang Crimes said you were with Homicide, but nobody knew where. Listen to me. *I found them!*"

"*What?*" Tow got to his feet, his heart already racing.

"The kids and the dog, I found them. I'm sorry, Tow. I'm so sorry I didn't believe you. But I found them. They were just here."

"Where are they?"

"Now listen to me. I don't know where they are right now. There's the boy with the dog, and there's another boy with him."

"That's right!" said Tow. "That's right!"

"The boy with the dog, he's a skinny kid about 12, right?"

"*Jesus Christ*," breathed Tow, settling down now.

"And the dog, the dog is scrawny with a section of its hide peeled off."

"Yes," said Tow, now certain Harold's information was good. "Harold, that's exactly right. I got a lead and spotted them myself one day, but then I lost them."

"And now the other boy. Get ready for this, that boy works for me. His name is Benjamin Foster. You arrested his mother for the murder of this Rosco Mink."

"Oh my god," whispered Tow. He knew that somehow there was a connection there. It was always some crazy thing. "Do you know where he is?"

"No, but he's a good boy. He may be back to see me. But the other boy, I don't know his real name, but Ben calls him Spider. The dog is Scab. The dog bit a few young gangbangers a while ago, and a big policeman in a suit who chased them in the park not long ago. I think that's why they're on the run. They think you're after the dog."

Tow first groaned aloud at hearing this.

"Tow, now listen to me. There's more. All this time we been looking in the wrong place. This boy, Spider, he lives in King Gardens, not LBJ. That's why there wasn't even a trace of him. And Benjamin told me they like to play with firecrackers."

Now there was no doubt. "I can't leave this Rosco Mink case now. Find them for me, Harold. I need to talk to both of them."

"I will, Tow. You know I will."

Tow hung up and just stood there for a minute, allowing all of this to register. Then he suddenly felt the need to sit down. Staggered, he sat heavily, and tried to catch his breath again.

30

The sole dissenting voice regarding Morrison's performance was that of Joe Guilliam, defense attorney for Patrice Foster. Guilliam announced to reporters one Monday morning that his client had twice been the victim of assault. A very intoxicated Rosco Mink had beaten her up the evening of his murder, and she had been raped and beaten at a north side bachelor bash the previous December. And there was something else. The witness who had identified her at the home of Rosco Mink the night of his murder was a participant in that December party, though not a participant in the rape. Tow, formerly the beneficiary of Guilliam's talents, was now painfully on the receiving end. Of course Guilliam, always theatrical but never frivolous, had made a devastating revelation.

It was Richard Landon who had placed Patrice Foster leaving the front door of the victim at about 9:00 the night of the crime. Richard Landon alone had established that proximity. The cab driver remembered only stopping for his fare somewhere in the Gold Coast area, not necessarily even on Astor Street. With the cover-up now uncovered, the credibility of Richard Landon would certainly be attacked by the defense.

• • •

"You should have told us about this," Tow complained to Richard when the news broke. "You lied to me again when I asked you if you knew any other way to locate this girl. You said no. Then you came up with this bullshit story of following her home. Lying to the police is obstruction of justice, I trust you realize that."

Richard didn't know what to say, so he just glared back at Tow.

"It would be a real good idea to tell us what you know about this thing," said Tow. "You're important to this case. Nobody here wants to prosecute you for anything, but we need to know the truth. And we need it now."

"Okay, okay, okay. I don't have much to tell, but I can tell you who does."

"That's a good start."

"Alright. It was a party. Just a party for Christ's sake. Right before Christmas. Gordon Wells, it was his bachelor party. Willow Creek, up north. You know, it was just a wild party. Lots of booze, lots of women. A bunch of hookers. Some drugs—I have nothing to do with drugs. I want you to know that now. I don't know who brought them, what they cost, where they got them. Nothing."

"Yeah, how about the hookers?"

Richard had to consider this for a moment. "I don't know. I mean there were a lot of people there I never saw before. Or since."

"What happened to Patrice Foster?"

"Patrice Foster I remembered because she was so goddamn good looking. She was a topless bar tender, not a hooker. When the party really got rolling, some of the guys were drunk and just got out of hand. Look, it wasn't me. I didn't touch anyone there."

"So what did happen?"

"I'm not exactly sure. I know Patrice Foster tried to resist, but they took her to an upstairs bedroom and pressed hundred dollar bills in her hands. Everyone was standing around watching. Even the real hookers were watching."

"Did Patrice Foster take the money?"

"I don't know how it ended up. The way she resisted, I doubt it. I left. I didn't want anything to do with it."

"So what do you think happened to her?"

"I think she got gang banged."

"That's pretty serious."

"Maybe if you did it. But I didn't do it. Do you understand me? I did nothing. I left."

"So who does know what really happened?"

Richard had anticipated this and was reluctant, but ready. "Ricky

Wells. Gordon's brother. That's the guy you want to talk to. Ricky Wells. That's how I found Patrice Foster. I got Ricky to talk. He told me about some escort service. Grayson something or other. It's a modeling agency that has this escort service on the side. I got an address out of them, and just followed the trail to her mailbox on Pine Street. You know the rest."

Tow considered all of this for a moment. He would have to report everything to Morrison. But first Tow wanted to be sure his information was good. "You expect me to believe this story? I mean, you aren't taking any liberties with the truth here, are you?"

"*Look, I did nothing wrong,*" said Richard with a sudden surge of courage, the result of being cornered too often. "I gave you guys the girl, the one who did it. Then I agreed to testify about seeing her leaving Rosco's. And you're still complaining. What's the difference how I found her? *She did it!* And I want you to know that I did nothing wrong. Not at that party, and not at Rosco's that night. *Nothing.* Do you understand me? Even Joe Guilliam admitted I did *nothing* wrong at that party."

Tow stalled. "I don't know how you do it," he said quietly, evenly. "You're always just on the edge of some lunatic event. I have just one question. What else? What else have you got to say?"

"Nothing," said Richard gloomily. "Nothing at all."

• • •

A very spirited Joe Guilliam, however, had a lot to say.

And, like any savvy pro, he continued to talk to any reporter who would repeat his story in print or on television. The testimony of a key witness was suddenly in doubt, and now he saw nothing that tied his client to murder. *Prostitution*, okay–big deal. *But not murder.* The cash found in his client's possession had been received for services rendered over time. And that was not murder. His client had not murdered anyone. Not Rosco Mink, or anybody else. And there was no evidence to the contrary. There was absolutely nothing that linked her to the first two victims. No one saw her kill Mink, and no weapon had ever been found. And now key testimony placing her there that night was severely compromised. Hair and Fiber reports indicated seven other women had been in that bedroom that week. *Seven white women.* Any one of them could have been the real killer. So either reduce the charges, argued Joe Guilliam, or let Patrice Foster go. Of course the real message here was obvious. Guilliam was threatening to play the traditional race card in a city that was still coping with the tensions from events of a year earlier.

• • •

One person who certainly got the message was Commander Anthony Morrison.

"Close the door and sit down," he told Tow in his office. "What the hell is this Joe Guilliam trying to do, start a war?"

"He's just doing his job," said Tow. "And he's good at it."

"You haven't been talking to him, have you?"

"Hell, no, Morri. Not once since the hearing back in July. I'm not crazy. And he doesn't need my help anyway. The kid is a natural. He's just telling it the way he sees it."

"Well, I think it's more than that. It's politics and it's racial and I'm getting tired of the tone of it all. So we can't find Benjamin Foster. There is no conspiracy behind that."

Tow did not disagree. Being the beneficiary of Guilliam's racial remarks was certainly better than being the target. "The boy will turn up," said Tow evading the first issue. "I have a snitch out looking for him."

"Well, I hope to Christ he's okay."

When Morrison fell silent for a moment, Tow took it to mean the meeting was over and got up. "You know, we still haven't followed up on Grayson and this Ricky Wells. Do you want me to check them out?"

"No," said Morrison. "I already have Baily and Silverstein on that. Right now I have something else for you. Guilliam is saying there was another girl assaulted at this party last year. Her name is Lydia Cooper. Here's her number and address. I want you to talk to her."

• • •

Lydia Cooper refused to open the door beyond the chain lock, and just peeked out at Tow. "My lawyer says I don't have to talk to you without him being here. And I already told the police everything I know. We were the victims in this, you know. We didn't commit any crime."

"It's not about December," said Tow. "I just have a few questions about Patrice Foster. You might be able to help her."

She considered this for a moment, then closed the door and unchained the lock.

Lydia Cooper was about the same age as Patrice Foster. Attractive, but lacking the extraordinary beauty of her friend. She invited Tow to sit down in the living room. "You have the wrong person, Detective," she began, wasting no time at all. "Pattie would never harm anyone."

"Is that right?" Tow just wanted to hear what she had to say.

"That's right," said Lydia. "I've known her since high school. She is the sweetest person in the world, believe me. She could not have done this under any circumstances. You have got to believe me."

"Okay," said Tow agreeably.

Lydia accepted this as an opportunity to continue. "I know she has had her problems since John was killed. Do you know about that? That her husband was killed by the gangs?"

Tow nodded. He had already seen the original police report on the shooting and knew all there was to know. Still, he let Lydia Cooper go on.

"Terrible. Just terrible," she began. "He was walking across the street and stepped into some kind of shootout between two gangs. Patti was devastated. John Foster was a good man, I'll say that. He was really so good with her. You know Benjamin is not his child. Pattie had Benji when she was barely 16. And there was no one to help her either. She lived in King Gardens–that's where Benjamin was born. Her boyfriend split as soon as she got pregnant, and she had the baby alone. And then she got a job and took care of Benjamin and got through high school at night. Lord, I couldn't have done that.

I mean, I really don't know how she did it. Then she met John and they got married right away. It was so good for them for those five years. They had a house in Oak Park, and Pattie wanted another baby. Lucky, that didn't happen. John was killed about three years ago, and she's been struggling ever since. But I'll tell you this: she would never harm anyone for any reason. You've really got to believe me."

"How did she know Rosco Mink?"

"The Grayson Modeling Agency. Patti found Grayson and a few others. She was just so desperate for work. She modeled for Sears for a while, but then that ended and she had to lower her standards. Grayson is mainly an escort service. That's how we got booked for the bachelor party last December. I really don't know much about this Rosco Mink. She never talked about him. But I'm sure that's how she met him. Big spender, you know."

"Do you know where Benjamin Foster is?"

"No. I was hoping he'd come here. I haven't heard from him. And I'll tell you something, this is a crime. If anything happens to that boy ..."

"Do you know where he might go?"

"I wish I did. I'd be there waiting right now. Patti's sister, Frances, lives in Milwaukee. I've already talked to her. She hasn't seen him, and I really doubt Benjamin would even try to find her there."

Tow gave her his card. "If anything comes up, call. Anytime."

Lydia Cooper accepted the card without looking at it. "She didn't do it, you know. That guy was a fiend. Someone had it in for him."

Tow left considering Lydia's story. Of course, he'd heard it all before. It was always someone else. But in this case, he was beginning to believe it. Things were not adding up.

• • •

Ricky Wells was nowhere to be found, but the results of Baily and Silverstein's investigation into the Grayson Modeling Agency were on the front page of the *Tribune* Wednesday morning. Initially they were unable to locate a list of the firm's clients, but they quickly determined the names and addresses of its employees. Of female employees, there were 26, and they began to run them all down.

Most addresses and phone numbers were dead ends, but a few actually panned out. One of these, Miranda Wallace, actually wanted to talk. No, she did not know Patrice Foster or Lydia Cooper. But yes, she admitted, she and another Grayson girl had been with Rosco the Friday evening prior to the murder on Sunday. She didn't know where Kathleen Kelly was right now, but said that Kathy and she spent the late afternoon and entire night with Rosco Mink at his Astor Street townhouse. Rosco locked his two German Shepherds in the laundry room, and all three of them drank a lot of champagne and did a lot of coke. Rosco consumed most of both. They had gone to bed together, but all bombed Rosco could do was watch her and Kathy go at it.

The girl's prints matched some found at the crime scene, and Hair and Fiber also confirmed matches.

And there was one other thing. Blonde and 20, Miranda was angry. Her boss at Grayson, a man named Bill Norbert, she said, had abused her. Norbert had promised her a modeling career, but had done nothing except take a few dozen cheesecake photos for her portfolio. He kept promising opportunity, but instead had exploited her sexually and cheated her financially for more than a year. Now she intended to return the favor. She handed over to police something she had obtained secretly. She actually *wanted* them to have it. It was an exhaustive list of clients and their phone numbers–Grayson's little black book. Therein were the names of prominent businessmen, politicians, commodity traders, doctors and even two judges and a priest.

Once again, the lurid scandal surrounding Rosco Mink exploded when, along with a color glamour photo of Miranda from her portfolio, the *Tribune* published every name in the book in a front page column.

31

It was just the next day that Robert Lanier, 57, walked into the offices of Block, Morris and Ferrel, one of the largest matrimonial law firms in Chicago, and took five divorce attorneys and one paralegal hostage. The standoff lasted almost three hours. In the end Lanier executed all five lawyers with a ceremoniously delivered bullet between the eyes, but spared the paralegal. The last bullet he drilled into the ear of an already dead lawyer, Daniel Pearson, emphasizing his frustration with his opponent's refusal to listen. Then he surrendered to police.

Taken into custody, Robert Lanier suffered a serious heart attack only minutes later.

The murders were big news, of course, but it was the motive that really caused the story to explode. That, as reported by the spared Pamela Harris, was anguish. It seems Mr. Pearson was stalling in the case of *Lanier versus Lanier*. Robert Lanier, dying of throat cancer, objected to Mr. Pearson's protracted delays in settling a substantial but simple estate of about $3 million. Discovery of almost two years involved numerous frivolous subpoenas, baseless motions and outrageous depositions. All while refusing even to meet with Lanier who offered to answer any question put to him in order to speed the process. In desperation, Lanier offered several letters proposing generous settlements, but had not even received a response. All of this was bad enough. However, his spouse's $240,000 in fees constituted, in the opinion of the dying man, nothing but racketeering. Robert Lanier, frail and hairless– without even eyelashes–and with only months to live, wanted to remarry with the intention of leaving the proceeds of his divorce to his new spouse. Of course, if Pearson could drag the settlement out, chances were good that Lanier would die in the meantime and there would be no divorce and no proceeds for his client to divide. And although there was no real issue in his case, Lanier had no legal recourse. So he sought a more original solution.

However, before resorting to his own methods, Lanier had visited Police Headquarters and complained bitterly about being shaken down in a divorce proceeding. A young officer had taken the complaint only to file it with four others Lanier had made in the previous two months. All of this became a sudden calamity for Commander Anthony Morrison who now faced the hot lights of the TV cameras.

Under enormous pressure, there was little Morrison could say— A terrible event, a suspect in custody. Yes, the suspect had complained to police about being extorted in the past. And no, the Department had taken no action. Morrison quickly withdrew in order to turn the podium over to Frederick Manson of the Illinois Bar Association who, in a single sentence, promised a full investigation and then bolted before reporters could question him.

But apparently the wheels of justice turned too slowly for some victims of this system.

Then the next day, Cecilia Fields walked into the same BMF office bearing a sympathy wreath. She was instructed to leave the flowers in a conference room in which three attorneys were just gathering.

There she, apparently inspired by Lanier, shot all three to death. A fourth walked in to investigate the commotion. He was expected to survive, barely, after being shot twice in the groin. The same day, a suburban office of BMF was cleared due to bomb threats.

Now Morrison was truly besieged, a situation that grew worse by the day as other reports of ignored complaints surfaced in the press. Most of the complaints were similar in nature. The legal provisions of divorce law were being flagrantly abused to the extent that the resulting fees constituted extortion. And among these, there were numerous references to outright blackmail. *Yield in settlement or some embarrassing information will be used against you.*

Privately Morrison fumed to Tow. "I've got the mayor screaming at me one minute, and the media the next. And now these goddamn lawyers are saying they get three or four death threats a week. What the hell am I supposed to do, provide body guards? I just can't believe what they're telling me is legal. They can conduct investigations that go on for years–at $300 or $400 an hour–*does sound like racketeering, for Christ's sake.* No wonder these fuckers get death threats. Isn't there an ethics association or something? *And what about the judges?* They're supposed to control these things. It does sound like a goddamn mob shakedown, that's exactly what it sounds like. I can't believe the Bar lets this go on. *Like they don't know!*"

Tow just let Morri rant, not saying much himself.

The following day the scandal went nuclear when WQQX, always outrageous, announced that it had received an insider tip that there had been 19 suicides related to cases that BMF handled over the previous five years. This info was confirmed the next day by 11 callers on the morning talk show, generally all furious spouses of BMF clients who had heard the same rumor over the years. QQX took no prisoners. Nearly 20 suicides within only five years, the station declared, was an achievement no other matrimonial firm, no matter how greedy and callous, could ever hope to approach. Accordingly, QQX deemed it an accomplishment that would stand forever in the newly instituted WQQX Matrimonial Court of Shame. And in BMF's honor, QQX announced that it had been inspired to produce a work of art. Borrowing heavily from the renowned classic, the staff composed a poem it called *Fees*. (*I think that I shall never see, a thing more beautiful than a fee ...*)

Following this ridicule, a local urban cowboy actually wrote a country western song, *Nineteen Dead at the Intersection of Love and BMF.* Normally heavy metal/rock and roll QQX made an exception for *Nineteen Dead* and aired it at least 30 times a day, introducing the song theatrically with its entire lengthy title prior to each playing.

By now the more conventional media were also asking serious questions about the scandal. Abruptly, the *Tribune* scooped the competition with its revelation that 12 of the 14 attorneys at BMF were registered to carry concealed fire arms. With this, QQX went into a kind of gleeful overdrive while the national tabloids joined the fray with blatant accusations of racketeering among Chicago matrimonial law firms. An assistant U.S. attorney legitimatized the grass roots allegations when he proposed the use of RICO to clean up the mess.

This circus had the consequence of abruptly edging Rosco Mink and friends off the front page.

• • •

And for some, the sudden shift in media coverage provided an overdue sense of relief.

"Listen," Beverly told Tow one evening. "It's time we had a weekend off. I just have to get out of the city–just to get away from the craziness. I mean, it's too much for me. Rosco again, and now all this violence. It's just way too much. Why don't we drive up to my place in Michigan? We could leave Friday morning and come back Monday morning. What do you say?"

"Sure, sounds good to me," said Tow automatically. But upon the briefest reflection, he had a few doubts. He had been spending every night with her, which was exciting enough in itself. But then in the morning she went her way, and he went his. Now this would be different. It would be the first time they traveled together–and all that that implied. Tow had a distinctly uneasy feeling about it. *A travel weekend.* Just him and her. It suggested intimacy and fun. But he wasn't sure just how capable he was of intimacy and fun for days on end. What if she finally got bored with him? Then what? He didn't want to think about it.

She went on. "It's a long drive to Maple Creek, you know. It's near Traverse City. That's almost eight hours if we drive all the way. Ten if we take the ferry across the Lake out of Milwaukee."

"Makes no difference to me," said Tow.

"The ferry will be fun. I just love the excitement–the sun, the water, the wind. And sometimes there's a late summer storm."

"Sounds great," said Tow.

What he wanted to say, and did not, was that he'd go anywhere with her, and that it didn't matter what she wanted to do. He knew that he was in love with her, but didn't really know how to tell her.

Beverly was so different from him in almost every way, and this worried him. She always had a preference, and often a passion for things he wouldn't think about twice. Planning this trip was typical. They would take the ferry because *she loved the excitement—the sun, the water, the wind. And sometimes a late summer storm.* On his own, he couldn't care less. But she cared, and that made it fun. That was the thing. She cared. She cared about everything. Maybe, he thought, just maybe he was learning from her. Everything in her life had meaning. So unlike himself, just trudging along every day, indifferent to opportunity or even to possibility. She was enriching him and his life, and he loved her for it.

· · ·

So Friday morning, they were up early and dumped their bags in the trunk of her vintage Mercedes. It took a few minutes to put the top down and button the snaps around the boot. This Mercedes was a big touring model, late '60s, ivory with red leather seats worn with age. Tow had never seen it before. Her other car was a new Lincoln.

"Where'd you get this clunker?" he asked her as he climbed in.

"I bought it restored. Isn't it great?"

"There can't be many of these still around."

"That's for sure. I just love it."

"It's a beauty, I'll say that."

"Well, are you ready to have fun? It's sunny and 70, not a cloud in sight. You can't ask for more than that," she told him as she put her shades on. "We're burnin' daylight, partner. Let's hit the road." Then that smile.

She looked great, thought Tow. Casual this morning, shorts and canvas shoes. But some make up, some jewelry, some perfume. God, she was fabulous. "How about some music?" she asked as she cranked up the stereo. She had a Beach Boys disc in, already into *Help Me, Rhonda.*

He actually laughed.

She smiled and rebuked him happily. "You just wait and see! I'm going to show you how to have fun! You don't know how to have fun yet, Tom Miller, but you're going to learn!" She was smiling happily and laughing. "We're going to have so much fun!"

They talked all the way up to Michigan. In the car, over breakfast, during the ferry ride, back in the car. All the way to Maple Creek, there always seemed something to share. There was politics. She liked politics and seemed to know a lot about it. She told him that she was a Democrat. "We need more women in government," she assured him.

"Couldn't hurt."

"Madeline O'Connor had a real chance to be mayor, you know. I mean, before your hearing. Now people are saying she doesn't have a prayer. You can't look like you don't know what you're doing if you want to be chief executive of a city like Chicago."

Tow just nodded.

"Now you're not going to tell me that you're a Republican, are you?"

He of course had no politics–he didn't even vote, but was too embarrassed to admit it. "No chance," he said. "Not me. I'm an Independent."

"My mentor in the investment business was an Independent. Independent in everything, not just politics."

"Is that right?"

"Oh, yes. Bill Redmond. I learned so much from him. Actually I'm a lot like him. Independence wise, I mean."

"I believe it."

"Among other ventures, Bill ran a mutual fund. That's how I met him. I was just a couple years out of college. He really taught me the money management business. He was so successful in so many businesses. A great example for me to follow. Really, I owe him so much. He taught me to set high expectations for myself. That has proven to be the most valuable of all the gifts he gave me. Set high goals. You know, shoot for the moon to hit the barn. He was so right. He always told me 'you can have anything you want in the world, but nobody's going to give it to you.' And I believe that. I love achieving, doing more than I ever thought I could. I've been at this money management business most of my life and I love it. And there's so much more that I can accomplish. Sometimes I can hardly wait to get to work in the morning. I never want to look back and think I didn't try my best. I want to do it now."

"Beverly," said Tow, smiling and confident. "You're amazing."

She had a zest for possibility that energized even him.

The conversation just rambled on.

Finally they got around to entertainment. "I love movies," she told him. "Alfred Hitchcock movies are my favorites. Mysteries–you know. Like Charlie Chan and Perry Mason–I just love them. And books. I love to read. I buy tons of books, but I don't have the time right now to read any of them. Someday, I'll have time. Then I'll write a mystery of my own. But not right now."

He let her go on. He hadn't been to a movie theater in years. If absolutely cornered, he was prepared to say he had read a few good books recently. The truth was that he wasn't much of a spectator of anything. Not movies, not sports, not politics. But with Beverly, further explanation wasn't necessary. He figured that she realized that she already knew him well enough, and didn't need to hear more from him. Instead, she went cheerfully rambling on about why she loved Impressionist paintings. He never got tired of being with her, listening to her, just looking at her.

Finally at Maple Creek, they stopped at a large grocery store. Now they were shopping together, going down every aisle at her insistence. Talking and laughing, with the whole weekend ahead of them. He couldn't remember shopping ever being fun. She could see he had loosened up and was enjoying himself. "See," she said. "I *told* you we'd have fun!"

Her cottage was approached by a long gravel road that curved through a thick forest growing out of the sandy soil. Despite the warmth of the day, it was cool and damp under the trees. She slowed to a crawl, and pointed ahead. Six deer were feeding in the tall grass in a clearing off to their right. They all froze, then looked up, but none bolted. She kept her same gradual pace, passing the deer which went back to feeding. Finally the cottage emerged from behind a sandy ridge. Tow was surprised. The sturdy cedar construction was recent, and it was actually less of a cottage and more like a large rambling two story house. They lugged everything in, and even before they unpacked, she wanted to take a hike. "You'll love these trails back through the sand dunes," she told him. "It's a fun way to relax. We'll take the binoculars with us."

"Great," he agreed. He hadn't taken a hike in decades. "Let's go."

• • •

They returned weary and ready to call it a day.

"You make the drinks, and I'll get something to hold us until dinner," she told him, disappearing into the kitchen.

The feature of the lower level of the house was a large living space organized around a wide stone fireplace. Firewood stood nearby in neat stacks. The bar took most of one wall. Tow poured wine for Beverly and opened a beer. He took a pull, and marveled at his good fortune. Then he drank some more. He selected a large easy chair and sat back. Could all of this really be happening to him?

A few minutes later she was back, and sat down in the chair squeezing next to him. "Finally, we're truly alone!" she said and, reaching for her wine, offered a toast. "To us, and to our first official weekend together!" An embrace lead to a kiss and then to another, longer, and more romantic. Before long she took his hand and led him to the bedroom.

• • •

Later they were hungry.

She gave him orders to start the grill out on the deck that opened directly to the beach. "I'll set the table," she told him, "But you're grilling the salmon."

"Beverly, anybody ever tell you you're pretty bossy?"

"All the time," she said happily, and came close for a kiss.

The sun had suddenly disappeared, but the evening was warm. They ate on the patio, around which she had strung colored lanterns. She even had speakers out there.

Later, they sat, just talking, watching the stars and listening to the surf until almost 2:00 a.m. "I love Traverse City," she told him. "It's beautiful all year around. In the summer we have the sun and stars and the waves. Sometimes we get these incredible thunder storms and the Lake rises and comes crashing in. It's absolutely thrilling, believe me. In autumn, the leaves turn and it's like the forest is on fire. And winter is stark and frozen and it snows for months. We get about six feet of snow here every winter. Sometimes a lot more. Then it clears and you can see the stars again. They are so bright in the winter that they light up the whole beach. It's all frozen and beautiful. I love to stay close to the fire and read. I'll write my mystery someday, right here. I'll do it over an entire winter. This is where I want us to retire. Not Florida or Arizona. Right here."

The last part of this did not escape him. He nodded. "It's sounds really great," he told her.

• • •

Saturday morning they were up late, and busy making breakfast when she surprised him with a proposal. "You know, Tom," she said as she casually cracked another egg on the edge of the pan, "We really don't need two places anymore. Don't you agree? I have more room than any two people could possibly use. So why don't you just move in with me?"

It finally occurred to him that this was her real purpose in wanting to get away. "Beverly," he said, "Are you sure that's what you want?"

She nodded and turned to him for an embrace. "Yes, I'm sure," she whispered. "I've thought a lot about it. And us. And I'm very sure." She hesitated. "I think it's time for us to be together. Is it what you want, too?"

He nodded. "You know it is."

• • •

Sunday afternoon came much too soon. "This was wonderful," she told him. "I can't wait to do it again."

And he agreed, almost astonished by how good he felt.

• • •

Monday morning they had just gotten seated in the car, about to begin the return drive home when, at Beverly's initiative, a serious topic came up. One of those difficult things that they had so carefully avoided for the past few days. Beverly was in the driver's seat. She put the key in the ignition, but didn't start the engine. Instead she turned to engage Tow with an earnest look. "You know, Tom, I want to say that when we get home, whatever happens, happens," she said. "Somehow I think we have a long way to go before this thing with Rosco is over. We both know there is something wrong there. You'll have to do whatever you have to do, and I'll have to cope. I just want you to know that I understand." She leaned over and kissed him, and gave him one of her best smiles. Then, resolutely, she started the old Mercedes and took the wheel for the long drive back to the city.

32

So just where was she that night?

Vicki never gave him much of an answer the night they argued after the Hawks game. "*Home.*" A pretty evasive response.

Richard Landon was seated at the bar, eating cashews and working on another gin and tonic. It was a little after 9:00 p.m. Friday, just over a week since their breakup, and he was drinking alone. Jax was new and already hugely popular, especially among traders. Already he could feel the press of the crowd behind him. When several couples next to him left, their seats were quickly taken by four young women. Richard evaluated them in a glance. Four babes on the prowl–bare shoulders–even on a cool fall evening. All brunettes but one. The blonde girl was truly exceptional in a short black dress and heels. She smiled warmly as she squeezed in next to him in order to climb onto the high bar stool. "Excuse me," she said with another warm smile. All exceedingly polite, but just so hot. She reminded him painfully of Vicki. He looked at her and smiled back, then returned to his drink and his thoughts.

At least Kate never walked out on him. No, there was no chance of that. Low maintenance Katie had only one desire–the ring and the cradle. Now in his loneliness and his pain, Richard seriously considered calling her. Of course he had not seen or even spoken to Kate in several months, but he guessed she would be receptive to a reunion. Then again, what if she had found someone new? That, he knew, was unlikely. It was far more likely that she would be very happy to reconnect. But then what would he do if Vicki came roaring back into his life with some midnight phone call, scorching hot and ready to fuck all night? This was something that certainly required thought.

He tried to be analytical. After all, he did have options. There were other women in the world. This place was already swarming with women, most of them hoping to find Mr. Right, but willing to settle for a little temporary romance on a Friday night. Again he considered the talent at hand. This blonde girl chatting away to his right had a great body and had clearly made serious preparations for the evening. Chicks who traveled in packs and dressed that well were definitely looking for action. And he knew he was pretty hot stuff himself. A Wall Street trader. A derivatives trader. A big trader. Women loved this stuff, even if they understood none of it. He could probably score right now if he bothered to try. Maybe that was the answer–a quick overnighter with some hot babe.

But he knew in his heart that it wouldn't change the longing he felt for Vicki. It was killing him. Just the thought of her, her body, her scent–god, he literally ached for her. He wanted her near, touching him, pressing herself against him, breathing in his ear, whispering to him as she played with his zipper. He wondered where she was right now, what she was doing–and who she was with. *Who was she with?* It was making him crazy. He considered calling her and making up. But he couldn't. He was angry. She had mocked him. Called him a baby. *A baby.* Christ. He had done nothing wrong, and despite that, he had a homicide cop on his back with all kinds of crazy accusations. *A baby.* What he really wanted was to tell her off. She could be pretty goddamned selfish. *A baby.* When the cops were picking on her, she had cried herself to sleep. He was also unhappy with her response to his question about that night–*home.* At least she was consistent in her alibi. He realized that she might be so consistent because that was the truth and that she had in fact done nothing wrong. Accusations in the face of innocence was a concept he could relate to. Could it be that he was doing to her what Detective Miller was doing to him? It was a disarming possibility.

Now his mind toggled wearily back to Kate and immediately he felt a sense of dread. Just why was that? The mere thought of her produced a sickening physical reaction. Was it Kate herself? Not really, he told himself. He actually did like her. He liked her a lot. But liking was not loving. Mostly he felt sorry for her, but even that did not account for his revulsion. There was something going on with Kate that had produced a dismal, almost nauseous feeling of dread. Was it her mother? The Widow O'Connor was a truly a bitch, but there was something more, something profoundly evil about Madeline. Maybe she seemed evil because she was so vigilant about evil in others, and so quick to seek punishment. Or was it Molly? There was something dark about her, too. There was a *lot* dark about her. The combination seemed to leave its mark on sweet Kate, as though she were contaminated by something toxic from which there was no escape.

Jax was growing loud and overflowing with people, and the band had just started their first number. Again Richard considered his options. He could easily ask the blonde chick to dance, buy her a few drinks and then make his play for the evening. He belted down his gin and tonic, then made his decision.

A one night stand, even with this gorgeous girl was not the answer to his problems. What he felt was profound loneliness and the pain of rejection, something for which there was only one solution.

33

"Morri says he doesn't have time," Sweeney told him.

"A writer?" asked Tow. "Morri wants me to talk to a *writer?*"

"That's right. That's what he said."

"Why?"

Sweeney shrugged. "I don't know. He just said for you to talk to this guy as soon as you got in."

"What kind of writer? *Newspapers?* I hate reporters."

Sweeney shook his head. "No. Books. This guy says he writes books."

"What his name?"

"Douglas. Paul Douglas."

"Never heard of him."

Sweeney shrugged. "He's waiting out there now."

Tow shook his head wearily. Another miscellaneous chore. "Alright, alright."

Paul Douglas was a slight man in his late 40s.

Tow invited him to have a seat. "So what can I do for you, Mr. Douglas?"

"First let me give you a little background on myself, Detective. I was a professor at New York University most of my career. My field was psychology with an emphasis on criminal behavior–that's how I came to know Commander Morrison. A few years ago I decided I wanted to write mysteries, the kind of fiction that would bene-fit from my field of study. I've published three mysteries since." Here Paul Douglas hesitated, expecting Tow to comment. When that didn't happen, he continued. "My first was *The Art of Murder*, then I wrote *Murder By Candlelight. Candlelight* was a political mystery. And then I wrote *Aftermath of Murder.* We're still nego-tiating the movie rights, but I'm optimistic. I expect the film will be out in about 15 months. *Aftermath* was a best seller, you know."

Tow didn't know, and was definitely not enthused. "You know, Mr. Douglas," he lectured bluntly, "What we have here is not exactly what I would call entertainment."

Paul Douglas suddenly became energized. "Detective Miller, you are at the center of one of the greatest, most lurid true crime stories of all time. Someday it will be entertainment for a lot of readers. And Hollywood will love it. I would like to write that story."

"Okay," said Tow indifferently. "So go ahead and write it."

Abruptly subdued now, Douglas continued. "Yes, yes, of course I could proceed on my own. That's true. But it would be so much better if I had your cooperation."

"My cooperation?"

"Now, don't get the wrong idea, Detective. I'm a veteran profes-sional. I understand police work. I won't get in your way. You won't even know I'm around. I just need to spend some time with you periodically to get the inside dynamics of the investigation. Read-ers expect to know just how you solved the case. Suspects, clues. Loose ends. That kind of thing."

"Well," said Tow giving Professor Douglas a polite brush off. "We do seem to have a few loose ends. Let me think about it, and I'll give you a call."

• • •

One particular loose end had occurred to Tow while talking to Paul Douglas.

He picked up the phone. "You still got that report?" he asked Barry Stern in Records and Systems.

The boy recognized him immediately. "You bet, Detective."

"Good," said Tow. "I'll be by in an hour or so."

• • •

The report was organized exactly as Tow requested. Very concise. It covered a fairly large area, but was limited to the Sunday and Monday of the murder. All citations sorted by owner of the vehicle. And there was not a single name that Tow could recognize. Not one.

Tow felt like a fool, such a fool.

So much for Sherlock Holmes, he thought.

There would be no more playing detective now.

34

The idea had been Spider's.

"You stay with me an' Scab," he said, putting a thin arm around Ben's shoulders. "You be safe."

With little choice, Ben agreed to go home with Spider rather than hide out alone in the boxcar. And if they had not been before, the police were certainly looking for him now. He was dead broke, unable to work for Harold Lamb and did not know where his mother was, or when she was coming home.

As Spider well knew, Ben was furious with the big policeman for arresting his mother while actually searching for him. Often Ben could talk of nothing else, requiring Spider to listen as he ranted for hours at a time. And to make matters worse, there was talk– *shameful talk.* On the television and even in the *Tribune.* The story the police had made up about his mother killing a man with a knife was humiliating. It wasn't true. His mother would never have done such a thing. She was a model! The police should just look in the Sears catalog. Her pictures were right there. Then they should let her go. It was not what they were saying. The real problem was that the policeman just wanted him, and Spider too, because of the fight with the Devils. Ben made this point repeatedly to Spider. And the police also wanted Scab, because Scab had bitten one of the Devils, and later had bitten the big policeman himself at the playground. These were the real problems, Ben told Spider, who listened without enthusiasm.

• • •

Just as Pine Street had no trees, Martin Luther King Gardens had no grass and no flowers. As prepared as he was, Ben saw a frightening landscape of concrete and asphalt. The community had been here a long time. Whatever was constructed of iron, now rusting, or of concrete, now crumbling, were the remnants. Everything else had been beaten into the ground.

"Dat where I live," said Spider pointing ahead.

Ben looked, both eager and anxious. His mother had warned him so emphatically about the projects.

It was a big building, and like those around it, it was ugly, with many windows covered with boards. Some windows were only partially covered with crooked sheets or blankets. Some had no covering at all and appeared to be dark holes. Ben was immediately fearful, ready to retreat to the box car. Still, something about this place was familiar, though he wasn't sure why. He had some kind of memory, one with a distant, absent quality about it, as in a dream.

As soon as Spider and Ben entered building, the brightness of the late afternoon quickly dissolved into cave-like darkness. The concrete lobby was filthy, extremely cramped, and damp. The walls seemed to weep, the grimy floor was slick. Dense gang graffiti covered every surface, including the low concrete ceilings. It reminded Ben of the subway which was often poorly lit, with gang graffiti covering every receptive surface, and rats running along the tracks below. Inside the slow noisy elevator was the strong repugnant odor of urine, which immediately made Ben feel that he was drawing his memory from some unpleasant experience with this very place.

The three of them got off on 11 and entered a corridor scorched by fire. It seemed there were no lights anywhere. Trash and junk accumulated everywhere. A wooden crate the size of a grown man stood outside one door, partially blocking the corridor. Then they passed several boarded up apartment doors on which were pasted red signs with yellow letters that spelled caution. Spider seemed not to notice these things, or perhaps not to care. Instead he nodded toward the end of the hall while Scab ran ahead. "We home. See? Scab know. He hungry."

Inside Ben could hear a television somewhere.

"Where Momma?" Spider asked a boy of eight or nine.

"Workin'," said the boy.

"Momma always workin'," explained Spider. "Come on," he told Ben, and proceeded with Scab to a bedroom where two soiled mattresses lay on the tile floor. Near the door, there was a blanket and a water bowl for Scab. Against one wall stood a chest of drawers painted bright blue. A small television sat on a wooden crate. There was a sheet covering the windows. These conditions made his own room on Pine Street look fabulous, but when Spider closed the door, Ben did at least feel safe.

• • •

Later Spider took Ben to a fast food place where they spent their last few dollars. Ben was too upset to eat, but thought it wise to wrap his leftovers and put them in his pocket for later.

Ben tried to sleep that night, but the surrounding noise kept him up. Televisions and stereos blared from the floors above and below. And voices floated constantly, coming and going outside and in the halls. There were horns blowing in the parking lot directly below. He heard shouts of kids playing and the angry voices of men arguing. And from the same general direction, though more distant, there was laughter. Then somewhere a girl screamed. A car engine revved over and over, followed by squealing tires. A bottle smashed against concrete. And later, after a moment of silence, a baby began to cry. It cried and cried and cried. How would he ever sleep with this racket?

Somehow he did.

Then he was awakened. Scab was growling low and mean. Ben froze, his heart already skipping faster. There was something there, something that Scab was confronting. Ben rolled slowly away. In the darkness, he could see something black, about the size of a large house cat. It retreated into a corner. Then, suddenly, Scab lunged. The scuffle, furious, went on for only seconds amid intense growling and high pitched squealing. Then it was all over and there was silence.

Spider, who had observed the fight while propped up on one elbow, hopped up and opened a window.

Ben, his heart pounding now, did not move, but he noticed his half eaten hamburger lay open on the floor near the scene of the fight.

Scab, the victor, went back to his blanket and laid down.

Spider picked the loser up by its long tail and dropped it out the window. Without a word, he laid back on his mattress. Then in the darkness, he said very quietly, "See, I tol' you you be safe. We got Scab, an' Scab here, well, he doan put up wit' no rats."

• • •

The next morning, Ben wanted to go outside for a while, anything to get out of the dismal apartment. So, as a unit, the three of them wandered out and joined in a rough game of kick ball on an asphalt parking lot. This was not soccer in the lush green fields of Oak Park. And if Pine Street had been dangerous, King Gardens was outright war. Trouble arrived almost immediately in the person of an older, bigger boy called Dennis. Shoved viciously from behind, Ben went sprawling.

Instantly Ben was on his feet, screaming, then rushing, then punching the very surprised much bigger offender. "*You cheated, Dennis*," screamed Ben, his anger surging. "*You can't do that! It's against the rules.*" Dennis began to fight back, and now fists were really flying. In his rage, Ben landed a serious blow to the larger boy's nose, and Dennis immediately went down hard. Instinctively, Ben jumped on him, still punching. Bleeding profusely from his nose, Dennis tried to curl up, but Ben continued to batter him fiercely about the face and ears.

"Enough!" Spider called. "Ben! That enough! Ben!"

But unlike the fight with Spider in the boxcar, enraged Ben did not stop. When the knuckles of his fingers were too painful to punch any more, he tucked his thumb into his fist and battered the boy's temples. Abruptly Ben realized his larger opponent was no longer struggling. Instead Dennis lay there limp, bleeding and unconscious.

Spider pulled Ben by the arm, and the three of them ran.

Someone else was after them, too.

Later the same day, Ben almost walked directly into Harold Lamb who was speaking earnestly with a young woman holding an infant.

The three of them turned directly around and slowly retreated.

A very close call, and Ben wondered how Harold already knew about the fight and where to look for him.

• • •

The next night, Spider had an idea. "You want to see stars?"

"See the stars?"

"Yeah, stars," said Spider. "Come on."

Spider led Ben to the Lyndon Baines Johnson Homes, two miles closer in the direction of the Lake. In the center building, the highest, they took the elevator to the top floor, then had to climb the back staircase in order to access the roof. This was the long way around but, as Spider explained, the front was locked. Ben wasn't really sure why Spider wanted to do this. It wasn't much fun. The rooftop was completely dark, and it was late. "We here," announced Spider.

Ben looked up, but saw only a dark night sky. "I don't see any stars."

"No," said Spider, turning Ben around in the direction of the city. "Now look."

Ben found himself facing not stars as Spider called them, but brilliant, glowing city lights. They were looking at the city directly from the west, and the view, thought Ben, was like seeing the Milky Way almost edge on. In the middle was the dense center consisting of the tallest buildings–all brilliantly lit. And surrounding this galactic core lesser stars were distributed in all directions as far as Ben could see. This view gripped him, and held him until he realized that Spider was saying something. "Here," Spider was saying. "It happen right here."

Ben wondered what was coming next. Clearly star-gazing had merely been a ploy of Spider's to draw him to this location for some other purpose. With Spider there was a purpose for everything.

"One night," continued Spider, "Me an' Scab, we visit dis boy. Calvin, him name."

Already Ben was wary. "Calvin?"

"Calvin, that right. The boy what got shot. Calvin. Calvin a lot like you. Him new kid–like you. Doan have no friends at all, 'cept me an' Scab. So me an' Scab, we visiting Calvin one night."

"The boy that policeman shot?"

"*Dat right.* Calvin." Spider could not be more direct. "Dat the boy."

Now Ben braced himself.

"We visit Calvin lots of times," Spider went on, "But da last time I had bag full of firecrackers. M-80s an' cherry bombs. Me an' Scab, we sneak up here wid Calvin that night. Nobody else around. It real dark wid no lights, like dis. I was lightin' M-80s an' throwin' em off the roof and they go off half way down. Now Calvin, he want to have fun, too, but he doan never know how to do nothin'. But he want to try so I let him hold a pack of lady fingers so I can light them. Theys just ladyfingers, but Calvin, he doan know to throw 'em. I say 'throw 'em!' but he doan know. He just stand there and smile to me. So I grab 'em away and throws 'em *fast.* Calvin, now he feel real bad, an' start crying. I say, 'Doan cry, Calvin. Doan cry.' I had a sparkler gun, so I gave it to Calvin. It wasn't nothin'. Didn't shoot or nothin'. Only make sparklers. Calvin, he like it though." Now Spider formed his hand into a pistol. "Calvin, he go 'round laughin' an' smilin', goin' '*Bang, bang.*' He like it a lot."

Ben wondered why Spider was telling him all of this, but said nothing. In the past, Spider had guarded this topic carefully. Ben knew it had to have something to do with the big policeman. Spider, in his own way, was trying to tell him something.

"We just playin' like dat when that big po-lice come and yell, '*Who dere?*' Me an' Scab, we quick hide over near dat door." Here Spider pointed as he talked. "Calvin, he run hide by dem stairs. In dark, po-lice say, 'We po-lices. You come out now. You put up you hands now.' I hang on to Scab collar real quiet. But Calvin, he come walkin' out and aim dat gun right at po-lices like before, *playin'.* Po-lices think it a *real* gun, an' Calvin, well there somethin' wrong with dat boy. He doan hear good, an' act funny, like a baby. He doan listen to po-lices. Po-lices say real loud. '*We po-lices. We won' hurt you none. You jus' put down you gun.*' But Calvin, he doan care for nothin' an' *aim right at po-lices.*" Here Spider, full of anguish, demonstrated just how deliberately the boy had pointed the gun. "*Bang!* Calvin fall down. Me an' Scab, we run. Dat big po-lice call to us, but we run fast."

"You mean you saw that policeman shoot that boy?"

Spider nodded. "Me an' Scab, we seen it all. Right here. Dat why po-lices huntin' us. All the time, huntin' us."

"But you didn't do anything wrong. Why did you run away?"

Spider hesitated, then quietly said, "Roosevelt."

"Roosevelt?"

"Like I tell you. Roosevelt tell me 'Doan you never do nothin' wrong or judge put you in penitentiary like me for 44 years.'"

Ben was out of patience. "Yeah, and you *didn't* do anything wrong."

Spider disputed this, sadly shaking his head. "Me an' Scab, we ripped off dem fireworks from some gang bangers in King Gardens." Spider counted off one finger. "Fireworks, dey against da law." That was two. "Dat my sparkler Calvin shoot against po-lices." He held up three fingers, and offered his conclusion. "Now Calvin daid." Spider was full of remorse about this. "Judge put me an' Scab in penitentiary for 'bout hunerd years fo' all dat. Be *just* like Roosevelt."

• • •

It was only later that Ben truly understood Spider's intention. This had been his closely guarded secret since the day they met. Revealing it had been an act of supreme confidence. But it had also been a rebuke. Spider was trying to explain that the big policeman had actually done nothing wrong either. There had been something wrong with that boy, Calvin. The boy had not understood what was happening around him. And in the darkness, the policeman thought the boy was about to shoot him, and nevertheless fired only after giving several warnings. That was the real point Spider tried to make. Weary of Ben's constant accusations, Spider was absolving the big policeman who had arrested his mother.

But not even Spider could persuade Ben now.

His father had been killed three years before, and the police had done nothing about it. Neither were they of any help when those two boys tried to steal his mother's purse a few months ago. Now they had actually taken his mother from him, leaving him with only misery and squalor.

And about all of this, Ben remained very angry.

35

The media's focus on the scandal at Block, Morris and Ferrel ended abruptly with the arrest of Edmund Chambers. Richard Landon heard the news that morning on television.

Chambers had been apprehended by private security guards on the Barrington estate of Madeline O'Connor about 11:00 p.m. the night before. Because of the private security, he never got near the house, and no one was hurt except for Chambers himself who was badly bruised and scratched when he tried to evade the mounted guards and patrol dogs. Chambers was armed with a switchblade knife. No charges had been filed, though trespassing was a possibility. Edmund Chambers, however, would face other more serious charges. He had already been positively identified by Carmen Lopez and her daughter, Beatrice, who was still recovering from the knife assault by Chambers.

• • •

Richard called Kate right away. "Thank god you're okay," he told her. He was surprised by the depth of his feelings for her. This threat suddenly caused him to feel a slight panic, a rush to protect her.

She seemed relieved to hear from him. "Oh, Richard. I'm so glad you called. I was going to call you, but it has been so crazy around here. No one was hurt or anything, but Mother is very upset. And the police made her even more upset with all their questions. She's not herself at all. She was really hard on Commander Morrison. I don't understand it. She ordered everyone off the property. She says she just wants to get away. She's even talking about leaving the country.

Some nonsense about the south of France. Molly and I don't even have passports."

Richard couldn't begin to guess what Madeline O'Connor might be thinking. "So what happened, anyway? First Rosco, now this lunatic. It's crazy."

"It sure is. No one knows exactly what he was doing here," Kate told him. "But Molly is sure she saw this Edmund Chambers at the mall yesterday, following her around for about an hour. This skinny guy in a blue T-shirt and a red baseball hat and long hair. She got scared, and came right home. The police think he followed her, then came back last night. They say he's a stalker. This is a very deranged person we're talking about here."

"Is there anything I can do?"

"No, really, Richard. We're perfectly okay."

"Well, I was going to call, actually. I wanted you to know. Vicki and I broke up." For some reason, it seemed important to tell her this despite his earlier resolutions to the contrary.

"Oh, Richard. I'm so sorry. These things are always so hard."

"Well, like I was saying, I was going to call. It's only been recently. Well, we'll talk soon."

"I'd like that. Let's do that soon."

"We will."

Richard hung up, already regretting telling Kate about Vicki, then sat down to consider what connection Vicki herself had to all this craziness, and just what he had done to deserve her, Rosco and all the rest.

$$\bullet \ \bullet \ \bullet$$

That evening was the black tie Economics Club dinner at the Hilton. Tow had been dreading this event since Beverly told him about it weeks earlier. "I have to go, so you have to go," she explained happily back then. "It will be fun," she said. "I promise."

This evening, however, she was unusually quiet while they got dressed. He knew she didn't want to do this either. Maybe another time, but not now with links to Rosco again in the headlines.

Tow fumbled his way into a rented designer tux while she was in the bathroom. He whistled when she came out in an ivory gown, looking terrific.

"Oh, Honey, you look great," she told him. Observing his struggle with his cuff links, she laughed and said, "Here, let me help you with that." Then she grew serious again as she finished the second link. "It's only a few times a year. Part of the job, you know. A girl has to do what a girl has to do. This is how I meet people who are decision makers. The ones who can do business with me or refer business to me. It's important, actually."

"I'm not much for fancy dinners," Tow confessed.

"Well, don't let these people get to you tonight. Most of them are really nice, but there are a few jokers in the deck. And I'll tell you something. A lot of these guys are good at what they do. No doubt about it. But they couldn't do what you do, Tom. There's no doubt about that either."

"Beverly," said Tow. "Don't worry. I'm going to do my best."

"That's good enough for me," she said, managing a smile.

• • •

They were in time for cocktails in the huge hotel lobby outside the dining room.

For Tow black tie events were a rare experience, and this evening he felt foolish in his rented tux with the striped trousers and snug cummerbund and ridiculous bow tie. But he told himself if Beverly was working, he was working. Still the hum of conversations emerging from the crowd was already intimidating. These were wealthy, powerful people. Heads of banks and corporations. The Economic Club, for god's sake. He just didn't fit.

But Beverly did. And she knew just what to do. She cranked up a smile for every power broker and always seemed to have some enthused comment for his wife. Tow shook hands and said little. Wisely, Beverly moved quickly from group to group.

Though he knew little about business, Tow could see Beverly was making an effort this evening. Clearly this was not easy, mingling with the city's aristocracy, risking indifference or even outright rejection. Not an easy thing at all. She said that there were some jokers in the deck. She knew she was taking chances. His regard for her deepened. Beverly had guts. And she was gorgeous. And unbelievably, this fabulous woman who could certainly have found companionship and comfort among the elite was interested in him in his ridiculous rented tuxedo.

• • •

They were seated at Table 25. Tow sat next to Beverly with an elderly woman to his left. This was generally a mature crowd, including a lot of seniors. The men seemed at ease with each other, as were their wives with one another. Tow guessed that they all worked together and regularly saw each other socially. If there were any more solo acts like Beverly, they were not evident. Clearly this was a club reserved for the boys.

They had just begun their salads when the evening's speaker was introduced. Tow turned slightly to the podium for a better view. Stephen McKinley, President of the Federal Reserve Bank of New York, looked like a banker was supposed to look. A dignified man. Tall, his gray hair turning white, with glasses. Imperial in his tuxedo.

Tow glanced back at Beverly who smiled at him.

Amid the genteel clatter of the silver striking fine china, Stephen McKinley began his remarks in the most conventional manner, saying good evening and commenting how much he enjoyed visiting the city. "I love Chicago," he went on. "This is where I began my career with the Federal Reserve, as an economist working at the Bank at LaSalle and Jackson. But of course that was 40 years ago, and a few things have changed here. And I must say that I'm happy to hear that some of the local mysteries seem to have found solutions recently."

It was like a punch.

Then, again drawing on the murders, McKinley told a brief joke about his wife insisting on selecting his hotel herself and got a huge laugh from the audience. Tow waited briefly then stole a glance in Beverly's direction. Disbelieving what she had just heard, she sat frozen in her pain and distress.

Understandably, she remained quiet through dinner.

Later they walked to the car in near silence.

"I really hope all of this lunacy ends soon," she finally said when Tow stopped for a red light on Michigan Avenue. "First Rosco, now this thing with Madeline. It's insane."

"That it is," he said, knowing to let her get it all out.

"Rosco is still my biggest problem. The scandal is just killing me. I mean, it *never* ends. Look at what happened tonight. Now I have absolutely no credibility with these guys. And these are people I really need," she said. "And there's more. When it rains, it pours. My biggest account walked out the door two days ago. And I won't be getting another I've been working on for six months. And tonight, I really didn't need personal ridicule from the President of the New York Federal Reserve Bank for all the world to hear."

Sharing her frustration, Tow took all of this silently.

"I'm afraid I'm going to have to do something drastic just to survive."

"Like what?"

"Well, for starters, I'll have to call a real estate agent to put the condo on the market. We can get something smaller, but still comfortable. I don't have a mortgage, but it is one of the assets I pledged on a loan that will be coming due in January. I know I have a few months, but the business isn't performing. I'm losing money–quite a lot of money. I'm bleeding money. I mean, you know what kind of overhead I have? The lease and all those people? So I have to think ahead. I'm one girl who pays her bills on time. I'll pay up, and the boys will let me play again another time. I'll also have to lay off four more people. That leaves five to run the whole place, to do the same work that 14 did back in June."

"Can you really do that? I mean, will it work?"

She thought about this for a moment. "Well, it will if I work 18 hours a day and weekends, too."

"Is that realistic?"

"I've done it before."

"I don't know. That seems to be asking a lot."

"I don't think so."

"No?"

"No. This business is very important to me. I've put everything

I have into it. It's what I've always wanted."

"I see your point."

There was a long silence, which she finally broke. "There's only one thing more important to me now."

He looked at her. "What's that?"

"Us," she said.

Behind them a taxi laid on the horn and Tow hit the gas.

• • •

It was later that night, when they were in bed that he finally found the words to tell her how much he really loved her.

36

If Tow was doubtful concerning the arrest of Patrice Foster, he was completely perplexed by the arrest of Edmund Chambers on the estate of Madeline O'Connor. Nothing in this puzzle seemed to square. On the advice of his attorney, Chambers wasn't talking. And further, no one seemed interested in challenging what appeared to be solutions. It was out of this sense of uncertainty and frustration that Tow entered the sealed apartment of Edmund Chambers.

This visit was pretty much the same dismal tour as the last time. Nothing particularly noteworthy. Mostly a strange collection of weird paraphernalia. It was on his way out that Tow caught sight of the stack of parking tickets, immediately recalling how foolish he felt the last time he played detective. Still, the tickets represented possibility in a case that seemed to offer no true answers at all. He counted the yellow envelops. There were 14 records of the suspect's activities. And they were rich in detail–dates, times of day, and locations–all of this information just begging for analysis. Tow made a short list of the dates and locations of the citations, and requested that all the suspect's mail, including the tickets, be sent to the lab as evidence. If any of the dates matched the dates of the victim's attacks, the tickets would be easily available for further review.

• • •

But they didn't match.

Not a single citation had been written on the date of an attack. Again there was that miserable sinking feeling, and Tow was tempted to toss his note and try to forget such a stupid tactic. He recalled Paul Douglas, the psychology professor turned mystery writer, and felt even more a fool. This wasn't a mystery novel and he wasn't Sherlock Holmes. However he did notice one thing. Several tickets immediately preceded the murder of Joanne Rice, an event that Tow remembered well. Three tickets, all within a week of the murder. The locations varied widely. Then he saw it. Of course the locations varied widely. Of course! *Chambers was stalking her.* According to Nancy Martin, Joanne Rice had told her that someone was following her. The physical evidence now supported the testimony. *So what?*

Tow was stuck. *So what?*

Well, what if someone had also stalked Rosco Mink?

But Rosco was killed in his own home.

So what if someone had staked out his home? A stakeout of the victim, prior to killing him, in order to become knowledgeable about him, his habits, his home? The kind of thing a careful killer might do?

But Chambers, for the most part, had been a skilled and careful killer, and he had accumulated a stack of tickets.

How to reconcile that? A careless stalker, but a careful killer? Why not?

• • •

"No problem, Detective," Barry Stern told him. "Anyone with two or more tickets. No problem. I can modify the program myself. I'll just expand the dates and reduce the boundaries in the existing routine and rerun today. Couple hours, it'll be ready. Maybe a $50 charge to your department, if that's okay?"

• • •

It wasn't a big report. Only scofflaws had multiple parking tickets.

Fearful of being wrong yet again, Tow hurried, almost evasively, through the report. He was just a little over half way, getting nowhere, when one name suddenly jumped off the page. There were four tickets, all within the two weeks preceding Rosco's murder in

July. Tow stared, his heart pounding.

And the name Madeline O'Connor stared back.

• • •

Tow decided to keep the ticket report to himself.

There were four tickets all together. All issued to the same late model Mercedes sedan registered in the name of Madeline Marie O'Connor. All issued within three blocks of the townhouse of Rosco Mink, between the hours of 7:00 and 10:00 p.m. Two tickets cited violations of residential parking restrictions, one for parking next to a fire hydrant, and one for parking in a handicap reserved space. The fire hydrant violation on Astor proved to be the exact location where Tow had received his ticket the morning of the murder. Three of the four had been issued by Officer Rita Martinez. Indeed, the heat had been on.

In addition to this information, Tow called Barry Stern in Records and Systems to provide any further information regarding the disposition of the four citations. "The disposition?" asked Barry.

"Yeah," said Tow. "Are they paid or outstanding? And if they're paid, who paid them, and when?"

Barry was getting all of this down. "No problem, Detective. Big case you're working on, huh? Just like Sherlock Holmes. You're following the clues."

"Sure," said Tow. "Just like Sherlock Holmes."

"No problem," concluded Barry. "I can't wait to see where all of this leads."

"Me, either," said Tow.

• • •

Of course the parking ticket report in itself was not proof of anything. However, linked with a motive–and there certainly was one in this case–it was suggestive. And what it suggested was that someone needed to have a serious conversation with Madeline O'Connor in connection with the murder of Rosco Mink.

But Tow had his reservations. What he needed was to discuss all of this just to evaluate the impact on another rational person. He could have approached a number of people. Beverly was a natural choice. But she had already done enough by providing Tow with Madeline's motive. In short, Rosco had been instrumental in providing young women to Robert O'Connor. Madeline's discovery with the help of a private detective agency almost destroyed the marriage and ultimately resulted in immediate termination of Robert's participation in Mink Capital Management upon his death just three years earlier. All of this constituted a pretty good motive. Additionally, Tow did not want to worry Beverly further. What he was considering–effectively reopening the case–would have been a reversal of the first order, resulting in a massive renewal of media coverage. Beverly would be panicked by the possibility.

Morrison was, of course, the most appropriate person with whom to discuss the topic. But Tow guessed that Morri, too, would not have appreciated what the report suggested. *Very influential, very powerful and very wealthy*, was the way Morrison had described Madeline O'Connor. *Has serious political ambition.* Tow would be proposing that Morri consider a candidate for mayor to be a suspect in a sensational murder. Not likely. Not on the basis of some flimsy possibility. Not with a suspect already in custody. Not with the kind of pressure Morrison had endured.

Regarding the link between Edmund Chambers and Madeline O'Connor, Tow did not have a clue.

And until something more surfaced, he had another task before him.

• • •

He arranged to meet Harold Lamb at the Rainbow Cafe, a greasy spoon across from the Everlasting Life Baptist Church on Madison, just a few blocks from the King Gardens. Harold was late, so Tow waited in the car. He had no particular desire to actually enter the grimy Rainbow.

Martin Luther King Gardens was a place Tow knew especially well. This was the turf of the Viper Kings who were entrenched in the universal industry of the projects. Drug wars here were common. Rivals all wanted a piece of the $20,000 a day traffic zealously cultivated by the Kings. The consequences of confrontation were predictably violent. The Kings, however, had one notable advantage over their endless competitors. They were led by a particularly savage ex-felon named Antwon Moon. *Nitro* to his associates, Moon was regarded by Gang Crimes as an unusually intelligent leader excelling in the organization and marketing of his products. His weakness was a phenomenal temper, that earned him his gang name and the respect of every gangbanger in the city.

• • •

"Was this really necessary?" Tow considered the question as he waited in the car for Harold Lamb. Was it still really so important to slug through the gang infested projects to find this kid? And then if he did find him, he'd probably have to wring the truth out of him. Was it really still so necessary? Others had put it to him in almost exactly the same way so many times before. Morrison, in particular, had made exactly these very same points in the Mink home back on his first day in Homicide. But Tow, burning with the need for vindication, had not seen it that way at the time. He had changed, he realized, and now he, too, was beginning to see it differently.

Without a doubt, it had been Beverly Nickols who had brought about this change in him. She had filled up some void within him, reducing those other needs. Sure, the shooting, the need for vindication–he still reacted strongly to all those things. But not like before. Not nearly like before. It was amazing how his life had changed in a year. And just as amazing was how little control he had over any of it. A late night call on the radio, a tragic moment of indecision, then a nightmare to live every day. But then later another uncontrollable event occurs and in the middle of an investigation of a vicious homicide, he meets the most desirable woman he'd ever known.

"What next?" he wondered aloud.

He didn't know. His instincts were sorely lacking on this subject. Beverly clearly wanted something permanent, but that seemed too good to be true. She could have whatever she wanted. Why him? What did she see in him? His life paled in comparison to hers. His was King Gardens and the Vipers and all the death and poverty and hopelessness that went with them. Hers was Wall Street and Lincoln Park and a cottage in Michigan. It didn't make a lot of sense, but it seemed real enough when they were together, and they were together all the time now. She filled up his life in a way he loved. But there was risk for him, too. After losing so much, he was still wary. Now she was the only person who could hurt him. But he knew she wouldn't do that. He was sure that he could trust her. If this search failed, maybe at last he could give up the past forever and concentrate on the future with Beverly.

• • •

Finally Harold showed up and climbed in Tow's Buick.

"*They're here*," Harold assured him. "I don't know just where yet, but I know they're here. The boys and the dog. *They're here.* People have seen the three of them together, but no one knows their names or where they live. One of the boys got in a fight just a few days ago. I'm afraid it was Ben. Hard to believe, but I think he was the one who beat up another youngster here. Ben fits the description of witnesses. They say Ben beat this boy senseless. The boy, he's still at Cook County. He's got a concussion and a couple broken ribs. He'll be okay, but it was a hell of a terrible beating. Still, it sure don't sound like Ben."

Tow's gaze drifted in the direction of the projects themselves. He knew what was there. It was not hard to imagine what might happen to a kid like Benjamin Foster fighting for his life in a place like King Gardens. "So now how do we find them, Harold?" he asked quietly.

This was a pretty fair question. More than 9,000 people lived in King Gardens.

"We jus' keep lookin'," said Harold. "They'll turn up soon."

"Spider and Scab," said Tow, sort of thinking out loud. "We can't exactly look them up in the phone book."

"No, but I'll find them. Don't you worry none. I'll find them alright. Kids will know. Maybe the school can help."

Tow nodded. Of course, these were exactly the right things to do. But there was one other thing. "Flyers," said Tow. "Hand out flyers with your phone number. And say there's a $1,000 reward."

"That should help," said Harold.

"It better. That's the bottom of the barrel."

Harold nodded, he understood.

But there was one other thing to consider. "What about Nitro?" Tow asked.

They both knew that nothing would escape the scrutiny of the Viper Kings. At the top of the food chain, their rule of terror on residents was absolute.

Harold Lamb hesitated. "I thought about that, too. But I figure that $1,000 should buy us a snitch or two who has it in for the Kings."

37

I n a single bond trade, Richard Landon lost almost $18,000
Monday morning, and had given up on the day in infinite
frustration. Following a few errands and an hour at the
health club, he was home, pained and miserable, surfing
channels late that afternoon. The loss had put him in an extraordinary funk. His normal response to such adversity was to scroll
through all his problems, examining each with critical care for the
purpose of re-ordering his life. Problems, Richard knew, did not
fix themselves, and his were about to overwhelm him.

It had been almost two weeks since Vicki and he had broken up,
and there still no sign of a thaw. Richard's remorse about this was
punishing. He missed her dreadfully, but when he recollected the
argument, he didn't feel he was all that wrong. *Just where in the hell
was she that night?* It was the question he kept coming back to. Was
it righteous indignation that had him so ticked off, or was it something else? After all, how often did he stand on principal? Was it
fear? Was he afraid of her? *Did Vicki kill Rosco after he saw Patrice
Foster leaving?* He couldn't stop thinking about it. She would have
had no trouble seducing a sucker like Rosco. He wouldn't have had
a prayer in Vicki's hands. And the way she stabbed those potatoes?
And what about that husband of hers in Texas eight years ago? It was
making him nuts. How, he asked himself, how could one guy have so
many problems when he had done nothing wrong?

And there was also something strange about this crazy thing
with Kate and Molly. That Edmund Chambers was a monster, a
first-rate lunatic. Why Molly? That was what he kept coming back
to. *Why Molly O'Connor?* Had she actually been a patient at the
clinic like the other victims of this creep? That was his angle, stalk-

ing women who had had abortions, not shoppers at the mall. But somehow, this possibility did not fit the Molly O'Connor that Richard knew. It just didn't fit, no matter how he considered it. Molly was not the type to risk getting pregnant. But maybe Molly was covering for Madeline. Kate said that her mother had acted erratically in the presence of the cops and was even talking about moving to the south of France. Was all of that a crazy emotional complication of some kind? But Madeline was too old to get pregnant. And further, Richard couldn't really imagine bitter, angry Molly coming to the aid of her hateful mother under any circumstances. That left Kate. Molly would certainly cover for Kate. *But not Kate.*

Suddenly, he saw it—as only he could.

Richard Landon put his head in his hands.

Oh my god, he thought. Sure, of course. She never told him she was pregnant. Of course by the time she knew, he was probably already with Vicki. Consumed with lust at the time, he could think only about fucking Vicki day and night. Now he *had* to think. They broke up in late March. He started dating Vicki in early April. It was so obvious. He groaned aloud. It *was* Kate. She had gained weight last summer. He had been shocked the day he had returned her things. Now it all made sense.

Then abruptly, he sat straight up, then stood up and walked briskly from the chair as if to escape further conclusions. There was something else. Something worse. Something far worse. Now he knew. It had to be. It all fit. *All of it.*

He picked up the phone, his heart skipping.

Kate answered after several rings. "Oh, *Richard*," she gushed. "Hi, how are you?"

From her enthusiastic tone, he could tell she assumed he was calling about the reunion he had so foolishly hinted at earlier. "Fine," said Richard, direct and serious. "I'm fine."

"Hold on, Richard," said Kate. He heard her tell Molly, "It's Richard." Then, still breathless, she was back. "Molly says hi."

"Listen, Kate. I need to see you. Something's come up. I want to see you now."

She knew something was wrong. "Richard, are you all right? You're not in any trouble, are you? Do you need money? Molly has some ideas if you really need to get some money."

"No. Nothing like that. I just need to see you. I could be out there in an hour or so."

She hesitated. This, she knew, wasn't about any reunion. "Well, all right. I mean, if you want to. Mother is in the city tonight. She's putting her condo on the market. She's selling the house here too, you know. She's planning to resign from the police board, and we're moving to Boca Raton. I was going to call you, to tell you, you know. Molly and I are making dinner tonight. Would you like to join us?"

"*Yes!*" He was barking at her, and quickly rebuked himself for it. Then, more patiently, "Yes, that would be great. I should be there around 4:30."

"Alright, Richard." Her voice was small and deflated, and held a timid sadness that wasn't there before. "See you in just a little while."

• • •

The drive, however, took longer than Richard expected.

It was bumper-to-bumper all the way on the Kennedy, then it opened up for a while, but then again Barrington Road was excruciating all the way to Lake Cook Road. Heading west, Richard was finally in horse country on this humid evening in Indian Summer. He recalled his previous trip out here last summer to return Kate's things and retrieve his own. And most importantly to end their dreary relationship. It had rained that day, he remembered. He'd gone there merely to appease Vicki. Had she not objected to the boxes of Kate's things, he never would have figured it all out. He had never expected this. Good god.

• • •

Normally the guard just waved him through.

This evening, however, was different. The gate, serious new galvanized construction replacing the old wooden frame, blocked his entry, and someone unfamiliar was stationed in the guard house. Richard stopped directly before a video camera, also new. "Richard Landon to see Kate O'Connor," he said.

"Do you have a picture ID, Mr. Landon?" asked the uniformed guard with professional politeness.

It could have been a military checkpoint, courtesy of Covington Security, Inc. The patch on the guard's uniform, the logo on the new video hardware, the sign warning that the property was under surveillance, all bore the bold red insignia of Covington Security.

Richard dug out his driver's license and handed it to the guard who carefully compared the photo to Richard. The guard seemed skeptical.

"Sorry, it's a few years old," Richard volunteered. "I had longer hair back then."

"Of course, no problem," said the guard recording his arrival time in a notebook. "Sorry for the delay, Mr. Landon. Mrs. O'Connor's orders. Everyone stops, even if you're expected. Have a good evening, Sir."

• • •

"Richard," said Kate greeting him warmly. "Come in."

He kissed her cheek, risking only the briefest glance into her eyes. They were guarded eyes, already worried.

"What do you think of Mother's new security system out there?" she asked, struggling to be casual. "She didn't waste any time. Think we're safe enough now?"

"I hope so," said Richard.

"How about a drink?"

He would have asked had she not offered. "Sounds good."

"Molly is getting ready to barbeque chicken out on the patio. Hope you're hungry."

Kate led the way to the bar off the family room. She was much slimmer now, thought Richard Landon. Just as he had feared. Almost back to normal.

"How about if I pour the drinks?" he asked.

"Sure, Richard. If you want."

Behind the polished teak bar, he splashed some bourbon for himself and poured a glass of chardonnay for her. "Let's sit down here for a minute," he said.

"Okay, Richard." She was nervous. "If that's what you want."

They settled in on a sofa facing the patio. Molly was starting the grill, and looking up, waved to them. Richard smiled, waved back and took a gulp of his drink. "Kate, listen to me. I have something to tell you. You have to listen to me. *I know.* I know everything. That's why I'm here. I want to talk to you about it."

She hesitated, then shrank slightly away from him. "Richard, what in the world are you talking about?"

He was prepared for evasion. "The clinic killer. Edmund Chambers. Kate, I know why he came here. *Can't you see that I know?* I know everything. I know about Rosco, too. Everything. What happened, and why."

Now she retreated even further, fear gathering in her eyes. "Richard, what are you saying? I don't understand."

It was Molly who spoke next. Her voice had a hard edge. "He's telling us that he knows, Kate." She was approaching them from behind, trailing an empty wine glass in her hand. When Richard turned around, Molly was addressing her sister, but looking directly at him as she made her way behind the bar, searching for, then locating the Chardonnay. "He knows everything. See, I told you he had it all figured out. I knew as soon as he called out of blue and wanted to come right over." Then she smiled warmly, and raised her glass. "A toast to Richard Landon," she proposed theatrically. "Congratulations, Richard. Good detective job."

"*Molly*," admonished Kate.

Richard began to feel as if everything had gone into slow motion.

Molly came around and sat down opposite them. "Relax, Richard. We trust you. We wanted to tell you at the funeral, but you were with *her*. The Blonde Bitch. We watched you two arrive. You were almost late. But now that she's no longer a problem, there's no reason we shouldn't tell you everything."

Kate reached over and touched his arm. "It wasn't your fault, Richard. I want you to know that. One thing just led to another. You couldn't have known. I didn't know I was late until later, weeks after we broke up and by then you were with her. And of course, I couldn't tell Mother. She would have disowned me. So I had to do something. Thank god I had Molly to rely on. She found that clinic.

It was the best in Chicago.

"It wasn't your fault, Richard, none of it. It was Rosco's fault. He ruined everything. He lost the money. Molly thinks he actually stole it and cooked the books."

"That's right. So he had to pay for his crime," concluded Molly. "And pay he did," she said suddenly gleeful. "He was great right to the end."

Richard just sat there, knowing and not wanting to know. Finally he found his voice. "So does anyone else know about this?"

Molly took a gulp of wine, then shook her head emphatically. "Don't worry, Richard. We were careful each step along the way. Really, we planned this for months. We staked out Rosco's place a dozen times. Then we waited until we got the perfect opportunity. Actually we were ready five other times, but Rosco kept screwing us up with all those women. We just couldn't get the little stud muffin alone. Finally our patience paid off and everything came together perfectly that night. His date left early and that storm gave us great cover. So relax. No one knows except we three."

Richard considered this gloomily.

Observing his solemnity, Molly was annoyed. "Really, Richard. We thought you would be pleased. After all, Rosco did fuck you and Kate royally. And we did your dirty work for you. Don't you think he deserved what he got?"

Richard struggled to compose himself. "No, no. It's not that. He did, he sure did deserve it. I mean Rosco was a son-of-a-bitch. It's just that this is a lot to comprehend at one time."

This seemed to appease Molly who nodded understandingly. "Another round?"

• • •

They had another, then another.

When the patio and pool lights automatically switched on, they all looked in that direction. "It's getting dark already," Kate commented and got up to turn on the Tiffany lamps on the end tables beside them. Then she struck a match to light several small bar candles in their little frosted vases. A bit of sun still reflected off the abundant brass and glass of the bar, giving much of the room a hazy golden glow.

Slightly drunk, Molly began to work on Richard again. "So you know why we did it, would you like to know how we did it?"

"Oh, Molly," said Kate. "*Really*."

Richard just listened, chilled.

"I don't think Richard needs to hear the details," protested Kate.

"Oh, yes he does. He needs to know everything. Don't you, Richard?"

He couldn't resist. "Okay, so how did you do it?"

"I'll tell you a little secret," Molly began drunkenly. "We saw you. That night? We saw you. We were parked right across the street. We couldn't believe it was you. Actually we were about to call to you to come join us, but that girl was just leaving. The black girl, the one they arrested. She got into a cab right next to us. Then we actually did call to you, as soon as she left, but you were already too far away to hear us. It was raining again and you had started jogging for home. Pity we didn't connect. You would have enjoyed yourself. I know we did.

"So we waited 10 minutes or so, and by then it was really pouring. We made a dash for the door and rang the bell like crazy. It took Rosco forever to let us in. I'm sure he thought it was the black girl coming back. "*Oh, Uncle Rosco, can we come in and use the phone?*" We said we had car trouble and we had forgotten to charge our cell phones. Rosco had already been drinking–we're sure he was drunk actually. I think he was doing a lot of coke, too. He had a really hard time getting his guard dogs into the laundry room so they wouldn't eat us alive. Then we asked for a drink and pulled a gun on him and marched him up to the bedroom. He put up no resistance at all. It was just so easy. We stripped him and tied him to the bed and gagged him. Just like we read in the papers about those other two guys. Then we took turns stabbing him with the ice pick from your tool box."

Richard sat straight up. "From *my* tool box?"

Molly giggled. "Yeah, we thought it was only fitting. Something personal, from you to Rosco. Because of what he did to you and Kate."

Kate looked away.

"What did you do with it when you were done?"

Molly laughed out loud. "Don't worry, Richard. I put it where no one could ever find it. Actually, you have it. I gave it to you the last time you were out here."

"*Molly*," said Kate, suddenly angry. "You *didn't*."

A smug Molly nodded to Kate, "Ah, but I did."

Katie, shocked and distressed, looked at Richard. "Richard, I'm so sorry. I didn't know."

And then Molly, returning to Richard, "Don't you remember?"

Richard nodded. He did remember Molly handing him a gaggle of various tools. And that curious smile. Thank god he had left all that stuff in his trunk–where it still remained. What if Miller had found the murder weapon when he searched the apartment?

"Rosco took forever to die," continued Molly. "We think he sort of sobered up about half way through. He started crying, really crying. I thought it was disgusting. Repulsive, a grown man like him, crying like a baby. He even offered to give you your money back, but we said it was much too late for that. And it was. Katie had already had the abortion, and you were with the Blonde Bitch. What good would money do at that point? Everything was wrecked, and Kate could never get away. We just wanted to watch him suffer. And suffer he did, for hours until the lightening hit the tree that crashed into the window and we had to get out of there pronto."

Molly drained her wine glass then closed her eyes, remembering. "I did the honors," she explained quietly. Then, to Richard's horror, she composed herself and became motionless, losing herself in thought. Her intention was clear. She was about to demonstrate the execution. Reliving the experience, she slowly raised her hands high, closed together as if grasping an unseen weapon. The pupils of her now gleaming eyes were enlarged, giving her a shark-like appearance. Her expression a wicked smirk. Then, trembling, with her face abruptly contorted into a fierce grimace and her eyes suddenly flashing, she brought her weapon down viciously, sinking it deep into a sofa pillow that served as her victim. "The classic dagger to the heart," she breathed, low and huskily, then halted and deliberately wiped her mouth with the back of her hand. Then, with her head hung low like a feeding animal, she glanced slowly from side to side surveying the corners of the room for the presence of any witnesses to this intimate horror.

No one said anything, no one moved.

Molly became motionless and closed her eyes, again breathing slowly and deeply, as if savoring fresh mountain air.

Richard took care to show nothing, and resolved to resist any eye contact.

Soon Molly opened her eyes and looked directly at Kate. She spoke in a little girl's voice, strange and detached. "I wasn't bad. Daddy wanted me to do it, so I had to. To protect you. He said so." Then with childish urgency, she blurted, *"But Kate, don't tell Mommy. Don't tell. Don't ever tell her anything. She hates me. You know that. She hates you, too. Don't tell."*

Molly closed her eyes was quiet again for a moment, and then began to gently rock back and forth. Then she began laughing, very softly. It was a child's laugh, that of a little girl, terrible, impossibly sad. Then she grew quiet again, and motionless, gradually becoming herself. At last she opened her eyes and smiled prettily, and suddenly gushing, she eagerly continued the murderous account as if rendering an amusing story about a prank on a friend. "And so, we split just in time. But we couldn't get the door closed because the tree branches got in the way. That meter-maid showed up a minute later. We almost walked right into her. That was really close, believe me. It was the only time I was really scared." She seemed completely herself now.

"And no one else knows about this?" asked Richard quietly, taking a chance. He had to know.

"Richard," exclaimed Molly, almost shouting, rebuking him outrageously. *"Stop worrying!* All is well. No one knows." She leaned toward him. *"Believe it,"* she hissed. *"We got away with murder!* The Police think they have their killer. And they must think she killed those other two guys, too." Then Molly sat back and changed her aggressive tone to something more intimate. "You know," she began, "It seems we did the real killer a favor. I'd say she owes us a thank you, if you asked me. Actually I looked for her at the funeral. I figured she'd be there, expecting that we'd be there, see? It was her one chance of at least getting close to us even if she didn't know exactly who we were. I figured the same thing–it would be our only

chance ever to connect, if we could only recognize each other. I really tried to spot her, but no luck. To tell you the truth, Richard, I thought the most suspicious woman in the entire church was the Blonde Bitch. She looked like a real sex killer–going to a funeral in a short dress like that without a bra. And all that mascara. She looked like a raccoon. A braless raccoon sex killer. All she needed to complete her outfit was a whip." Molly gave a wicked, contemptuous laugh. "Maybe it really *was* her. You're lucky you got away, Richard."

Richard, still cautious, chose not to respond to this nonsense, and looked away.

"Anyway," continued Molly, "*Stop worrying*. It's an open and shut case for us all."

"Well, not if Joe Guilliam has his way," said Richard quietly, now carefully crafting his challenge.

"We know," said Katie, still visibly unhappy, in a rare interjection. "I hope she goes free somehow."

"Well, I *don't*," said Molly suddenly again cold and remote. "Too bad she didn't kill him, and save us all this trouble."

"What about finger prints?" said Richard, taking another chance. "I assume you wore gloves of some kind.

"No, but we've never been finger printed for anything," Molly responded. "And we were careful, so how are they ever going to know? Actually we did think about wearing gloves, didn't we, Kate?"

Kate nodded, but reading Richard's grave reactions, now appeared to again be uncertain and afraid.

Molly returned to Richard. "You know, like a murder mystery on television," she said dead-panned. "But gloves, you know, seemed a little dramatic."

• • •

It was the thunder that returned their attention to the patio.

The rain, unexpected, came a few seconds later, sweeping heavy torrents that pounded the patio and lashed the windows. "Well, I guess we can forget the barbeque," pouted Molly, disappointed. Then, abruptly, she rallied. "Hey, guys, *I know*. How about if I heat up a pizza?"

38

During his late night trip home from Barrington, the rain had cleared, and Richard Landon drove beneath a moon so full and bright that he hardly needed headlights. Speeding down empty streets, his thoughts bounded from one shocker to another. *Kate!* He just never expected this from her. Of course he had not been wrong just on Kate. *He had been wrong about everybody.* Patrice Foster—now in jail due to his efforts—*was innocent.* Just as this Joe Guilliam had been saying all along. And Vicki. *What an idiot he had been!* The best thing he'd ever known, and because of the way she ventilated potatoes for baking, he accuses her of murdering Rosco Mink! The very crime that his former girlfriend committed *as a result of her relationship with him!*

Now Richard longed to call Vicki, but realized that he could not. How could he credibly reverse himself? How could he tell Vicki that he knew that she did not kill Rosco because now he knew who did? No, he would have to wait for Vicki to call him. There was no other way. Still, in his heart, he was euphoric. Vicki was innocent of this crazy deed! *Innocent! Innocent! Innocent! Goddamn innocent!* Now there was a good chance they could have a future together. That future was what Richard Landon wanted more than anything, and now it was up to him to make it happen.

Good god, what a night! And it wasn't over yet. Although the murder weapon had resided in his trunk without incident for almost three months, its presence there now prompted all sorts of distressing possibilities.

Discovery, if a zealous cop gave him a speeding ticket and decided to search him for drugs.

Discovery, because Miller realized he missed the car in the first search and was there now, waiting with a warrant for another.

Discovery, because Molly decided to set him up and simply called the cops.

Molly. Molly was the ring leader. Kate would never have even thought of something like this. It was all Molly's fault. Christ, the way she had contorted her face when she re-enacted the dagger to Rosco's heart. And those eyes! Thrilled, she had relived the murder right before his eyes, and savored every moment. Molly, he concluded, was truly crazy.

And in spite of his connections to all of these things, he was completely innocent. This was not fiction. It was fact, though understandably hard to believe. He had in fact committed no crime despite the appearance of motive and opportunity. But right now, the trail had better not lead to him, because he was fresh out of explanations for appearances and coincidences. Instead he began a game of "If Only." If only he had not left that message on Rosco's machine. If only he had not gone over there and run into Patrice Foster. If only Kate had taken her books and crockery with her back in March. If only Vicki had not so bitterly complained about the presence of those very things boxed in the closet. If only ...

At the end of the trip, nothing had happened, and he fell into bed exhausted at 2:15 a.m.

• • •

Richard had already determined what to do with the murder weapon at the bottom of the tool box in his trunk. Fingering Patrice Foster had been his personal mistake—a devastating error that could result in a devastating consequence. Not something he wanted to live with the rest of his life. Fair was fair. Patrice Foster had been wrongly accused by Richard, but she had not wrongly accused him when she easily could have. She simply told the truth. He had been at the bachelor party, but had not participated in the rape. That's what had happened, and that's what she had said. Not more, not less. So Richard meant to return the favor, to correct his mistake, and he meant to reverse it without implicating anyone else.

The next day he poked around until he located the ice pick in the corner of the toolbox, then picked it up with an old sock and brought it inside where he put on plastic gloves from the drug store. This precaution did seem a little dramatic, as Molly had so dryly commented. And besides, he had probably already grasped the handle that day she handed it to him a few months ago.

On the kitchen counter, the tool didn't look like much. Short, maybe four or five inches long, kind of narrow and slight. A scarred burgundy handle made of cheap soft wood, grooved for a better grip. He studied the weapon carefully. It was cheap in every respect. And brittle. The very tip had broken off. Richard absently tested it for sharpness and managed to inflict a small wound to his thumb. The bleeding was profuse and he had to get a band-aid. Again, he cursed himself for his stupidity. The jagged broken tip was probably sharper now than in its original condition. This thing that had caused him so much trouble was just piece of junk that happened to come in the boxed set of 50 tools for the well-equipped basement workshop. He was certain he himself had never used it. In fact he had not even known that he owned it. Over the years, he had already lost half the other tools. It was too bad he had not lost this one, too. Richard sighed in frustration as he went about his plan. Why him? *Really, why him?* Though it could not possibly be receptive to fingerprints, he wiped the ice pick carefully with a spray cleaner of industrial strength.

Next was a small plastic bag, selected from a new box, destined for a remote trash bin together with all other new purchases.

Then an envelope, also from a new box. This he addressed carefully, left-handed, in awkward block letters. Next about $3.00 of stamps, at least five times the likely amount necessary. The stamps, also new, had adhesive backs so no moisture was necessary. Richard mailed it Tuesday afternoon from the main Chicago post office to a *Tribune* reporter who had been covering the case.

And then he waited.

• • •

Thursday afternoon, a somber Morrison showed the weapon to Tow.

"There is no question," said Morri. "Lab says there is no doubt whatsoever. This is it."

Tow considered this development. The murder weapon, at last. He knew its implications were huge, and wondered how Beverly would cope with the news when it broke.

• • •

Joe Guilliam was, of course, euphoric.

As soon as the new evidence was introduced, Guilliam brought the prosecution's attention to another object, something already inventoried from the kitchen of the accused. It was a wicked seven inch ice pick from a kitchen drawer. "My client already has an ice pick as anyone can see. Laboratory tests determined weeks ago that it is not the weapon used in any of the three murders in question. And as anyone can see, my client's ice pick is a much larger heavy duty professional kitchen utensil compared with the real murder weapon, a cheap hardware store version. I submit that if she did have both–and I ain't sayin' that she did–but if she did, why would she choose the short, squat, hard to handle pick over the longer sleeker alternative that she kept handy in a kitchen drawer? I ask you to think about that.

"What I'm sayin' here is that that thing you got in the mail ain't hers. What you got there is a message from the real killer. She's sayin' you all got the wrong person. And I'd say this murder has just been *unsolved*. So now why don't you all do the right thing *and let my people go?*"

• • •

Then, later that afternoon, Joe Guilliam got his wish. Murder charges against Patrice Foster were dropped, and she was released.

• • •

The validity of Joe Guilliam's suggestion was demonstrated for the world to see the next day. Alexander Scott, a middle-aged insurance executive from Minneapolis, was found murdered, stabbed 33 times in a Midtown Manhattan luxury hotel. Under the bright lights of TV cameras Friday afternoon, New York Police Commander Lawrence Pinto held a news conference to confirm the details.

No, the weapon had not been located.

Yes, it was thought to be an ice pick.

And true, two small lighted candles were found on the night-stand.

The investigation pointed to a prostitute with long dark hair.

39

The serious beating that Ben had inflicted on Dennis over the soccer infraction resulted in immediate consequences. The police were now searching for them in King Gardens, making it too dangerous to return to Spider's apartment. "Dis bad," Spider told Ben. "Dis real bad. We cain't stay here now. Po-lices find us for sure." Individually, each of the boys was fairly inconspicuous. Even together they were still not especially noteworthy. But with Scab, they knew they had no chance. That left only one place to go.

• • •

In the boxcar they had no food and slept on the wooden plank floor with Scab snuggled between them. Spider quickly went to sleep, curled up with his head on his arm. Unaccustomed to such hardships, Ben had an especially difficult time. He made a pillow of his jacket, but sometime during the night he became so cold that he put it back on. The dropping October temperatures were miserable, but there was yet another distraction. Trains passing in the dark were simply terrifying. Sleek lighted passenger coaches streaked by in seconds while long shadowy freights rumbled on forever. In the darkness all of them were scary and the old box car seemed to shudder in a way that it never had on a warm sunny afternoon. Ben wondered how trains coming and going managed to stay on the right track at night, and imagined one of them colliding with the boxcar at any moment. Finally in his exhaustion, he slept hard.

They awoke hungry and chilled, and determined that Ben would go out for doughnuts and chocolate milk while Spider stayed with Scab.

• • •

The boxcar plan, however, did not last long. Ben was already broke, and Spider's money had run out in three days. "There one other thing we can do," Spider told Ben.

"Then we better do it," said Ben.

But Spider was hesitant. "Theys' name Viper Kings," he explained. "Kings for King Gardens. Can be Kings or Vipers. Either one, Viper Kings."

Ben understood. "Yeah? So?"

"Nitro, he need us to run for him."

"Nitro?"

"Right, Nitro. Nitro head of Kings."

"And what do we have to do?"

"Nitro, he need us to run for him."

"What do you mean?"

"Run. Dat what he always want from young boys. Dey all the time askin' me to join Vipers. Happen all the time."

"What does *run* mean?" said Ben.

"*Run.* Drugs. We young. Po-lices look mostly for older kids. When car come down street, we go up an' say '*What you want? Rocks or blow?*' Den we take da cash and toss da bag in da winda and go back to sidewalk."

"What do we get?"

"We get $40, maybe $50 fo' a good night. We jus' better doan get caught, dat's all."

"$50?" Ben was astonished. "For one night? $50?" Now he was excited. This sounded pretty easy.

Spider however showed no such enthusiasm.

Baffled, Ben looked at him.

Spider met his eyes. "Roosevelt a Viper King," he explained quietly.

• • •

On Sunday morning they made a cautious return to King Gardens with their new plan. When the predictable happened, they would accept. If nothing happened, they would have to take the initiative themselves. They were standing around a broken swing on the asphalt playground outside Spider's building when they were approached by the Kings. Instead of a solicitation, however, they received a direct message. The emissary, a sullen boy of about 16, simply walked up to them and said, "Nitro want to see you two chumps tonight."

Spider took a moment to answer, as though he were thinking it over. Finally, reluctantly, he nodded an acknowledgement.

The boy just turned his back on them and walked away.

When Spider remained silent, Ben quizzed him. "What's the matter?"

Spider just shook his head.

"Well, come on," Ben urged. "This is just what we wanted."

"I doan think so," said Spider, unhappy.

"Sounds to me like they want us to join. Just like you said."

Again Spider shook his head. "Something wrong."

• • •

Ben realized that if Spider was worried, they must be in real trouble. But what could he do? His home and mother had been taken from him. He had no money and only one friend. Now his sole recourse was to join the Viper Kings, which presented another problem—a very personal problem. Gangs like the Kings had killed his father. Ben kept thinking about this. It was a street gang that had done that terrible thing. After some thought, he managed to rationalize his plans only by concluding some *other* gangs had done that, not this one. He could join the Kings and still loath whoever had killed his father.

• • •

Spider knew exactly where to look for the Viper Kings. They operated out of a large second floor apartment in a middle building in the King Gardens. As the boys approached with Scab, Kings of all ages eyed them suspiciously.

Ben was frightened. He could see that he was surrounded by thugs and misfits. Many of them were young, but all were older than he and Spider. Most were loud and profane. All were intimidating, instantly focusing on them as if they were an opportunity for exploitation. It reminded Ben of getting trapped by the bill collector, only worse.

Then a young man stepped in their way, blocking their path into the lobby. "What you doin' here?"

"We here to see Nitro," said Spider.

The man looked at them doubtfully.

"Nitro, he want to see us," said Spider. "He tell us to come."

The man snorted contemptuously. "Wait here."

After a while, he returned and led them into the dark lobby, and again told them to wait.

Spider held Scab by his collar. Ben tried not to show fear though he was trembling.

Then it was their turn.

They followed the same man up the stairs to the second floor, then down a long corridor to the last apartment. The door was open. There were five or six men sitting and talking in the living room, and a few young women, too. The room grew silent as they entered. All deferred to a man sitting alone in the middle of a sagging sofa. The man was an adult, bearded and heavily tattooed about his arms and shoulders. He also wore a lot of jewelry, Ben noticed. Gold ear rings and several gold chains around his neck.

"Now what you got you here?" asked Nitro, already menacing. His voice was deep and raspy. "This here Lassie you got here?"

There was laughter all around.

"*Scab my dog,*" said Spider. Ben could see that Spider was already prepared for a fight. Now he was truly frightened. There was no possibility of surviving a confrontation with these people.

Apparently surprised by Spider's defiance, Nitro just snorted with contempt and looked away. He shook his head sadly. "Well, you all in trouble," he said flatly. Then he returned his penetrating gaze to them. "Why you in so much trouble?"

Spider was shaking, and drew Scab closer. "We didn do nothin'."

Nitro laughed, mocking him. "*You didn do nothin'?*"

Spider was at a loss to respond.

"Well, if you *didn do nothin'*, why the po-lice lookin' fo' the three of you?"

There was more laughter in the room.

Spider was shaking. "It wasn us started it. We jus' defendin' our-selfs."

"You got that Gang Crimes police after you, too." Nitro's raspy voice suddenly hardened. "They handin' out theys phone number, lookin' everywheres for two boys with a dog. *$1,000 reward.*"

Ben was frozen with fear. But he got Nitro's point. The police were searching for them, and he knew all about it–and he wasn't happy because of it.

Abruptly less intimidating now, Nitro continued. "You know, you lucky boys. You know me. You can work for me, belong to Kings."

Spider nodded.

"You want dat, Spider? You want to join Kings? Do like Roosevelt?"

Again Spider nodded.

Nitro looked to Ben.

Almost paralyzed with fear, Ben was silent.

"What you name?" asked Nitro, actually acknowledging Ben for the first time.

It was an effort to speak. "I'm Ben."

Nitro nodded. "Okay, I have a job fo' you two tonight. You go into city and smash car windows. Bring me what you find. Phones, CDs. Other stuff. You bring it all here tonight."

They both nodded immediately.

"And best you don't fuckup," warned Nitro, again serious and menacing. "I be waitin' on you."

They turned and rushed out, the laughter trailing behind them.

• • •

Out of the building, the boys kept walking until they were alone.

Under a street light, Spider explained the reasoning behind their assignment. "Nitro, he testin' us. He want to see if we got guts."

"So what do we do?" asked Ben, tremendously relieved, but still nervous.

"I show you," Spider told him.

・・・

The self-park lots were the easiest. A brick was all Spider needed to accumulate three phones and at least a dozen CDs. Ben also had some success in this way, and even stole a gym bag, perfect for carrying all their stolen loot. Phones and compact discs did not seem particularly valuable to Ben. He had another idea. "Why don't we just take some woman's purse?"

Spider thought about this, and surprised Ben by shaking his head. "That a lot more dangerous."

"Look, it happens all the time. It happened to my mother, and nobody ever caught those guys. The police don't even care if you rob a black woman."

Spider didn't respond.

Ben refused to give up. "I'll do it myself, then."

And he did. He stole three purses. The first was the easiest. He just jogged slowly past a young woman, grabbing the strap of her purse which broke as he ripped it off her shoulder. And then he sprinted away, leaving the aggrieved cries behind him. Next Ben approached an elderly couple in a parking lot. The woman never had a chance. Her husband was too feeble to even protest. The last episode however was much more involved. Like the first two, his victim here was simply no match for Ben. This time it was a black woman with a young boy of five or six. Ben came up fast from behind and knocked the woman to the ground with a vicious forearm. Then he picked up her purse. Her face contorted in pain, the gasping woman clamored to protect her little boy while Ben stood over them both. As the woman collected herself to call for help, Ben made a threatening move in her direction, his fists clenched, his face fierce. The woman shrank away and covered her child. Then Ben ran.

・・・

It was after midnight when they dumped their loot on Nitro's table. Six phones, 14 CDs and three purses.

"Well, what we got here?" asked Nitro.

"What you tell us to do," Spider responded.

When he saw the purses, Nitro seemed surprised. He opened each and emptied the contents on the table. The wallets still contained cash and credit cards. Seeing this, Nitro seemed particularly satisfied. "Good job," he told them. "You punks come by tomorrow night," he said, still nodding in approval. "And we get down to bidness."

40

Hoping it was Vicki, he picked up the desk phone in his study on the first ring. "Hello?"

But it wasn't Vicki.

"Richard!" screamed Molly. "You fucked us! We trusted you, you son-of-a-bitch, and you fucked us!" She was screaming and sobbing at the same time. "You are a rotten son-of-a-bitch, you know that?"

Stunned by the ferocity of this assault, Richard stood up at the desk to defend himself.

"*Molly*," said Richard, now physically bracing himself by leaning forward and planting his feet as if to meet a rushing opponent. "Take it easy. Nothing is going to happen."

"*You fucked us, you son-of-a-bitch! After all we did for you, you fucked us!*"

"Molly stop. Kate, are you there?"

"I'm here, Richard."

"Look, you guys. You are in no danger as a result of anything that I did. Do you hear me? I didn't talk to anyone. Let me tell you exactly what I did."

"You are a miserable rotten son-of-a-bitch. We did all of your dirty-work for you, and you fucked us."

"Look, all I did was send the pick to a newspaper reporter. First I wiped it clean. Then I mailed it. No note, no trace, no nothing. No one knows anything."

"See, Molly," said Kate. "I told you Richard wouldn't betray us. See?"

Molly didn't say anything, but he could hear her breath coming in gasps.

"Molly, Kate is right."

Molly sniffled.

They waited for her.

"Oh, yeah, so then why did you do it?"

"I had to. Patrice Foster was in jail because of me. I put her there. I couldn't let her fry."

"He's right, Molly. It wasn't right for her to pay for our crime. You know that."

Molly just scoffed at this. "*Yeah, right.*"

Richard tried again. "Look, they had to let her go anyway. As soon as they found that guy in New York on Friday, they would have had to let her go. Now the heat is off here, and on full blast there. I still have the Sunday *New York Times* right here. Big article. It says right on the front page that the killer probably moved to New York after things got too hot for her in Chicago because of Rosco. Now it looks like the same woman committed all four crimes and that woman is now in New York City. The cops there say they're looking for a prostitute around 30 or so with long brown hair. You are actually safer. The description doesn't fit you and the search has shifted to New York."

Molly's response was only a contemptuous snort.

"Look," said Richard. "That's what the *New York Times* says. Long brown hair, early 30s. That's not either of you. You can read it for yourself–I'll save the paper for you."

"You do that, you son-of-a-bitch," snarled Molly, and hung up.

"I better go, Richard," said Kate, obligated as usual to comfort her distraught sister.

Richard Landon sat down at his desk for a few minutes to compose himself.

• • •

He reread the *Times* article again. For future reference, with a red pen he circled the title and severely underlined the discussion of the prostitute with long brown hair. Then put the paper in a drawer for safe keeping. He sat back, and reflected for a moment. He had hoped that Vicki would have called. There was no way to vindicate Vicki without revealing Kate and Molly's secret. He would just have to wait for her to call him.

And Molly! Molly, he concluded, was crazy. Completely crazy. She frightened him.

41

Nitro lined them up side-by-side and gave them their instructions. "You work together," he said.

Very nervous, Spider and Ben both nodded emphatically.

This response was a little too enthusiastic for Nitro, and he tried to slow them down some. "Okay, now here three bags of crack. You know what's crack?"

Again, both boys nodded vigorously. Spider seemed to know all about everything. Ben, however, had no idea what crack really was. A drug, something dangerous. Something so inappropriate that his mother had never even included it in her rules.

With clearly high expectations, Nitro spoke most directly to Spider. "Now you know what to do?"

Again, Spider nodded, then recited their instructions. "We just playin' on the sidewalk and wait."

"That right." Nitro assessed them for a moment, and then continued reasonably. "Each bag $200. You got it? $200 for each bag. Three bags. That $600. Your share $50–if you do right."

The boys, just so anxious, nodded immediately.

"You turf Adams and Monroe on Lane. You understand?"

Spider managed to speak. "Uh huh."

"Just doan you fuck up," warned Nitro.

• • •

It was just twilight when they got started.

Spider seemed to know what to do. Inside his light jacket, he had the three bags, and a ball. On the corner was a four-way stop sign around which operated several businesses. There was a liquor store, a small grocery and a tire repair shop. All dilapidated, but thriving. Spider selected a spot on Lane Street just down the block under some trees and near a street light. "Okay," he said nervously. "We here."

Ben was following silently, but observing intently.

Again Spider surveyed his choice. Something was bothering him. "We got to move away some more," he told Ben.

"Why, what's the matter?"

Spider pointed to the brick wall of the building across the street. Ben looked. The dark brick was nearly white with graffiti. "What?"

Spider led the way across Lane Street to get a closer look. "There." He pointed to a drawing of a crown with five curved points. It was the kind of thing a king might wear. "Vice Royals," said Spider. "That their sign."

Ben tried without success to absorb what he saw. It could have been a wall of Egyptian hieroglyphs.

Again Spider shook his head. "Look," he said. "This bad. Vice Royals movin' in. See, they make Viper King sign upside down. Insult to Kings."

Ben looked. It was a drawing, a very good drawing, of a cobra-like figure wearing a crown, but the whole thing was inverted.

"We got to be careful," said Spider. "Fo' sure, theys Vice Royals aroun' here."

Ben didn't know what to think, and as always, he deferred to Spider.

Spider's next choice in locations was similar to the first in most respects, but provided an alley as an emergency exit. "Okay," he said. "This better—we can get out. Now we play ball with Scab. When car come and stop, I go over. You stay right with Scab."

"Okay," said Ben, very nervous.

• • •

Their first customer showed up just minutes later.

A gray Ford with two men accelerated from the corner stop sign, and then slowed suddenly. Both men, young white men, watched the boys intently as they cruised by. Spider stopped and returned their stare. With this the Ford suddenly accelerated and bolted down the block only to reappear at the corner stop sign a minute later. Again the car drew near, slowing for them. Spider was bolder now, walking in the direction of the street.

The Ford stopped and Spider approached.

Ben watched Spider lean over, but could see nothing else. It was all over in seconds. Spider promptly returned to playing ball with Scab while the car sped away. Essentially the same scene was re-enacted twice more before dark, and they were through for the night.

When they returned so early with $600, Nitro was pleased.

Their share was $50 as agreed, the cash coming from the grimy bills they had collected.

• • •

The next night they were provided eight bags by a handler named Rapper. Rapper was a frightening, strange looking character, thought Ben. Rapper had a serious case of acne, but he also was badly scarred along the whole of his right arm and neck. These were huge ugly welts that were disturbing just to see, and reminded Ben somewhat of Scab's injury.

On the street, Rapper kept his distance.

Spider explained to Ben that there was always danger in contacting another gang member because the police were eager to crash a meeting that would yield carriers, handlers, money and drugs. But there was also danger in just holding either drugs or money. Rivals were constantly robbing carriers. The boys were strictly accountable for themselves once in possession of the goods. That much was very clear.

Again they started just before dark, repeating the ball playing with Scab. This time it was Ben who approached the first car. In seconds he had made the sale, and rushed back to the safety of the sidewalk.

They had sold six bags when they heard sirens and quickly ducked down the alley.

Moments later three blue and white squad cars arrived from different directions to break up a fight at the tire repair shop. Although they were never in any danger, it took the boys an hour to sufficiently recover their nerve to return to business.

. . .

Ben learned fast, and between them they had made $150 in three days. That was $75 for each of them! Ben could not earn $75 selling *Tribunes* for Harold Lamb in a week!

Now he was eager to do the business. Further, their teamwork with Scab was very convincing as well as effective. Most people simply drove right by them, while real customers knew just what to look for. On their fourth night they were given 12 bags. They started work at their usual time, but it wasn't long before competition arrived wearing a baseball jacket. He was about 17, and glared at them from across the street.

"Bad," said Spider. "Vice Royals, they cuttin' in on us."

. . .

It was a warm autumn night, and there was a lot of traffic looking for drugs. It didn't take long for the boys to determine their plight. When a car approached, their competition raced ahead of them. He was a lot faster and bolder, forcing them to move quickly and to take more risk.

By midnight, they were down to their last two bags, and weary of the new pressures. They should have been done hours earlier. Ben was making another sale when his customers, two black men, were distracted by the other boy who had also approached their car. Ben, too, looked in his direction. It was then that one of the men suddenly reached into Ben's open jacket and grabbed both bags. "Go!" said the man to the driver. Immediately, the driver saw his advantage and the car sped off.

Ben was left just standing there, his jacket open and his eyes wide.

Observing all of this, Spider looked stricken, and typical of his reaction to extreme stress, was almost unable to speak. They were

$400 short.

"What do we do?" asked Ben.

Spider shook his head unhappily. "We in trouble. Nitro, he warn us. He say 'Doan fuck up,' and we fuck up bad."

"Come on, it wasn't our fault. We were robbed."

"Nitro, he doan care about dat for nothin'."

"Why don't we just take all the money and run?"

Spider was visibly appalled by this suggestion, and quietly rejected the idea. "When Kings find us, Nitro, he kill us for dat."

• • •

Later they turned over their proceeds for the night.

While Rapper was occupied counting the wad of cash, the boys made their escape into the night, retreating to the one place they were safe.

• • •

The next morning, they were again cold and hungry, and right back where they had been a week earlier. However now they were certain to be hunted by the Kings. Only hunger was a more immediate concern. At least with money, they could eat. So Ben walked seven blocks to a McDonalds and hurried back with bags of pancakes and sausages. Starving, he couldn't wait to open the bags.

When he returned to the box car, he discovered that he had crawled directly into a trap. Observing Ben's sudden shock, Nitro said, "That right. You in real trouble now. Get you scrawny ass in here."

Spider and Scab now sat in one corner under the gaze of Nitro, Rapper and two younger thugs. Ben joined Spider, realizing that they had been followed the previous night.

Nitro immediately turned on them. "*You two owe me*," he snarled. He was very angry, standing over them. "*You stole from me*."

Spider looked sick.

Seeing this, Ben immediately despaired. Still, he managed a response. "We didn't steal from you. Two men stole from us. They took two bags and drove off without paying."

Nitro just snorted. Then suddenly he leaned down, screamed at Ben. "I tol' you doan fuck up. An' you didn listen for shit, did you?"

Ben tried to withdraw without much success. He was squeezed with his back to the wall when Nitro took out a gun and pointed the barrel directly at him. *"You stole from me and from the Kings! Admit it. Admit it or I'll kill you right here and now."*

Terrified, Ben tried to speak, but could not.

"Ad-fucking-mit it or you're dead."

Ben nodded emphatically. "We did it," he managed to say quietly. "We stole from you."

Nitro again leaned over, and with one hand, lifted Ben and threw him across the width of the car. Ben landed hard on his back. The pain shot up to his neck, and he realized he was out of breath. He was too frightened to move.

"You little bastard," Nitro screamed. "I should kill both of you right now."

Then there was a long moment when nobody said anything. Rapper and the other two guys quietly backed away from the action.

Finally Nitro spoke again, evenly, but menacing. "Now I have a job for you," he said still holding the gun. "Vice Royals, they cutting in way too much. This here Slasher's plan."

Ben took Slasher to mean the head of the Vice Royals.

"Theys six shells in here. I want you to go to North Park tonight and put all six in Slasher head. Rapper show you who. You two be dere. You kill dat fucker. He cuttin' in on da Kings and he got to die."

Spider stared morosely at the gun until Nitro put it away.

"You understand me, Spider?" asked Nitro. "You two owe me. You know dat. You be dere and you do right." He glared at them both, waiting for their response.

Too frightened to speak, both boys nodded.

This Nitro accepted. "Now get da fuck outta here," he growled.

Immediately they both got up to leave. Spider discretely patted his thigh, signaling Scab to join them.

Observing this, Nitro stopped them. "No fuckin' way," he said. "You two punks take off, but Lassie here go wid me."

42

It was Barry Stern calling. "The results are back, Detective. You know, your request about the disposition of those four citations. I just got the results."

"So what did you find out?"

"They're all paid. All four, the same date. Remitted by Covington Security, Inc."

Tow couldn't believe it. "You're telling me that a detective agency paid those tickets?"

"Covington Security. That's all I have."

"All four, paid together?"

"Yeah. One check to the City of Chicago. I have a copy of the check right here. Two hundred and ten dollars."

"Don't tell me. I'll bet the date of the check was the first Monday in July."

It took Barry a moment to confirm this. "Yeah, that's right. How did you know?"

• • •

They met again at the Rainbow Cafe.

"Do you think it's good?" Tow was asking Harold Lamb if his information was reliable.

Harold nodded. "I think so. I mean, it all fits. She's a Viper King. She says Nitro has gone ballistic about the Vice Royals moving into King drug turf. She says tonight is the night. The boys are supposed to hit a Vice Royal in North Park. Tonight, 11:00, under the angel. That's what she says. She's the bait. She's risking her life seeing me and wanted the money before she would talk. So I paid up."

Tow nodded.

It all did fit, thought Tow. A young girl desperate enough to risk information for money. A gang snitch reporting that two young boys–Nitro had their dog–were being forced to kill a rival gangbanger over drug turf. Nothing uncommon here. Employing children to kill rivals was a good strategy for gangs. And North Park, infested with street gangs, was a premiere location for a hit. Drug deals under the huge marble statue of the angel were frequent. Shootings and stabbings were normal business practices. It wouldn't be the first time several kids shot a gangbanger to death in that very location.

"I'll be there at 10:00 with plenty of backup," said Tow, mostly thinking out loud. "I want to stop this thing before it happens. Get Ben back to his mother and get some protection for Spider. Maybe even put Nitro where he belongs."

Then he turned to Harold Lamb. "You've done a great job, Harold. I owe you for this. You know that. I owe you."

"Just you be careful, Tow."

"Don't worry about me, Harold. I'll be fine."

"I'll tell you somethin'," said Harold Lamb.

"What's that?"

"I believe we're getting too old for all this street gang carrying on. That's what I believe."

Tow thought about this. "I know you're right, Harold. And you've done your part and more. I'd say it's time you got out."

Harold Lamb was slow to respond. "It just never ends, do it? After all these years of tryin', it just never ends."

"No, I suppose it never really ends," said Tow. "It's the drugs, that's the problem. Some day that will change. Look what happened with prohibition. Gang warfare, back then. Blood in the streets. Just like drugs now. Same thing. They repealed prohibition to stop the killing. Someday this will change, too. They'll make drugs legal, put a lot of restrictions on them and tax them to kingdom come. Presto, no more blood in the streets."

"You're right," said Harold with a rare hard edge in his voice. "But how many people got to die in the meantime?"

Tow thought about this for a minute. What do you say to a man who has buried two children murdered by gangs? "You made a difference, Harold," Tow said quietly. "And you helped me make a difference. You've got to believe that."

Harold Lamb looked away and considered this for a moment then returned to Tow. Again, in his good natured way, he said, "I do. I really do. And now, my friend, you be careful, you hear?"

43

Of course, they realized that only one of them could pull the trigger. Nitro had ordered Spider to do the job, but still Ben offered, only to be refused. "No, it my job," Spider said. "Scab my dog."

"Then we'll go together and do it together," said Ben. "It'll be safer if we're together."

Spider didn't say anything, but Ben knew he was grateful.

Clearly, Spider did not want to do this. He grew especially quiet, as he typically did under great stress, and seemed to want to be alone. All of this Ben could understand. But they had no choice. Nitro would kill Scab if they failed, and probably kill them, too.

• • •

North Park was beautiful at this time of year as the trees turned colors yielding leaves that lay in crisp bunches everywhere. The Park was old and vast, and included a swimming pool and a greenhouse as well as numerous gardens and fountains. But there were many less communal places as well, and that isolation was the attraction of the location.

At about 8:30, Ben and Spider found Rapper in a parking lot.

"It's about time," complained Rapper as he handed the gun to Spider.

The pistol proved to be much heavier than Spider expected, and he immediately struggled with the weight. "Use two hands. And get up real close," said Rapper. "Aim for his head. And pull the trigger until all the bullets are used." Rapper looked at Spider. "You understand me now? Keep pulling the trigger until all the bullets gone.

You'll hear click, click, click. You understand me?"

Spider nodded and carefully put the heavy weapon inside his jacket as though it were a bomb ready to go off.

Ben's heart was already racing.

The plan was to loiter around until the target arrived. According to Rapper, Slasher had been set up to expect a young woman who wanted to join the Royals. On a mild autumn evening in the middle of the week, there would be a lot of people around. Witnesses were an issue here. Slasher would push the girl for an early meeting, with many people still around. Nitro would want a later time with fewer observers. But if the meeting were proposed late into the evening, Slasher would certainly take more precautions, or might even refuse altogether. Already the timing of the hit had been changed twice. It was set now for 9:00 p.m. Rapper would identify Slasher. Spider and Ben would fall in behind him, and Spider would open fire from behind at point blank range. Then they would run.

• • •

Ahead of them now, a girl lingered under a lighted statue of an angel. She was pretty, thought Ben, just a teenager. She wore a short skirt and high heeled boots. Ben recognized her as one of the girls they had seen with Nitro that first night. Other people were strolling past, in no hurry, just enjoying the park. Just minutes later, two men walked passed them in the direction of the girl who now stood still as a frightened fawn. Rapper pointed to the taller of the two, and the boys walked out of the shadows and fell in behind the men. Hearing footsteps in the leaves closing behind them, the men turned sharply. Spider was still fumbling with the heavy pistol as the men bolted into the darkness. Instantly there was a shot, then Spider fell, dropping the pistol without firing it. "My leg," he cried rolling away. Ben dropped down beside him. Spider was curled up, holding his thigh and grimacing with pain.

Then there were more shots, rapid shots coming from the same place. They were quick pops, like firecrackers going off. People were scattering into the darkness.

Ben picked up Spider's gun and turned toward the two men who were now on their feet running in different directions as they passed the lighted angel. Ben ran, too, following Slasher out of the Park, into an alley. At the end of the alley he had the man cornered under a light. Slasher was a big man, and very muscular and scary, but unarmed. Conquering his fear, Ben moved closer. Slasher had nothing in his hands. If he had been armed, Ben reasoned, he would have already been shooting. Instead he was panicked, backing up against the brick wall of a building. "Look, man," he told Ben. "We can make a deal. You don't need the Kings. Nitro is fuckin' crazy. He'll turn on you and kill you. He will. He's fuckin' crazy. You know that. He'll kill you sure as shit. You come join the Royals an' me an' you, we'll forget all this shit."

Ben said nothing and instead took careful aim, just as he had done with the bill collector. He knew just what to do this time, and closed the distance on his target. This time he would not miss.

Reading this, Slasher was completely panicked.

Ben was just about to pull the trigger.

"*Don't shoot!*" a voice called from the street. It was a man's voice. The voice of a man severely out of breath. "*Don't! Police! Don't shoot!*" The words came between gasps.

Ben froze.

The voice was closer now. "Benjamin, I'm a policeman," shouted Tow. "Put–the–gun–down."

Ben looked behind him. He recognized the figure. It was the policeman. The one. And he had a gun in his hand.

"Don't pull that trigger, Benjamin," Tow called again. "I'm a policeman. I'll arrest Slasher for shooting at Spider and you. He'll go to jail for that. Just let me do it from here."

Ben was listening, but kept the gun trained on Slasher who screamed, "*Don't shoot me! Shoot the fuckin' cop!*"

Abruptly Tow realized that once more he was facing a young black boy–again with his weapon drawn–the same nine millimeter Smith and Wesson semi-automatic pistol that he had drawn on Calvin James. *No,* thought Tow. *Not again. Not for anything.* "Watch, Benjamin," he said. "I'm putting my gun down." Tow laid the gun carefully on the ground, and put his hands at his sides.

Now Ben's gun wandered slowly in Tow's direction, until the barrel was pointed right at him.

Slasher made a move, but Ben instantly refocused his aim on him.

"Shoot him," screamed Slasher. "Do it! Shoot the fuckin' cop now."

"Don't shoot anyone, Benjamin," said Tow.

"He shot Spider," said Ben not taking his eyes off of Slasher.

"Spider is okay. And Slasher will pay. I know all about the Vice Royals, and I saw everything that happened tonight. I'm a witness. He'll go to jail for shooting Spider."

"They have Scab. They'll kill him. Nitro said so."

"I'll arrest Nitro, too. And I'll get Scab back for you and Spider. Just don't pull that trigger, Benjamin. Do what your father would tell you. I know about your father, too. Lydia Cooper told me what happened. How he was killed by a street gang. By a creep like Slasher here. Now do what your father would want you to do, and I'll put all these gangbangers in jail for him."

Ben was surprised that the policeman knew all of this, and hesitated, considering what he had heard. There was one more matter. "You arrested my mother."

"*Your mother is free.* She's home. She's been looking everywhere for you."

Now Ben's anger yielded. Justice for his father, his mother back home. And Spider would approve.

Tow's heart pounded.

Ben lowered the gun.

Tow picked up his own.

"*Oh, man,*" moaned Slasher.

44

They had to hurry.

"It's now or never," Joe Guilliam told Tow. "Her resignation is effective at the end of the week."

Guilliam insisted that Madeline O'Connor could not really deny them this. And Tow agreed with his assessment having witnessed Guilliam's mastery over the media in the Rosco Mink affair. Guilliam would crucify her in public if she had resigned without hearing them out. So Guilliam called and arranged a late Friday afternoon meeting, Mrs. O'Connor's last official act as Chair of the Civilian Police Board.

• • •

They met in Madeline O'Connor's private office, the same place in which she had exploded in fury following Tow's hearing only four months earlier. At that time she condemned Tow as a disgrace to the Chicago Police Department, and snarled that she personally would make sure that he never would be allowed to return to the Gang Crimes Unit. Now she sat at her desk, a court reporter to her right, and two members of the Civilian Police Board to her left. Before them, Tow sat with Beverly's hand in his. Next to her sat Commander Morrison. Having relocated to Fort Worth, representatives of the James family were unable to attend on such short notice.

• • •

"Madame Chairman, this young man is Paris Williams," began Joe Guilliam. "He is among several key witnesses for the prosecution relating to the major gang bust involving the Viper Kings a few weeks ago. We should all be grateful for his courageous testimony against this violent element of our city. We should also be grateful to Detective Miller and Commander Morrison for their roles in that case, which also has yielded what I believe will be the final resolution of another case that we are all quite familiar with."

Despite Guilliam's professional demeanor, the tension in the room was considerable.

"Paris is here with us now to provide testimony regarding that matter. There is no question that he is the person who witnessed the events surrounding the shooting of Calvin James a year ago. His fingerprints match several of the unknowns on the toy gun in evidence. He is here because he wishes to tell us something important.

"Paris, just tell us in your own words," coaxed Joe Guilliam. "Just tell us what happened."

Paris Williams, slumped in a wheel chair with one leg propped up, nodded, and then for the next few minutes, recounted what had happened that July evening on a rooftop in the Lyndon Baines Johnson Homes. How he and his dog, Scab, were visiting this boy, Calvin. How Calvin and he had been playing with fireworks. How Calvin had behaved—so often like a baby. How the big po-lice had told him twice to put his gun down. How Calvin had aimed it so directly, just as when they were playing. How the big po-lice didn't know. How he and Scab had run away.

Then there was a tense silence while they waited for Mrs. O'Connor to speak.

Finally she asked the obvious. "Young man, why didn't you come forward with this information before?"

Paris struggled for words. "I was afraid."

"*You were afraid?*" Now Madeline O'Connor took this opportunity to glare at Tow. Then returning to Paris, she coaxed, "Afraid of Detective Miller?"

Paris shook his head. "No. I wasn't afraid of him. I wasn't never afraid of him. Not that. Roosevelt, he my brother. He in the penitentiary. He tell me, 'doan do nothin' wrong or you be like me, an judge ain't *never* gonna let me out of this place.'"

Joe Guilliam intervened quietly. "Paris's older brother is serving

42 years for murder in the first degree. I believe we can all understand what Roosevelt Williams was trying to tell his younger brother. However, Paris received his message literally, and thought the act of providing the fireworks involved on the night of Calvin James' death would result in a sentence similar to that of his brother."

Tow listened with dismay. Beverly gasped quietly. Morrison shook his head and grimaced. It was, thought Tow, somehow always something like this.

Mrs. O'Connor was silent, obviously considering her situation. There was no way out–she had to reverse her July decision. "The court reporter will amend the record to include the testimony we have heard today." Here she stalled briefly; she had no choice but to go on. "And Detective Miller, you may return to your former position in the Gang Crimes Unit, if that is still your wish."

They all looked at Tow.

No one said anything, allowing him a respectful moment for reflection. It had all come to this. All the pain, the remorse. All the second guessing, and all the punishment. It was over. A year ago, he would have been euphoric with this vindication. But now it was an oddly empty victory, and Tow already realized why. There was something–someone–now more important, far more meaningful in his life. She was sitting next to him. Last night she accepted his proposal. They would marry in a few months. But now the question before him was Gang Crimes.

Was it still his wish to return to Gang Crimes?

Tow began to speak, but found he had to clear his throat. Finally he managed to quietly say, "No. It is not my wish to return to Gang Crimes. I have a new job in Homicide, and that's where I intend to stay as long as Commander Morrison wants me."

Smiling, Morrison offered a handshake and his congratulations. "You've done a great job, Tow. I'm just glad to have you on board," he said. "You have a home as long as you want it."

Mrs. O'Connor seemed surprised and unhappy with this development. "Very well, Detective Miller, if you're sure that's what you want?"

"It is," said Tow, declining this second invitation.

Then Tow was aware that Beverly was leaning over to kiss him.

"I love you," she whispered.

"And now," said Madeline O'Connor, "This case is, at last, closed."

• • •

Only Joe Guilliam thought to applaud.

His was a vigorous applause, theatrical and robust, and accompanied by several hoots and whistles. Then with that fabulous smile, he cheerfully proposed they all accompany Mrs. O'Connor, who was not smiling, to the podium just erected outside in order that she might address the many waiting TV and newspaper reporters who had somehow been tipped off about the story.

Peter Gallagher

45

T he next morning they were still in bed, sipping coffee and reading the papers.

"Oh, Tom, listen to this one," Beverly said holding the *Tribune* up in order to read the story. *"Mayoral Candidate Resigns. Madeline O'Connor, Chairwoman, resigned from the Civilian Police Board effective yesterday. Widely considered the first viable woman candidate for mayor since Jayne Byrne, Mrs. O'Connor also announced her retirement from the Democratic Party and active politics in order to pursue personal and business interests. The long time Chicago resident plans to relocate to Boca Raton in the near future.*

Mrs. O'Connor was influential in the racially charged case in which a Gang Crimes Detective was removed from his position in connection with the shooting a year ago of an 11-year-old boy in the Lyndon Baines Johnson Homes. Detective Thomas Miller was completely exonerated in eyewitness testimony before Mrs. O'Connor late yesterday. 'It was my greatest pleasure to finally see justice done,' said Mrs. O'Connor."

Tow showed little interest in reading the article.

"There's another column about her here. 'Mayor Praises Retiring O'Connor.' Politicians are always happy to see other politicians retire, you know. Lots of photos. Now look what time it's getting to be," she said lowering the paper as she looked at the clock. "I'd love to lie around and chat, but this girl has to get to work. The name on the door changes Monday morning, you know. Now it'll be Nickols Capital Management."

"That's great, Beverly," said Tow. "Really, that's marvelous."

She smiled happily and returned to her coffee and a last look at

304

the paper. "Oh, look, Tom. I *told* you Richard Landon was engaged to one of the O'Connor twins. See? It was Katherine. *I told you so.*"

"What did you say?"

"I said Richard Landon was engaged to Katherine O'Connor. He's right here in this picture. I told you so back when."

Tow put down his coffee. He didn't remember any of this. "Can I see that?"

Beverly handed him the paper. The photo was from a political fundraiser for a congressional race a year earlier. Tow read the caption carefully. Centered was Mrs. O'Connor flanked on the right by a daughter, Eleanor, and her husband, Paul Steward, and on the left by twin daughters, Molly and Katherine, with her fiancé, Richard Landon.

"Jesus Christ," said Tow. *"Holy Jesus Christ."*

"What?" said Beverly, already alarmed. "What's the matter?"

"Well, I think your problem is finally about to be solved," he said. "Permanently."

She considered this for a moment. "If this is really the end, we'll manage." Then she seemed to fold. "Oh, Tom, do you really think it'll end this time?" Her tears were just beginning. She reached over and touched his arm. "It's all so crazy. And now we're going to go through it all again? Do you really think it will finally be the end this time?"

"Beverly, I think so," he said holding her eyes. "I really think so."

• • •

Tow called Morrison at home.

"It's Saturday," Morrison complained. "It's time we all had a break. I promised Beth last week that we'd drive up to the lake today. I hope this is important, Tow."

"It is, Morri. Trust me, it is."

• • •

Morrison was even more unhappy when Tow walked into his office a little later. "I hope this is good."

Tow slapped the paper on his desk. *"Take a look at that picture."*

Morrison picked up the paper and looked closely at the photo. "Madeline O'Connor. She's retiring." He looked up at Tow. "So what? We should all be grateful."

"Look again. *Who else is in that picture?*"

Morrison made an attempt to study the photo, but again returned to Tow. "This isn't sour grapes, is it? I know the woman made your life miserable, but she made it up to you yesterday, I'd say. That Joe Guilliam is goddamn ruthless. The way he set her up was vicious. She sure as hell had it coming, but I mean, those reporters worked her over like a piece of meat in front of the cameras. Her career went out on a stretcher."

"Morri, look," said Tow. "This has *nothing* to do with any of that. *Who do you see here?*"

Morrison looked closely, but recognized no one.

"Well, read the caption."

He did. "Richard Landon?"

"Right. *Richard Landon engaged to Katherine O'Connor.* The same Richard Landon we suspected of killing Rosco Mink who lost $300,000 of Richard's money. Richard Landon whose engagement to Katherine O'Connor must have ended sometime before Rosco Mink was killed." Here Tow paused, allowing it all to sink in. "And after we connect all these dots, I think we'll also find out what Edmund Chambers was doing on the O'Connor estate."

Morrison was pale. This was all leading to a place he really didn't want to go. Understandably, the last thing he wanted to do was to challenge Madeline O'Connor just as she was about to disappear. Cornering an already defeated foe was simply not wise. Why not just enjoy the victory?

"There's more." Tow told him about the ticket report, explaining how Edmund Chambers had carelessly accumulated parking tickets while stalking Joanne Rice. "Madeline O'Connor had four tickets in the immediate area of Rosco Mink's home," concluded Tow, "all within four weeks prior to his death."

This was too much for the reluctant Morrison. "Well, shit, Tow," he snapped. "That doesn't *prove* anything."

"Well, then why would Covington Security pay all four tickets the Monday morning after the murder? Come on, Morri–*this is a detective agency trying to hide evidence the day after the crime.*"

Now Morrison sat back and shook his head slightly. Then he exhaled slowly, and looked out the window for a long moment. It was drizzling. A crane was lifting a steel beam to the roof of the building across the street. Finally he looked back at Tow and in a quiet voice he said, "I sure as hell don't know what's going on here. But I think you're absolutely right on the big picture." Again he returned to the crane, studying it. "Madeline O'Connor," he said solemnly, his gaze fixed on the crane. "May god help us."

• • •

Morrison took an understated approach.

No sirens or flashing lights. Just he, Tow, Sweeney and Lynch. They found Mrs. O'Connor at her North Michigan Avenue condominium. The doorman phoned the residence and advised her that she had visitors. "Commander Morrison and several other police officers are here to see you."

She didn't even bother to fake anything.

"It's 43A," the doorman said as he buzzed them in.

The elevator was plush–smoked beveled mirrors, dark woods and a burgundy carpet. No one said anything. Morrison, thought Tow, looked nervous.

At 43A, Tow rang the bell.

Madeline O'Connor opened the door and let them in. She seemed to recognize only Morrison. "I've already called my attorney," she told him. "I really have nothing to say until he gets here."

"You must understand that we will need to interrogate your daughters as well," Morrison said politely.

She nodded.

Morrison then turned to Lynch. "I want search warrants for this apartment and for the house in Barrington as soon as possible. Both in connection with the murder of Rosco Mink."

Hearing this, Madeline O'Connor sat down heavily on an ornate sofa that offered a spectacular view of the Lake. Her tears came in long anguished sobs, interrupted only by the briefest sorrowful glance in Tow's direction. It was a look that said everything.

So, thought Tow, someone else had been playing detective, too. *She knew.* It was just what he suspected. She didn't do it herself, but she certainly knew who did.

46

I t was almost midnight.

Richard knew it was her even as he was reaching for the phone. He had planned to call her tomorrow, but she, the aggrieved party, was already calling him.

"Hi," Vicki said softly. "I can't sleep. All of this about Rosco is just all over television."

"I'm sorry," he said, struggling to compose his apology. "I was an idiot. I'm sorry. I wanted to call this afternoon when I heard the news, but I guess I just didn't know where to begin. I'm sorry."

"I told you I had nothing to do with Rosco," she said quietly.

"I know. I don't know what I was thinking. I was just an idiot."

"Well at least now the police know we didn't do it."

"That's a relief, but the rest of it is pretty bizarre. The Twins thought Rosco cooked the books. By screwing me, he screwed Kate. So they took revenge."

"I doubt that Rosco cooked the books, but I don't have any sympathy for him." Here she paused for a moment, obviously composing her thoughts. "I think we've all made some mistakes," she said completely changing the subject, "and I also feel that it's time for you and I finally to put all of this behind us."

Richard's heart leapt at this suggestion of a reunion.

Vicki's abrupt dismissal of so many serious issues surprised him, but he promptly accepted her reprieve, and their midnight reconciliation rambled on quietly for a few minutes. Then Vicki, as usual, soon wanted more than to talk. "How about if I come over?"

• • •

Finally she was back, and they were together again. And now that was permanent, just what Richard had always wanted. Vicki moved in with him, and put her condo on the market. It sold in three days. The young woman who bought it, Sarah Stone, was an investment manager from Manhattan who just loved the frescos in the master bath. Vicki of course happily provided the name of the artist in order that Sarah might customize the golden goddess to her own auburn requirements.

At last Richard Landon finally had exactly what he had hoped for back in July when all the craziness started over Rosco. And it did get crazy. Even to the extent that at least for a while he had actually believed that Vicki had cooled Rosco! It all seemed so ridiculous now, but who could blame him at the time? She certainly appeared to be guilty. It had all been so crazy. Since that first Sunday in July, life had become for Richard Landon a voyage of discovery. A troubling journey, from eager certainty to sudden doubt, then off again to the fuzzy fringes of certainty only to be wrenched back to the shadows of newer, darker doubts. At last, the craziness was over.

• • •

As Richard understood the newest developments in the case, it had been Detective Miller who had pieced it all together, completely severing Rosco from the three other crimes that to this day remained unsolved. But not so Rosco. Once the cops knew where to look, they found plenty of evidence regarding Rosco's murder. At the O'Connor house in Barrington, they confiscated the bar candles and clothing still bearing microscopic traces of blood, as well as an unregistered hand gun. And Madeline's Mercedes yielded even more blood. And of course the girls also had left abundant evidence behind in the form of prints and hair at the scene of the crime. Predictably Molly continued to deny everything, while Kate followed her lawyer's advice and said nothing. Joe Guilliam got on television to gloat, pronouncing the murder what he termed *re-solved*—this time, he said, for real.

• • •

Much of the evidence related to a private security firm that Madeline O'Connor had hired. According to the in-depth investigation published by the *Tribune*, she had used this Covington Security over the years for all kinds of sneaky stuff. Surveillance on political rivals, trailing her husband–that kind of thing–exactly what Molly criticized her mother for at Richard's apartment that night. That was the detective agency, recalled Richard, that Molly had named, Covington Security. But Molly never guessed that her mother instructed Covington to trail her and Kate as well. And because she had her daughters under continuous surveillance, she knew all about the clinic. Madeline O'Connor understood very well Edmund Chambers' deranged motives on her Barrington estate. And of course she knew all about Rosco, too. She had probably been shadowing the twins uneventfully for years. For Madeline O'Connor, the murder of Rosco Mink must have come as a profound shock.

• • •

In the end she was arrested for obstruction of justice because the cops claimed that through Covington, she knew about Rosco's murder. Something to do with a lot of parking tickets the twins had racked up casing Rosco's place. And all of this clandestine reporting explained Madeline's sudden interest in travel and a new home in the south of France, as a baffled Katie related to Richard. And then in a unavoidable admission of guilt, Madeline turned around and accused Covington Security of blackmailing her for five million dollars to keep it all quiet. It was all pretty crazy.

• • •

So Miller had cracked the Rosco case. Of course he confronted Richard in the process. "Boy, you really get around. Why didn't you tell me you had a relationship with Katherine O'Connor?"

"I didn't tell you because you didn't ask," Richard responded. "And I didn't think it was important."

Miller grunted. "Well, I suppose you should know that Madeline O'Connor had you under surveillance, too. All the time you were engaged to Katherine, Covington Security was watching your every step."

"*What?*" exclaimed Richard.

"Yeah," said Tow. "That's what their records show. Two guys, around the clock. Watching your every move." Actually Covington's records showed a great deal more, but this was all that Tow chose to share with Richard.

"Can they do that? I mean, is that legal?"

"Worried?"

"*Look,*" snapped Richard Landon. "I did nothing wrong. What happened between Kate and me, well I accept my responsibility for that. But only that. And that's not a crime. But I had nothing to do with Rosco's murder. Nothing. All of this is as big a surprise to me as it is to you." This much was certainly true.

"And you wouldn't know how the murder weapon got into the hands of a *Tribune* reporter, would you?"

Richard was already thinking. Miller suspected him of having something to do with the murder weapon! "Not a clue," said Richard, risking an unavoidable lie.

"You were out there at the house in Barrington just a few days before it turned up. The guard's log book shows you arriving one afternoon at 5:30 p.m. and not leaving until 1:12 a.m."

But the girls could not accuse him without admitting the crime themselves. He was safe! "Just a friendly visit," said Richard with sudden confidence.

"Long talk?"

Richard was now quietly smug. "You could say that."

"What else?" asked Miller. "That's what I want to know. What's next?"

• • •

Fortunately for Richard, there was no proof that he had done anything, or even knew anything. Covington had followed him until Kate and he had broken up. So what? But there was one last bizarre development. It seems Molly poured much of her rage into a notebook. Rosco, of course, was the main subject, but there were also others on her agenda of murder. Foremost was her mother, but Vicki, too, was condemned for execution at the earliest possible opportunity. Then in the last pages, Richard himself was targeted. This, in Richard's view, was a lucky break because it tended to invalidate anything Molly might say about him in the future. Molly, Richard concluded, was truly crazy.

And Kate, well, reluctant loyal Kate was too sad to be true.

• • •

What Tow chose not to share with Richard was this.

Richard had not been the only one under the surveillance of Madeline's Covington Security. Tow himself had also been shadowed. The same impounded Covington records that revealed the hours billed to Mrs. O'Connor relating to Richard Landon also revealed that Covington had followed Tow continuously since the hearing back in July. No doubt at that time with the hope of spotting him in some incriminating activity. Tow was stunned when he was told about this. It was outrageous. He couldn't believe it. He had had no idea that someone was on his tail day and night for months. Day and night, without his slightest knowledge! But that's what had happened. There were even Covington gasoline and motel charges in Michigan, and additionally a $48 fee for the ferry out of Milwaukee. These people had even followed Beverly and him up to her cottage! They were on the same ferry with them! But this was the only solid evidence in the record that proved he had been followed. Just to satisfy his own curiosity, Tow succumbed to playing detective once more. He began at Baroque's Crockery in the mall. And he was in luck. Debbie still worked there. "I was here one day last summer," he began.

"Oh, I remember," Debbie said. "Mrs. Brock helped you then, but she isn't here anymore You had the question about the ice pick."

"That's right," confirmed Tow. "The ice pick."

"So did your friends and you ever find one?" she asked him.

"My friends?"

Debbie appeared confused. "The two men who were here looking for you. They just missed you. I told them what Mrs. Brock told you–try a hardware store for an ice pick. They said they would, and if you returned, to tell you they would meet you later at your place."

The girl's expected confirmation of Covington's shadowing gave Tow an unexpected chill.

• • •

Then, taking this process one step further, Tow went back to Collins Hardware.

He had shown the clerk there his badge before, but the man was now immediately apprehensive. "Just what's going on here?" he asked.

"You tell me," said Tow.

"You told me last time you were here that you were a cop."

"I am," said Tow producing his credentials once more.

The man looked carefully at Tow's photo. "Well, right after you were here the last time, two other guys came in asking me what you wanted. I said you were a cop. They said you weren't, and offered me a hundred dollar bill to tell them what you wanted."

"Yeah, and?"

The clerk began to protest. "Look, I didn't do anything wrong."

"I know you didn't," said Tow. "You took the money and said that I had asked about ice picks. Then the two guys just left."

"That's right. That's exactly right."

• • •

These two episodes convinced Tow that Madeline O'Connor had no doubt known what he was up to all along. Not that he was really hot on her trail, rather he had been just too close for comfort. No wonder she was annoyed that he chose to remain on the job in homicide instead of accepting her repeated offers to return to Gang Crimes.

47

The anniversary of the November 8th slayings of the two Chicago call girls was remembered with a shocking rampage across the nation. A movie producer was murdered in L.A. A lawyer slain in Dallas. In Washington D.C., a lobbyist for an oil firm. In Chicago, an advertising executive. And in New York, a Wall Street trader, a fashion designer and a literary agent. In Santa Fe, a software engineer and in Atlanta, a retired police officer. It was truly a grisly harvest. In each case the victim was male found bound Friday morning in a hotel room stabbed multiple times with an ice pick. Local cultural preferences also surfaced. In Santa Fe, a scalp was taken. In Atlanta, a bible was found open to Exodus 21:24 highlighted in yellow: "a life for a life, and eye for an eye." In every case two small candles were found burning on the dresser. Apart from sketchy descriptions of prostitutes with long dark hair, additional evidence was scarce.

• • •

Of course the recurrence of the original pattern in Chicago put Morrison and Tow back on the hot spot. And WQQX, irreverent as always, again went into overdrive.

• • •

Aware of these headlines that same Friday morning, Richard Landon allowed none of it to distract him. Stocks rallied big on larger-than-expected auto sales, and suddenly he was up almost 50 grand in an equity option position that he had purchased on Tuesday. September through early November had been his most profitable period in more than a year. It seemed everything he touched turned to gold. He was just killing them in stocks, and making almost as much with his long bond position as the Federal Reserve cut interest rates. He had even scored big in a conservative currency spread short the dollar. Finally, it seemed he had his touch back, and the money was rolling in. Still, Richard knew, today was spectacularly lucky.

And there was a little more to look forward to. Vicki would be home tonight.

She was doing her usual Wednesday to Friday itinerary, but because of a customer request, she had scheduled her monthly Manhattan visit a week later than normal. Business seemed to have improved for her, too. She left a message just a little earlier, very excited. "Everything went so well," she gushed. "Things just could not have worked out better. I just can't wait get home and see you!"

• • •

Oddly, the Rosco affair seemed to be a catharsis for Vicki and him. Both had been very shaken by the Rosco accusations. Vicki, Richard realized, had indeed been very, very rattled. What a relief to have all of that over. Maybe, thought Richard, their current success was because all doubts surrounding Rosco truly had finally been resolved. Richard felt such a fool. First he had been sure Patrice Foster had killed all those guys. Then he thought Vicki had cooled Rosco—without even considering who might have killed the others, or why. And this thing with Kate and Molly—why couldn't he have seen that earlier? It was so obvious now, yet he had suspected nothing. Could anyone be a worse judge of character than he? Maybe, thought Richard, he should just stick to the simplicity of buying and selling bonds. But still, because of that trauma, both had changed, grown more mature, and ultimately closer together. Vicki now clearly put their relationship first. Selling her condo was an important demonstration of that commitment.

• • •

And today, at last, Richard himself also was ready to commit. He knew he was profoundly in love with Vicki. *Could-not-live-without-her* in love with her. *Stupid-crazy* in love with her. *Ready-to-take-a-bullet-for-her* in love with her. Now he resolved never to lose her again. His recent success, he told himself, was an opportunity for a new future. A time to get serious. He was determined to make the most of it. After work that Friday, he hurried directly over to Tiffany's on Michigan Avenue where he spent three times what he had intended.

• • •

Then, later, in the rain, the late Friday afternoon traffic out to O'Hare was murder.

And of course her flight was over an hour late. None of this, however, fazed Richard who rehearsed his lines while he waited patiently at the passenger exit. Finally, there she was. He could see her coming down the stairs lugging her little Chanel carry-on, her blonde hair so conspicuous in the crowd even at this distance. She saw him as she approached, now hurrying, waving, smiling. Richard Landon felt a sudden rush of happiness—an unreasonable, almost unbearable happiness. They embraced and kissed while passengers streamed around them.

Then in the car, Richard blew all his carefully prepared lines and simply opened the Tiffany's ring box and showed her. Vicki took one look at the stunning marquise, then happy and teary-eyed, gushed, *"Yes, yes, yes!"*

• • •

About a week later, they were at the crowded bar at Ergo's one evening after work.

Waiting for their table, Vicki was seated with Richard standing, one arm protectively on the back of her chair. Vicki strategically placed her left arm on the edge of the bar, prominently displaying her glittering new ring. They had just ordered their second gin and tonic when she said, "Guess what? I have some news."

"Oh yeah, so what kind of news?"

"Well," she began, "it occurred to me that it's time to make some changes at work."

"Vicki, we don't need more money, you know. You work too hard the way it is."

"Well, that's what I want to change. I'm cutting back. I'm going to focus just on trading. That means no more client entertaining, and no more travel."

"Stuck in the office? Are you sure you're gonna be happy with that? You love those trips to Manhattan."

"I'm sure I'm doing the right thing, Richard. I really am. I don't need the long hours, and I don't ever need to go to New York again. I love you, and I have never been happier in my life. We're going to be married in just a few months, I really don't need anything more."

Just then the tuxedoed maître d' was there with the menus. "Mr. and Mrs. Landon," he announced, "Your table is ready."

His was an understandable mistake, thought Richard. That was a lot of ring.

But Vicki, smiling happily, was far more enthused. "I just love it all already," she said happily. Then she turned and whispered to him. "And I love you."

48

"Momma, I'm going outside for a while," Ben told his mother.

She was in the kitchen making meatloaf, one of Ben's absolute favorites. He loved the light toasted crust and the way she baked croutons and onions inside with tomato sauce covering the outside. And with meatloaf, his mother always made mashed potatoes, another absolute favorite. And there was leftover carrot cake for desert. Could anything be better?

Many things were better now. His mother was home, and Ben was in school again and working weekends for Harold Lamb. And Ben had met Joe Guilliam, and liked him. Mr. Guilliam had represented him in the fairly serious matter of the fight with Dennis. Until he met Dennis in court, Ben had not realized what a mismatch the fight really was. Dennis was at least six inches taller, and outweighed him by almost 50 pounds. These facts were not lost on the judge who ruled Ben's actions a matter of self-defense, which it was, though Ben himself still felt profound remorse about beating someone unconscious and fleeing the scene. Fortunately Dennis had recovered fully. And also through Mr. Guilliam's efforts, his mother had a new job now, and they would be moving soon.

But there was more. His mother had taken him aside and spoken to him a few days earlier. It was time for a family discussion, she had explained. There were some things he was now old enough to understand. So she told him that his father was really his stepfather. She had no current knowledge of his real father who had abandoned her when she was 16. She told him that he had lived in Martin Luther King Gardens alone with her until he was three years old when she married John Foster whom she still loved *"very,*

very much." And she said that Ben, too, should love him very much because he was a good man who had loved them both very, very much. Then she started to cry, and could not stop for a long time. Overall, this discussion filled Ben with a profound sadness, but he knew there were worse things in life. About that, he was very sure.

"You bundle up, Benjamin," called his mother from the kitchen. "And you be careful. And be home before dark. That's a little more than an hour. And you just remember my rules, Benjamin. You stay away from trouble."

• • •

It was a bleak Saturday afternoon in November. Low fast clouds of steel blue and gray permitted only occasional sun on their fringes. When there was direct sun, it was golden, but lacked any kind of warmth. Ben shivered as he turned into the wind, and pulled on his gloves. Both his down jacket and the flannel lined leather gloves were among the new winter things his mother had gotten him for his birthday last week. He was 13 now.

• • •

They were waiting for him at the box car.

Scab leapt to greet Ben even before Spider climbed to his feet to give him a high five. Then they sat in a patch of sunlight to talk, with Scab squeezed between them. Both boys shivered as wind knifed through broken sides of the car. Spider was wearing only sweatpants and the same light jacket he had worn the night of the Vice Royal shooting weeks before. Beneath the inadequate jacket, he wore only his usual tee shirt. "Here, try these," said Ben offering Spider his gloves. "I have another pair at home." Of course he did not have another pair and would have to tell his mother that he lost his new gloves. She would be upset, Ben knew. Very upset.

It had been several weeks since they'd been together. Ben had arranged this meeting through Harold Lamb, requesting that Spider meet him at their *safest location.* "How's your leg?" asked Ben.

"It okay."

The sun abruptly disappeared.

"I brought some stuff," said Ben, taking a bag out of his jacket. To celebrate their reunion, he had taken a few leftovers. Several of his mother's funny little sandwiches with the crust cut off, and a couple especially large slices of cake because the sandwiches were so small. For Scab, he'd taken some lunch meat from the fridge.

All three of them were hungry.

"Now what dis?" asked Spider examining the cake. "It gots little orange bits in it."

"Those are carrots. It's carrot cake."

"Carrot cake?"

"Yeah, you know. Carrot cake."

Spider just looked at him doubtfully.

"It's sorta like banana bread."

Spider nodded, then smiled at the recollection and laughed. "Right, banana bread."

Scab finished first and begged for more. Spider fed him part of his cake.

The sun was suddenly back, illuminating much of the car in a golden brightness. It was the bright sun that allowed Ben to notice something different about Spider.

"Hey, what do you have on your face?" Ben asked, and then looked closer. In the strong sunlight, he could see small blue teardrops tattooed beneath Spider's eyes and on his cheeks.

"Roosevelt daid," said Spider explaining these symbols of permanent mourning. "Kings kill him. Right in the penitentiary, they kill him. Nitro, he say to do it. He in the penitentiary now. He so mad he tell Kings to kill Roosevelt."

Ben didn't know what to say. Who did it, and how didn't really matter much. Death, to Ben, was essentially something that was unnecessary, and for that reason it could not be explained. His father, Spider's brother, Jason, and now Roosevelt. Each was unnecessary. The *real* reasons, if there were any, were a complete mystery. What was very clear to Ben was that the shooting incident brought a new burden of guilt which now rested with each of them, demanding additional sacrifice. "Maybe one of us will die, too," said Ben.

Spider answered immediately a soft, *"Maybe."* Then he went on.

"Nitro, he tell Kings to hunt me an Scab, but that big po-lice, he come an' tell my momma we can move to a different place far away where we be safe. He show her where, an' we move. Then he come an' say 'good, now doan tell nobody where you live now.'"

Ben of course had been cautioned by Mr. Guilliam about the possible consequences of his own testimony against the Viper Kings. Fortunately he and his mother would be moving soon, and Ben had no reason ever to return to the territory of the Kings. But he knew well that King Gardens was Spider's whole life. Ben knew that was impossible for Spider to hide forever, but still he had to ask, "You didn't ever go back there, did you?"

In response to this, Spider refused to meet Ben's eyes and just looked away.

Right away Ben knew.

Then he considered the probable consequences. "Are you afraid?" he asked.

Spider nodded. "Always," he acknowledged quietly. "Always afraid. Always lookin' out. Never safe, not fo' sure. You know. You know everything now. You like me. You smart, you strong, you tough. You jus' like me."

Ben agreed solemnly with a nod. Now he was just like Spider, exactly what he had always wanted. "Yeah," he said. "Now I know. Now I know everything."

They were both quiet for a long moment.

Then Ben said, "It'll be dark soon. I gotta get home."

Spider nodded slowly, and finished his carrot cake.

As the left, they made plans to meet the next day at noon.

• • •

Sunday afternoon flurries were in the air, swirling in bitter gusts from the north.

Ben was on time and waited in the box car, freezing with his hands jammed in his pockets, for over an hour.

But Spider and Scab never showed up.

49

It was a Friday, the last day in November.

"A low of 20 degrees tomorrow," Sweeney was saying. "And more snow on the way for the weekend—another three to four inches tonight alone."

"Christ, snow already," grumbled Tow as the phone rang. "It's too early for snow."

"Yeah, you're right about that," said Sweeney, "Traffic is gonna be brutal."

Breaking off his conversation, Tow reached for the phone and got it on the next ring. "Miller."

"Detective Miller, this is Paul Douglas calling. It's been some time. You remember me, don't you? The writer."

Tow did, of course. The crime writer. He remembered him very well, Tow assured Paul Douglas.

"This is just a call to catch up," said Douglas. "I've been following recent developments in this case very closely as you can imagine."

Far less critical this time, Tow sat back and said, "So what can I do for you, Mr. Douglas?"

Hearing this conversation begin, Sweeney waved goodnight.

Tow returned the gesture as he continued to listen.

"Well, as you know, Detective, I am very interested in writing a book about this case. True crime, you know. I'm pretty far along. The working title is *Our Girl*. But I need more information."

"Well, as I'm sure you know from the media, Mr. Douglas, we arrested a suspect in the November 8th murder here two days ago. Cynthia Defasio."

"Do you have a confession yet?"

"No, she denies everything, but she did have the murder weapon in her possession, and there are two witnesses who place her at the crime scene."

"And did she know the victim?"

"We don't know at this point."

"And motive?"

"Well since the murder was on the anniversary of the deaths of the two call girls, I'd say motive is closely aligned."

"And can you link Cynthia Defasio to any of the other crimes there in Chicago or in New York?"

"No, but it's still pretty early in the investigation. As you can imagine, we're working on that."

The writer's tone shifted from inquisitive to direct. "What we saw on November 8th, Detective," lectured Paul Douglas, "is the copy-cat syndrome gone wild. Cynthia Defasio is just a crude plagiarist. I think another woman is responsible for all the other unsolved crimes in Chicago. I am also certain that she is responsible for the unsolved murder in New York on the eighth day of November, and all the other unsolved murders there as well."

"Well, that could be," said Tow patiently taking this all in stride. "Right now, our suspect is our main focus. She could well be responsible for at least some of the other crimes here in Chicago."

"I just don't think so," argued Paul Douglas. "November 8th was largely amateur night. In addition to your suspect, the D.C. killer has been caught, two of the three in New York as well. And my contact in L.A. tells me they have a promising lead there. I'm sure none of them is the original killer. No, 'Our Girl' is far, far superior. Highly motivated. A zealot of the highest order. And smart—very, very smart. A professional among professionals, 'Our Girl' isn't going be caught as a result of a careless mistake like so many of her primitive admirers."

"I don't know about that," said Tow. "Sooner or later, all criminals make mistakes."

Paul Douglas shook his head. "No way. Not 'Our Girl.' She's safe. And she's through with all of this. She doesn't have to do another thing. She's recruited a nation of wounded vigilantes to do her bidding. Next November 8th there will be even more. Eventually there will be international incidents. 'Our Girl' hasn't made any mistakes, and she isn't going to. She will never be caught. And although we will never have any evidence, we still might be able to figure out who she is."

"And just how do we do that?"

"If we'll never catch her on the job, so to speak, we'll have to backtrack. Do some research. What we want is a *link*. The O'Connor girls copied the original killer. And as a result, 'Our Girl' has to have been interested. Maybe afraid. At least flattered. Very likely flattered, I would think. I imagine that 'Our Girl' may even have attended the funeral of Rosco Mink, if only to survey the crowd for the presence of her imitator. It would have been a natural point of reference for both killers. You might call it an opportunity for bonding, even though it may have been indirect. There's a connection there somewhere, I assure you, Detective. It's often just a matter of connecting the dots."

"Could be." Tow was already considering this suggestion.

"So I'm wondering, Detective. Are there any remaining loose ends? Anything left over, so to speak, from the Rosco investigation that might offer a link to the others? Even if it's a long shot. I just have this intuition that there must be something that points to 'Our Girl.' I would be happy to help. Believe me, I have a real sense for these things."

"Actually, there are a few loose ends, Mr. Douglas. Now that you mention it. I think I see what you mean. There's something I have to check first, and then I'll get back to you."

Paul Douglas was immediately enthused. "Like I say, Detective, I'd be happy to help. Call anytime. Anytime at all. You have my number?"

"Actually, better let me have that again."

• • •

Tow finally found the video in a box from his old apartment.

Sweeney had been right on the weather. It was a terrible night for Beverly to be working late, but now she almost always worked late. The snow was really coming down and the wind was howling out of the north. But not for Tow. For him, with the click of a button, it became a day in July. A sweltering high humidity scorcher. He had actually forgotten about the video–so had Morri–until Paul Douglas caused him to think of it today.

Back then they had assumed there had been one killer responsible for all three victims. It was just Jankowski, McNamara and then Mink. Morrison's theory at the time was that someday they'd look at the tape and see the killer walking right up the steps of the church to say goodbye to her victim. Well, it was finally time to have that look.

The screen at first revealed the interior of Tow's Buick with an especially close examination of the dash. Aware of his errors then, Tow now heard himself curse, "Damn it." This was followed by a much too rapid panning of the street in the direction of the Cathedral. Police vehicles were smeared into a blue and white streak. Then finally in focus was a guy with a Cubs hat and an ice cream push cart featuring a gaggle of high flying red balloons. A mounted police officer trotted over and ordered him to move, but soon the guy was back and vigorously protesting police brutality.

Among the first mourners to arrive were the Mink wives. The two older ladies were still cheerfully gabbing on their way to see Rosco off. Then the young bombshell with her 80-year-old husband.

Next came the Mayor and company. The flags on his limo again wilted in the heat.

Following His Honor was a stream of the city's business elite.

At last came the O'Connors. Madeline and the girls. Tow watched this part carefully. Madeline's diamond brooch was still glittering in the sun. Morri of course had been right. There with their mother were the two young killers of Rosco Mink, both in black, both looking so innocent, both walking right up the steps of the Cathedral to bury their victim. Morrison had been so right.

Then with a shock, Tow stood up. "Son of a bitch," he said aloud. "*Son-of-a-bitch*." There in the crowd watching guests arrive lingered another celebrity killer. Edmund Chambers in a blue baseball cap could be seen keenly surveying the mourners. Was he there, wondered Tow, hoping to achieve some proximity to the killer of Rosco Mink? Was he at the funeral to bond with his competitor in a bold variation of Professor Douglas's theory? Then there was even more–Chambers could be seen specifically observing the O'Connor girls, drifting in their direction, even risking attention by craning his neck to keep them in view. Now there was no question that Chambers had stalked his victims. And Tow had had the evidence on tape all this time without knowing it! It was amazing, he thought, what you could find when you knew where to look.

And then, quickly, there was Joe Guilliam, accompanied by the red-hot babe, rounding out the spectacle. The camera's audio had even picked up most of Guilliam's shameless speech at the very doors of the Cathedral. He had been right as well. Rosco Mink had indeed become the biggest Chicago murder mystery in years, and Patrice Foster had certainly come to need his services as a good defense attorney.

Then, toward the end as Tow recalled, there was Beverly with her fiancé and abruptly his concentration was broken. He leaned forward to see just a little better. Beverly looked spectacular. Now with his earlier focus interrupted, Tow looked at his watch. It was almost eight. Beverly would be home soon.

Working late hours and weekends was finally producing significant results for Beverly's business. She was excited about the two big accounts she had recently landed, and hopeful about two more. And a week ago, she rehired three staffers whom she had laid off months earlier. Now she spoke with enthusiasm about clearly seeing what she called "the light at the end of the tunnel." Still all this effort was exhausting. She would be beat after such a long day, and getting dinner going was the least Tow could do. With this sense of obligation, he stood up and clicked off the video, then stopped. Something had barely, just barely, caught his eye. He clicked the machine back on, and reversed it slightly.

It was what he had thought.

There on the screen, still hurrying after all this time, appeared Richard Landon with his striking blonde girlfriend, Victoria Moss. Richard Landon, who always knew more than he was telling. And Victoria Moss, accused of stabbing her husband in Texas.

Very slowly, Tow sat down.

He had not known about the stabbing the first time he reviewed the film for attendance. Victoria had appeared so beautiful then. Did she somehow look more guilty now? Was that possible, was it just his imagination? Or was it really intuition?

Morrison had been absolutely right in his prediction. What if Paul Douglas were right, too? What if the original killer had shown up just to have some physical connection to her imitator? Maybe. Maybe not—maybe just too great a stretch. Playing detective, Tow now resolved, had its rewards if you didn't mind the risk of making a fool out of yourself from time-to-time. But some hunches were simply worth the risk he decided, watching Richard and Victoria once again hurrying up the steps of the cathedral. Sometimes it was all there, right in front of you, but for whatever reason, you just couldn't quite see it. There was something going on there with Richard and Victoria. Now he was certain. There had to be, Tow just didn't know what it was. Where there was smoke, he reasoned, there was fire.

But Paul Douglas was right. They had no evidence against Richard and Victoria. And neither was the video itself evidence—not anything even close to the kind of probable cause necessary to get a search warrant. And a second investigation now was especially remote following the spectacularly failed results of the first.

Still he was intrigued. Was Victoria "Our Girl?"

50

Saturday Richard Landon was home watching college football highlights on a snowy afternoon. Undeterred by the forecast of gusting winds and heavy snow, Vicki was shopping with Sarah Stone, the girl who had bought her condo and who was now becoming a good friend. The bride-to-be already had the dress, now she was completing a honeymoon wardrobe. The wedding was planned for late January in Maui.

For later that evening, they had dinner reservations at Restaurante Augustino. Auggie's was close enough to walk to no matter how much it snowed. Afterwards they planned to see a movie at the Mercury Theater, another walk-able destination over on Wells. The Mercury was dated and not plush in any way, but it was only 10 minutes away. At first Richard had proposed that they cab-it to the new Metro Cinema Complex on Michigan Avenue where they had 18 flicks to choose from, but instead Vicki wanted to walk in the snow over to the Mercury. Presented with a choice of just three films there, Richard preferred the techno-thriller, or even the murder mystery, but Vicki already wanted to see the romantic comedy. So Richard, as usual, deferred to her wishes. They would see the ultra-fluff *Aspen Ski Holiday*.

• • •

It was the snow that finally motivated Richard to make the effort of going down to his basement storage locker. It was time to get his winter boots and other heavy clothes. Accessing his condo storage locker was always a hassle, and for that reason he had put off this chore for as long as possible. He took the elevator to the lobby, requested the doorman's key for the basement door, then took another elevator to the basement. Finally there, he unlocked his locker, and opened the door. Locating the winter boxes required removing several suitcases piled in front of the door. Even empty, the two big Tumis were surprisingly heavy, and Richard noticed something leaking from one of them. His closer inspection revealed that the leak was not coming from either of the Tumis, but rather from above.

Vicki's favorite little New York carry-on was light as a feather as he pulled it down. Richard was surprised to find the case in storage, and reasoned that Vicki must have rolled it down here herself a few weeks ago when she abruptly ended her monthly commute to New York. Now he could clearly see that there was something leaking from its synthetic construction, something that looked like shampoo. What a mess–Vicki would be pissed when she saw what had happened to her phenomenally expensive little Chanel carry-on. As he set the case down, he could tell a bottle was rolling around inside, undoubtedly the source of the leak. Opening the case, he found the cap loose on an almost empty bottle of Dovette wig detergent, as well as a beige cardboard box fairly saturated with the leaking solvent. When he opened the box, he found a mesh bag containing a wig. This he withdrew carefully. It was a shoulder length brunette wig. What was this doing in Vicki's favorite New York travel bag? He had never known her to cover her hair, her gorgeous long blonde hair. Why would she ever want to do that? It didn't make sense. What use could she have possibly had for a brunette wig in New York? And why did she leave it in her carry-on when she put it into storage?

It was only then that Richard Landon saw the connection. The *New York* connection. New York travel led him to the *New York Times*...

It was that *New York Times* article that leapt to mind. The article that he had saved for Molly–*the suspect was in her thirties with long brown hair*. He had underlined it all in red ink back then, and had argued its significance forcefully to Kate and Molly.

"*Oh, no,*" he said to himself. It was as if he'd been clubbed in a dark alley. "Oh, no."

Stunned, he just stood there, thinking. She wasn't innocent, as he concluded following Kate and Molly's confession. Not innocent at all. And she wasn't just storing the wig–she was *hiding* it. Hiding it for what future purpose?

Richard was profoundly disturbed by this discovery, but, he had to admit, not terribly surprised. She seemed guilty about Rosco in so many ways. He had been right about his suspicions, just wrong about the victim.

So now what to do? What to do? What to do? Everything had changed.

He could just clean up the detergent, and put it all back and forget it. Just go on.

Instead he decided he couldn't do that. This, finally, was something that could not be negotiated. He would have to face the music. He was, he knew, risking everything.

Abandoning his original purpose, he rolled Vicki's suitcase back to the apartment, into the bedroom, and placed it open on the bed, displaying the only two objects within. To these, he added the *New York Times* that he had saved for Molly, the big story already circled in red ballpoint with references to the brunette prostitute underlined severely.

• • •

Later when Vicki returned from shopping, she called a happy hello to Richard who happened to be in the kitchen, and, as usual, breezed into the bedroom with her packages.

Silent, Richard followed her.

He found at the bed her reading the *Times* article. Deep down, he hoped she would tell him how wrong he was, and deny everything.

Instead she dropped the paper to her side, turned quickly to face him, and said a confident, "*I can explain.*"

Richard's heart dropped. She didn't look like a killer. In a pink sweater and faded jeans with her long blonde hair tucked behind her ears, she looked like a college girl.

"Okay," he said quietly.

She didn't try to deny anything, but drew her arms to her chest, her right hand clutching her left as if to protect her ring. "I admit that what you think has happened actually has happened, but I want you to know that it's over, Richard," she said with eerie composure. "It's been over for some time."

Richard looked at her gravely. "So then–*why?*" he said.

"Because I had to," she said, tears quickly welling up in her eyes. It took her a moment to continue. "When I heard what that creep did to those two girls last year, it just made me sick, Richard. Just sick. It made me think of what my husband did to me. Jack was a bully and a prick. He liked to beat me up and rape me. He did it all the time, and he got away with it. A couple times he almost killed me. And he enjoyed it." She was sobbing now. "There was nobody to help me. I was absolutely alone. I'm lucky to be alive. So this time I had to make a statement. I had to stand up for those girls. I could never hope to find Edmund Chambers, so I targeted other predators. But now it's over. I've done my part. I don't have to do anything more."

"Vicki, this is so crazy. I mean, how can I believe you?"

"My work is finished, Richard," she said solemnly, sounding like a messiah. Tears ran down her pretty cheeks. "You saw what happened on November 8th. Now other women all over the country will carry on. My job is finished."

"What does Sarah have to do with all of this?"

"Nothing. Nothing at all. I know what you're thinking, but I did not know her from New York. I just met her here when I sold my condo. Sarah doesn't know about any of this."

Richard tried to be thorough. "Vicki, tell me the truth. Is there anything else I need to know?"

She thought for a moment, her tears slowing. "Yes," she said, "just wait." Then she went into the living room.

Richard just stood there permeated with a feeling of dread.

Vicki returned with her purse. "*Here,*" she said withdrawing a wicked looking ice pick, and handing it to him. "Take it," she said. "You get rid of it. I just don't want it coming back."

Though he was filled with a sense of revulsion, Richard had no choice but to accept the murder weapon.

"I just didn't know what to do with it," Vicki went on. "You know, this is not the kind of thing you can get through airport security. The one I had in New York I just dropped over the side of the ferry into the river one night. We don't have a ferry here. I've been carrying this around Chicago for months looking for a chance to bury it."

"Then why keep the wig?"

"Same thing. I'm not really *keeping* it. I'm always very careful, Richard. Really very, very careful in every way. I bought it in London last year. I paid cash and took the manufacturer's tag out so it would be really difficult to trace. It's actually an expensive human hair wig. A wig is not an easy thing to dispose of. Not really. I'd prefer to burn it, but that's not easy. I probably would have eventually cut it up into a hundred pieces and tossed them away one at a time. I was just waiting to find a good solution, that's all."

"So what else is there? The wig and the pick. What else is there that we have to get rid of?"

"Nothing, Richard. That's all."

"What about clothes? What did you wear?"

"Clothes were easy to unload. I already got rid of everything, Richard. I had a box of candles and I trashed those, too."

"What about your shoes?"

"Gone. Everything else is gone. I was very careful. It's over, Richard. I promise." She was clutching her ring again. "It's all over. It was already over when I told you at Ergo's that I had stopped all travel, including New York. I told you then that I never had to go back."

Richard considered this. She did tell him that night at Ergo's a few weeks ago that she did not intend to return to Manhattan. And, as warped as it was, her zealot's view that others had taken up her cause provided a respectable way out, a permanent escape that she could accept. It was all so crazy. So Molly-like. "That's right," he said, "you did tell me that." Richard paused, reflecting, searching. "It's got to be over, Vicki. Never again."

"Never again," she agreed, sobbing quietly, coming into his arms. "I'm really relieved that I don't have to do anything more. It's over. It's all over."

He had only one more question. "Vicki," he said. "Listen to me. Does anyone else know about this? Anyone?"

Slowly, she shook her head, then whispered, "just you."

He stood there holding her for a few minutes, realizing that he was only beginning to suffer the pain of his discovery.

• • •

The clock read 2:11 a.m., and Richard Landon was wide-awake, mentally scrolling through events while a furious blizzard stormed outside. It was better, he had finally convinced himself, much better now that he knew everything. Now he could get rid of the rest of the evidence, cover for her, take care of her. In a way, she was sick– *very sick*–but she didn't scare him the way crazy Molly did. And she needed him. And there was no question that it really was over. She could retire now, and allow others to carry on. What really worried him was what he didn't know and couldn't anticipate. Something that could blindside him. What if some evidence surfaced that lead the police to his door in the middle of the night? That was frightening. He couldn't stop thinking about it. Then another thought occurred to him. Was *this*, he wondered, how it was always going to be? Always worried, always sleepless, always calculating?

Next to him Vicki lay snuggled close, dead to the world. Even under the down comforter, he could see the lush shape of her hips and his desire stirred. *He was still in love with her.* There was no doubt about that. Still *ready-to-take-a-bullet-for-her* in love with her.

He checked the clock again.

Only minutes had passed. He got up very quietly and went to his study where he had put Vicki's suitcase. From it, he withdrew the ice pick. Richard studied the weapon carefully. This agent of death was about eight inches long, sturdy and fairly heavy, capable of immense damage. Her crimes, he realized, had been monstrous. Profoundly monstrous. But now it was over. He could not change what had happened, but neither would he allow her to be taken from him. That would accomplish nothing. No, he resolved, he would never lose her again. In the morning, he would get rid of the murder weapon and the wig.

Abruptly, there was the faint sound of a distant siren. Startled, Richard quickly fumbled the ice pick back into the suitcase and made his way back to bed. He had somehow become suddenly warm, very warm, and found that he did not need the blankets and comforter. The siren was little more than a whisper in the wind, almost smothered in the fury of the blizzard. It was nothing, Richard convinced himself. A single siren in the night in a city filled with sirens in the night. No more than a scary coincidence that played to his fears.

In the darkness, he considered the facts. Everything made so much sense. It all fit, especially the New York connection–on the surface a clever bit of misdirection on her part. However, if ever discovered, the murder weapon would be enough to indict her, and her undeniable itinerary would be enough to convict her. Still the siren, approaching from the north, just kept coming. He could hear it clearly now, piercing even the fury of the storm. Impossibly, it seemed to be headed directly toward him. This was just how the whole episode with Rosco had begun, recalled Richard, with sirens in the middle of the night. Still he tried to ignore it, and returned to his thoughts.

And the rest of it fit too. All of it. The *why* of it all. He had no trouble understanding her reasons. The disenchanted zealot of women's causes, dismayed with the ineffectual system. And within her marriage, a victim of repeated brutality herself. The first two guys in Chicago were her enraged response for the murder of the two call girls last November. Then later she became a vigilante at large, resourcefully extending her range to Manhattan. She had been abused herself, and was now standing up for women against predators wherever she found them. It all fit. The night person revealed. Had she been *hunting*, he suddenly wondered, that rainy night last April when she picked him up in the hotel bar? Had he been an intended victim, spared by only some last minute change of heart? Good god, this was crazy. The siren was growing more urgent now–constant, clearer, closer. Plowing relentlessly through the blizzard, it was impossible to ignore, and Richard was becoming very warm. Still he tried to return to his thoughts.

His discovery tonight had been disturbing, a profound moment of reluctant certainty. He still didn't want to believe any of it. And what were the odds? Really, what were the odds? He had been sleeping with not just one killer, *but two*. What were the odds that this could happen? And why him?

In a way, he realized, he had seen tonight's calamity coming all along. There were just so many signs, so many things he had willfully neglected. The truth was that he had always known that there was something very strange about Vicki. And in her own way, he recalled, Molly had realized the same thing. Crazy Molly, who had been so eager to bond with the original killer at Rosco's funeral. She had been exactly right in her catty comments about Vicki's attendance that morning–*the braless raccoon sex killer.* Molly, realized Richard, had been unknowingly drawn to exactly the person she had sought for all the right reasons. The two of them had always been so alike–and for this reason, Richard wasn't really surprised at all. But there was still more to consider. How had he managed to become so involved in dual tragedies while having no real role in either? Now the threat was wailing no more than a block away! In a minute it would be at his door–and the murder weapon was still in his study! If the siren stopped, he determined in a rush, he would wake Vicki and they would grab the car keys and run.

Almost paralyzed with fear, Richard Landon lay perfectly still. The siren continued its relentless approach, less than a block away, and still coming. Slowing for an intersection, it passed very nearby, and then groaning with renewed energy, it proceeded south. Relieved, Richard listened until it gradually receded into the fury of the blizzard.

Then there in the darkness next to Vicki, another thought surfaced.

Suddenly chilled, Richard Landon felt the need to reach for both the blankets and the comforter. He knew that he could get rid of the wig and the weapon, but he would never get rid of the sirens. And in a city filled with sirens, he realized that it all would be bad, day and night. But the nights would be the worst. No siren, especially a late-night siren, would ever again pass unnoticed.

He lay there, staring at the ceiling, thinking about how it was going to be.